The Grooms Wore White

Charlie Lyndhurst

First published in the United Kingdom in 2022 by

Hera Books
Unit 9 (Canelo), 5th Floor
Cargo Works, 1–2 Hatfields
London, SE1 9PG
United Kingdom

A CIP catalogue record for this book is available from the British Library.

Print ISBN 978 1 80032 966 9
Ebook ISBN 978 1 912973 97 2

Look for more great books at www.herabooks.com

Printed and bound in Great Britain by Clays Ltd, Elcograf S.p.A.

1

To Tim, I heard about an author's husband complaining his wife had received an advance for a novel she'd written without telling him and he felt betrayed and unable to share her joy. You're not that person. And for this, I'm very grateful.

Chapter 1

'The happy couple will now cut the wedding cake!' a man in a red jacket and tight trousers announced.

The guests assembled next to the table, upon which was a three-tier wedding cake and the bride stood in front of her new husband as they held the knife together.

As it cut through the cake, the guests cheered and cameras flashed.

Jason smiled at the bride – Caroline – as she caught his eye.

He'd made all of this happen. From the simple ceremony in the village church, to the powder-blue Rolls Royce that had taken them to the country barn where they stood now.

Jason left the guests clicking away as the bride and groom wrapped slices of cake, handing them around with laughter and chat.

The barn was decorated in white and pink. White chair covers with light pink ribbons gave the impression of snow and confetti. The tablecloths were white, each table had a centrepiece of pink and white chrysanthemums.

Jason collected a wedding favour someone had left on the table, unopened. A brown paper package tied up with string, inside was a small chocolate bar, a book and some gift vouchers for a wine company.

The groom – Karl – walked past, looking very dapper in his grey morning suit, white shirt and pink cravat. 'All right?'

'Just taking one for him indoors,' Jason said, blushing slightly at being caught. 'Hope it's okay.'

Karl shook his hand. 'Course. Help yourself. We've got bags of 'em left over.'

'I didn't want you to think I was nicking it.'

'You're a guest, so it's yours.'

They'd wanted to give each of their guests a night in and since Caroline worked in publishing and Karl was a wine taster, it hadn't been too hard to source the wedding favours. Ironically, the chocolate had been the hardest, a specific sweet in those chocolate assortment tubs sold at Christmas that Caroline really loved but hadn't been available during summer.

Except Jason had called in a few favours, and now each brown paper package contained one of the nutty purple chocolate sweets Caroline so loved. Just part of the service making him one of the best wedding planners in the area.

'You should have brought your other half,' Karl said.

Jason shook his head. 'Not when I'm working. Although he'd have enjoyed the bus.'

'Same.'

There had been an old Routemaster red bus taking guests from the church, through the countryside, to the barn. Karl was something of a public transport aficionado.

'Geek,' Caroline had said with a smile. 'If I'm getting the colours, he needs that.'

Karl had blushed, said it wasn't so important. 'I'm not fussed. As long as you're happy.' He'd stared at his fiancée.

Jason had dealt with this before, men pretending not to be bothered about having parts of the wedding they wanted, leaving it all to their brides. Some sort of macho bullshit. It never worked, because nearer the day they'd start making subtle hints about changing the DJ, or could they have their mate's car to drive them to the church. Or did they really have to wear a crushed velvet cravat with the suit…

Jason had said, 'I can definitely source a bus. A train, not really. Unless you want a trip on a heritage route. Although there aren't any near your venues.'

Karl's face had lit up at the mention of trains. 'Bus. That sounds good, right?' He turned to Caroline.

'Bus it is then.'

'Did you get plenty of pictures?' Jason asked Karl now.

'The driver waited while I took them.' Karl smiled. 'Caroline wanted to get here, but I said everyone would wait for us.'

The guests had waited at the barn, for an informal commitment ceremony – the church had been too small for more than just family. Caroline and Karl stood in front of their guests, restating their vows to one another. They'd written them – Jason had given them help with that, suggesting some popular songs, poems, quotes from books his previous clients had used before.

Guests helped themselves to a buffet because Caroline didn't want everyone formally sitting in set places, she wanted the guests to circulate and for friends from the different parts of their lives to mix. This allowed Caroline and Karl to move from table to table – there was no 'top table' at this wedding.

'Are you staying for the disco?' Karl asked now.

Jason liked a dance, but he had to drive home, and he knew that by the time the music started, most of the guests would be pretty jolly, having drunk the Cava upon arrival at the barn, the free wine on the tables, and probably been to the bar to top up with their own money a few times.

'I'll wait to check it's all right, and then slip off.'

'Whatever works for you. Thanks mate.' Karl shook his hand. 'For everything. I never thought I'd cope with the stress. That's why we never bothered before. I couldn't deal with all the aggro.'

Jason smiled. That was what he did. Worked out what the clients wanted and made it happen, taking on all the aggro himself, so they didn't need to. 'That's kind of the point.'

'Will you say goodbye to Caroline before you go?'

'I will.'

Karl grinned, waved, and left, slipping into the melee of people standing by tables, talking, eating the last bits of food left.

Pete would have enjoyed a dance, Jason reflected. Early in the days of them dating, Pete had once led an impromptu kick line at a pub when the latest number one 'I'm A Movie Star' from The Fridays – his favourite girl group – had started.

Jason had leaned against the wall and watched Pete on stage, gathering others by gesturing and dancing alone on the stage. By the chorus, there were a dozen men and women kicking and dancing, arms looped together to the chorus singing – shouting mostly – that they were movie stars and that's what they really are.

Jason smiled at the memory. He knew then that life with Pete would never be dull, that he'd love Pete and one day they'd marry.

The music started. Jason checked the time, exactly on schedule. He walked past the tables, onto the dance floor – a corner of the barn with shiny wooden flooring, surrounded by chairs against the walls.

The DJ stood behind a wall of flashing lights, and glanced at his laptop screen, looking up as Jason approached. 'Everything okay?'

'I'm about to go. Just checking you know about the change in music for their first dance.'

'"Going Underground" isn't it?'

That had been Karl's attempt at a joke to wind up Caroline. Jason shook his head. 'It's "All You Need Is Love" by the Beatles.'

The DJ scrolled with his mouse pad. 'Sorted. Thanks.'

Jason shook his hand, walked across the dance floor. He stood by the door as the DJ announced the first dance.

Caroline and Karl walked onto the dance floor, holding hands. They stood in the middle, staring into one another's eyes as the song started.

His work here was done. He waved goodbye to Karl as he looked over Caroline's shoulder. Jason knew he should say goodbye to them both, but didn't want to interrupt, nor did he want to stay much longer. The night wasn't about him, it was about them, and they shouldn't need to worry about saying goodbye and thanking him. Seeing their perfect wedding day all come together was reward enough for Jason.

He grabbed his jacket, thanked the bar staff, and left.

His final wedding with Cotswolds Curated Weddings. Although his boss didn't know that yet.

Jason was determined to have a new job before his next wedding took place, which gave him four weeks.

He walked to his car. Guests stood outside smoking, drinking, dancing, chatting. Men in suits, women in formal dresses, all manner of hats, fascinators abounded. He loved seeing how people's versions of dressing up could vary so much. He'd seen one guest at a wedding arrive in a tracksuit.

Leaning against his car, he turned to look at the barn, surrounded by countryside, crunchy gravel in the car park, the faint chorus of 'Come On Eileen' filled the air and he smiled. God, he loved his job. It was just that he'd done the Rolls Royce, church, barn reception wedding dozens of times. Of course, they were all slightly different, the wedding favours, the music, the colour scheme, but he'd done it. Again and again, and although locally he was known as the Fairy Godfather of weddings, he wanted a new challenge, a bigger pond where he'd be, for a while, a smaller fish. That was the phrase, wasn't it? He frowned, as he tried to remember what Pete had said, starting the car, slipping into gear and leaving the car park.

As he turned onto the road towards home, towards Pete, where he'd want to know how it had gone, and why couldn't he have come too, Jason glanced at the signpost – left towards Oxford, right towards London.

He turned left, in the direction of the small Cotswolds village where he and Pete had made their home, but he knew if he wanted a new challenge, some variety in the weddings he planned, the people he planned them for, he'd need to turn right, back to where he'd spent his twenties.

Towards London.

Chapter 2

Mel Waltham had managed to get her two youngest children fed, bathed and almost ready for bed, when her husband returned from work.

Her hair stuck up, she had baked beans on her face and T-shirt, and she was contemplating sunglasses to disguise the bags under her eyes. Cold teabags, metal spoons and attempting to get enough sleep had all failed to reduce their size from eye-openingly exhausted to simply sleep-deprived.

Today, forty-bloody-six felt like eighty-six.

'Hello,' Steve said as he hung his jacket by the door. 'Are you alone, or…?'

'Are our children still awake?' Mel shook her head. Why did he always treat the kids as if they were hers to look after, as if they'd arrived without any intervention from himself?

'Getting ready for bed. Would you like to read them a bedtime story?' She tried to keep her tone hopeful, optimistic, in case it was different from the last fortnight.

He sighed. Frowned. Slumped his shoulders. 'I've had—'

'If you say you've had a long day I'll… Well I don't know what I'll do. But you won't like it. Do you want to hear about my day?' He never did, but she thought she'd ask in the hope it would result in a different answer.

Steve strode through the hallway into the kitchen and made himself a large gin and tonic.

'Would you like to see *your* children?'

A child's voice shouted for her from upstairs.

Mel shook her head. 'I tried explaining they have two parents, and that Dad would be home to tuck them in before bed. Tonight I said he'd be home.' Unlike every other night that week.

He clinked the ice in his glass, sipping in thought for a moment. Shaking his head, he said, 'I've got some stuff to finish off before bed.' He removed his laptop from his suitcase, opened it and placed it on the work surface.

'Hello Mel, how was your day, Mel? What did you do today with our children? Would you like a drink too, Mel?' The sarcasm was strong within and outside of her today.

He stared at the laptop, crouching forwards, having pulled out a chair on which to sit. Another sip of his gin and tonic.

'Shall I tell them Dad is going to tuck them in?' She sighed. A thought she'd tried to ignore for some time, floated, unbidden through her mind. *Does this marriage need fixing?*

A child shouted from upstairs, this time her tone more insistent and tinged with desperation.

Without another word, Mel glanced at Steve, raising an eyebrow in serious need of plucking if this morning's brief glance in the mirror was anything to go by.

Between sips of gin and tonic, he tapped with two fingers at the keyboard, peering at the screen.

Going splendidly, as ever! She debated throwing some passive-aggressive comment as she left, but knew it wouldn't make any difference. She'd be accused of nagging and why couldn't she see he was busy. And so, with a sigh, and another large glug of wine, she left the room.

As she climbed the wide spiral staircase, following the noise of the loudest child, she knew it was pointless trying to discuss anything with him at the moment. He'd say he was doing his best, work was work and what needed to be done, needed to be done. And she'd point out everything she did for the children, for their family, wasn't optional. Although she knew she should do it all without any longing for more in her life. She should find motherhood, in all its wonderful varied complexity, perfect, fulfilling and everything she dreamed of.

But the reality didn't quite match up. Piles of washing, food shopping, school drop-offs and collections, three meals a day for four needing to be not only cooked, but bought, cleaned up and thought about.

'Hello, darling,' she said as she entered her daughter's room.

Lily's curly brown hair fell over her shoulders, her blue eyes looked up in sadness.

'Is Dad coming to tuck me in?' Lily asked.

Mel shook her head, rubbed Lily's hair, settled onto the bed and opened a book. 'Maybe later.'

Lily seemed to accept that, nodding enthusiastically.

A while later, Mel reached the end of the story, kissed Lily's forehead, brushed a hair away from her face, stood.

'I miss Pete,' Lily said, as she snuggled under her duvet.

'So do I.' Although she'd never tell anyone this if asked, Pete was her most special child. She wouldn't use the *f* word *favourite*, because even thinking it she worried the other children would notice. But Pete, for myriad reasons, was her most special child. Her first and so kind and sensitive. She left the room.

Popping her head around the next door, Thomas was staring at his TV, playing on his games console.

'Bed.' She stood in front of the TV.

'I'm in bed,' he protested, leaning to one side to continue playing his game.

'Asleep.' She held her hand out for the controller.

He looked up, his brown eyes pleading. He knew exactly how to push her buttons. 'Let me save it, will you?'

She wasn't a monster, so she indicated he could.

She removed the controllers from his bed, perched on the edge. 'Did you do your homework?' She'd meant to supervise him but had got distracted by, what was it again? Something… Lily had told her something about a girl at school being unkind. Then dinner, then tackling the Mount Everest of laundry, then the uniforms and Steve's shirts needed ironing, then the post had remained unopened for the last three days. So she'd opened, sorted, paid, filed, actioned it all. Knowing if anything was overdue, or unpaid, or the car didn't get taxed, or the house insurance renewed, she and she alone would be held responsible for it.

Because Steve was working.

She looked to the ceiling, blinking back tears that had appeared from nowhere.

'Are you okay, Mum?' Thomas put his hand on her arm.

Guilt at even thinking Pete was her most special child stabbed her heart. They were all perfect in their own way. Thomas had watched her cry not two weeks ago, when Steve had said he'd be back very late and could she get on with things without him… Hugging her, telling her she shouldn't cry, he didn't like seeing his mum upset like that.

Am I really happy?

She nodded, blinking away more tears. It was because everything related to the household, the children, fell firmly on her shoulders. It wasn't so much the doing of it that left her teary, exhausted, overwhelmed, feeling thoroughly done with everything, it was the having to *remember* to do all the things. All. The. Things.

She'd tried lists, read every article online about how to get organised, bought Post-It notes and coloured highlighter pens, downloaded various apps and had, at one nervous exhaustion-inspiring point, six separate to-do lists on the go.

'*Fine.*' She nodded. 'Fine. Very well in fact. Did you do your homework?'

He shrugged. 'Why are you sad, Mum?'

She stood, smoothed down her T-shirt, noticed a large yellow stain she'd missed earlier. Her jeans – originally bought when she'd gone up one size to tide her over until she slimmed down – were, she'd acknowledged last year, now her normal size.

She didn't even know where to start, so simply said 'Night,' kissing Thomas's forehead.

He shook his head. 'Disgusting. Do you have to, Mum?'

She stood by the door. She did. Very much have to. Because otherwise what would it all be for? 'Love you.' She waited for him to reply. They'd discussed it didn't make him soppy or cissy, it meant he loved his mum. Which was perfectly normal for any boy, no matter his age.

'Love you.' He sat up in bed. 'Pete messaged me. He wants to come round for lunch at the weekend. And Uncle Jason too.'

That sounded nice. 'Why did he message you?'

'Said you weren't answering your phone.'

She'd dropped it in the sink two days ago and hadn't had time to have it fixed.

'Will they come round?' Thomas asked. 'I'll help. Uncle Jason said he'll help me with football practice.'

'Did he, that's lovely, darling.' She kissed his forehead, turned out the light, closed the door. She stood on the landing for a moment. *Is this my life? How did I let it get to this?* She bit her lip, she needed to have The Conversation with Steve. Even if he was up to his neck in work, the bloody work would have to wait. She couldn't wait, because she was at breaking point. End of tether territory. Crying in her car, waiting for the kids outside their school, having left the house like a bomb site.

Not to mention Steve's behaviour of late. That phone call he'd dashed off to take a few weeks ago had alarmed Mel. He'd explained it away as work, but he rarely had calls at the weekend. Then she'd found a third mobile phone. So now he had a work, personal and another one. 'A dumb phone for when I'm running. Digital detox,' he'd said.

At the time she'd thought it laudable, minimising his screen time. But then, with the hotel receipt in his coat, 'Conference, very boring,' he'd said, although Mel was sure he'd never mentioned an overnight conference.

I'm overwrought. Imagining things where there's nothing to explain.

She stood resting her hands on the banister, contemplating if she could face *this* conversation.

And then there was the earring in his wallet – she'd needed cash to pay the window cleaner and had found it among the change. It was not one of Mel's. Bright green plastic triangle. Very tacky.

She hadn't asked about that, since she didn't know how she'd deal with the response.

She grasped the banister tightly, her knuckles whitening with pressure. Or was she, perhaps, joining up the dots, where there was no drawing to make from them? No conclusion.

Best tackle the total lack of help issue first. He won't be having an affair, when would he have time? Mel barely had time for a wee most days, never mind an affair. And Steve was busier than her, or so he told her anyway.

Definitely a coincidence.

She carefully stepped down the stairs. Steve sat in the darkness, the only light coming from his laptop, casting a blue glow over everything.

'You'll ruin your eyesight doing that.' She sipped the wine. She still cared for him. Loved him even. On a good day.

He shook his head, didn't look at her.

Like now. Mel sighed. 'Lily missed you. I'd said you'd read her a story tonight. I don't think Thomas's too bothered. As long as he has his PlayStation. Apparently there's a new one just out. So he's campaigning about wanting that.' She sighed. It sort of never stopped, did it? A school trip to pack for, a new device to buy, a bit of the house in need of fixing… Life continued with its endless list of tasks, some related to each other, others entirely separate. The skill, she reckoned, was working out which ones *weren't* critical and which ones *were*.

'Can you look at me, please?' She stood to the side of his laptop.

Sighing, he sat straighter, glanced to her, properly making eye contact for the first time since arriving home.

She had loved him. At twenty-three he was handsome. At twenty she knew she'd always love him. Twenty-five years, four children later and…

Fondness definitely. She'd married him for better or worse. This was one of the worse periods.

Do I love him still? I definitely don't wish him any harm, if that's a start perhaps.

She bit her lip. 'Pete and Jason want to come for lunch at the weekend.'

He sighed, shook his head. 'When?'

'Saturday or Sunday.'

'I realise that, darling, but which one?'

'Why? Do you have plans?' If he did, they weren't on the wall calendar where they put all family appointments. She'd started adding the kids' too, but realised since they all fell to her, there was no point ensuring Steve knew they even existed, never mind asking him to take care of some himself.

'I'm busy on Saturday.' He returned to the laptop.

'No you're not.'

'I am.' Terse tone.

'Doing what?' she asked, trying to keep the irritation out of her voice, but failing.

'Out with the boys.' He grinned, too enthusiastically she reckoned.

'Doing what?'

'It's a surprise. Geggsy mentioned something about paintballing. Or that thing with the rope tied between two trees, you swing down on it. Like Boris Johnson did…'

'Zip wire.' She frowned. 'You're doing that? Voluntarily?' It seemed unlikely since he'd never expressed any interest in such outdoorsy pursuits in the time she'd known him. All two and a half decades of it.

'Maybe.' He turned to face her. 'What do you want, I am busy, you know.'

'I need some help. I can't do it all. I'm basically doing MVP parenting at the moment.' The guilt at saying it shot through her like a spiky shard. *Why do people bother having children if they're going to do such a bloody useless job at it?* Words she'd said BK – Before Kids. And then she'd realised it was far easier said than done.

'MVP?'

'Minimum Viable Product. Bare minimum.'

'Picked that up today, did you?' Was that a sneer she detected?

'I'm not stupid.' One of the articles on how to get organised had mentioned it in relation to developing an organisation app. The phrase had stuck with her.

'That's not what I meant, darling. I—' He gestured at the laptop. 'I'm—'

'Busy, yes, I can see. Only, I've not exactly been sunning myself by a pool with a paperback. I've been—'

'Must we *really* do this? Chore wars are so tedious, don't you think?' He frowned, tilted his head to one side.

For a brief moment she imagined not quite slapping or punching him, but if she could blink and he'd disappear. Smug grin and patronising tone and everything. 'Only because I'm the one doing them all.'

Steve closed the laptop, turning to face her. 'You have my undivided attention.' He folded his arms.

'Window cleaner came last week.'

'Gripping.' He raised his eyebrows. 'Can we *please* get to the point? I've had a very—'

'Long day, yes, you said. Same here. Not that you'd know. I only mention the window cleaner because I had to dip into your wallet for the cash.'

His eyes widened, he bit his bottom lip.

She waited, to see if he'd give anything else away in his body language, but his arms remained tightly folded across his chest.

Mel took a deep breath. 'This isn't working for me.' That felt like a reasonable in to a conversation about him helping a little more around the home.

'I wondered when you were going to say something. I'm so relieved. I'm not saying I left some clues, but I'm not saying I didn't leave them.' He shrugged, smiled like a pleased child. 'I was worried you'd take it badly. This'll make things much simpler.'

What on earth is he talking about?

He smiled. 'A clean break will be best, I think. I've sought advice. I'm sure you'll want to speak to someone.'

She wouldn't mind speaking to someone now, someone who could tell her what he was talking about. 'A clean break? We've got a cleaner, I don't—'

'Us. Apart. Separating. I'm sure you'll meet someone else. I mean she sort of fell into my lap. Earring's hers of course. Very lucky of me really.' He frowned. 'Isn't that what you meant when you said it wasn't working for you?' He looked confused.

She hadn't meant that. Although Steve was far from a perfect husband, the thought of being a single mum of four, three who still lived at home, just north of forty-five, and without any prospects of work, left her full of cold dread.

'Are you okay?' He peered at her, concern clouding his face. 'You seem miles away. I'd like to separate. I shall move in with Sally, she's already asked me, still see the kids at weekends, we can work something else out more permanently once we've—'

'Sorry, what did you say? Sally, who the hell is Sally?' She raised her voice, knew the children wouldn't bother checking as they often argued. Sadly.

'My girlfriend.'

She couldn't stop herself, it must have been a nervous reaction to the shock, but she laughed. Great loud guffaws, almost so she couldn't catch her breath. '*Girlfriend!* You're nearly fifty. Is she calling you her *boyfriend*?' More laughter. She was definitely having an out of body experience. This must be normal for the point at which your life falls apart. This was some sort of joke, wasn't it?

He stood in silence, stroked her arm in an attempt to calm her. 'Isn't that what you meant? I assumed you wanted to separate. Divorce eventually. I'm so relieved it's not working for you too. We've had a good innings overall.' He raised an eyebrow.

She would be happier single than with Steve. He could bugger right off, with his sodding girlfriend. Even if it felt as if she'd just hit rock bottom. 'Is that what you're doing at the weekend? Or should I say who.'

'Let's not get into the whole who's doing what, and timelines. It can all become so messy.'

'You're the one who's been having a bit on the side. While I've been here, looking after your, our children. Your, our house.' A silence as she thought about what to do next. Rage at the injustice of looking after Steve for all these years only to be discarded when she had no other options. 'When did you start seeing her?'

'Like I said, we don't need to go into the timeline, it can become so sordid.' His superior tone made her want to slap his smug face.

She didn't, but it took all her restraint. 'Fuck off!' she shouted, really letting herself go, secure in the knowledge the children would think it was just another of their rows. 'You're the one fucking someone else. You're certainly not sleeping with me. Haven't done for ages. Just tell me two things and then you can go to her. How old is she and when did you start seeing her?' Mel paused for a moment. 'Anyway, I don't want you back this weekend; I shall tell the children.'

'If you don't mind, I'd like to speak to Pete and Isaac myself.'

Of course, the two fully grown offspring would probably side with their father. 'When will you understand you're not in charge of this? I'm not some stupid PA you can boss around. I'm your wife. This isn't for you to control. This affects both of us, the whole family. I'll tell the two older boys. I was thinking about inviting Isaac and his girlfriend around since Pete and Jason are coming.'

There was silence.Steve hung his head forwards, fiddling with the laptop's keyboard. 'Thirty-ish. Last year. That summer weekend you went to your mum's.'

That was eighteen bloody months ago. She'd left the kids with Steve and spent the weekend at a health spa with her mother – a very, very late birthday treat. Steve's present was still to materialise.

'How? You had Thomas and Lily. Tell me you've not brought her inside this house. Tell me.' The thought of him shagging this so-called Sally in their bed had her feeling sick with rage.

'I have not. I left the kids with next door, she rang, needing a hand with her oven. She lives all alone. I went round to install it for her and—'

She put her hand up. 'You ended up installing much more than a bloody oven.' She rolled her eyes, shook her head. 'I really don't need to know the rest. She's obviously a secretary from work.'

'How did you know?'

She shook her head, put her head in her hand. 'Because it's so obvious. Thirty-ish. How "ish" are we talking?'

'A bit under thirty actually.'

She wasn't sure why these details were so important, and yet here she was pressing for them. Running on pure adrenaline, she forged onwards. 'I don't know why I'm asking, but since we're having it out, we might as well have it all out. A bit under thirty? By how much? Precisely.'

'Couple of years. Or so.'

'You've told me you want a divorce, why is this nugget so difficult to extract from you? We've not spoken this much in months. This is a whole new experience for me. It's almost like having an actual real live husband. Someone who converses with me.'

'Five years.'

'She's twenty-five?' Mel heard a pinging sound inside her head. She was sure it was someone upstairs signalling this, for her, was the last straw. 'Twenty-fucking-five?'

'Your maths is good.'

'I've fed you, looked after our four kids for twenty-five years, washed, cleaned, done everything for you, watched you progressing in your career, while I stayed at home, some days going out of my brain with no intellectual distraction, and now, not me, but you are the one who ends it?'

Steve shrugged. 'These things happen.'

Having marshalled her temper up to this point, she now failed. Without thinking she slapped him, cleanly across the face. It made a satisfying thwack sound and her palm stung, so she imagined it would have hurt Steve's face.

'You're mental.'

'I am. But not for that. I'm mental for obediently sitting by your side, doing exactly as you've wanted, and waiting until you can find a younger model to replace me.'

She was so shocked, so incandescent at Steve, that she simply left the kitchen, storming upstairs to their bedroom where she threw all of his suits onto the bed, grabbed his toiletries from the bathroom and chucked them into a suitcase. Wiping her cheeks of tears, the suits were rolled into sausages then thrown into a second bag. Holding one in each hand, she descended the stairs, leaving them in the hallway.

He joined her, his hands on his hips and a bemused expression on his face. 'What's this?'

'You, leaving.' She waved, wheeled the bags into the porch, then pushed him by his behind, out of the door, closing it then locking it.

'Don't be ridiculous.'

'You're leaving me, so you're leaving the house. Fuck off. Now.'

Although much larger than her, he seemed so confused that he put up no resistance, simply following her lead and the suitcases outside.

He banged on the window, shouting something about his car keys.

She rang a locksmith and asked for an emergency appointment. She posted his car keys through the letter box. Turning her back to the door which was banging from Steve's fists, she closed her eyes, slipped down and onto the floor. *I've locked my husband out of the house. He's leaving me for another woman.* And yet, although it felt pretty big, as far as Wednesday nights went, the main emotion she felt was relief. Sweet, warm relief that she could walk away from Steve, without any guilt, knowing she'd done more than enough, more than her fair share for their marriage.

Steve's shouts and banging had ended. He sat in his car, staring into space.

And then the relief was replaced with deep, ugly, painful, stabbing guilt. For bringing up the children in a 'broken home', for ignoring her vows at the first opportunity...was it the first...she wasn't sure.

Another man's voice interrupted her thoughts.

She opened her eyes. A check of her watch told her half an hour had passed.

'I'm here about the lock,' someone said outside.

Wiping away tears, she opened the door, showed the locksmith inside, nodding to indicate Steve could follow.

He sprang out of his car, walked past. 'What were you thinking, locking me out of our house?'

The locksmith was removing tools from a rectangular metal box, looking back, doing his best to ignore the argument in mid-flow.

Mel smiled. 'Sorry. Don't mind us.' She tapped the front door. 'This one, if you don't mind.' She led Steve away.

In the kitchen, she said to him, 'What were you thinking, ruining our marriage?'

19

'Be fair, love. We've not been right for years.'

She shook her head. 'Don't you *love* me?'

Steve remained silent, his hands in his pocket he stared at the ground, then glanced at his belongings in the hallway.

That told Mel all she needed. 'I've spent my whole life bending my will around you. Making allowances for what you wanted.'

'Don't be so ridiculous. I've given you everything. House, holidays, cars, clothes, jewellery.'

'You finished your degree and look what that got you. And I dropped out because I was pregnant with your child.'

'Our child.' He stared at her. 'Didn't you want Pete?'

'Don't be so stupid. Of course I did. But I also wanted a degree.'

'You could have finished it.'

'How? With breasts leaking milk, a baby stuck to me, and no-one to look after him?'

'Your parents would have looked after him.'

Mel sighed. She'd been through this with herself decades ago. And still, Steve was too blind to see. 'Fat lot of use they'd have been three hours away.'

'Mine too, would have helped,' he said.

She wouldn't have trusted them with a dog, never mind her first born but for the sake of her marriage she'd never told Steve that. Because she had loved him, at the start, very much, hoping they would create a family together, that she'd return to her studies without too much of a delay. 'Maybe. I thought we'd work something out and I'd go back to uni.'

'So did I. I wanted you to. But then I got that job and the promotion and then...'

'I was pregnant again.' Mel sighed. She definitely had loved him. Otherwise why would she have been with him all this time, created a family together? It was just that who she and he had been then was nothing like who they were now.

Steve looked away, shook his head. 'What should we have done?'

'If we'd both looked after the baby maybe I could have finished my degree.'

'In 1997?' He laughed. 'I wouldn't have got onto the bank's grad scheme unless I put my all towards it.'

'And so I was left giving my all towards our son, and dropping out of uni.'

'You're a better mum than I could ever be.' He shrugged.

'Don't do that. Don't you dare do that now.' In a mocking voice, she went on, 'You're such a great mum, it's been your life's work, it must be so rewarding. What have I got to show for it now? Mid-forties, unemployable, and single because you've found a new model.'

'I wish it could have been different... I wish—'

'You hadn't accidentally fallen into bed with this woman?' Shaking her head she said, 'Doesn't matter. Get your things and go, will you?'

'Now?' He frowned.

'This minute. Why do you think I'm having the locks changed? I don't want you swanning in and out like you own the place. Changes will happen.' Too late for them in the marriage, so they were being forced on her outside of the marriage.

He shrugged. 'I do own it though.'

'What?'

He motioned with his arms. 'This place.' He strode upstairs.

Bile rose in her stomach, her throat tightened, and she was violently and uncontrollably sick into the sink.

The locksmith's voice shouted from the hallway: 'All done, I can show you how it works.'

What works? 'With you in a minute.' She caught her breath, put her head under the tap for some water.

'The new key,' he added.

Right.

Mel wiped her mouth and strode to the hallway, folding her arms across her chest, determined to take everything and anything this mess threw in her way. After she'd paid him, Mel stood by the door in the hallway.

Steve walked slowly downstairs, stopping in the entrance hall. 'Are you sure?'

'That I want you to leave now that you've admitted to having an affair for the last eighteen months?'

He shrugged.

'Yes. Yes I am sure.' She opened the door.

He collected the belongings she'd thrown on the lawn, walked to his car and drove off.

Mel shut the door, walked into the living room and curled up into a ball on the sofa. There she wailed loudly, like an animal in agony, as the betrayal, shock, sheer gall of the man, hit her bodily. It left her winded. The grief at the end of this life she'd had up until an hour ago hit her like a hammer, filling her stomach with sickness and pain.

'Mum, what's wrong?' Lily asked, shaking her shoulder carefully.

Mel wiped her eyes and nose with her sleeve, blinked away tears, took a deep breath, then said: 'Dad's gone.'

'To work?'

'No, permanently.'

'What does that mean?' She jumped on the sofa and cuddled up next to Mel.

'Forever?' Thomas said.

'When did you arrive?' Mel asked, gesturing for him to join her.

Reluctantly he did. 'I heard it all.'

'All?' Mel wiped her cheeks.

'Dad's a shitbag and a selfish twat.'

She was about to tell him off for swearing, but instead nodded, pulled him in for a hug with her other arm. And there they sat, on the sofa as Mel tried to work out what to do next.

And mostly failed.

Chapter 3

Harriet listened as the bride and groom discussed how much they loved the venue she'd brought them to.

'We'd like all of the these,' the woman said, motioning to the ornate archways above the doors.

'Can we have that song, "Perfect Moment" when she walks down the aisle?' the man asked.

They were paying, so as Harriet knew, the client was always right. And they could have whatever they wanted. She nodded. 'The archways come with the venue. You can't opt in and out of having them. They're sort of part of the building.'

'Right.'

They were in the main room, floor to ceiling windows, pillars along both walls, gilt edged paintings on the ceiling, the walls were covered in patterned fabric.

'How much does this one cost?' the woman asked.

'Twenty-five thousand pounds.'

'For the whole place?'

They'd walked around the stately home before arriving at the ceremony room which the venue used for wedding receptions. Harriet summoned all of her patience and explained this.

'So it's just this room?' the man asked, rubbing his stubbly chin.

Harriet nodded.

'For twenty-five grand?'

'Plus VAT. But it does include catering, and staff to serve. Plus decoration of your choice. How would you like it decor-ated?'

The woman's face clouded over, she stared at the ceiling. Pointed to the painted fresco. 'Can that go? I'd like something really elegant and simple. Pink. Everything pink. With silver. And white. And a little bit of blue.'

Harriet's phone rang. 'I need to get this. I'll definitely check with the venue.' She turned, rolled her eyes, strode out of the room and answered the phone.

Robert's deep gravelly voice reverberated through her. It was certainly more exciting than this couple of parvenus. 'I'm working,' she said with a curt tone.

'Do you want to see me tonight?' His cheeky and lascivious tone told her this meant one thing.

She hadn't seen him in more than a week and knew she'd enjoy their time together. But also knew it would leave her feeling a bit... repulsed by herself, used perhaps. She'd never actually asked if he was married, didn't want to think he could be and therefore make it her problem. Something she'd need to worry about. *Don't ask don't tell.* But he always seemed to need to return to something, someone possibly, disappearing for days at a time, to then resurface as now.

'Where and when? Assuming I'm free.' She added the last part to retain some level of self-respect.

'Are you free?'

'Possibly.' *Definitely.* If she kept him long enough, did she think he'd ask to become serious? So she finally, having planned hundreds of them, would have her very own wedding.

Possibly.

'I'll bring a bottle of something fizzy.' He laughed. 'Eight at your place?'

That was how they always arranged it. She hated that she'd become so predictable already, having only been seeing Robert for thirteen months. 'Dinner out first I think.'

'Oh.' The disappointment was obvious in his tone. 'Can't you finish work and meet me now?'

She wasn't short of money to eat out in nice restaurants, didn't really need to work for the money, it was more for the display to show her parents she was capable of doing so. In readiness for running Electrovax, the family company. In theory, she could walk out, meet Robert, find some other job tomorrow. But she didn't want to. 'I can't. Dinner. Somewhere nice. Up west, surely? Bibendum. Quags. You choose.'

'I thought since you've not seen me for a while you'd…'

Want to jump straight into bed as soon as she saw him? He wasn't wrong. One of the advantages of him being a more distinguished man, greying temples, silveriness to his trimmed beard, was that he was a much better lover than any men her own age. Boys, more like, in their late twenties, rushing straight to the finish line, forgetting to take the scenic route.

Robert, although sporadic, mysterious and possibly married, was a man who relished the journey, taken along a wonderfully circuitous route, rather than simply the destination.

Harriet's toes curled in anticipation. She bit her bottom lip, twirled her hair between her fingers.

The client shouted from inside the building.

'I'm working. I said. Which reminds me, why aren't you doing the same?' He did something in the city to do with money, or investments, or mergers and acquisitions. Or both. He'd not said, she'd not asked. He had money, she enjoyed money. It worked for them.

'That's why I wanted to get the fizz. I've got something to tell you.'

'Stop. No more. Don't tell me on the phone. I'll sort us a table at The Ivy. Eight for eight thirty?'

'And then back to yours?' From his tone she could imagine the lascivious lustful grin on his face.

And she didn't hate it. 'Perhaps.' She ended the call, strode back into the building.

The couple were in conversation with the venue manager.

'He says they can't cover up the walls and ceiling.' The woman scrunched up her face, pulling the man closer, looping her hand through his. 'I don't want it.' She shook her head.

The groom-to-be shrugged. 'Back to the drawing board, I guess, babe.'

They left the room.

'I'll join you shortly,' Harriet said to their backs. She turned to the venue manager and said, 'What did they want?'

'A Disney princess wedding. In a fifteenth-century stately home.' He grimaced.

She patted his shoulder. 'Sorry. I have plenty of other couples who will adore your friezes and columns and architraves.' She winked, said goodbye and left.

Meeting the couple outside, she said, 'What would you like to do now?' She had a few other venues she could show them, but they were all very similar. None would quite live up to Disney princess.

The woman sighed. 'Flowers, is that a good place to start?'

Harriet plastered on her best service sector smile, nodded. 'It absolutely can be.' She led them to the car park. 'If you'd like to return to the office, we can agree some of the periphery items, and perhaps that'll give me a better idea of suitable venues.'

The man frowned.

'Cakes, clothes, invitations, music, those sorts of things.'

They climbed into her dark blue BMW. Birthday present from mother and father. Top spec, but without the badges because she didn't want to seem ostentatious. She may have been brought up like a little princess, but she didn't live her life like a Disney one. People didn't need to know she was in line to inherit an empire. Even if she didn't want it.

At the office they'd managed to agree half a dozen key items for the wedding, and Harriet felt more confident she could find them a suitable venue within their generous budget.

They left and she surveyed the cake, flowers and invitations brochures laid on her desk. Her screen had three dozen windows open with further options.

Not bad for an afternoon's work. These clients' budget was top tier, and with Tailored Weddings taking a percentage for organising, they'd make a handsome profit to go towards her annual bonus.

Not that she needed it, but the recognition from a job well done always gave her a little buzz. Plus, something to tell her father about to convince him, if she wanted, she'd be more than capable of running Electrovax when she was what he described as *the right age*, thirty-five. Leaving her six years to work up the desire to actually run the company for her father.

Her phone beeped with a text from Robert: *what time did we say for dinner? Where? Xxx*

Three kisses. *God, he's keen.* And, truth be told, so was she. Itching to eat, drink, chat and forget this whole day in the pleasure of his company. Ignoring completely what sort of person or life he had outside of their time together.

She tidied up the brochures, called the maître d' of The Ivy. They chatted about how they were; she'd gone to boarding school with his sister. They had used to summer in the Algarve – an enormous villa with a swimming pool, two families, five children. Hadn't she sort of got off with him once? Or was that the other brother, the one who hadn't got into their school? Or had he gone gay… She'd heard some such distasteful rumour about him but she lost count. Those summers felt like a lifetime ago.

'What can I do for you?' he asked.

'I know it's terribly cheeky, Toby, and unbelievably short notice, but you would not believe the day I've had.' A long sigh. 'Optional architectural features in a stately home and that gives you a picture of what I've dealt with. The only thing keeping me going is the thought of chef's shepherd's pie, a fruity, oaky Cab Sauv and lashings of pav for dessert.' She smiled. It was what she always chose when at The Ivy. It provided a sort of comfortable hark back to a childhood she'd wished to have enjoyed. Home-cooked simple food. Rather than endless dinner parties and seven courses.

'I'll tell chef to put one aside for you.' He chuckled. 'Any news on us having that hol you mentioned?'

Last time she'd visited she'd ended up terribly tight on Cab Sauv and had suggested revisiting the French villa they'd enjoyed as children. It was now an Airbnb and Toby, the maître d', had always harboured a crush on her. His brother – yes he had gone gay, she remembered now – he was meant to come with his... man friend. She couldn't bear to say *boyfriend* when it was two men. It felt so... distasteful in her mouth.

'We'll talk about it tonight, Toby. Is that okay?'

'Course.'

'Two, if you could put two of the shep pies aside please. Well, a table for two, I'm not sure what my friend will want.' She knew precisely what he'd *want*, but it probably didn't involve slow cooked lamb topped with crispy mashed potato.

'Table for two. Eight thirty. Done. Anything else I can do for you, Harriet?'

'Not unless you can find a wedding venue for a Disney princess, Toby.' She ended the call.

Flicking through one of the industry's many bridal magazines, she came across an article with two men tying the knot. She refused to say *married*, because marriage was about a man and a woman. Said so in the Bible. Or some such.

The men wore well-tailored blue suits, pink flowers, and had been walked up the aisle by their mothers.

Aisle. She shook her head. You don't get aisles anywhere except churches or cathedrals. And those men couldn't have married in one of those.

She flicked through the article, reading the picture captions: met in a pub in Soho... been together for twelve years... all their friends joined them... didn't want anything too ostentatious.

She shook her head, flipping the magazine shut. *Well, perhaps pink and purple flowers, enough baby's breath to open a factory and mothers dressed in matching pink wasn't the best idea.*

A sigh and she pushed the magazine away.

Men marrying men. Women marrying women. Why couldn't they leave marriage and weddings for the rest of us; a unity between a man and a woman. When will all this nonsense end?

–

Next day at work, Harriet stirred her instant coffee.

A tall and muscular man was being shown from one meeting room to another. The HR person ushered him gently.

He wore dark fitted jeans, white shirt, rolled up at the sleeves, revealing tattooed forearms. He made eye contact with her as he looked across the office, while the HR person spoke to him. And had he smiled at her too? Surely not. Blue eyes and dark hair were such a dreamy combo.

He strode across the office, cleared her desk, sweeping everything onto the floor in one strong arm movement. He placed his hand on the small of her back, pulled her closer, lay her backwards onto the desk and then he kissed her. First her neck, then her lips, gently prising open her mouth so his tongue could explore.

This was it, she closed her eyes and leaned right into the moment. She'd met her romantic hero, her future husband, he was precisely what she had in mind. Her father would surely approve of this man. Perhaps hide the tattoos for the first few times they met...

She felt a rocking motion.

'Harriet, Harriet, I was asking you a question!' a voice seeped into her consciousness.

'Sorry, what now?' Harriet asked.

'Do you want the milk?' Her colleague gestured to the carton.

Tattooed forearms man was nodding as the HR person continued talking. He walked into a meeting room, the door closed.

Later, she looked out of the window to see him leaving. His white shirt and dark jeans stood out against the sea of grey suits. A man walked up, hugged him, and then—

Kissed him.

Briefly, Harriet turned away. Disappointment lodged itself deep in her gut as her dream of this man being her perfect husband was swept away like a sandcastle as the tide came in. She knew it was totally irrational, but honestly, what business did a man like that have being…

'All right?' a voice behind her asked.

She nodded. 'Looking at where I might eat for lunch.'

'Are you okay? You look like you've just received some bad news.'

'Don't be ridiculous. What on earth makes you say that?'

'You look… disappointed.'

'How can I be disappointed for something I've never had.' She strode towards her desk, wishing to avoid any further interrogation for fear she'd let it all spill out in an emotionally incontinent mess.

–

That evening she opened another bottle and rang Sophie.

Determined not to burden her friend with this unbidden wave of sadness, Harriet put on a bright smile. 'Are you still at work?' The noise of keyboards and chatter in the background told Harriet Sophie was still in the busy newsroom of the national paper.

'Look, I'm on deadline, but I can ring you later. Have a proper natter. What's happened? You sound as glum as a wet weekend in Widnes.'

'Would you cover the wedding of those two reality TV stars?' She felt tackling it at such an oblique angle would help.

'The two men from *Filmed In Kensington*?'

'Indeed.'

'No.'

'I see,' Harriet replied, suddenly feeling brighter.

'Not for the reasons you're thinking.'

'You don't know what I'm thinking.'

'I do.' A pause, and then, 'It's a bit... lowbrow for us. We're more royalty, crown princes and princesses from across Europe, actors, actresses, musicians. If we have to list which TV show they're from, we've lost our readers.'

'I see.'

'Harriet, what is this *really* about? Has that chap dumped you? Because I told you how unsuitable he is, and how you're wasting your time with him – how long is it now?'

'Thirteen months.' Their anniversary had been splendid – oysters and champagne before catching the train to Paris for a weekend of sightseeing, fine dining and staying in a five-star hotel.

Sophie scoffed. 'And how you'd never meet someone more appropriate while you're associated with him.'

She had. She'd told Harriet all of those things, at length, and still Harriet persevered with Robert. 'It's not *him*.' Although he hadn't taken her away for a whole weekend, Friday night and he'd had to rush back for something by Saturday evening.

'Right,' Sophie said.

'Traditional values, traditional roles, why can't men be men and women be women?' *There's always a proper way of doing things, so why do so many people insist on ignoring it?* Harriet poured herself another large glass of wine.

'I think it's a lot to ask of a man to take on a traditional role, while women, us included, have demanded more progressive roles for themselves. With change comes change for all.' Sophie sighed. 'I'll call you later.'

'I'll let you go.' Closing her eyes, she enjoyed the light-headed sensation the wine gave her.

Was it really that simple, Harriet wondered. In a world where girls were told they could be anything, it was reasonable to expect boys to be told the same. Progress. And although she wasn't the sort of woman who'd ever been interested in becoming a car mechanic, or a doctor, it had been comforting that if she'd so desired, they were options. But, just as she preferred the traditionally female role, she still longed for men to maintain theirs.

Chapter 4

'So how did it go?' Pete asked over dinner.

Jason thought about the job interview for a moment. 'Once I met them I knew I'd sparkle.'

'Something about selling snow to the Eskimos, isn't it?'

'Some people hate a presentation, but I give great Power-Point. I know. I've been told.' Mainly because it didn't involve writing long words, and he could use pictures and talk *around* the subjects.

'Have you got any more interviews lined up?'

He did, but they were local firms, and this was London, and all that represented. Growth, change, different ways of doing things, a wider range of clients and their dream weddings.

Jason had done the traditional church, registry office, white dress, morning suit, flowers, disco reception at a hotel dozens of times.

'A few, but I really want this one,' he said.

Pete held his hand. 'I have a good feeling about this one, right.'

The last job application only took him half an hour since he had the standard paragraphs Mel had written and his new kick-arse CV. Satisfied with a good day's work, he poured himself a large gin and tonic and waited for Pete to return.

He finally received a call the following morning, having resigned himself to not getting the job.

'Your presentation style was relaxed and confident,' a man who'd introduced himself as Christopher said, 'your knowledge of the wedding industry unparalleled, and your assessment put you in the top quartile, despite some spelling and grammar issues.'

Jason braced himself for a big fat 'however' since he wasn't great with quartiles, and knew his spelling and grammar had let him down in the assessment.

'We'd like to offer you the role. We think your different approach and point of view will provide us with the valuable diversity of opinion we're aiming for.'

'Thanks, I mean yes, of course! Great.'

'We'll send a letter with all the details, for you to return a signed copy.'

Jason ended the call and despite buzzing on the high from the offer, he couldn't help fixating on some of their words. No point getting too hung up on that, until he saw the letter.

Later that evening, when they were having drinks in a bar to celebrate – at Pete's insistence, since Jason was still a little reserved – Jason said what had been preying on his mind since the phone call.

'I think I'm ticking some kind of box for them.'

'What do you mean?' Pete topped up their flutes with Cava.

Turning forty had lowered the number of fucks Jason gave about many things. 'I think I'm a diversity hire.'

'You're white, and as far as most people can make out, straight. So I don't think so.'

'Except I was very open about myself in the interview.'

'In what way, open?'

'Told them I'd done events for London, Manchester and Brighton Prides.'

'Everyone does those. Doesn't follow you'd be gay.'

'What about if I told them I lived with my partner, Pete?'

'How did that come up?'

'Flexibility to travel and overnight stays as part of the job. It felt like the right time to show them who I am.'

Pete nodded, sipping his Cava in thought. 'So you leave the last job because it's too… What are we saying?'

'Restrictive, dull, boring?'

Pete nodded. 'And now you're hired for being creative, different and yourself and you're unhappy? Is that about right?'

Jason hadn't thought of it this way before. Perhaps he'd been focusing on the negatives and being out of work had made him doubt everything, including himself.

'Did they offer you the job?'

'They did.'

'So you've worked somewhere that doesn't want you to be yourself, let's see if this place gets it right. Why don't you wear Ruby on your first day?'

Ruby, his bright red suit. 'I could. I should. I will.' Even if he was a diversity hire, he'd show them he deserved the role more than anyone else. Because not only was he the best person for the job, but he also had that undeniable quality no one else could bring to the role: himself.

'I always worry someone's going to tap me on the shoulder and ask me to leave, cos the game's up,' Jason said.

'Why?'

'When I was an events assistant, TV show runner, corporate events manager, I'd do anything, keep my mouth shut to get in with the right people. No one gives a shit about the real you when you're organising a press conference for The Fridays.'

'Love them. Teeth, big hair and a fabulous chorus — those girls can sing, right?' Pete winked and smiled.

'Right. And no one wants an events manager to turn up to work in a red suit, diamond studded earrings and heels.'

'You didn't?'

'No. I didn't. But I wanted to. Plenty of times. But it wouldn't have gone down well with the biggest food manufacturer in Europe who wanted us to organise a tasting event.'

'Do they do those ice creams that you slice? With the chocolate, ripples of ice cream?' He closed his eyes in thought. 'The Misteletta.'

'They do *everything*,' Jason said with a glint in his eye.

And he'd loved it, the corporate events, gradually working up to bigger and more complex ones, until a friend had asked him to plan her wedding. He'd done it so well, and enjoyed it so much that he showed his boss the pictures and videos and explained how much he could have marked up the price, if it weren't for a friend... his boss had no choice but to move him to wedding planning.

They called him the Fairy Godfather of wedding planning in the Cotswolds. But he'd outgrown it, wanted the variety working in a London firm could offer.

Jason folded his arms, sighed. 'I held back the real me. And now I always wonder how differently things would have been if I hadn't done that.' He'd compromised himself in so many little ways back then, living in London in his twenties. Not telling people where he danced (Heaven, Pop Stars and sometimes Fiction) and drank with friends (The Black Cap, Molly Mog's, 79 CXR), changing the pronoun for the boyfriend he had at the time, toning down his clothes, removing his ear piercing, jewellery. Although it wasn't that long ago, almost twenty years felt like a different age from now, and Pete couldn't understand because he'd been five.

'You can't re-do the past. It is what it is. But you can do things differently now.'

'Maybe that's not accepting this job.' Jason shrugged.

'You really can be stubborn sometimes.' Pete shook his head.

'Comes with having principles.'

'And being such a grumpy old man.'

Jason raised an eyebrow.

'Joke. Promise when I turn thirty you can do the same to me.' Pete nodded. 'Your principles are one of the reasons why I love you so much.' Pete kissed him.

'Enough about me, how are you?'

'I'm fine, but Mum, on the other hand.'

'What's wrong with her?'

'She's not said. She wouldn't. But I think she's taken on too much and won't ask for help. As usual. She thinks she's up for super mum of the year award and if she needs any help then it shows she's a terrible person.' Pete shook his head. 'I'm sure it's just a blip. Her and Dad are okay. After all those years, it can't be so bad, can it?'

'Parents are people too. Messy, imperfect and fallible just like their children.'

'Yeah, but do they have to be so messy and imperfect *right now*? I'm sure they'll muddle on together.'

Jason shrugged. He didn't know what to say.

Pete shook his head. 'If she asks, I want us to help her and Dad. But not in a way where she feels she's imposing on us. She's always thinking of others, she never considers herself until it's too late, or not at all.'

Chapter 5

It was Saturday and Mel's eldest children were arriving any moment. She thought she had something of a plan to deal with the separation and divorce.

Mel had sat Lily and Thomas down and explained what had happened. 'Your dad and I have decided it will be better if we don't live together any more.'

'Why?' Lily had asked.

Mel felt she should have prepared for this. 'Sometimes parents meet other people and they decide to live with them instead of each other.'

'Why?' Lily asked, perfectly reasonably.

'People change how they feel over time. This is normal. Dad has a new friend and he's going to live with her.'

Thomas flicked his hair from his eyes and shrugged. 'Dad's got another woman, right? What about you?'

'I'll be fine,' Mel said, trying her best to mean it.

'Can I see him?'

'Every other weekend and one night during the week.'

Thomas shrugged. He looked at her from the corner of his eye. 'Have you got another man?'

Mel shook her head vigorously. 'No. This is entirely your father's doing.' Although it blamed him for this, it felt fair.

Lily shook her head. 'I miss Dad. I want to see him every night. Why can't I?'

Mel could feel Lily resting on the precipice of one of her tantrums. 'You didn't see him every night before, because he's always working. But now, you can see him, all alone, without me, at every other weekend, and one night in the week. How does that sound?'

She seemed to think for a moment, smiling possibly at the thought that would be more than she'd seen him before. A nod and then: 'Okay. Will he buy me a name necklace, new pink and white bike and a smart watch?' Her eyes shone.

'Very possibly.' Mel turned to Thomas. 'We both love you both very much. This doesn't change that. Understand?'

Lily asked, 'Will we see Dad at the weekend?'

'Yes. But not this one. Next weekend.'

'He's not gonna start playing board games,' Thomas said staring at his phone, 'or take us to museums and art galleries, is he? At school Carter's parents split up and his dad went a bit mad. Took him to all these really boring places and it was worse than school.'

Mel hoped Steve would know how to amuse their children after all this time, but there was always an outside chance he'd be as useless as Carter's father. 'Perhaps you should tell Dad that.'

And then, content she'd done all she could to explain it, conversation had moved onto TV, dinner and whether they'd done that night's homework.

Ironically, Steve agreeing to take the children alternate weekends meant they'd see more of him than when they were married, but he didn't seem to realise that when he'd agreed. 'Of course I want to see them, they're *my* kids too.'

Mel had thrown the phone across the room at that. They'd always been his kids too, but quite why it had taken him finding a younger mistress to realise, was beyond her.

A spike of regret at years wasted with Steve shot through her.

Guilt flooded her stomach as she knew everyone would expect her to be sad at being single, in her mid-forties. Battling with the dating game again. Getting used to online matching programmes and services.

Except Mel wasn't sad at all. All the meeting new men, dating palaver terrified her of course. But not the bit about being single. About being separated. States she knew should make her sad, hopeless, feel like a failure, and yet she didn't.

She couldn't tell her friends she'd not been happy for a while, worried that it would make her look weak for not taking charge and telling Steve. But unhappiness, Mel now realised, was something you got used to. Gradually, week by week, decade by decade. Until she was used to a permanent state of misery as her normal way of living.

The front door opened and Pete and Jason walked in carrying casserole dishes of food.

'I said not to worry.' She took the food, set them in the kitchen, then hugged Pete and Jason.

They stood in the kitchen.

'I swear you keep growing.' She looked up at Jason. He looked taller and broader than the last time. Perhaps it was his clothes, they were always so tight, his muscles seemed to bulge out of them.

He blushed, shaking his head, pulled Pete close and put his arm around her son.

At least some people could make a relationship work. This was going to make what she had to ask even harder.

'Why the big mystery?' Pete looked around the kitchen. 'Is Isaac here yet?'

'He's coming late. He split up with—' she narrowed her eyes '—what was her name again?'

Pete shrugged. 'Never met this one. You look… nice.'

'Thanks. Brush up all right, don't I?' Mel had decided to wear make-up and straightened her hair, even though she wasn't leaving the house. She wanted to look her best, give herself a confidence boost for the big ask of her family.

Thomas ran into the kitchen and gave Jason a hug. 'Uncle Jason, can we play football?'

He looked at Mel, raising his eyebrows.

Mel said, 'Twenty minutes. As soon as Isaac's here, we're eating.'

They ran outside.

Pete helped himself to wine from the fridge, pouring Mel one too. Handing her a glass, he said, 'What's going on?'

Mel took a deep breath. 'Can we wait until your brother's here? I don't want to say it twice.'

'So there *is* a something to tell.' He frowned. 'Where's Dad?'

She turned away, not able to make eye contact and continue keeping this from him. Taking a big sip of wine, she turned her attention to the food they'd brought. 'What are these?'

'Macaroni cheese with bacon, and tuna pasta bake with broccoli spears. Gotta try to get your five a day, right?'

'Right. Can you check on Lily, please? She's in her room.'

There was a silence. Pete stroked Mel's back. 'Whatever it is, we'll be okay. Did you say where Dad is, I don't remember?'

'Away.'

'Away? Like, on holiday away?'

No, with his bloody girlfriend, who's your age. 'Golfing with the boys. His university friends. It's like a lunar eclipse to get them all together. So I said he should go.' She shrugged.

He left the room.

Just about managing to keep a lid on her emotions, Mel heated the macaroni cheese, grated more Cheddar on top, and made a green salad. She reckoned tearing lettuce, slicing onions and green peppers wouldn't be too difficult.

She *could* do everything. Had already been for years. Without Steve. Except the blasted money part. If it wasn't for Steve's bloody career she'd have half a chance at getting a reasonably well-paid job. That had been the deal; she would bring up the children and run the house and he would go to work. But now, as she looked back at her life, the regret at not making more for herself stabbed her gut. But there had never been time. Barely enough time to dress herself, never mind work, or do an evening class in… What would she have done? With sadness she realised she wouldn't have known where to start.

Hopeless. Myself, and this situation.

With the salad made, she walked to the garden to find Jason and Thomas playing football. They looked so happy. And then she was going to tell them what had happened and it would all end.

She'd asked the two younger children not to mention their dad had gone away because she wanted to tell the others all together. Because it would mean working out how to be a family again.

Now, announced with a loud blast on his modified car horn, Isaac turned up in his black, lowered Ford hatchback. It was his pride and joy and if he put as much time and energy into his relationships with women as he did with that car, he wouldn't be arriving now single. He'd moved out to decide what to do with his life, and so far had only managed to get a job delivering takeaway food that seemed to pay enough for his living expenses, and no more. She hoped it would help him work out he definitely wanted to go to university.

Mel pulled him into a hug in the hallway.

'Where's Dad?' Isaac raked a large hand through his wild ginger hair. 'His car's not here is it?'

'Come on inside.' She gestured for the others to follow. Shouting for Lily and Pete as they sat in the living room, they sat in silence waiting for the final two to arrive.

Pete perched on the arm of a chair where Jason sat, and Lily sat on Jason's lap.

'Did somebody die?' Pete asked, chuckling.

'Your father and me are separating.' There, get it over with. Like ripping off a plaster. Done.

'Why?' Isaac asked.

She looked at the two eldest kids. 'I can go into details later. Assuming you're all staying the night?'

'We didn't bring stuff,' Pete said, looking to Jason who shrugged. 'But we could.'

'Isaac?'

He bobbed his head to one side. 'Can we get McDonald's tomorrow for breakfast?'

42

Mel closed her eyes in despair.

'Focus on the big issues, there Isaac,' she said. 'Okay.'

'Why are we here? Is it something you and Dad can fix?' Pete asked.

She knew she should feelsadder that her husband had left her, but honestly, she was relieved.

'This is actually the best all round. I can focus on my future.' She looked at Lily and Thomas. 'Our future. It will all be fine.' *All will be well.*

'You seem very calm, Mum,' Isaac said. 'If you're totally okay with this, why have you invited us round, why are we all made to stay the night?'

'I wanted everyone to be together when I told you. We're a family, and Dad will always be part of that, just it'll be different.'

Isaac said something to Pete who nodded.

'What was that?' Mel asked.

Pete shook his head. 'Nothing. It'll keep. Until we can have the 18 version of what happened. Is this PG13 version done now?'

'You seem pretty relaxed about it,' Mel said.

'I will be, until I know what actually happened. I can't get angry at Dad until I know.' He glanced at his younger siblings. 'Details.'

'The main thing you all need to know is that with a few adjustments, everything's going to stay as now. This house, everything.'

'Yeah, about that.' Isaac narrowed his eyes, stood and leaned against the wall, tapping it. 'How's that gonna work, exactly? Seeing as you don't work.'

Dammit, Mel had hoped to get everyone full of food and a little tipsy before laying out her big ask. 'We've been discussing dividing assets. Financial arrangements. You know.'

'Like we know, Mum?' Isaac shook his head, slid down the wall and sat on the floor.

Pete stood. 'Sounds very... amicable? And quick?'

'Adult.' She was still livid he'd cheated on her, but she wasn't about to share that with everyone. 'Practical.' She also wasn't about to tell them she felt relieved to finally be able to give up on their marriage. Not least because it made her feel terribly guilty for reneging on her wedding vows. For finally admitting *forever* didn't mean quite until one of them died. What sort of an example was she setting for her children – until death us do part, or until one of us has had enough...

'We talked it through. It makes sense if we carry on our lives... separately. Your dad is going to pay child maintenance for Lily and Thomas until they're eighteen. Generously.' Only because she'd pointed out quite how much she'd probably get if they went formal since she was the wronged party and he'd cheated on her, a devoted loyal wife who'd put her own career aside to raise his – their – children for twenty-five years.

'Right,' Pete said, looking at his watch.

'Sorry, am I boring you?'

'I'm hungry.' He rubbed his stomach. 'Go on. This is important. Remind me why you're so attached to what's only bricks and mortar?' He gestured at the house about him.

'I'll keep the house. Since I decorated and looked after it.' And designed it. And had it built. As well as the children, this home was one of Mel's most proud achievements.

'Sounds perfect, you've obviously got it all sorted with Dad,' Pete said. 'Can we eat?'

'Wait,' Isaac said. 'Let her finish. There's gonna be a big catch. Wait for it.'

'Thank you,' Mel said, 'for that trailer for the good news, Isaac. Yes. He's right.'

Mel's life seemed to have led up to this point. To this ask of her family, having done so much for them.

Mel closed her eyes, sent up a wish for good luck to whatever higher power she felt she needed that week. 'I can't work. Or even if I could, I wouldn't be able to afford the mortgage.'

'What about the child maintenance?' Isaac folded his arms. 'Generous, you said.'

'More than. But it's not income. Not classed as income for me. So the bank won't allow my name to be on the mortgage because I have no income to cover it.'

'But you do. From Dad.'

'Only on paper. And honestly, it's not enough. Not to eat and heat and other wild luxuries.'

'So you sell and move?' Pete said.

'Or,' Mel said. 'You move back in.'

She looked at Pete, then Isaac. 'Come on, what do you say, boys?'

'Boys… Moving back in with my mum, at my age?' Pete shook his head. 'No offence, Mum. What about Jason?'

Jason held his hands up in surrender. 'Don't get me involved.'

'I'm up for it.' Isaac stood, walked towards the kitchen. 'More money left for me. There's so much stuff to do when you leave home. I'm going thirty hours a week for the delivery company and at the end of the month I have nothing left. I mean, council tax, what's that about?'

'You'd have to pay rent. Otherwise I'd still lose the house.'

'So lose it, it's only a house,' Pete said.

'Easy for you to say, you didn't have it built, designed, decorated, conceived from scratch. Did you dream about the layout of every room? Do you have marks on the walls from your heights at each and every birthday until you left?'

'Sorry,' Pete said. 'But it's a place to live. We're the family, surely?'

He wasn't wrong, and yet Mel couldn't separate the emotional ties to the house from the actual bricks and mortar. Besides, she'd imagined growing old there, why should Steve's stupidity stop her from doing that?

'Anyway,' Isaac returned. 'I'm going to uni. Unless you don't want me to go?'

'Isn't one of your choices nearby, could you go there and… live in?'

'The crappiest and last choice one, yeah. But I don't want that. If I get the grades I'll—'

'Fine.' His education, of course, came first. She turned to Pete and Jason. 'What about you?'

Jason shrugged.

Pete looked at him. 'Like I said...' He looked at the floor. 'We've got Jason's place. It's how we like it.' Turning to her he said, 'Mum, I'm twenty-five. Jason's forty. Do you *really* think we'd get along living with you? I've got a job offer our side of Oxford. It'd be hours from here.'

'Have you?' Jason frowned.

Pete nodded. 'Branch secretary and regional organiser. I didn't want to bother you, with your new job stuff.'

Jason rubbed Pete's neck, then stood. 'I'm starving, do you think we could carry this on later, maybe? With wine.'

Everyone seemed to think that was a good idea, so they left for the dining room.

Mel remained sitting in the living room as the bustle of everyone else continued elsewhere.

That had gone better in some ways, and much worse in others. At least she'd said it. Having her problem out in the open wasn't exactly a problem halved, but it was definitely shared.

They ate and talked about everything and anything except what Mel had discussed earlier.

As Pete checked his macaroni cheese was finished, he stood. 'Shall I get the dessert?'

Mel looked up. Taking on this house financially seemed like something she should have considered before casually agreeing to the separation. Except Steve hadn't given her much choice, and had run off into the sunset with his younger model. Having the house for the two youngest children had made sense, at the time. Steve hadn't disagreed, apparently it was usual for the mother to stay in the matrimonial home. It had seemed so simple when they'd discussed it. Almost as if he'd thought it all through months ago and was waiting to be caught.

But why remain in a marriage for financial reasons? And yet, she realised, with regret, this was what she'd inadvertently done for a while. Rubbing along with him, thinking he'd improve, he'd show her kindness, attention, even half as much as he did to his bloody work laptop.

Pete stood by her elbow. 'We can't move in, but I can totally give you some money.'

'I'mma get a part-time job when I start uni, so I can send some money to you. Not much though.' Isaac shrugged, helped himself to another spoonful of potatoes. 'If that's any help.'

Mel smiled. 'Thanks. Yes. I reckon I'll have to get myself a job.' Only she'd had nothing on her CV for more than twenty-five years. She'd get a job stacking shelves in a supermarket, delivering food with a bike, anything. As long as she could keep this house.

Her house.

Because for some reason, although she wished she'd had a career, the thought of losing what amounted to her life's work, seemed too sad to contemplate.

Chapter 6

'Harriet, this is our newest employee, Jason.' Christopher stood by her desk.

Mr Tattooed Forearms stood next to her in a bright red suit.

Harriet arranged her face into something approximating a smile. Held out her hand. 'Pleased to meet you.'

His handshake was firm, he made eye contact throughout. Piercing blue eyes with slight crinkles at the edges. Were there flecks of grey in his beard, on his temples?

'What's your role?' Harriet asked.

He put his arms behind his back, stood with his legs apart and was still smiling. Those perfect teeth couldn't be natural. No one has teeth that straight and white. No one. Not even Sophie, and she'd had the best dentistry money could provide.

'I'm an account manager,' he said.

Harriet blinked. An account manager? Like herself. 'You're joining this team?' She wanted to check she'd not misunderstood.

'Is that what you are?'

She nodded, forcing herself to blink.

Christopher laughed. 'I thought you knew. Didn't I tell you?'

'I'd have remembered that,' Harriet said.

'Jason is here to bring some much-needed sparkle to our wedding planning department. I'd have snaffled him for our corporate events department except… Anyway, I'll leave you to it.' Christopher left.

'Apparently you're showing me the ropes!' He raised two perfectly plucked eyebrows. 'I'm not sparkly all the time. In fact most days I'm plain old me. Hope that's okay.' He shrugged.

'Where are you sitting?'

Jason pulled the chair out next to Harriet's desk. 'They asked me to go through my presentation that got me the job. Feels a bit stupid to be honest.' He blushed.

The seat next to her had been empty since her colleague had left and Harriet had become nicely used to the extra space. Sharing it with someone didn't fill her with the most charitable thoughts.

He sat, glanced at a piece of paper and logged onto the computer.

She smiled, taking her seat. With as little interest as possible, she asked, 'What was it, your presentation that got you the job?'

Jason shook his head, staring at the screen as he logged on. 'It's nothing too major.'

Major enough to mean you're sitting beside me, taking half of my job off me. She grinned.

'How to bring Tailored Weddings into the twenty-first century.'

She mentally rolled her eyes. Externally she grinned. 'Do tell more.'

'Now?'

'As good a time as any.' She sat back on her chair, preparing to listen to whatever codswallop he was about to tell her.

Jason stood next to the computer screen showing his first slide. 'Shall I stand?'

'If you want to,' Harriet said, immediately disliking the typeface he'd chosen – all fake historical with swirls and almost illegible, and the image of two cartoon men holding hands, next to a pair of women in wedding dresses doing the same. *Oh God, this is going to be dreadful.*

'As you can see,' Jason gestured to the slide 'Weddings are about all sorts of people. So my vision is to deliver a bespoke service to clients, working with them in partnership, from storyboard, to delivery.'

Of course. How else can you plan someone's wedding? 'Assuming you describe how to do that?'

'It's on the next slide.' Jason moved the presentation on and started talking about how to do this. 'I always think it's like a good salesman – or woman.' He chuckled nervously, staring at Harriet, then turning back to the screen. 'If you give the customer what they want, it doesn't feel forced, you're helping them with a problem they've come to you with.' He rubbed his hands on his trousers.

Big thighs. Such a waste... 'Right.' Harriet leaned forwards. 'Do you have a sales background?'

Jason shrugged. 'Bit of this, bit of that. I've got slides for the dreaming bit. How to work with clients to really understand what they want from their wedding.'

Harriet nodded, indicating he should skip to that slide.

It showed a Pinterest board with words, images, book covers, film posters, celebrities, stuck at various angles.

Harriet nodded. 'What's this?' She had to admit, it did look more interesting than the wedding commissioning form they currently used.

'I ask my clients to bring magazine cuttings, wallpaper, quotes from books, films, music lyrics, anything that is the vibe they're looking for with their wedding. Then together we build a Pinterest board until we have a clear shared vision. This makes it much easier for me when I'm talking to suppliers, so I know if they'll fit in with the clients' vision.' He smiled and talked through the example on his slide.

Begrudgingly, Harriet admitted it was a good idea. Once he'd got going, he'd also relaxed a little. Sophie often said she could be brusque and a little scary. Harriet had never understood this, but took her best friend's word for it.

Jason had moved on a few more slides about providing value for money, a tailored budget whatever the clients can afford, and was now talking about suppliers. 'Suppliers are so keen to show they're inclusive. Sometimes it's a bit pink-washy, but most of the time it's really genuine.'

Harriet frowned. 'Pink-washy?'

'Like green-wash, where it's pretending to be environmentally friendly, but it's only sticking a green label on something. Pink-washy is where it pretends to be inclusive of LGBT people – the pink pound, you've heard of that, right?'

Harriet pursed her lips and nodded, staring directly into Jason's eyes. 'Of course.'

'Right.' He straightened his tie, buttoned and unbuttoned his jacket. 'So, it's about working with suppliers to create new and innovative weddings. Since same-sex marriage, the book of who does what has been ripped up. People can make their own traditions, create their wedding their own way. And I believe more opposite sex couples want to do the same – why have the father of the bride walking her up the aisle? Why have a best man? Why have bridesmaids?' He shrugged.

Harriet could think of dozens of perfectly reasonable reasons why, but she kept them to herself. 'Very good.' She sat back. 'I can see why you got the job.'

Jason sat at his desk.

'Your PowerPoint skills are certainly better than mine...'

'If you want, I can show you how I did it.'

'Maybe later, I've got quite a lot on at the moment.' Harriet returned to her screen and viewed her empty diary for the day. *What to do now?*

–

Later, over lunch with Sophie she recounted what Jason had told her. 'And he thinks I know nothing. Talk about grandmother sucking eggs.' She shook her head.

Sophie ate the cucumber in her goblet-sized glass of gin and tonic. She was having a liquid lunch, only allowing herself the cucumber and ice until suppertime. 'Have you got any pictures?'

Harriet narrowed her eyes. 'If you're asking me if I took a picture of my new colleague, then the answer is no. Excuse me, I think you're really handsome, despite you being on the wrong bus, please can I take your photo so my friend can drool about how much of a waste your being gay is.' Harriet rolled her eyes. 'Perlease.'

Sophie crunched on the ice. 'I doubt his boyfriend thinks it's a waste. You can't say stuff like that nowadays. It's all live and let live now.'

'He's totally a diversity hire. No way they'd have given him the job if he wasn't…' She waved, not wanting to say the word. 'You know.'

'Gay?' Sophie offered.

Harriet nodded. 'It's political correctness gone mad. Since when do brides and grooms want a man to plan their big day? Since never, that's when. I've been doing this for long enough to know most people won't want *him* to plan their wedding. What does he know about flowers, colour palettes, confetti, wedding favours, bridesmaids' dresses, wedding dresses?' She shook her head. 'It's nonsense of the highest order, that's what it is.'

Sophie raised her hand indicating to the waiter she'd like another drink. 'You?' she asked Harriet.

'Best not.' A pause, and then, 'Second thoughts, go on then, I've got an empty afternoon.'

'Rare for you.'

'Not since Romeo arrived. He's taken half my clients, and suppliers. We divided them earlier. That was of course after he told me how to do my bloody job.'

'Grumpy, much?'

'Wonder what Karen's up to.'

Sophie frowned, thanked the waiter for their drinks, resumed hers. 'Who?'

'Used to do all our admin. Under my supervision of course.'

'She had a baby, didn't she?'

Harriet shook her head. 'And never came back. Honestly, some people. Why are these women surprised when they prefer being a mother to work? The role we've been playing for millennia. Wouldn't it be simpler for all concerned to simply stick to being a mother in the first place? Rather than messing everyone about?' She shivered.

'You're hardly an earth mother, keen to start a family. Why must women choose just one and stick with it? Isn't progress that women now have the choice?'

'I have a career because I choose not to have a family. Thinking they can have both strikes me as having one's cake and eating it, don't you think? Attempting to juggle both it seems inevitable one, or both, will suffer. How's that progress for the fairer sex?'

'So, you're never going to want a family? Always sticking with the career choice?' Sophie shook her head and rolled her eyes.

'I don't think it's possible to have both, at the same time. If I had a family I would give up work, without any pretence otherwise. Focus on one thing and doing it well, that's what I say.'

There was silence.

'Still knocking about with Robert?' Sophie asked.

'Knocking about' did seem to sum up their relationship. Much to Harriet's chagrin. 'I'm very happy with him. Very happy with my sex life. Very happy with my relationship. With my boyfriend. Very happy with everything.'

'Right.' Sophie nodded. 'In which case, can you explain why you've been such a terrible moaner since midday?'

'Men. I'm sick and tired of being told what to do by them.'

'I think that's rather broader than this poor Jason, don't you?' Sophie looked out of the corner of her eye.

She wasn't wrong. Harriet pouted.

'So now what? You can't kill him. You shall simply have to learn to work with him. He's not marrying you, until death you do part. He's some man you sit next to five days a week.'

Sophie always had the enviable quality of being able to see the wood for the trees and taking the emotion out of any situation. Harriet, on the other hand, was nothing but emotion. And most of them, at the moment, weren't very positive.

'I have no idea,' Harriet replied feeling very glum and defeated. Seeing perfect manly Jason kissing his perfect boyfriend had been the start of it. Jason kept dropping the boyfriend's name into conversations in the office – it was all 'Pete this' and 'Pete that'. It was all so perfect and sweet and nauseating.

She knew it was uncharitable, and nothing to do with her current man-based quandary, but perfect colleague Jason and his perfect relationship were doing nothing to endear him to her.

–

Later, she returned to her desk with a determination to not quite become *friends* with Jason, but at least put aside her unattractive jealousy at him and find some way to work together in a version of harmony.

'Tea or coffee?' she asked.

He didn't look as if he'd left for lunch. Irritating.

'Have you eaten?' she asked.

'Protein milkshake. Quick run, shower and back here.' He smiled eagerly. Bright-eyed and bushy-tailed didn't even come close.

So irritating. Oh God, could he please just not? Raising an eyebrow, she said, 'Would you like a drink?'

'I'm trying to cut out caffeine. I've got some herbal teabags.' He handed her one.

Waving it away, she smiled tightly.

'Are you okay to go through some questions with the clients you've handed over to me?' he asked.

She knew saying she'd prefer to listen to chalk scratching on a blackboard was pretty unreasonable, so she said, 'Of course,' and left to make their drinks.

They went through his questions, most of which were pretty understandable and in some ways highlighted Harriet's poor note-keeping and filing system, but thankfully Jason glossed over that.

'Are you sure you're okay with me taking on Lux-Lodge Hotels and the photographer?'

'You'll do a much better job than I ever could, I'm sure.' Sarcasm was so unbecoming, her father had always told her, but she couldn't help it. Besides, they were only the two biggest suppliers and giving them to Jason to nurture and develop would either show how out of his depth he really was, in which case he'd soon leave, or would bring in money for the company, reflecting well on how Harriet had managed the accounts beforehand.

—

That evening on phone, Sophie listened to Harriet's plan and said, 'Isn't that a tad risky?'

'Why?'

'If he loses the hotel and photographer you could lose your job.'

'If he loses them he'll lose *his* job. Sink or swim.' It was cut-throat, but she wasn't going to watch him ruin their department with his reckless behaviour and ridiculously modern vision of what marriage should mean. 'Marriage is an ancient institution, about a man and a woman joined for their lives. Anything else makes a mockery of it.'

'I love you, but sometimes your views are a little old-fashioned.'

'Not everything needs bringing up-to-date. There's a lot to be said for tradition and doing things properly, in favour of always wanting to do things *differently*.,. Why throw away tradition, it's served us very well for many years. Cricket, afternoon tea, the Royal Family, our two-party political system – these are not things that need reviewing, changing, modernising. And neither does marriage. There's plenty of things much better exactly as they are.' Harriet ended the call and poured her second large vodka and orange of the evening.

Robert had texted, asking if she wanted to see him. She hadn't replied, too angry after the day she'd had to endure, so she had a long bath, sipping a large glass of wine, reading a thick book about a knight rescuing a maiden from an arranged marriage, and wondered when everything in real life had gone so terribly wrong.

Chapter 7

Jason had successfully kept his job for three weeks. He and Harriet, although not exactly friends, had come to an arrangement of how to work together.

They'd bonded, one afternoon, after Harriet had used Jason's Pinterest board approach for a new client.

'They loved it,' Harriet had said, sitting at her desk, holding a folder.

'What?' Jason asked.

She opened the folder. 'They couldn't do Pinterest, but have left me with this.' It had scraps of wallpaper, pictures of flowers, a cake, pictures of small fluffy dogs.

'Why couldn't they do Pinterest?'

She shrugged. 'This... is a goldmine. I know exactly what colours they want for their flowers, the chair covers, everything. I can look for a wedding car that fits with this whole vibe, it's great.' She smoothed the paper, sticking down some stray magazine clippings. Carefully, almost under her breath, she said, 'Thanks.'

Jason blushed slightly, pride making him grin. 'Do you need to file it electronically somewhere, so if you're off I can—'

Shaking her head she said, 'Let's not spoil it, eh?'

The following week, after Jason had returned from a client meeting, bursting with ideas, he had to tell someone who he thought would be interested. Carefully, checking she wasn't in the middle of something, he said to Harriet: 'You know when you have a really good meeting and it's the best job in the world?'

Harriet stared at her screen, typing quickly.

Jason coughed. 'Like, it's like, almost as if we should pay them to work here.' He chuckled, leaning back on his chair with his hands behind his head.

Harriet continued in silence.

Jason was just about to give up, and he stood, picking up his mug. 'Tea, coffee?'

'Sorry, what were you saying before, some rot about us paying them to work here?' She frowned.

She had been listening. He explained he'd had a great meeting and couldn't wait to get started on the client's wedding.

Harriet smiled, closed her eyes and hugged her mug to her chest. 'It's the best feeling, isn't it? Although I wouldn't go so far as to say they shouldn't pay us.' She raised an eyebrow.

'Do you have a mood board for your perfect wedding?' He'd wanted to ask her this a few times since she'd mentioned a friend, and going out, but hadn't said his name. Perhaps they weren't that serious.

'Perfect wedding. I'd settle for an okay man first.' She pursed her lips.

'Why, what's wrong with the one you've got?' Jason indicated her mug.

She smiled tightly, signalling a lot more behind what she'd not said. 'Small church, countryside, horse-drawn carriage, big party with everyone I've ever known in a barn. Like the ball in P&P with Colin Firth.'

Jason frowned.

She stared at him. '*Pride and Prejudice*. BBC One.' She looked out of the window. 'I want an empire-line dress, hair tied up with little ringlets.'

He liked the sound of that. 'What do the men wear in P&P?'

'Tight trousers, boots, jackets, shirts. It's splendid fun. You, I'm sure, would approve very much indeed.' She returned to orbit, handed him her mug. 'Yes please.'

He made their drinks with a smile. Perhaps he'd stop referring to her as Horrible Harriet when discussing his day with

Pete every evening. 'Friendly colleagues' was how Jason would describe their relationship.

-

Jason arrived at a five-star hotel in the home counties to discuss the requirements of two clients. He could have done it over the phone, but since the Lux-Lodge hotel chain was one of his key suppliers, having wrestled them from Harriet's clutches, he wanted to get to know the events manager since he'd be putting a lot of bookings their way.

Jason gave his name at reception and explained he had an appointment to see Eric.

He took a seat in the light reception area, low black sofas, a glass coffee table and fronds of palms added to the impression of luxury he knew the clients would want. And all at a reasonable price, if Jason had read Harriet's previous client contracts correctly.

Eric – a red-haired clean-shaved man in his fifties – held out a hand for Jason to shake. 'So pleased to see you. I understand you've taken over from Harriet.'

With extreme reluctance, it had to be said. At one point, he'd wondered if he may need to sedate Harriet while logged onto her computer for access to her contacts and client notes. Fortunately it hadn't come to that, once Jason had explained he didn't want to take all her client relationships off her, only half of them.

'I was surprised Harriet had left. She always struck me as part of the furniture,' Eric gestured for Jason to follow.

Jason did as indicated. 'She's not left, she's lucky enough to have me to share her workload.' He thought that nicely summed it up.

They walked to an office with a floor to ceiling window overlooking a lake surrounded by landscaped gardens. A row of small wooden cabins perched on the far edge of the lake.

Once seated, Jason said, 'I'm lucky to work with her of course.' It felt a little too arrogant how he'd phrased it earlier.

'Of course.' Eric made them proper coffee from a fancy machine with more buttons than Jason's first phone.

'Lovely view.'

'The riverside log cabins are part of our Platinum service. For clients who want the privacy of their own accommodation, with the convenience of a hotel nearby.'

Jason opened his notebook, glancing over the list of clients who were interested in a hotel venue accommodation package.

Eric explained they had hotels throughout the UK ranging from budget, mid-range to premium, as with this, their flagship hotel.

'I'm assuming you're interested in some kind of discount, or similar?'

Jason hadn't expected to get down to business so quickly, but he liked the honesty of Eric, so followed his lead. 'You'll be one of our preferred venue suppliers, of course. And since you have such a wide variety of specs, and locations, I'm sure most clients will find a Lux-Lodge hotel for their needs.'

'Indeed. It is what we aim for.' Eric folded his arms in his lap, reminding Jason of a yoga retreat when he'd spent Christmas in total silence.

Jason talked through the half dozen clients' requirements and Eric suggested Lux-Lodge hotels to match. 'How many weddings do you and dear Harriet plan a year?'

Jason had asked Harriet this, so felt comfortable doubling the figure as it roughly correlated to his last year's number at his previous employer. 'I understand we have a ten per cent discount currently agreed.'

Eric nodded.

'Since we're doubling our numbers I wondered how you'd feel about a thirty-three per cent discount.'

Eric shook his head, tutted loudly. 'I admire your chutzpah, but I can't agree to that.'

Jason hadn't expected him to agree, so countered with, 'Twenty-five?'

'Fifteen?'

'Thirty.'

Eric laughed. 'That's not how negotiations work, you know as well as I do.'

'How about you show me around and I'll reconsider?'

Eric's eyes lit up. He stood. 'I think you'll find we're located far enough from London to avoid all the unsavoury elements in so many large cities nowadays. We're within a stone's throw of some of the Cotswolds' most wonderful market towns and historic cities. Small, traditional cities, you understand.'

That was odd. His phrasing sent something buzzing inside Jason. He didn't mention it since Eric was in full flow.

Eric took them to one of the hotel's rooms and it was larger than Jason's first flat. A queen-sized four-poster bed, separate dressing room, spacious bathroom with separate bath and shower, mood lighting and a desk with all the required plug sockets.

'Of course this is our Platinum room. Would you like to see the others?'

'What about the log cabins?'

'Lakeside log cabins.' Eric raised an eyebrow.

'Of course.'

'I booked one for my anniversary. My wife was very happy.'

'Congratulations, which anniversary was this?'

'Thirty years.' Eric walked past reception, outside to the lake.

'You don't look old enough.'

Eric laughed. 'Would you like to see the lakeside wooden cabins?'

'I would.'

The bed had rose petals scattered and the pillow had a 'Mr and Mrs' sign in red joined-up text. There were two towelling bathrobes hanging in the enormous wardrobe, one blue and one pink.

'Very nice.'

'Indeed,' Eric said.

They talked prices for a short while, with Eric outlining what he felt to be a reasonable group discount. Jason made a mental note.

'Of course, the finishing touches can be flexible according to client requirements?' Jason asked, but more as a statement since he knew this would be the case.

'Indeed. What were you thinking?'

Jason felt the bathrobes. 'Two pink ones or two blue ones perhaps?'

Eric frowned. 'I don't follow.'

'We are a modern wedding planners and our clients come from a wide range of backgrounds, budgets. We believe everyone should have their dream wedding.'

'Of course.'

'I have two clients, for instance, who wouldn't require a pink and blue bathrobe. Or the Mr and Mrs on the pillows for instance.'

Eric shook his head. 'I'm sorry, but I don't follow.' He smoothed the bed cover, moving some red rose petals that had fallen out of place.

'My clients are called Adam and Ryan.'

Eric scoffed, 'I don't think someone called Ryan would be able to afford this.' He waved his arms about, nodding to the lake.

Jason smiled tightly. 'Why would you say that?'

'There's never been a King Ryan, has there. Nor a Queen Tracey or Sharon.'

Jason bristled at the snobbishness. 'You're right, but I can assure you they can afford this.'

Eric raised an eyebrow.

'Am I right in thinking,' Jason asked, 'the Lux-Lodge chain includes reasonably priced hotels in its portfolio, in some areas where there are likely to be plenty of people called Ryan, Dave, Sharon and Tracey?'

'Correct.'

'However, I'm considering this venue for a wedding. I'm sure my clients would find the cabins right up their street. I can imagine them loving the Grand Ballroom too.'

'Why?' Eric narrowed his eyes.

'Adam is a professional dancer. He's on *Simply Ballroom*. Do you watch it?'

'I used to. It seems to have become so politicised. I've not watched it since—' Eric stopped himself, almost undoubtedly at the fact that the show now included same-sex couples.

'Political, how do you mean?'

'An agenda.'

Jason wished there had been men dancing together on TV when he'd been a boy. It would have shown him he wasn't wrong, that what he wanted was okay and although less common, still healthy and normal. 'Visibility is important.'

Eric said nothing but smiled briefly.

Jason realised he'd have to actually spell it out. 'I think what I'm *trying* to say is we plan weddings for two men, two women, as well as men and women. So I'm assuming you could arrange for two men's blue bathrobes. Or perhaps they'd like two pink ones...'

'Who?'

'Adam and Ryan. Their colour palette is pink and mauve so...'

Eric stood, ushered Jason out of the cabin, locking it firmly behind them. He looked at his watch. 'I'm very sorry but I have another appointment. Are we nearly done?'

They were far from done. Jason hadn't agreed the deal, nor secured Adam and Ryan their venue at a significant discount. 'Sorry, I'm not sure if I'm sure what you're saying.'

'The wedding night bedroom is laid out in a particular way. For all our clients. Of course, roses can be tulips, the less expensive rooms may not have flowers or a hot tub. But the rest is... as it is.' His face was red.

'Are you saying you wouldn't be able to provide the wedding for my two named clients?'

Eric raised his eyebrows. 'I believe you had a bigger list of potentials. Perhaps we can return to that once we're back in my office.'

Jason followed as Eric walked back to the reception. There, Jason gave him the list of potential clients.

Eric glanced at the names. 'We'd be delighted to host these weddings. We guarantee we'll make their dream day a reality.'

'All of them?'

Eric shook his head. 'We wouldn't be able to help with those.' He pointed to Adam and Ryan's names.

'Why?'

'It's a very busy time.'

'What is?'

'When they want to marry.'

'I didn't give you any dates.'

'I'm sure you did. I distinctly remember you mentioning them.'

Jason decided to give him one last chance before making his mind up. Surely Jason was misinterpreting this. 'September. First two weeks.'

Eric shook his head. 'No can do, I'm afraid.' He stood. 'We aim to remain neutral, non-politicised with our activities.' He shivered briefly. 'If you don't mind I've got someone else I'm already due to meet.' He ushered Jason out of the reception and practically marched him to his car.

Well, that hadn't gone as well as he'd hoped. No discount, no bookings, and a definite 'something off' about the gay clients. Jason wondered how Eric would have reacted if he'd mentioned Andrea and May's plans. Two pink dressing gowns rather than two blue ones. He doubted Eric would have been able to fit them in either.

Jason took a deep breath, sighed and set the satnav for his return journey home.

He was relieved not to return to the office since he wanted to process what had happened. Really check if what he thought was happening had actually been what was happening. He didn't hold with people who searched for offence where none was meant. He recognised the difference between a well-meaning but clumsy discussion and genuine homophobia.

Arriving home, he decided he'd give Eric the benefit of the doubt, and arrange a time to continue the discussion about the discount.

Jason set himself up on the dining room table and ploughed through the emails he'd neglected since this morning's trip. Among them he saw one from the company's favourite photographer, Ray.

> Dear Jason,
> Further to your enquiry about the wedding of your clients as discussed on the telephone, I'm afraid to let you know we don't have any available photographers.
> Best wishes,
> Ray, Managing Director of Ray Photography

It seemed very terse. Probably busy or something. Jason rang, charmed his way through the switchboard, did the same with Ray's secretary and was shortly speaking to Ray himself.

After checking how they were and Ray saying it was a pleasant surprise to hear from Jason, he said, 'I'm assuming this is about my email? Look, no hard feelings, but we're really busy at the moment. All my best photographers are booked that weekend.'

Jason had given Adam and Ryan's preferred September weekend priority, as landing a quality photographer was very important since Ryan's family lived in Australia and wouldn't be able to attend, so they'd asked for video as well as photographs. Which Ray's company was normally very happy to help with.

'All of them?' Jason asked. Usually Ray could find someone who could do the job. His reliability was one of the reasons Harriet spoke so highly of him. That and his consistently high-quality photographs, with his photographers always meeting with the clients to discuss the mood they wanted their pictures to evoke, plus any specific shots they must have.

A long pause, and then, ''Fraid so. I think you'd be better finding another company.'

'Who would you recommend?'

'It's a bit out of the ordinary for us.'

'Two men getting married?'

'I've nothing against it. Live and let live, that's what I say. Except we have other clients and they… It would put us in an awkward position.'

Jason would love to know who these clients were and why they had such a problem with men marrying and women marrying. 'Would it change your mind if it were two women?'

A long sigh, and then, 'Not really. Although… It's nothing personal. I don't mind what people do in their own homes. I've got a nephew who's a bit theatrical, and it's no problem. Really, it doesn't bother me. But it would put *us* in a difficult situation. The other client is one of our longest-standing ones.'

'Who is the client?' Jason's patience was wearing thin.

'I can't reveal. Confidentiality, like. As I said, it's not personal, it's business. If it was up to me I'd send someone to cover those two men's wedding, just like that. Except it's not that simple.'

'It really is.'

'Like I said, I wish I could, but I can't.'

Jason's patience had run out. 'You realise this is illegal. What you're doing. You can't deny services to someone based on their sexuality.'

'Like I said, I've got nothing against them. I like a musical as much as the next person. But there's no one available for that wedding.'

'Right.' Jason gritted his teeth.

'Anything else I can help you with?'

'Suppose it's pointless having a conversation about a discount for all our clients.'

'I'd love to chat with you about that. But not right now.'

'Right.' Jason ended the call, staring at his phone in disbelief. He wished he'd recorded the conversation. But would it have been useful since Ray had been at pains to explain it wasn't personal, it was due to availability? Plus the other mystery client. Jason wasn't sure if that was a smokescreen too, disguising Ray's true feelings.

He decided to leave that conversation to reflect a little before doing anything. He went on a brisk run to clear his mind, having missed out on his usual run to the station and walk from the London terminus to the office.

The rhythmic thudding of his feet on the pavements made him replay the earlier conversations. He knew some people felt this way, but perhaps he'd been shielded from them through the bubble of his friends and family. Attitudes like these reminded him of his school days, knowing he wasn't like other boys, listening to them shouting 'gay' and 'poof' and 'queer' and 'bender' as insults and ways to describe anything that wasn't normal for boys their age.

Later, as he forged on through the thicket of emails, he thought it was easy to become protected from this prejudice by living and working in big cities. But as soon as you left them the worst of the small-minded views were beneath the surface of some people.

Jason lived a much more out and proud life in the Cotswolds than he had in London. Only now he considered it, was it ironic? The villagers where he and Pete lived had welcomed them with open arms, inviting them to the gardening group, cricket club and local pub's quiz night. Except for one particularly excruciating moment where someone had invited them to the Scottish dancing group before realising one would need to play the role of the female partner, suggesting Pete ('Oh he's almost a woman anyway, look at him!') them being a couple was never mentioned in any way other than how the others in the village were discussed.

And here he was, a twelve-year-old boy, ashamed of himself, once again. The power that Eric and Ray had over him really knocked Jason sideways. He'd thought he was big enough and old enough to not let shit like this affect him.

Except the shame he felt about who he was, about Pete, that those two men had made him feel, had made him angry.

Harriet called him at the end of the day, asking how his meeting with Lux-Lodge Hotels had gone.

'Well, I'll tell you properly tomorrow when I'm in.' He tried his best to keep the pain out of his voice.

'Wonderful. I was thinking of you working hard next to the splendid lake and fountain.'

'Yeah. Right.' He forced a chuckle.

There was a silence, and finally Harriet said, 'I'm sure you want to get on, I'll see you tomorrow. Don't work too late.'

'I won't.'

'Are you all right? You sound a bit... off.'

'Tired.'

'Sure?'

He nodded resolutely, to convince himself as much as anything. 'Speak tomorrow.'

She ended the call.

Maybe she wasn't as bad as he'd initially thought. He felt guilty about calling her Horrible Harriet. Perhaps Hard Work Harriet was fairer. The more he knew about her, the more he wanted to know. She stuck him as a sort of Head Girl kind of woman, strict, old-fashioned, traditional values. But actually she was much floatier and more romantic than that, if her plans for her own perfect fantasy wedding were anything to go by.

Jason smiled in satisfaction at the challenges this job provided. If he'd simply swanned in and met Lux-Lodge

Hotels and Ray Photography without an issue, securing a hefty discount, then where would the challenge be with that?

Perhaps he *had* misinterpreted their responses. With the benefit of hindsight maybe he'd got the wrong end of the stick.

The door opened and Pete shouted, 'I'm home!'

I'll leave it for a while before running this by Pete. 'In here!' Jason shouted.

Pete arrived in the dining room, looking as handsome as the first time they'd met at the book launch. If Jason hadn't been organising the event and if Pete hadn't been such a superfan of Sara, the lead singer from Appledrama, they'd have never met.

Isn't life great like that sometimes, Jason reminded himself.

–

The next day, Jason was meeting his clients in a café.

'What happened about the lakeside log cabins?' Adam asked, holding his fiancé's hand.

Ryan grinned and squeezed it back. 'They looked amazing.'

Jason now had the unenviable task of telling these two men the hotel wasn't available for their dates. Even though he'd not given them the dates. 'About that,' Jason began.

'We can be flexible with dates. We talked to Ryan's family and they want to fly over from Oz.'

Ryan nodded.

'They're having refurbishments during September, so there's no bookings.'

'Push it back,' Ryan said. 'More time to book flights.'

'Let me call them.' He rang, asked to speak to Eric, the manager. After an awkwardly long pause, he heard Eric's voice.

'I thought your colleague Harriet was taking over this negotiation.' Eric sounded very put out.

Jason gritted his teeth. 'It's about a booking. It was in September, but I know you're having works then.'

'Works? What are you talking about.' A sigh, and then, 'Can I have the clients' names and dates and I'll call you back?'

Jason gave them, adding, 'It's not a wedding.'

'I see. What is it?'

'A birthday.'

Ryan shook his head and began to speak, but Jason politely silenced him.

'The two men, whose names you've given me, are having a joint birthday. Have I understood correctly?'

'Precisely.' He gave a number of dates and ended the call.

'What's happening?' Adam asked with a worried look on his face.

'As soon as you mention wedding, the venues add twenty percent to the price. We'll get a quote and then tell them.' The lie lodged itself in Jason's throat.

'Clever. I'm so excited. We've been saving for this so long.'

The thought of them spending their money at a place that denied their existence and believed they didn't deserve love was too much for Jason. 'We'll wait to hear, but I think they'll still say no.'

'How come?'

'My fault. Sorry.'

'What's wrong?' Ryan asked.

The hotel called back. 'We can do those dates for a birthday. However, if it were to transpire that it required the wedding package, which I'm sure you're well aware of, I'm afraid we wouldn't be able to accommodate them.'

'For that date, or for those people?'

'As I said, the birthday party we can facilitate. I believe those client names seemed similar to the ones you showed me.'

'Thank you.' Jason ended the call, took a deep breath.

'And?' Adam asked.

Jason explained what Eric had said.

'A joint birthday for two men is okay, but an actual wedding isn't?'

Jason nodded. 'I'm really sorry. I was trying to suggest you go with another hotel chain. Plenty of others have the log cabin option. Some aren't part of a hotel, but it's almost the same.'

'I wanted to leave our reception in the Grand Ballroom and walk to our honeymoon the other side of the lake. I'd been imagining how it would be.' Ryan blinked quickly. 'Mum and Dad said it sounded beaut.'

'It does,' Jason added. 'But it'll have to be somewhere else.'

'Isn't it illegal what they're doing?'

'Technically yes. But they're not saying they don't want your wedding, they're saying they can't do it for their own reasons. A company can refuse a customer's business, as long as it's not for discriminatory reasons. They can say no thanks.'

'But refusing based on sexuality, race, religion is unlawful.'

'It is.'

'So now what do we do?' Adam asked.

'I understand if you want to go elsewhere for a wedding planner,' Jason said.

'We came here for you. I saw the weddings you'd planned with your previous firm. Besides, I appreciate your honesty. Others would have given us a load of old flannel. You should hear what others told us when we enquired.'

Jason dreaded to think. 'I'm so sorry.' He'd included pictures and descriptions of his previous wedding clients, added to their section about services they provided. Harriet had done the same, agreeing it was a good idea. Rather than being the gay guy talking about gay weddings, he wanted to be a good wedding planner showing others the variety of weddings he'd planned.

'Not your fault. We can find another hotel. I'm not happy about it, are we?' Adam looked to Ryan who nodded emphatically. 'But our wedding will happen, won't it?'

'Plenty of other hotels.'

'With lakeside log cabins?'

'Yes,' Jason said confidently. He'd plan them their perfect wedding, spending money as he would if it were his own big day.

Later, after refining their plans, as they prepared to leave, Ryan said, shaking Jason's hand, 'Should we complain or something?'

71

Jason was cautious of pissing Harriet off even more, but as soon as he had something in writing from the photographers or hotel chain about not wanting to supply services to certain clients, Jason would have them by the balls.

'Not unless you want to,' Jason said, knowing they wouldn't make trouble unless he asked for their help.

'I want to live, love and laugh.' Adam's eyes shone as he looked at Ryan.

'I'll be in touch.' Jason shook their hands, then was pulled into a hug by the two men. He walked them to the door with a scary realisation *this* was definitely bigger than he'd first thought. Lying to clients was pretty crappy behaviour. Deceiving suppliers ranked almost as high. Why was Jason doing this, when usually he was such a principled man?

He told Harriet what had happened. 'What are we doing about it?' Jason asked her who he'd followed into the kitchen.

'*You're* doing nothing.' Harriet stirred her coffee furiously.

'I lied to a client, and tried to deceive a supplier. This can't go on.'

'So stop doing it.' Harriet shrugged.

'What I need you to understand, is this puts us in a difficult situation with our clients. If we're selling ourselves as wedding planners for everyone, yet we're working with two massive clients who won't—'

'What I need *you* to understand, Jason, is I'm handling it. And if you interfere any further I shall have no choice but to report you to Christopher.'

Telling tales in school. At work. One of Jason's favourite sort of colleagues. Not. He knew she'd totally do so without a moment's pause. 'If you don't resolve it I'll...'

'You'll lose your job is what you'll do.' She left the kitchen.

If that were true, Jason was beginning to feel it was worthwhile. Because not only did he not want to work with suppliers like that, but he also didn't want to work with a company that continued to work with suppliers who thought they could pick and choose whose weddings they approved and disapproved of.

Because that meant, by extension, they didn't approve of him, of his lifestyle, of his relationship with Pete.

their could pack and I have three volumes. I'm dressed and dejected.

I hear the music. By the window. Up, and I appear to run. I had I said or I turned out my son. I'm.

Chapter 8

Paper, pens and Thomas's laptop were strewn over the dining room table, next to a strong coffee.

Mel shook her head at the brown ringed stain on what had been her fifth attempt at an updated CV.

Why was it so difficult to find a job now? Application forms weren't something you filled in and posted any more. Create an account and username to complete your job application.

Never mind creating an account, Mel needed to create a credible work history to stand a chance.

'I've three Bs at A level, plus two years of a degree in English,' she'd said earlier to someone at a local estate agent.

'Do you have experience of selling houses?'

Mel thought for a moment, then said, triumphantly, 'I've lived in three during my marriage.' That word still seemed to stick in her throat. She was gradually getting used to not being Mrs Waltham, but she missed the security that seemed to afford her. The ease with which she and Steve had slipped into a couples dinner party, children at the same school as ours, circuit.

'As an estate agent, not your own homes,' came the reply.

'I had one designed and built myself. The other two we bought. Then, in that case… no.' The light streamed in through the patio windows, casting a pale rainbow across her dining room.

'If you'd like to email me your CV, we'll keep it on file in case anything comes up.'

Mel had grinned, remembering the nearly empty fridge, and said, 'Brill!' before taking the details and ending the call.

Now, a morning of similar conversations and she'd called a few temp agencies, offering her services. Sadly, none were too impressed with her almost English degree from twenty years ago.

'Mum, when's dinner?' Thomas shouted from the hallway.

'In here,' she replied.

Thomas joined her, dressed in his uniform. 'How did you get on?'

He'd given her a crash course on using his laptop.

'It's a bit different from what I'm used to.'

Thomas sat next to her, scoffed, raked his hands through his hair, like his father. 'Don't be ridiculous. You've got a phone, a tablet, it's all the same.'

It really wasn't. Browsing videos for recipes, emailing friends and using Facebook were nothing like trying to master what complicated monstrosity Word had turned into in the intervening two and a half decades since Mel had used it.

'What's up?' he asked.

She hadn't the heart to recount how it had taken her three attempts to work out how to save her CV in a place where she'd be able to find it. She couldn't bear having to explain she'd written the CV first by hand, then typed it, then rewritten it, by which time the laptop had locked her out, having left it unattended while searching for her old university and college papers. Flicking through them she'd felt a pang of longing wishing she'd finished her degree. But that would mean she didn't have Pete, which was even more ridiculous to imagine than having a degree.

And she definitely wasn't going to tell Thomas how she'd shouted at the printer, near to tears, when it had refused to cooperate and actually do its bloody job and print out what she'd taken the previous two hours writing.

Finally, she said, 'I think I'll leave it until after dinner.'

Thomas turned the laptop to face him, clicked onto her document and scanned it quickly. 'Is this all you've done?'

With shame, she nodded. 'I've got loads of notes.' She gestured to the paper covered in her handwriting.

'Why don't you tell me, and I'll type it and make it look profesh.'

She ruffled his hair, smiling. She had, after all raised good children. Not all bad for twenty-five years' work, out of the workplace. Gritting her teeth, she said, 'I think I'll need to know how to use the computer if I get an office job. And unless you're going to sit under my desk and do my work for me, I fear that won't work.'

He clicked and swiped a few times. 'How's that?'

It certainly looked more like a CV, but the gap in her employment history remained glaringly obvious. No amount of fiddling about by Thomas would mask it. 'Better, but not good enough.'

'There must be something else you can do, Mum.'

One of the temp agencies had suggested cleaning. Mel proudly kept her home spotless without any help from a cleaner, despite Steve offering to pay for one. Mel had wanted someone vacuuming under her children's beds as much as she'd wanted someone putting them to bed.

'Someone suggested cleaning,' she said absently.

'But you hate it, don't you?' He shook his head.

'It's different when it's here, because it's never ending.' A laundry mountain that needed crampons to tackle, four bathrooms to clean and a marble-tiled hallway that showed all manner of marks weren't the biggest joys of her life. However, cleaning for other people would mean walking away, once she'd finished. Being paid for it, unlike here.

'No need for software there.' He shrugged. 'Once you get the hang of it, you'll pick it up.' He nodded at the laptop. 'If Lily can use it, you definitely can, Mum.' He smiled.

She was less convinced of that.

It wasn't that she was a snob about cleaning. Good honest work, job satisfaction, no worrying about bloody software or computers. 'Maybe,' she managed. The niggling feeling that surely she could do something else lingered. Having studied Shakespeare, Milton, at least two if not three of the Brontës, meant she'd imagined waltzing into an office, with open armed co-workers immensely grateful for her knowledge of the correct use of an apostrophe, helping them with their semicolons and understanding when to use 'yours faithfully' or 'sincerely'.

'What about something with kids?' Thomas asked.

She shrugged. It wasn't the worst idea ever.

She could work in a nursery, or become a childminder perhaps. Childcare was, apparently, like paying for a second mortgage. And that was precisely what she needed. Given she wanted to use being single as an opportunity to create a new life, returning to what she'd devoted her life to for her four children, felt like something of a fail.

She'd read wonderful things about becoming an air steward, and think of all that free travel. No, she was surely too old for that.

'Where's Lily?' she asked. A vague memory of Lily having something happening this evening crept across her mind. A letter had been brought, thrust into her hands and signed.

'Round a friend's house.' Thomas reached into the cupboard for a jar of peanut butter, stopped for a spoon and was about to leave for the living room where he'd eat most of the jar with little trouble, when Mel stopped him.

Mel shouted, 'Have you heard from Dad?' A change of subject felt as good as a rest.

'Should I?' Thomas chewed peanut butter thoughtfully.

Not more than usual, since you're his child, no.

'Do you want me to ask him for some money? I'll give it to you,' Thomas said.

Her heart burst with pride. She blushed. 'I'll be fine. Got to be.' She removed the jar from his hands. 'No spoiling your dinner, please.'

He left, the noise of his games console soon filling the living room.

Lily duly arrived courtesy of her friend's mother, who, obviously sensing Mel looked tired – which was always code for old – asked: 'How are things?' The woman's head tilted to one side tipped Mel off she really was laying on the sympathy and anything she revealed would no doubt be all around the village by the end of the week.

'Adjusting, you know. Cutting cloth accordingly.' Seemed nicely vague and much more polite than telling the nosy woman to sod off and mind her own bloody business.

'It's hard to get back in, once you've been out of it for such a long time.' Head tilted to the other side now.

Mel frowned.

'Pete's twenty, isn't he, so you must have been not working since he was born.' Narrowed eyes, pitying mouth shape.

'Twenty-five.' Mel gritted her teeth. 'I've not stopped working actually. Bringing up four kids is—'

'Of course, I know. Myself, a devoted mother to three girls. And I wouldn't have it any other way. Except I was fortunate because I was able to keep my hand in.'

As an assistant director if Mel remembered. *Keep my hand in, my arse.* 'I've got a job actually.'

'Great news, what is it?'

Not a bloody assistant director. 'Oh it's not much. A stepping stone. While things settle down, and Steve works out maintenance payments.'

The woman smiled.

Mel decided to try this on for size and said, 'I'm helping people out at home. Keeping on top of things for the busy professional.'

'At home, how great. It's marvellous what can be done now, with the internet and video conferencing. I hardly need go into the office now.'

'I'm going to be cleaning,' Mel said deadpan and without embarrassment.

78

'I've lost our lady who helps, would you consider doing people around the village?'

She'd only just invented the job, so Mel felt a little premature to be offering mate's rates. 'We'll see. New dawn and all that.' She nodded backwards at the children's shouts. 'Best get on.' She closed the door.

As it turned out, the woman who offered Mel a job at her cleaning company was called Dawn.

–

Mel turned up at their office when they opened the next morning, explained the situation, said she'd work anywhere locally except in her village.

Dawn had short blonde hair, wore surprisingly generous amounts of make-up and scant amounts of clothing, with a particular penchant for leopard print if her blouse, boots and skirt were anything to go by.

Dawn had taken her details, explained she'd be in touch about a criminal records check, and then she'd be in touch with her first assignments.

'There's no shame in it,' Dawn said.

'I know.' She'd gone for house cleaning as it seemed more friendly than offices. Plus, she reckoned it less likely she'd feel envious of the people sitting at their desks doing stuff with their computers that Mel could only dream of.

'I left school at sixteen, got a job cleaning a nursing home then started this place. Cleaning is what pays for my BMW, mortgage, four holidays a year. Do you know what I mean?'

'Where there's muck there's brass,' Mel said in quiet ad-miration.

'You'll never be out of work. People always need cleaners.'

Mel stood but felt Dawn had more to say.

'My husband left me too.' Dawn inspected her long red nails. A shrug. 'Not for a younger model, I wanted kids and he didn't.'

'Oh.' Mel replied, resuming her seat.

79

'He's got two with her now.' Dawn raised her perfectly pencilled eyebrows. 'Men, eh? I'm on better terms with my husband now than when we were married. She's welcome to him.'

Mel wondered if there would ever come a time when she would wish Steve well with his next partner, whether she'd civilly work out who had the children over her kitchen table, while Steve and his new wife or girlfriend held hands.

'I'll come round your house to finish the rest of the paperwork,' Dawn said.

'Why?'

'I like to meet new employees in their own homes. Gives me a better idea of who they are. Do you know what I mean?'

'Do you walk around with white cotton gloves checking for dust?' Mel laughed nervously.

'Only sometimes.' Dawn smiled, shuffling her papers then picked up the gold pen she'd used.

—

Next day, Dawn arrived, walking from room to room of Mel's home – no white gloves. They sat in the kitchen drinking coffee and Dawn completed the paperwork.

'Beautiful pad you've got here.' Dawn photographed Mel's passport.

'It's why I'm working. Don't want to lose it.'

'Makes sense.' She shuffled the application form, checking through each page at a time. Dawn looked up. 'If you're ever feeling lost, want someone to talk to, not sure if you can carry on, give me a shout, will you?'

'I don't follow…' Mel was certainly not planning to feel any of those things.

'Some of your friends may think of you different, if they find out you're working like this. Screw 'em, I say. You do what you gotta do, right?'

Mel smiled. 'Right.'

'Once you're on my books we look after you. If it wasn't for people like you, I wouldn't be where I am. I never turn anyone away who's looking for work. I wanted my agency to be somewhere that anyone could find work.'

'Very kind of you.' Mel lifted the cafetière, indicating if Dawn wanted more.

'Not for me, ta, I can feel the ulcer inflaming.' Dawn rubbed her stomach. 'Plenty of agencies won't take people who've not worked. They can't get work until they have the experience of having the work, to get the work. Catch 22.'

'Indeed.' Mel poured herself a glass of water, leaning against the sink, wondering if Dawn was ever going to leave, or if there was another agenda here.

'Stick with me and you'll always have work, whatever you want. I once placed a woman in an office as a secretary when she'd not worked since the eighties.'

'How?'

'She came into my office and I taught her computers, everything, working for me, and then I placed her in a client's office. She's a board secretary now. Governance, all that jazz.' Dawn smiled, rattling her long nails on the table. 'Stick with me and you'll go places.'

Chapter 9

Harriet slipped into her coral pink silk nightdress.

She'd enjoyed a thoroughly pleasant meal out with Robert, ending with him sweeping her into bed for another splendidly imaginative, effective and varied horizontal performance. And then he'd slid into the bathroom, dressed and left.

Leaving Harriet feeling rather... flat. She wouldn't permit any deeper feelings of gloom. *Buck yourself up*, her mother had always told her.

There were clear advantages to dating a man fifteen years her senior: Robert had taken her coat, paid for dinner, the taxi, made perfectly interesting conversation over dinner, made perfectly good love to her earlier. *With* her, would she say?

She rolled over in bed, her body aching from their earlier exertion.

Sliding off the bed into her dressing gown, she walked to the lounge, switched on the TV, poured three but definitely not more than six fingers of vodka, added a splash of orange juice and took a large glug.

It stung slightly, but immediately lifted her mood.

The TV showed a property programme, people debating whether to size up or size down, go rural or go urban. It was all too tedious to contemplate. She supposed having a budget meant you needed to consider those options. She'd simply told her father where she'd secured the job in London and he'd secured her the perfect roomy two-bedroom Kensington apartment. Portered mansion block, off Kensington High Street, views into Hyde Park. 'To make your commute easy,' her father had said, handing her the keys.

She switched channels and an advert from Electrovax implored her to buy one of their all singing all dancing vacuum cleaners – this one even washed upholstery!

She rotated the glass between her fingers, enjoying the cold against her skin.

Reminding her of Robert's kisses.

Enthusiastic, adventurous, long-lasting, imaginative – they were all words she'd use to describe Robert's technique. But she always felt... Not distant, because he sort of took over all her senses, filling her with his woody scent, touching her with his furry body (salt-and-pepper temples and silvery-grey body hair were surprisingly more attractive than she'd at first imagined), overtaking her sight with his size, his weight pressing against her... And yet...

To her, she reckoned. Not *with* her. Making love. It was almost as if he were trying to outdo his personal best, regardless of whether she was joining in or not. She did, of course, join in, only he wouldn't notice if she hadn't.

She sipped the vodka, its bitterness was more jolting than wine, probably better – harder to drink as much without even noticing as she'd started to with wine.

She changed channels again and sighed.

Her phone rang.

'I was thinking about you, Dad,' she said, silencing the TV and clinking the ice cubes in her glass as she'd finished it already. Surely not.

'Should I worry?' he asked.

'I saw one of your adverts on the television. The new machine reminds me of a spaceship. Is that intentional?'

'I'm not calling to talk shop. Not about my shop anyway. Plenty of time for that yet.'

Five years at her next birthday and she was due to take over Electrovax. She'd tried very hard to take an interest in the company, and perhaps if it manufactured jewellery, or luxury cars, she'd have found it easier. But vacuum cleaners – she hardly knew where hers was kept, never mind how to use it. 'Yes,' she said wearily.

'I wanted to see how you were.'

She was absolutely fine. Job, apartment, boyfriend of sorts. Plenty of friends she could see to distract herself. The wooziness of the vodka caught up with her, a downside when compared with wine. 'I saw an interesting article about gay weddings.' She wanted to check if her feelings on this whole thing were at odds with most others.

'Right.' He coughed. 'Go on.'

'In an industry magazine. Apparently it's a growth area. Pink pound or some such. I can't see it myself. We don't have many. Well, I've not worked on any. I wouldn't know where to start, you know?'

'Who pays for the wedding for a start?'

She'd heard a joke on the socials about this which she'd not fully followed. It had sounded rude. At best offensive. Something to do with top halves and bottom halves, or some such. She didn't want to repeat it to her father. 'I have no idea. Mums walking men down the aisle. Not an aisle, but you know what I mean.'

'Quite. And the gentleman friend, is he still hanging around?' Clearly he didn't want to carry on with that conversation. He'd only ever taken a cursory interest in her job since it was really a training ground until she joined the family business.

Years ago, he'd told her in no uncertain terms she couldn't sit around being a socialite until she turned thirty, which was when her father had said he'd offer her a job at Electrovax. So shortly after her father's stern words, she'd drifted into events, then wedding planning.

'Robert is okay,' she said with as much feeling as she could muster. Anything else was too depressing to consider... She walked to the kitchen, poured another measure of spirit, added fresh ice cubes, a splash of lime cordial – made the vodka taste less bitter.

'Not becoming serious, I hope?'

'Hopefully. In time.' She needed to believe it because the alternative was all too depressing to think about. Why was it too much to ask that she find someone who loved her as much as the couples she met every day through work? Why did she seem to attract a certain type of man who... Well, didn't?

'I've told you before, your gentleman friend is entirely unsuitable for you.'

Harriet sighed. 'Why?' she said with a slight slur.

'*Must* I repeat this?' He sounded terse.

Her father had seen a picture of Robert and commented he was too old, lacking prospects – why wasn't he married by his age? – and entirely unprepossessing for a woman as pretty as Harriet.

'Are you tired? You sound odd, darling.'

She sat upright, took a deep breath, couldn't let him know she was three or four vodkas deep at this stage of the evening. 'It's the phone. Microphone needs replacing.' She bit her bottom lip.

'Are you drinking?'

She scoffed. 'Cocktail hour, isn't it? Six o'clock. Isn't that what you taught me?'

'It's nearly nine.'

Harriet put the glass down, folded her hands in her lap and cradled the phone against her shoulder. 'I think I'm coming down with something.' She coughed, at length, almost making herself sick with the effort.

'Surely it's moot. The pink pound. Your place doesn't do weddings for gays, does it? I thought you were classy, traditional, elegant.'

That was their ethos. 'Those are my *mots du jour. Du semaine.* And in fact *de* l'année.' Fluent in three languages, a master's in business, a degree in classics... She was honestly so wasted at that place.

'Sorry? I don't follow, darling.'

'The words of the day, week and year.' Those holidays to France and he still couldn't order a coffee in the language.

'I see. A fad I'm sure. Surely the appeal of such a lifestyle is to not be like everyone else? I've seen those parades with the rainbows. It's piercings, leather, tattoos, shaven heads on the women, and the men. I can't look at most of them. You're better off steering well clear.'

'What I thought.' There was a silence. She thought he probably wanted something bigger than to check on her. 'Anything else? I think I'm going to have an early night with an audiobook.'

She'd been secretly enjoying a young adult series about vampires in love with one another. She hadn't told anyone since she was mortified how much she loved it.

'Anything interesting? Audiobook?'

'Non-fiction about ancient Greece. It's part of a series going through a grand sweep of history. It finishes in 2001 which is regarded as the beginning of the modern age. For obvious reasons.' God, she was good at bullshitting. The lie had sprung, fully formed, from nowhere.

'I'm glad you're happy. Working is so important.' He ended the call.

Happy. It was such a subjective description. She definitely felt happy now. Laying here, on her sofa, lightheaded with the room slightly tilting to one side. She hiccupped – probably all the lime juice.

Happy. Yes, I am. Even if some of the people I'm working with make me question why they don't introduce licences to permit people to have children.

Throwing the remote onto the grey sofa, she slowly crawled back to the kitchen – for some reason the floor seemed to have tilted and she felt steadier on her knees than feet – she made herself another drink. Somehow the other had disappeared.

She'd deserved it, for putting up with her father's disappointment, questions, criticism of her life. Mind you, he wasn't too far wrong, Harriet wouldn't have arrived at this life if she'd planned it. Searching for love, being disappointed by men who only wanted her for one thing, which she gladly gave them time after time, with the mistaken belief they'd want to see her again. At least Robert had lasted longer than a night. Even if she had niggles about him.

Best not think about that now.

She slipped into bed, naked underneath the sheets, disappearing into the world of teenage romantic vampires.

It was taking more and more vodka each night to help her sleep. To silence the voices, the unanswered questions, the fact that she wasn't a son, that she didn't really want to run Electrovax, that she'd failed to marry the perfect man because they were all married, or gay, or both...

Chapter 10

Jason received an email from Lux-Lodge Hotels:

> Dear Jason,
>
> I regret to inform you we will not be able to continue the business arrangement between our companies. We will honour all weddings currently booked in our hotels, however we are unable to take further bookings from your company for your clients.
>
> This decision has not been taken lightly.
>
> Yours sincerely,
>
> Eric Harestock, Group Events Manager

Harriet arrived, holding her notebook, looking annoyed. 'I've been trying to speak to Lux-Lodge Hotels and they're not returning my calls.'

Dread filled Jason's stomach. 'It might be my fault.'

'What did I tell you? I was taking over their accounts.'

She had said that, and unfortunately Jason had ignored it. He had tried to speak to Eric, had attempted to make him admit he was refusing to work with their gay and lesbian wedding clients. But he'd failed. Eric wasn't stupid, he wasn't going to put it in writing. Or even say it, when he knew Jason could record their calls.

'I know, but I thought if I spoke to him, since I'd met him, he'd change his mind.'

'Thanks for making it so much worse.' Harriet said, 'Can you get me their number and I'll ring them?'

'Before you do, I need to tell you something,' Jason said carefully.

Harriet's eyes narrowed as she resumed her seat. 'Does it get worse?'

Jason explained how upset he'd been at lying to his clients, and how they'd wanted to remain with him. 'I think it's for the best in the end.'

'What is?'

'We don't want to be associated with companies like that. Even if it's not illegal, it's pretty shitty business practice.'

'I think I'll be the one who decides. What have you done now?'

'They're refusing to work with us.' He showed her the email from Eric.

'Bloody brilliant. First of all they're refusing to work with a tiny percentage of our clients. And now it's all of them.'

'I think,' Jason said, 'it's about the principle, not the numbers.'

Harriet remained silent.

'It is illegal. What they're doing.'

'You want to fight them in court? By then we'll have lost all our clients and we won't have jobs.'

'Come on,' Jason said. 'It's only a hotel chain. There are plenty of other wedding venues.'

Harriet rapped her nails on the desk. 'But are they in every region of the UK, with budget, mid and luxury hotels? Do they usually give us a twenty-five percent discount?' She waited for a response, and when none came, went on. 'I thought not. They're over half our venue business. Didn't you think of this before jumping on your little hobby horse?'

Jason felt the anger rising as his face heated. 'It's a bit more than that.' He kept his voice calm, knowing if he raised it he'd have lost the argument by becoming aggressive. Although it took all his self-control not to raise his voice.

'It's business, that's all. That's all this ever is. It's not about providing weddings to everyone, it's about us showing we're modern and welcome diversity. But really it's so we can get more clients.' She stood. 'I'm telling Christopher.'

'Please don't,' Jason said.

'What do you propose? I'd love to hear *your* great idea.'

Jason had no idea what to do. But he knew he didn't want Harriet misrepresenting him to Christopher. Plus he wanted to state his case for why it had been so important to him and why he'd persevered, regardless of what Harriet had told him.

'I wanted a quote for my new client. Normal, bog-standard wedding. Lux-Lodge would have jumped at it before. We'd have made our five percent and everyone would have gone home happy. I should have been done with that by now. But instead here I am clearing up your mess.' She shook her head.

People like Harriet would always hide behind traditional values, but the implication of the opposite of 'normal' made Jason even angrier.

'Are you coming?' Harriet asked. 'Face the music like a man.'

Jason was well aware what she meant but didn't rise to the bait. 'We'll see Christopher together.'

In their boss's office, Harriet explained the problem, then Jason added why he'd tried to fix it alone, despite Harriet's request.

Christopher looked from one to the other. 'What's the biggest gap this leaves us with?'

'Budget and mid-range venues. They're the most modern hotels in every major city across the UK. Without them we're left with non-chain hotels and you know what's wrong with that.'

Too expensive or sub-standard quality and having not been refurbished since the nineties in most cases. Jason always avoided them, instead preferring the Lux-Lodge hotels. The irony of the Lux-Lodge hotels being the most modern wasn't lost on Jason.

Christopher said, 'This isn't a total surprise.'

'Sadly it's not to me either,' Harriet said.

There was something else going on here, Jason reckoned. 'Sorry, why isn't this a surprise?' he asked Christopher.

'I knew they'd behaved oddly. Harriet thought it was a storm in a teacup. It may have been if you'd not stirred it with your size twelves.'

Jason turned to Harriet. 'You told him?'

She folded her arms. 'Had to.'

Not without speaking to me first. Jason became subdued as he felt stitched up. Worse than receiving a bollocking from their boss, having a colleague tell tales on him, without speaking to Jason first. His jaw tightened as he considered what to say, then decided better of it and kept silent.

They talked about contingency plans and Jason felt as if he weren't there.

'I think we should contact all our clients,' he suggested, 'tell them we're reviewing our business relationship with the Lux-Lodge hotel chain and Ray the photographer. That way we're taking charge rather than us being dumped by them.'

Christopher narrowed his eyes. 'I don't disagree that's a potential approach. I like us to be seen as the ones moving away from them. But I need to think about how it leaves us as a business.'

Harriet left upon Christopher's request.

Jason stood.

'Can you sit, please?' Christopher asked.

'I'm very sorry,' Jason said, 'I thought I could handle it. I've not—'

'No, you haven't, have you? I wasn't sure about you, but the others said you'd give us a nice leg up. I didn't expect you to go on some one-man crusade. This is a business above everything else, do you understand?'

Jason nodded. He understood enough. He was a diversity hire and now he was actually trying to ensure all clients could have the wedding of their dreams, regardless of who they were, he was coming up against this... this bollocks. The message was very clear. *Be yourself at work, unless it doesn't fit with how we operate.* Jason almost told Christopher to stick his bloody job, but he reckoned he'd be better off inside the tent pissing out than outside the tent trying to piss in.

'I'm sorry,' Jason said, meaning it. 'I would have told you at this point. Promise.'

Christopher smiled. 'We'll never know, will we?'

No, since bloody Harriet had beaten him to it. 'Harriet should have spoken to me first.'

Christopher shrugged.

'Please, let me sort it, rather than her?' He felt a responsibility to clear up his mess. Besides, he was sure once he spoke to Eric it would become clear the intent behind it was different from what Jason believed. It struck him as Lux-Lodge cutting their noses off to spite their faces to turn away all their business. 'What do you think of my suggestion to contact all our clients?'

'I don't disagree it would be good for us to take control of the narrative. But I need to think about it.'

'I'd really like to help. Think it should be me contacting my clients about—'

'I think you've done enough, don't you?' Christopher said, indicating he could go.

That evening, when Jason spoke to Pete during their nightly wine and chat, Pete said, 'I think it's sweet you don't think they meant to be homophobic. It's kinda cute you don't want to see the worst in them. But if it looks like a duck, quacks like a duck and swims like a duck, it's—'

'A homophobic duck?' Jason poured them more wine.

'Pretty much.' Pete nodded.

'I'm pissed off Harriet's dobbed me in to Christopher.'

'But is it surprising, though?' Pete shrugged, sipping his drink.

'I thought we were friends. Okay, maybe not friends, but friendly colleagues, and I thought she'd speak to me before telling Christopher.'

Pete raised his eyebrows. 'Think away. What are you going to do?'

'Whatever, I'm not telling Harriet. She's not to be completely trusted.' He shook his head, walked towards the fridge. 'What do you want for dinner?'

–

'I need to show you something, make sure I understand it.' Jason told Mel. He'd arrived at her house early evening.

'What?' Mel let him in. 'Has someone died?'

'Not yet.' Jason placed his work phone on the table, opened an email from the director of events, Ashley Ashford.

'Who's he?' Mel asked.

'*She's* the big boss. Christopher reports to someone else and then her.'

'Right.' Mel peered closely. 'What's this about? I'll need my reading glasses.'

'I'll read it: *Dear etc, it has come to our attention you have been undertaking activities with Lux-Lodge Hotels and Ray Photography which are not authorised by your managers. We understand this has affected Tailored Weddings' business partnership with these organisations, and as such may put us at risk. Although we understand employees may have political views and opinions that differ with the company's, it is not for employees to pursue their own campaigns during working hours, or on behalf of Tailored Weddings. You are instructed to cease all activities related to this disagreement with Lux-Lodge Hotels and Ray Photography. Failure to comply will result in disciplinary action, which may include dismissal. Yours etc…*'

'Shit,' Mel said.

Thomas arrived in the kitchen. 'You said we can't say that word.'

'Why are you out of bed?' Mel asked.

'Can't sleep.' Turning to Jason, he said, 'Why are you here so late?'

Jason raised his eyebrows, waiting for Mel's lead about whether to tell him the truth. Mel nodded.

Jason said, 'I've been told off for doing something at work.'

93

'What?' Thomas asked.

'Some people I work with don't want to do some of our clients' weddings.'

'Right. Why though?'

'They disagree with that sort of wedding.'

'But it's money for them. Why would they refuse it?'

'They don't think people like me and your brother Pete should be able to marry. They think me and Pete getting married spoils weddings for—'

'Normal people?' Mel said. 'Not normal, I mean, other people. Like me and your dad.'

'Straights?' Thomas rolled his eyes. 'You're not marrying Dad, are you? Wait – are you even divorced from him yet?'

'No, and no.'

Thomas opened biscuits from a tin, chewing on them as he thought. 'Why do some people even care about stuff like that? Like, if you disagree with gay people getting married…maybe don't marry a gay person.' He rolled his eyes.

'Because some people feel as if they're losing *their* rights, when others are given the same privileges, like marriage, they've taken for granted.' Jason raised an eyebrow.

Mel smiled, winking that he'd pretty much summed it up.

'Will they fire you?' Thomas asked Jason.

Mel and Jason shook their heads.

'Definitely not,' Mel said. 'As long as he behaves.'

'Good.' Thomas took three more biscuits, walked to the door. 'Hello Uncle Jason by the way.'

'Hello.'

Thomas left the room, only crumbs remaining on the table.

'What do I do now?' Jason put his phone away.

'You do what you've been asked to do.'

'Which is? Just to be clear.'

'Nothing.'

Jason nodded. 'I've got to keep this job. After all the fuss I made to Pete when I was offered it.'

She beckoned him in for a hug. 'It's all going to be fine. Make sure you don't do anything stupid.'

'Understood.' Jason left to go home. He decided not to tell Pete about it at this stage since technically there wasn't anything to tell. He'd been asked not to do anything, so that's precisely what he'd do, as Mel had said.

—

The next day, somehow, Jason found himself at the centre of a social media shit-storm, going from quietly scrolling through social media to receiving death threats from complete strangers.

'I didn't think anyone would see it,' he said that afternoon at work.

'See what?' Harriet asked.

'My conversation with Ray.'

'Why did you contact him?'

'I didn't. He came at me on Twitter, accusing me of lying. I wasn't going to sit by and watch him misrepresenting what I'd said and done.'

A colleague looked up from her computer. 'What now?'

Harriet said quietly, 'Just Jason losing his job.' She gestured at her screen.

Harriet and Jason gathered around.

@Rayphotograph: Dear @jasoncheriton I am a modern photographer and work with a wide variety of clients. Always have, always will. Your lies have lost me clients. Do you always lie to your clients?

@jasoncheriton: why have you lost clients? If you did nothing wrong, you have nothing to worry about

@Rayphotograph: because you claimed I was homophobic with no proof. I'm a traditional photographer w family values, and use traditional shots for weddings – my clients want that

@jasoncheriton: bc you are homophobic

@Rayphotograph: prove it!

@Rayphotograph: Hi @jasoncheriton why did you tell lies about me and my photography? Is it because you can't take a photograph – look at your profile pic LOLS?

@Rayphotograph: hi @jasoncheriton what does @traditionalweddings think of you spreading lies about its suppliers? How long do u think @traditionalweddings will last w/out photographers?

@jasoncheriton: @Rayphotograph it's the 2020s – wake up!

@Rayphotograph: @jasoncheriton I know what year it is. What's your point?

@jasoncheriton: You turned down my client wedding with no justification.

@Rayphotograph: lots of reasons for that: schedule, clients' requests, venue…

@jasoncheriton: It was blatant HOMOFOBIC!!!

@Rayphotograph: lies

@jasoncheriton: Hi @Rayphotograph WOT LYES exactly? what lies do u mean???

@Rayphotograph: saying I'm homophobic

@jasoncheriton: YOU refused 2 photograph gay couples at their own weddings.

@Rayphotograph: lie. I didn't.

@jasoncheriton: You stated you wouldn't do 2 WEDS for my LGBT CLIENT.

@Rayphotograph: which ones

@jasoncheriton: 2 MAN, 2 WOMAN!!!

@Rayphotograph: names

@jasoncheriton: I HAVE EVRYTHING in a chain of EMAIL.

@Rayphotograph: lies. More lies.

@jasoncheriton: ur EMAIL 2 me.

@Rayphotograph: prove it

Jason frowned at the screen. Surely not. Not for having an argument on Twitter. 'I've got like three hundred followers. Ray has more, but whatever. It's done now.'

'Not quite,' Harriet said carefully.

'What?'

'It's a story in *The Overseer*.'

Harriet clicked through the other tweets in the thread until she reached a web link. 'The Overseer. You're so fired.' She shook her head.

'West London Overseer actually,' Jason added. 'What does it say?'

'Let's read it, shall we?' Harriet said.

Jason put his head in his hands. 'That's where Ray lives. Oh shit. Do you think it's serious?'

'It won't be long until national papers pick it up. They trawl social media for stories. Apparently that's what passes for journalism nowadays.' Harriet closed her eyes slowly. 'Which bit of "don't interact with Ray and Lux-Lodge Hotels" did you not understand?' She clicked on the link:

West London Overseer
Local photographer accused of discrimination by events planner after 'refusing' gay clients

A London-based photographer has been labelled 'homophobic' after allegedly refusing to photograph two LGBT couples at their weddings, an events planner has claimed.

Jason Cheriton, a 40-year-old events manager from Oxon, made the claims public via Twitter in a heated exchange with Ray Meon (57), of Ray Photography.

Cheriton is employed as an events manager at Tailored Weddings, and has spoken online several times previously about working as a gay man in the wedding industry.

The pair came to blows when Meon claimed Cheriton had lost him clients with his accusations that he refused to photograph '2 men, 2 women'.

Due to the nature of the accusations, Meon has been contacted for a response.

Ray Photography is a local company and has been used to photograph international celebrity events including ex-girl group member Melly and her footballer husband Sharp's wedding and the glamour model Danielle Double D's marriage to her fifth husband Big Boulder the boxer.

Jason felt his face redden and heat up. 'He started it.'

'How?' Harriet asked.

Jason pointed to the first tweet Ray had written. He read it: '@Rayphotograph Dear @jasoncheriton I am a modern photographer and work with a wide variety of clients. Always have, always will. Your lies have lost me clients.'

'You couldn't have just ignored him?' Harriet asked, shaking her head.

Jason shook his head. 'His homophobia was all there if you read between the lines.' He searched through his emails. 'And I've got the receipts!' He read the email describing what he'd said.

'Tell me you didn't tweet the email,' the colleague said.

'He could,' Harriet said, 'but he'd be lying. It's right here.' She pointed at her screen. '*Daily* bloody *Post*.' She shook her head.

The Daily Post
Celebrity Photographer exposed as
'homophobic' by Gay Events Planner

Well-renowned photographer Ray Meon, of Ray Photography Ltd, took to Twitter last night to claim an events manager had lost him clients by wrongly accusing him of homophobia.

Jason Cheriton, 40, an events manager working at Tailored Weddings had accused Ray of being homophobic after he allegedly refused to photograph two homosexual couples for their weddings.

Meon aired the spat to his 20,000 followers, where Cheriton defended his assertion that Ray Photography was homophobic by quickly sharing the email discussion in which the photographer explained he wasn't homophobic, but was instead interested in his work being 'along traditional and family lines'.

'Here's the email,' Harriet said, pointing to the screen. 'At least they've redacted the names of your clients. That's at least something.'

Jason's mouth fell open. 'I didn't think anyone was watching us talking on Twitter.'

'Talking.' Harriet shook her head. 'I think fighting is a better verb.'

Jason stared at the screen as his skin prickled in horror while he read.

From: Ray@rayphotography.com

Dear Jason,

Thank you for your enquiry about the wedding of your clients [redacted] and [redacted]. I am afraid that I will not be able to take photos of these clients, nor will any of my associates and esteemed colleagues. The reason for this is that we have a traditional client base who have what some might say are old-fashioned family values. I'm very sorry, we don't have anything against your clients from a personal perspective, it's simply that our approach to photographing weddings and the list of shots we've developed over many decades of this sort of work, would not be compatible with your clients.

Best wishes and kind regards
Ray Meon

Jason's throat tightened; he loosened his tie and top button. 'I was only defending myself. He was lying. I needed to make him realise how hypocritical he was being. I'm a very honest person – accusing me of lying to my clients, am I expected to sit by as someone libels or slanders my character?' He couldn't believe this.

'That is precisely what you're expected to do,' Harriet said. 'To the letter.'

Harriet had printed out the two news articles, with screen-grabs of Ray and Jason's tweets.

Jason scanned the words, they were swimming before his eyes for some reason. The pictures showed every one of his two or three dozen tweets in response to Ray's. He remembered typing them. His spelling deteriorated down the thread, and his use of capitals increased. He'd seen red and lost control of what he was doing. Surely they'd understand?

'I'll tell Christopher, and Ashley, that I lost control. It was a moment of madness. Politicians, celebrities get away with far worse. It'll be fine. Won't it?' He felt the uncertainty in his voice as it wavered.

'Did you contact Eric from Lux-Lodge Hotels?' Harriet asked.

Jason shook his head. Not through any deliberate choice, but mainly since Eric didn't use Twitter. Lux-Lodge Hotels obviously had social media, but they were very corporate.

Jason told her, adding, '*I* didn't start it. You can see in the pictures what Ray said about me. Lies. All bloody lies.'

'I don't think, at this stage, that matters. You're linked to Tailored Weddings, so you're bringing us into ill repute by being part of this fight.'

Jason banged his fist on the table. 'But I'm bloody well right.'

'It doesn't matter.' Harriet squeezed her neck briefly. 'What do you want to do?'

'How do they know I work here?'

Harriet said, 'Third picture down, your Twitter bio says you're a wedding planner for Tailored Traditional Weddings. Sorry.'

'I'm going to be fired, aren't I?' He couldn't believe it. For something so small, correcting an untruth about himself, and then it had spiralled into a subtweet fight of dozens of messages.

'Do you want me to come with you?' Harriet asked.

'That's very kind of you, but I think I should go alone.'

Jason stood, fastened his top button, adjusted his tie and shrugged his jacket on. He caught his reflection in the window: *So this is what I'll look like when I lose my job. Right.* He swallowed the tight ball of anxiety in his throat. 'Are these all the stories?' He held the printouts aloft.

'Hang on,' Harriet said. 'There's a few more that have sprung up. Do you want me to print them?'

Like a condemned man, Jason said, 'Yep. Let's have them all.' He waited for the printer whirring to finish as he considered how he'd tell Pete he'd lost his job. How he'd explain to Pete that, after getting this far with the fight, he'd tripped himself up at the last hurdle with a stupid misjudgement. A misjudgement that, on paper, was morally right, even if it went against his director's instructions.

Harriet handed him a pile of papers. 'You okay?'

'Will be. Thanks.' He smiled at her weakly. He'd never felt less ready for anything, particularly something he held the moral high ground on.

He knocked on Christopher's door, said his name, then entered.

Christopher said, 'I was wondering when you'd arrive.' He gestured for Jason to sit.

Jason shuffled the papers. 'Can I explain?'

Christopher placed a phone on the table and pressed a button. 'I'm recording us. It's what I've been advised to do for protection. For us as much as you.'

Jason doubted they needed much protection since later today, Christopher would retain his job, whereas Jason would be unemployed again. He explained what had happened, stating his case about refuting the lies Ray had tweeted about him. 'I'm so sorry. I didn't mean to. I sort of got caught up in the moment. Forgot it was online. I saw red.' He'd been shouting at his phone, fingers shaking with rage as he'd tried to defend himself. Ray's Twitter followers had piled in, calling him names, threatening to kill him, saying he and his boyfriend should die and leave normal people alone.

'As much as I appreciate your intent, I'm afraid after the email we sent, expressly asking you to refrain from further engagement with Ray and Lux-Lodge Hotels, you have ignored this, leaving me with no option but to dismiss you. Sadly, because I think you did bring something new to the wedding planning department. I'll give you half an hour to collect your things. Ask HR for a box.'

'That's it?' Jason asked.

'I'm afraid it is.' He handed Jason a letter. 'It's all laid out. Including, I think you'll agree, paying you in lieu of notice isn't bad, in light of the circumstances.'

The letters swam in front of Jason's eyes. The first line said something about termination of employment with immediate effect.

'Would you like someone to fetch the box for you?'

Christopher stood, walked him out of his office, nodded to someone from HR, who handed him a cardboard box, accompanying him to his desk.

There, in silence he put his pot plant Pete had bought him for his first day, three months ago, a picture of them on the beach after a Pride weekend in Brighton, his notebook, some pens he'd bought, into the box.

'What about stuff on the computer?'

'Is there anything personal you'd like?' the HR woman asked.

He shook his head. He couldn't remember. Maybe. 'I don't know. Can I—'

Harriet stood. 'If you tell me later, I'll put it on a stick and post it.'

That was kind. Among this terrible, shitty, unbelievable day, Harriet's kindness affected Jason in ways he'd not expected. He blinked and a tear fell down his cheek.

Harriet handed him a tissue.

'Sorry, I'm really sorry. About everything. I didn't mean to I—' Jason wiped his eyes angrily. *God who cries about stuff like this?*

'I'll walk you out,' Harriet said, putting her arms round his shoulders.

At the security barrier, Harriet placed his cardboard box on the floor.

'So this is it?' Jason asked, composing himself, trying to leave with at least a strip of his dignity remaining.

'I'm so sorry. If it makes any difference, I did tell Christopher it wasn't your fault. That you hadn't started it.'

'Thanks. So did I.'

Harriet hugged him. 'Take care. Chin up, eh? Stay in touch.'

Jason nodded. He would stay in touch. Harriet had turned out to become a good colleague. Still not what he'd call friends, perhaps they should have got drunk together and stayed out in the bars of the West End until too late. That would have cemented their friendship.

Jason took a deep breath, pushed the rotating glass door with his foot, walked through and left the Tailored Weddings building for the last time.

Chapter 11

The chorus of Girls Aloud singing 'Jump' blasted as Mel reached the final flight of stairs, sweeping from side to side with the vacuum cleaner nozzle. As she reached the landing, she met a small child who'd left red hand prints on the wall.

He was saying something to her because his lips were moving, but Mel couldn't hear.

His mum, with freshly styled shiny brown hair and white blouse and jeans, held his hand and led him to the bathroom. She turned, smiled at Mel, mouthed 'thanks' and then she was gone.

A few hours later, Mel left the house in a much better state than when she'd arrived. With a sense of satisfaction she'd rarely received from housework in her own home, Mel walked to her car.

Pete rang and she put him on speaker phone as she drove to school.

'I know you're busy, but I wondered if you'd give Jason a hand.'

'Can't he ask for help himself? What about his parents?'

'He's embarrassed. They're miles away too. And they're only just getting used to smart phones. If you saw their messages you'd know why he doesn't ask them to help. Besides, he thinks he can do it on his own. You know he never asks.'

Besides, Jason knew he was probably dyslexic but didn't talk about it. 'Has he got a job yet?'

'Not even an interview.'

'Why?' She arrived at the school, parked and waited for Thomas and Lily.

'He's never got a job without knowing someone as a way in.'

'Never?' This was going to be harder than she expected. 'I'm hardly a model for finding the perfect job.'

'Don't do that, Mum.'

'What?' She rapped her shorter-than-before nails on the dashboard.

'Put yourself down. You're out there, working, sorting out ways to keep the house. Not that you need to, but I understand why.'

Mel was buggered if she was letting Steve make her lose her beautiful home. The place where she'd brought up four children, almost singlehandedly.

'We've been through this. What would you like?'

'I've looked at his applications and they're full of spelling mistakes, and well, it's like Lily wrote them. In fact, I think Lily would have done a better job.'

'Oh.'

'Precisely.'

Lily climbed into the back of the car, shortly followed by Thomas.

'And he won't let you help?' She loved Jason, but he could be stubborn and pig-headed sometimes.

'I offered and he said he was fine. I don't think he knows how bad he is. He spent hours on one application. He showed me it and it was terrible. I asked if he'd sent it and when he nodded, I mumbled it was fine. I mean, too late to change stuff, right?'

'Right.' She looked into the rear-view mirror. 'Seat belts on.' To Pete she said, 'I'll use mother-in-law prerogative.'

'Love you. Thanks.'

'My computer skills are a bit rusty...'

'I'll do the tech, you do the words. You can write it with quill and ink if it gets him a job.'

'Leave it with me.'

Thomas looked up from his phone. 'What's that about?'

Mel shook her head. 'Uncle Jason being Uncle Jason.'

Chapter 12

Harriet leaned her elbows on the table, stirring the milkshake absently. They were eating before going to the cinema.

Robert peered at the display in the distance. 'Are you sure you want to see this? We could slip back to yours and...' He rubbed her bare forearm.

She knew precisely what he'd want to do when they slipped back to hers. 'It's getting rave reviews, I thought you said you wanted to see it.'

He nodded, sighed. He always did that, when he was pretending not to be bored. He quickly changed the subject. 'My friend showed me something I never thought I'd see, back when I was your age.'

'Oh?' She perked up. *Who is this friend*, she wondered.

'Big twelve-page spread in *Greetings!* magazine. Lovely wedding. Thought you might have seen it, given your line of work. Two men. One's a reality TV star. Maybe they both are. Anyway, my friend showed me the magazine. I flicked through and, well...' He struggled for words.

She certainly wouldn't struggle for words for such a ridiculous spectacle as two grooms at a wedding. There was a word, or rather many words for that, and none of them very complimentary. 'What friend of yours reads *Greetings!* magazine?' *This ought to be good.*

Robert blushed, raking his hand through his greying hair, then stroking his silvery beard in thought. 'Colleague. Didn't I say it was someone at work?'

He had not. And she knew that was a lie. 'Do you have the magazine to hand, by any chance?'

He shook his head. 'Bet it's online though.' He pulled his phone from his pocket and turned it towards Harriet.

Two men in tightly fitting cream trousers and matching waistcoats, white shirts and cravats. *God, why did people think those were somehow more classy than a well-presented tie?*

'It's pretty cool, don't you think?' he asked.

'Why?' Except for the men being well trousered, and the photography being well put together, Harriet failed to see anything even remotely cool about two men marrying.

'It's like the radio DJ, you know.'

Harriet finished her milkshake, carefully avoiding the loud slurping noise her mother had told her off about as a child. 'I don't know.' She had time to kill, so why not ask for further explanation. She pushed the phone away, not wanting to see such a degradation of the concept of marriage any longer.

'That guy who's on the radio every Saturday afternoon.'

'Which station?'

He named a well-known show running from Saturday lunch through to the evening. She'd had it on in the background a few times, while lazing about her apartment, knowing it was too early to start drinking, but not sure what else to do with herself. 'I've listened. More as background than anything else really.'

'He was talking about the big match. The Arsenal and Chelsea. Said his husband was an Arsenal fan and if they lost, his hubby would be like a bear with a sore head.'

Harriet shook her head, failing to see what this had to do with, well, anything really. 'Does this have much more conversation involving football, do you think?' She knew she was being terse, and often wondered why Robert didn't dump her.

'I mean, the DJ just said it. Talked about his hubby and football, without making a—'

'Big song and dance about it?'

He nodded. 'Like it's nothing.'

'Hubby.' *Honestly, what a word!* She shuddered. 'Some people are so common.'

He glanced at the two grooms on his phone. 'I think it's nice.'

Nice. Honestly, why even bother saying it if it's such an anodyne word? 'I don't think it's *nice*. Not at all.' A picture of the two men holding hands caught her eye.

'I didn't know you felt like this.'

'I don't feel like anything.' She knew how careful she must be about voicing a dissenting opinion about this sort of thing. What had happened to men being men and women being women? When did it all become so muddled? *Hubby* and *the missus* were the start of it, she reckoned.

'When I was your age, if someone had said there'd be a radio presenter talking about his hubby, I'd have laughed. Never mind women marrying women and men marrying men. I think it's nice.'

That bloody word again. *Nice.* Harriet pursed her lips, a myriad of thoughts swirling around her mind.

'You do have a problem with it, I can see.'

She paused, wondering if she should verbalise her concerns, but since he was the one driving this conversation she decided she'd forge on. 'Who gives whom away? Who walks down the aisle? Not that they can marry in a church. Whose parents pay for it? Bridesmaids when there's no bride? Groomsmen when there's no groom.' The fashion for groomsmen was another Americanism Harriet didn't approve of either, only worse when there was an absence of a groom for them to men about with. She shook her head and pursed her lips in disgust.

Robert's eyes went wide.

'What?'

'Your face.'

'What about my face?' Her patience was rapidly running out. Perhaps slipping back to her place would have been preferable to this... Whatever this was.

He checked his chunky diver's watch. 'Best go if you want something to eat with the film.' He stood.

What about my face? She caught her reflection in a mirror. Her face was perfectly all right. More than all right. Her mother had said her gamine features reminded her of a young Audrey Hepburn and she had her maternal grandmother to thank for that.

Harriet didn't want anything to eat while watching the film, but Robert did, so he returned to the queue holding a large container of popcorn.

'Sweet and salted. Wasn't sure which you preferred.' He proffered the container, shaking it. 'Dig in.'

'I've not washed my hands.' She felt sure she should be enjoying this date, her time with Robert, more than she was. Increasingly she didn't enjoy most things: life felt like a long list of things she was compelled to do. Work, see Robert, eat, sleep. Nothing had the shine it once had.

'It's fine, grab a handful.' More shaking of the popcorn.

They were a few people away from the ticket inspectors so Harriet rushed to the ladies' loos, washed her hands, reapplied her lipstick, brushed her hair and powdered the shininess off her button nose. She removed a tiny bottle of vodka from her handbag. Checking no one was about to join her, she took a few large glugs, the warmth and bitterness burning the back of her throat and taste buds. And then the delicious coolness, the relief at having held off all day until this moment.

The door opened and a women entered, nodding politely before disappearing into a cubicle.

Harriet slipped into a cubicle, finished the bottle. She guzzled two more, sitting on the toilet with the lid down. She'd become rather proficient at this, nipping off for alone time to enjoy her handbag bar as she called it. Feeling happier than she had all day, she sprayed herself generously with perfume and chewed a stick of gum. *Now I can face whatever the rest of the evening throws at me.*

Slipping out of the ladies' loo, she joined Robert near the front of the queue.

'You look nice. What have you done?' His gaze darted over her face, hair, clothes.

Nice. That bloody word again. 'Thanks.' She held his hand, squeezed it tightly.

He rattled the popcorn, encouraging her to take some.

'Later.' She pushed it away.

Once seated in the darkness Harriet held his hand, placing it on her lap. The alcohol was lowering her inhibitions, letting her relax a little. Did she have another bottle in her bag, could she sneak out mid-film and drink it? Too obvious doing so in here.

Robert kissed her cheek. 'You were right, you know.' His beard rubbed against her cheek as he whispered.

She inhaled deeply the distinctive lime and woody scent of his aftershave mixed with something she recognised as Robert himself.

'Have you been drinking?' he asked, obviously perplexed.

'Of course not!' She laughed very loudly. 'Why? Why on earth would you say that?'

'Maybe it's me, but there's a distinct whiff of alcohol on you.'

'Perfume maybe?' More of that and oodles of chewing gum next time. She couldn't have Robert thinking she was an...

'Of course.' He pulled her closer and kissed the top of her head.

She thought vodka was odourless, which was why it had become her preferred tipple while she was on the go. 'I was right, you said. About what?' Perhaps wasting time here with the film was foolish, given how thoroughly proficient his love-making skills were. It would certainly take her mind off the irritation at their earlier discussion that had settled in her stomach.

'Coming here, rather than going straight to your place.'

'Why's that?' She smoothed her dress fabric on her lap.

'It's more romantic, isn't it?'

Harriet frowned. Had she really said that? She wanted moonlight, roses, expensive chocolates, men scaling fire escapes, proposals on crowded planes, and instead she'd seemed to have settled too comfortably in a rut of booty calls and takeaways gobbled in her apartment after bouts of mechanically mediocre sex.

Where did I go so wrong?

'It is,' she said tightly.

The film started, and Robert held her hand. She knew she should feel something more than she did. Happiness, satisfaction, contentment, a little of each probably. And yet, all she could think about was the two well-trousered men walking down the aisle and kissing in front of their friends and family. And all she wanted to do was rush to the ladies' loo and drink the second tiny bottle of vodka.

Men talking about their football-loving husbands, it didn't make sense. And if it did, she didn't want to have anything to do with it.

Later, after they'd returned to Harriet's apartment and Robert had attentively and methodically made love to her – it was definitely *to* this time, since Harriet had felt she was floating above her body during the whole thing, probably the two other miniatures she drank during the film – she was standing in her night dress by the door, not wanting to beg Robert to stay, but also not wanting him to leave.

'I said I needed to get home earlier.' Robert looked at the floor. His eyebrows rose in an expression of what Harriet took to be genuine contrition. Even if she wasn't quite sure why he felt so sorry.

He had said that, upon arrival at the cinema his opening gambit had been, 'I can't stay at yours tonight. I've got a *thing* early tomorrow. Need to sort it out.' A pause and then, 'Work.' A shrug.

Of course it was work.

Now, Harriet said, 'Are you married?' She said the words before she could stop them leaving her mouth. She wasn't sure if it was the alcohol, the popcorn or the sex that had her closely controlled persona slipping.

'Don't be so silly, darling.' He blushed, looked away, shrugged on his suit jacket.

No eye contact. Interesting. 'Your friendly colleague, with the progressive views on marriage, are you sure she's not your wife? Who you're returning to now, having showered here, so you can slip into bed next to her and not smell of me and sex and red wine.'

The red wine, perhaps that was why her tongue was so loose now. A bottle between them upon arrival had disappeared almost instantaneously, making the second one seem almost as if it were nothing.

He shook his head. 'This was fun.' Without a kissed cheek, lips or even a hug, he left.

Harriet stared at the door, a shard of loneliness and unhappiness shot through her, wondering where she'd gone so wrong that *this* snatched moment, being left alone after having sex, part-time relationship was whatever passed for her unremarkable love life. Perhaps she had watched too many rom coms, read too many romantic books, dared to hope there was a perfect man out there who'd love her as much as she loved him. Perhaps she held out hope against reality that Robert would turn into that perfect man.

Fun, she decided, returning to the kitchen to pour herself the dregs of the second bottle of wine, was as tragic as *nice*. As tragic as two men or two women thinking what they had was a marriage. A proper relationship.

Tragic, and more than a little distasteful.

She swirled the wine around the glass, drank it in one gulp, closing her eyes and wondering how much more she had in the apartment. Whether she could avoid nipping to the local shop and making small talk with the friendly man or his wife, or feeling the need to justify why she was buying six bottles of wine: 'Having a party, lots of people,' she'd said the last time, before returning to an empty apartment.

–

Harriet waited at the central London cocktail bar her mother had suggested. Perhaps afternoon tea would have been better. Except Mother wasn't an afternoon tea sort of woman.

The waiter arrived, offering another drink.

'I'm waiting for my mother. Perhaps some mineral water in the meantime. Sparkling.'

'Of course, madam.' He left.

If only sparkling water gave the same feeling, escapism, obliteration, joyful uplifting confidence, as champagne. Harriet sighed. Two cocktails and she was feeling a little bolder. She needed that if she were to face Mother.

The waiter arrived, holding a silver tray with a bottle of sparkling mineral water and a glass. 'Madam. I have brought your friend.'

Her mother stood next to him, smiling. Jet black hair tied back, a black cocktail dress that she had no business looking that slender in at her age, and a feathery bolero jacket. A diamond necklace sparkled as she sat. 'When he said you'd ordered that, I wasn't sure if he meant the right woman.' She frowned. 'Are you okay?' She laid her black-gloved hand on the table.

Harriet held it briefly. They never kissed or hugged, only if her mother was particularly tight.

'Didn't want to be too far ahead of you. Wasn't sure when you'd make it.' Harriet sipped the water, eyeing her mother over the glass, wondering how she was going to express what she'd been trying to voice for so long.

'I've ordered us a cocktail each. Your usual of course.'

What if I didn't want another one? But she did. She always wanted another one.

'Father said you're still seeing that gentleman friend.' She tutted, shook her head. 'I've told you, he's wildly unsuitable for you. He's not appropriate.'

'You've only met him once.' Harriet decided she'd prefer another drink before embarking on this conversation again.

'I said then and I'll say now, he's too old. I asked my friends and they'd never heard of his family. You can't marry an unknown.'

'He makes me happy.' She said it with as much feeling as she could muster. Robert did make her happy. Sometimes. So why did she want to down her cocktail when it arrived?

On cue, the drinks arrived.

Her mother said, 'We must do this more often. How else am I to know what you're doing?'

'You know. It's just that you don't approve.' Harriet carefully put the glass on the table.

'I do. We do. I think it's marvellous that you've got a little job. It's certainly more than I could be bothered with. And having a partner is better than not, I should think.'

Of that Harriet was sure. Although, the loneliness when Robert left her was like a sharp spike that she needed to be anaesthetised against. 'Quite.' Harriet finished the cocktail.

'Steady on, I've only just arrived. I thought you were being sensible, with your sparkling water.' Her mother sipped her drink, staring at Harriet over the rim of the glass.

Harriet sat back in the chair, folded her hands in her lap, more for something to do with them than anything else. 'Did you have a specific reason for suggesting drinks, or...?'

'Can't a mother simply want to see her daughter? Without any hidden agenda?' She scoffed, shaking her head and twirling the glass between thumb and forefinger.

'I know Robert isn't suitable. I know I should take more interest in Electrovax. I know I should have been a son. But I am not. I am me. And you're stuck with it.' As she was also stuck with herself, she reflected briefly.

'That has nothing to do with anything. I've told you, your father was thrilled to have a daughter, to have you. Still is. We both are. Of course. I wish you had more shared interests with your father.'

Harriet narrowed her eyes, waving a hand, ordering another drink.

'I can't speak to Father about this, because it feels...'

'You can speak to me about anything, you know that, don't you?'

Harriet really wanted to believe her. Ever since her mother had given her the 'You're growing up now, there are going to be changes to your body' speech, she'd hoped to have an open, supportive, emotionally mature relationship with her mother. Except, every time she tried to talk about those sorts of things, her mother failed to understand Harriet's issue. First boyfriend dumping her, second boyfriend wanting to trick her into bed, third boyfriend, having got her into bed, simply disappearing. These had all been conversations her mother had replied to with: '*Get a grip and get on with it.*'

'Promise me you won't just tell me to get a grip,' Harriet said now.

'I can't promise. But I shall promise to listen. I'm afraid I don't hold with all of this emotional incontinence nowadays.'

'I'm your daughter – if I can be emotionally incontinent with anyone, surely it should be you.' Harriet's eyes widened.

Her mother put a hand up to signal for Harriet to stop. 'That's as may be. But I can't change who I am. You must understand that.'

Harriet wished more than that... if she could change who she herself was. Because then she wouldn't have this gnawing sadness that ate away at her, that she needed to escape by drinking. 'I want The One. I want rom com, happy ever after, seeing him across a crowded room and locking eyes with him and knowing, to the depths of my soul, that he's the one for me. And that I'm the one for him.' She blurted it all out, tongue loosened by the three cocktails.

Her mother sat back in her chair, obviously in thought. 'That's quite a lot to live up to. Don't you think?'

'If it's not that good, why bother? Why be with someone who you're unsure about?'

'Such as your Robbie, perhaps?'

'Robert,' she said through gritted teeth. 'I'm not unsure about him. He's good to me.' *When he's with me.* 'He's better than being single.'

'So he's Mister Right Now, and not The One?'

'He could be The One.' She said it and meant it. She really wanted it to be true… Was holding out for it to become true, despite her niggling doubts.

'Really?' her mother shook her head. 'Do you seriously believe that?'

Harriet nodded emphatically, because the alternative was too sad to dwell on. 'Being with someone is better than being alone, even if being with that person hurts.'

'Even if Robert is The One, he's most definitely not The Proper One. As your father was – is – to me.'

Harriet stood, as tears formed and before they fell onto her cheeks, she strode to the ladies' loo.

She splashed her face, dried it, reapplied her make-up. She really was stuck with herself, who she was, what she wanted, what she didn't want, in spite of the great heavy pressures she felt from others. It would have been much easier to simply go along with her father's plan to take over Electrovax, to take up her mother's offer of setting her up with the proper sort of man. But she couldn't. No matter how hard she tried, she couldn't not want the things she desired for herself. Independence, love, meaning in her life.

And yet, she considered, staring at her reflection, she didn't seem any closer to reaching any of them.

'Darling, are you all right?' her mother's voice came from outside the loos.

'I'm perfectly okay,' she said with feeling.

Her mother entered, staring at her. 'What are you doing in here? I thought you'd climbed out of the window, so awful am I to spend time with.'

'We're four floors up.' Harriet looked at her, wishing with a great deal of hope that she could be more like her mother and less like herself.

'Would you like something to eat? I'm feeling slightly wobbly after two, or is it three, drinks.' She held out a hand.

Harriet took it, and was led back to their table.

They shared grilled oysters. 'It's the only thing on the menu that's not enormous,' her mother had explained.

An aphrodisiac, and she was enjoying them with her mother. The irony was not lost on Harriet.

'Could I have some of your mineral water, please?' Her mother held her cocktail glass. 'Actually, wait.' She waved for a waiter, when he came over she said, 'I'd like a highball for some water please.'

The waiter left.

'I had dozens of men courting me before I settled on your father,' she said after an awkward silence.

'Why did you choose him?' Harriet hoped her mother would say love, but seriously doubted it.

She poured another oyster into her throat, awaiting her mother's answer.

'Why did I choose your father?' Her mother dabbed her mouth with the serviette. 'I chose him because I knew he'd make me happy.'

'Because you loved him,' Harriet said optimistically.

'Goodness no. I'd barely spent any time with him. We'd had half a dozen dates. He could hold a conversation, and was generous, but I didn't know him to love him.'

'And yet you married him?' Harriet scrunched up her face in disbelief.

'Of course.' She placed a credit card on the tray the waiter had brought with their bill. 'Why ever not?'

'Because you didn't love him. It's…' Harriet struggled for words.

'People marry for many other reasons than love. If it's right, that comes later.'

'So you love him now?'

She shook her head, chuckling briefly. 'What a ridiculous thing to ask.'

Is that a yes, or a no?

'It's a mystery to me where you've got all this rot about happy endings, The One – it's an impossible dream sold to women to sell books and cinema tickets.'

'You really think that?' Harriet asked.

'Do you really think your Robert may be The One?'

'I have to.'

'Why?'

Because otherwise it's too sad to think about. She'd spent her twenties being far too fast and loose with her affections, so had decided to try and do something approximating settling down, and Robert had seemed like the most appropriate man for that.

'Darling, I asked you a question,' her mother said.

'You can't enter into a relationship believing it will end. One has to enter with the belief that it will be forever.' She bit her bottom lip.

'Forever.' Her mother tutted, shook her head. 'Nothing's forever.' She stroked Harriet's shoulder with a gloved hand. 'Will you be okay making your way home? I brought a car if you need a lift.'

'I think I'll sit here for a bit.' Harriet did all she could to disguise the dejected tone in her voice.

Her mother left, pressing some money into the waiter's hand as she passed.

She'd never really understood how her two parents could create her. As a girl, she'd asked – many times – if she was adopted. They assured her she most definitely was not. Although there was some resemblance in her nose and eyes with her mother, there was nothing about her personality that appeared to owe anything to her parents.

She held her phone and looked at Robert's last text: *Want me to get you popcorn? X*

He'd been in the queue at the cinema. The kiss at least meant something, she knew, hoped. That date had been enjoyable, she just wished she hadn't needed to nip to the ladies' for her handbag bar.

Her head felt light and she felt slightly sick – perhaps oysters didn't sit well atop four or five dry cocktails.

She could call Robert, arrange for him to come round, but she really was very much more than a bit tight, a little tipsy. She was swaying and her lips felt numb. He'd commented once to her that she only ever seemed to want to have sex when she'd had a drink. That had stung. More so because it was true.

No.

She wouldn't call him, she didn't need Robert, or any man. She would wait here, have some water, compose herself and then make her way home, in the sure knowledge that her mother was never going to understand what she wanted in a relationship.

She closed her eyes briefly, mainly to stop the room from spinning.

Sometime later, a hand on her arm woke her.

'Would you like me to call Madam a taxi?' It was the waiter, she recognised his voice.

Opening her eyes, she shook her head. How very improper of her. What did she think she was, some common drunk? 'Can I have a drink?'

A look of concern crossed his face. 'Water, I think, is best.'

She was about to request a vodka orange – vitamin C, practically a health drink – when his look of pity, more than concern she decided, stopped her dead in her tracks.

'I can order you a taxi. It will be here soon,' he said, staring into her eyes.

'Fine. But tell them to take their time, okay?'

He nodded. 'Understood.' He left.

There was nothing to rush back to at her apartment. Except sitting with her own thoughts and wanting to escape them, just as she had tonight.

Chapter 13

Jason waved Pete off to work, having made a packed lunch.

Since being fired, Jason had become a cross between a perfect house husband and an entrepreneur.

Pete had been shocked he was fired but understood why. 'I'm proud of you,' he'd said.

'For getting fired?'

'For having principles.'

'They don't pay the bills.'

'We'll be fine. You're right to walk away, it's not worth some big legal battle. Besides, we don't have the money.'

'I'm still thinking about sharing the emails from the hotel. Exposing them for what they're doing.'

'Maybe not today. I think you've done enough for one day. Getting fired and carrying your stuff out in a cardboard box is a lot for a Tuesday, right?'

'Right.'

Pete kissed him and they hugged and Jason felt surer than ever before he'd ended up with the best man he'd ever met.

Jason had spent the next few months working out how to set up his own wedding planning business. He'd always wanted to do this, but it had been easier to accept his next job offer. Now, having applied for some jobs, while not really wanting them, Pete had said, 'Just do it. If you don't do it now, you'll get to fifty and regret it.'

'But money?'

'I got this,' was all Pete had said.

Jason hadn't quite believed he meant it, assuming since he was older, it fell to him to be the big provider in their relationship. Until Pete had said one evening, after Jason had forced himself to apply for another job he'd not really wanted: 'Ten years you'll be fifty, I'll be thirty-five. Do you want to do what Mum's done, leave it until then, or do you want to grab this by the balls and go for it?'

Jason shook his head, mumbled something about needing to earn money.

'Yeah, eventually. But at the moment I've got this. If this isn't the universe telling you to do this, then I don't know what is. Besides, I'm telling you to do this. We'll manage.'

And they had.

So while managing on Pete's money, Jason had looked into limited companies, local networks for small businesses, met with people, spoken to other wedding planners about how they'd got started, looked into insurance schemes and now he was ready to launch Extra Weddings onto an unsuspecting Cotswolds and surrounding areas.

Jason hit publish on his Extraweddings.co.uk website and held his breath. He'd included testimonials from previous clients from all his jobs and pictures from some who he'd got on with particularly well, including Adam and Ryan.

That afternoon, Jason hovered over his inbox, waiting for enquiries to flood in. Finally, in desperation he rang Pete at work. 'Nothing.'

'I'm at work.'

'I went live and not a single bite. That's it, we're going under. I'll call a recruitment consultant after I put the phone down to you.' He knew he sounded a little manic, but after putting so much work into the big launch, he couldn't help but feel disappointed.

'Who did you invite to the launch?'

'What do you mean?'

'Didn't you organise an event to tell everyone Extraweddings.co.uk was live and open for business?'

Jason closed his eyes, shaking his head.

'Are you still there?' Pete asked.

'I got so carried away with the legal stuff, and the website I...' He was so tired, his brain was fried. He'd not even put 'launch party' on a list.

'Honestly, if I were you, I'd pack a bag and leave me when I got home.'

'I thought it was your weddings that are meant to be extra, not you?'

Jason took a deep breath.

'Can you leave the drama to me, please?'

Jason smiled. 'See you tonight.' He ended the call.

The rest of the afternoon was spent effortlessly doing what he'd done for so many years, organising an event. And by the time Pete arrived home, he'd arranged a launch party for a fortnight's time, invites sent out, Mel secured for catering... He'd gone with a nice hotel surrounded by countryside, had even called in a few favours with the local newspaper, promising the features editor a night in the hotel, once he was up and running.

Snow to the Eskimos – yep, pretty much.

Over dinner that night, Jason kept checking his inbox for enquiries.

'Nothing?' Pete asked.

Jason shook his head. 'But then again, I've not told anyone, because I forgot!'

'It'll be fine. I bet within a year you'll have too much work to handle.'

That would be a nice problem to have. One last check of his inbox and he saw an email. His heart soared. He told Pete. Opening the email he scanned through, deleted it.

'And?' Pete held his wine glass aloft, poised for a toast.

'Spam.'

Pete replaced his glass on the table. 'Tomorrow's another day.'

Indeed it was. 'Another day when I should have told people about Extraweddings.co.uk…'

'You've had a lot to think about. Give yourself a break. I decree you will take tomorrow off so you can slob out, watch TV all day.' It was very kind of Pete to say this, but Jason knew he'd find it difficult, with the constant worry about whether he'd actually have a business, or if he'd just set up a pretty website with no clients.

–

A fortnight later, Mel said, 'Will you please stop panicking?'

Jason's jaw tensed, butterflies filled his stomach and he had no appetite. He wiped sweaty hands on his red suit trousers. Because, of course, he was wearing Ruby, since she had started the chain of events leading him to this moment.

'No one's going to come,' Jason said. He gestured to the empty room.

'It's six. No one arrives when a party starts,' Mel said.

'Says the big party woman.' He hugged her, thanked her.

Mel smirked.

'What is that about?' Jason asked.

'Nothing, this is *your* night.'

There was something going on there and Jason would find it out. Jason saw the journalist from the local paper and collected his favourite red wine, handing it over.

'I can't stay too long, but I thought I'd show my face.' He sipped the wine. 'Not bad. Is there nosh too?'

'Of course.' He glanced at Mel who was talking to someone by the buffet table. 'Mother-in-law made it.'

'When did you and Pete get married?'

'De facto.'

They chatted about the wedding business, why he'd finally taken the plunge, then, after Jason had greeted his guests, he turned on the music, quiet instrumental versions of pop music played by string instruments. He wanted it to say 'Classy, classic and also modern'. Because that was the ethos of Extra Weddings.

Marriage is for everyone – if you can dream it, we can make it happen!

Mel had helped him with the words. As she had with the invitations, the press statement, the catering and a hundred other things to make today run smoothly.

It was half past six, and there was still no sign of Pete.

Nothing on his phone. He sidled up to Mel who was circulating with tiny hamburgers on a tray. 'Have you heard from your darling son?'

'You know as well as I do, he's a rule unto himself. Do you want me to call him?'

'I have. But nothing.' He was five minutes late, he'd have to start the speech now with or without Pete.

Jason stood on the raised stage, behind the microphone. The room was pleasingly full, he reckoned about half the people he'd invited had turned up. Journalists, friends, previous clients.

The crowd fell silent and the music stopped.

Jason pulled his speech from his jacket pocket. Mel had written it after he'd said what he wanted to cover. 'Thank you everyone for making the Tim – time – to be here tonight. This is the result of a dream I've had for about forty years… No, twenty years, but haven't had the goats…' He coughed, blushing slightly. '…guts to put into practice. And then some stuff happened…' He chuckled nervously. Mel had advised him to cut out all the stuff about Tailored Weddings and Cotswolds Wedding Company, since it sounded like sour grapes. 'ExtraWeddings.co.uk is here to make everyone's wedding day that *extra* bit special. Seclar.' He peered at the paper, then spelled it out, one syllable at a time: 'Sec-u-lar.' Looking up, he felt proud. 'Non-sec-u-lar – I always get mixed up which one means what. Basically, religious and non-religious, straight, gay, lesbian… If it's legal to get married in this country and you can dream the… I mean your perfect day, we can make it a realness.' *Bloody words.* 'Re-ali-ty.'

The crowd cheered.

Jason saw Pete arriving, mouthing sorry and slipping to the back of the crowd, standing against the wall, next to his mum.

'Before I propose a toast, I wanted to thank two people, without them this wouldn't have happened. Mel, who's helped me organise this, catered, done the music, decorations, everything basically. And my partner, Pete, Mel's wonderful son, who told me to go big or go home when I was worrying about whether now was the right time to start Extra Weddings.'

More clapping rippled through the crowd.

'Thanks everyone, please pick up a business card, tell all your friends, eat, drink and dream your perfect Extra wedding!'

'Dream your perfect Extra wedding!' Everyone responded to the toast, raising their glasses.

The launch party passed quickly in a blur of networking and talking to people who were thinking about getting married.

–

A few weeks later, Jason had half a dozen enquiries and a couple of firm bookings. His worries about no one turning up to the launch party, and nobody wanting to employ him, were both unfounded. Exactly as Pete had told him.

Jason had returned from a wedding car company that sourced classic cars from enthusiastic owners, through classic car clubs, providing a one-off fleet of vehicles, at affordable prices.

He'd booked enough white Rolls Royce cars and horses and carriages to open a factory. And for those who wanted it, there would always be that option. However, Jason wanted Extra Weddings to be quirky and different from the other wedding planners. Because he was in charge, he spent more time at the initial consultation, trying to dream big what the clients wanted for their wedding. He used wallpaper, fabric swatches, film posters, album covers, pictures from celebrity weddings, each to give the clients an idea of their personal mood board.

Jason checked his desk phone voicemail and wrote down the messages. Two clients he'd met through Tailored Weddings who'd only wanted Jason to organise their siblings' big day. When Tailored Weddings realised they wouldn't be able to offer them the hotel they'd wanted, they'd reluctantly allowed Jason to continue through Extra Weddings.

I could really do with some help, although being busy is a nice problem to have. He made a strong coffee and stared out of the bedroom window as a florist van arrived.

He'd taken the best photographers he'd worked with before and added a list of others, who could take traditional, right up to avant-garde photos, using equipment ranging from state-of-the-art electronic to black-and-white film cameras. He'd interviewed these photographers, asking them what unique qualities they brought to the photos, and selected only the best.

Sipping his coffee, Jason plugged a flash drive into his laptop to check photos from the latest photographer who'd pitched to be on his roster. Not bad, could do with a little bit more variety of the shots they took, but he could discuss that.

Jason's stomach rumbled. He'd not eaten since Pete had fed him toast at breakfast.

He opened a proposal from a caterer.

He worked with local restaurants, sourcing local food from small suppliers rather than big catering companies. He could deliver everything from a hog roast, to a vegan sit-down meal for a hundred via chocolate fountains, curries, Mexican finger food and French haute cuisine.

Jason replied to the caterer's email: *Looks great, I'll be in touch to confirm numbers.*

His stomach rumbled, so he left the bedroom they'd converted into his office and made a very late lunch, while speaking on the phone to a waste management company he wanted to partner with.

Because he'd seen so much waste and unsustainable practice in his career, he recycled decorations, gave leftover food to the local homeless shelter and used clothes suppliers who repurposed vintage items and upcycled high-street looks, which was far more accessible and creative than the traditional wedding clothes options of white dresses for women and grey suits for men.

He thanked them and ended the call, chewing on the apple he'd grabbed. He closed his eyes, savouring the moment, the dream he'd dared to bring into reality.

Footsteps clattered closer, and then Pete was at the door. 'How are you getting on?'

'Busy. Happy to see you.' It was as if Pete had left the house ten minutes ago. 'How was your day?'

Pete talked about a member he'd been helping with an employment tribunal and how he hoped to achieve the outcome they wanted.

'You love a good fight, don't you?'

'Only if I think it's the right thing to do.' He coughed. 'And I'm sure I'll win it.'

'Clever too.' He rested his arms on Pete's lap, staring up at him.

They sat in silence for a few moments.

Jason really wanted to marry him. With all of his heart. He couldn't imagine ever being with another man as long as he lived. He wanted in sickness and in health, till death us do part, with Pete and only Pete.

Jason bit his bottom lip. *Do I say it now?* He'd jokingly asked if Pete would marry him and Pete had laughed and said they didn't need that, because they loved each other and marriage wasn't for him. Old-fashioned institution, all that stuff. Jason had agreed, although deep down he wanted to be Pete's husband.

'I've been thinking,' Pete said, crossing his legs.

'Right.'

'You know how I say I love you?'

Jason nodded.

'And that I'll always love you. And I don't want anyone else?'

Jason's cheeks heated and he smiled, holding Pete's hand, staring into his eyes.

'I wondered, seeing as you're an expert at these weddings now, if you had space to organise another Extra wedding.'

'Who for?' Jason brushed Pete's cheek.

'The client is going to be a nightmare. He's totally extra. Never satisfied. A bit of a diva actually. Drama queen. You won't want him as a client.'

Is this really happening? 'I do want him as a husband. I was just...'

'What?'

'Doesn't matter,' Jason said.

'So it's settled,' Pete said with a grin. 'Will you marry me?'

Jason nodded. 'I'd love nothing more than to marry the heck out of you.'

Pete was blushing. 'Good.' He hopped off the desk, walked to the door and downstairs.

Jason's heart pounded in his chest, his mouth felt dry and it was as if he was flying. *Has that really just happened?* He stood on the landing.

'What do you think a really extra fiancé deserves for dinner?' Pete shouted from the kitchen.

Yes, it had happened!

Chapter 14

'Come round if you want to – it's still your house, legally.' Mel pressed her forehead in anticipation of a stress headache.

'I need to drop them off anyway,' Steve said.

'Them? Your youngest children have names.'

A silence, and then, 'Is that a yes?'

Mel gritted her teeth. Keeping civil during the separation and soon divorce was the top piece of advice her friends had given. Even if sometimes she wanted to throttle him.

'Of course.' She ended the call and decided she ought to tidy up a little before he arrived.

A week of cleaning other people's homes and unsurprisingly the enthusiasm for doing her own had somewhat dwindled. Helping Jason had been great fun. She'd forgotten how much she enjoyed words, language, writing. Once Jason had shown her the software it had seemed pretty simple. She was a while off a mail merge or nested tables, whatever they were, but Jason's CV had fancy headings, bullet points and everything. Plus all the good words. And they were in the right order. Thanks to her.

The cleaning was precisely what she needed: money and quick. Although a part of her niggled that she should do something with her English perhaps. *I wonder if I could, someday, return to uni... An impossible dream.*

Not a CV doctor as Jason had suggested, but something that didn't require being on her feet all day pushing a mop or vacuum around.

Speaking of which...

A lightning-fast vacuum, quick flick with a mop and damp cloth over everything and she resumed her position on the sofa. For some reason, despite there only being one fewer person in the house since Steve had left, there seemed to be about half as much mess. Perhaps it was because she no longer had to hold out hope he'd do some of the chores, she simply accepted she would do it all, with the kids pitching in occasionally when homework allowed.

The door was opened by Thomas and then Lily, who ran across the hall for a hug.

Steve stood at the entrance, bags beneath his red-rimmed eyes, unshaven, hunching forwards.

'Come in,' Mel said. To the children she said, 'Washing in the utility and unpack your bags.'

They ran upstairs.

'Don't leave them all week until next weekend.' She tutted loudly, indicating for Steve to follow. 'They think some butler is going to unpack them.'

He chuckled and followed her into the living room. They sat on the sofa at opposite ends.

'How's it going?' she asked.

'You look very well. Have you done your hair differently?'

She'd had a bit of an accident with a home highlighting kit, but with Dawn's help – she was an expert in anything to do with peroxiding hair – she'd rescued it and now looked as if she spent all day in the sun. 'Bit sun-kissed.'

'That's it. Suits you. You look well.'

'Thanks.' Wearing make-up, as she wanted, for herself, was obviously working too. A good foundation and some eye shadow would, as Dawn pointed out, cover a multitude of sins and hide many years. 'How are you?'

'Fine. You?' he said quietly in an unconvincing tone.

'Fine.'

'Wonderful.' He rocked back and forth on his feet.

There was an awkward silence.

'Well, that's great.' Mel shook her head. 'It's been lovely having this little chat.' It was like getting blood from a stone.

'We went out for food,' he said with a false brightness.

Nice for them. She couldn't afford that and was stuck with plain old cooking in the kitchen. 'You wanted to talk, so I'm here, talking. And you're not, it seems.'

He stared out of the window, then at the floor. 'Is it always *this* hard?'

'Is *what* always *this* hard?'

'Looking after the children.' He looked at her with a view of desperation.

It didn't seem reasonable. Why was he struggling so much? 'Lily is ten. Thomas's practically driving. They're hardly babies.'

He looked at her, then at the floor. 'I wanted to have a countryside drive with Sally.'

'Right. And so?'

'They were bored. Didn't like the restaurant we visited. Lily didn't eat anything. Was really hungry and grizzly when we arrived home. Thomas spent the whole time staring at his phone. It's like they're deliberately behaving so badly.' His eyes widened as he raised his eyebrows.

So, this really was serious. With a sigh, she said, 'Has it, by any chance, occurred to you to maybe become better acquainted with your offspring?'

'Where would I start? It's as if they're from another species. Is it harder at this age than when they were small?' He bit his bottom lip.

'Maybe spending more time talking to them, and less time trying to impress Sally?'

'What should I talk about?' He shook his head.

Mel took a deep breath. This really did beggar belief. Perhaps it was her fault for being such a great mum they'd not noticed the lack of dad. 'What do you think I've been talking to them about?'

He shrugged. 'Sally isn't into children, so it's difficult.'

Mel almost said that surely Sally was practically their age so she'd have a lot in common with the kids. But she bit it back. 'This is difficult for all of us.'

'It is, isn't it?' A pause, and then, 'Do you think you could have them for *my* next weekend?'

They'd agreed he would see the children on alternate weekends, plus one weeknight. But a few weeks in, and with the limited contact, he'd started cancelling mid-week time and now this.

Mel bit her lip so hard it bled while she considered what to say. *Is he going to ask how I am? Will he be wondering if I'm coping okay financially since that's the area I've missed out on, having raised our children for most of my adult life?*

'Are you okay?' he asked.

'Thinking. For someone who's so keen to get to know his children, dodging the next time you're due to spend time with them strikes me as somewhat short-sighted.'

He leaned forwards, placing his elbows on the table. 'Please. I wouldn't ask unless I *really* needed your help.'

'Sometimes the easiest thing isn't really the easiest thing, because it's a shortcut and makes things more difficult in the long run. You can see that, surely?' She stared at him.

His shoulder slumped and he leaned forwards with raised eyebrows in obvious desperation. 'Please?' A pause and then: 'Please. I'll be forever grateful.'

'I'm working, in case you wondered. Cleaning other people's houses. I'm determined to keep this house. I'm tenacious. But then again, you probably know that since you've been married to me for most of your life too.'

He sat back. 'Well done.' He raised an eyebrow, blowing out his cheeks and exhaling.

'It is, isn't it? I'm looking after the children most of the week and working. And here you're telling me it's a struggle to have our children four days a fortnight. A fair summary?' She narrowed her eyes.

Briefly he counted on his fingers. 'It's all so much to remember. School times, play dates, sports practice, everything. And then there's—'

'If you're about to blame it on that woman, you can stop right now. You were the one who decided to bail on this marriage. You made your bed, and it has her in it, so you need to lie in it.'

'Is that a no to taking them for my next weekend?'

'I will always look after our children if they need it. I have before and I will now. But what I can't understand is how you seem to think it's my fault you can't manage.'

'I didn't say that.'

'What are you asking for then?'

'A little more time to get used to—'

'Co-parenting our children?'

'What it's like to be a proper father.'

That was, at least, an admission that prior to now he'd very much avoided that role. She narrowed her eyes. 'My not helping now will aid you in this endeavour in the long run.'

He nodded. 'Right. A no it is then. Fine.' He stood, raked his hands through his hair. 'I'd better go. I'll be in touch.' He left, slamming the door, which echoed throughout the hallway.

Mel's rage turned into frustration, then disappointment, then sadness. Pure undiluted sadness that Steve was so monumentally useless about his own children. Had she set herself up for this all along? Being the perfect mum and letting him get away with doing nothing. It was, she reflected now, like having a fifth child.

I'm fine. I've got to be fine. Because what alternative is there?

But as she sat on the sofa, replaying the conversation, staring at the ceiling she'd arranged someone to paint when Steve had excused himself out of doing it for the fifth time, she couldn't work out her own escape plan. She was going to be stuck in this hamster wheel of working and never quite having enough time to do everything, while barely keeping her head above water and clinging onto the house.

She had other skills, but no time to develop or explore how to use them. Even less time now than before the separation, when ironically she hadn't needed to use the extra skills since she was financially, if not emotionally, more stable.

I'm doing fine, because I have no choice.

She stood, following the noise of a TV in Thomas's bedroom. After knocking and him saying she could enter, she leant against the door frame.

He was playing a computer game, miles away in his own world.

A pang of jealousy flooded her heart. Oh to be fifteen again. 'All right?'

He nodded, pausing the game. 'You look tired.'

'Old, that's what it means when people say tired.' She sat on the edge of his bed, beckoning for him to come closer.

He did so and she hugged him to herself, kissing the top of his head.

'I can do dinner if you want,' he said. 'Beans on toast and cheese. Make a change.'

'From what?'

'We ate out all weekend. Junk food's only fun for so long, right? It's not helping my spots.' He pointed to an enthusiastic outburst of acne on his face.

Steve's uselessness seemed to know no bounds. 'What's she like?'

'Not you.' He pulled away and resumed his game, staring at the TV.

She stood. 'I'm going to have a bath. Are you okay to do dinner? Anything out of the freezer. Just heat up a casserole and I'll steam the veg when I'm out of the bath.'

'I can do that. Peas and carrots okay, Mum?' He was staring at the screen, engrossed in play.

She stood, 'Peas and carrots would be great. Thanks, love.' She left the room.

As she lay in the bath, listening to the clattering from the kitchen as Thomas − surprisingly − did as he'd offered, she reckoned she'd not been a bad mum. A pretty good one actually. It was that she'd somehow lost most of the rest of who she was along the way. The wife part hadn't been too bad, but the woman, friend, daughter, sibling parts had somehow disappeared. And now she had the opportunity to be whatever she wanted but she had no idea *how* to work out *what* that could be. The possibilities were endless, which made it too scary to even begin. She was so used to putting herself second, third, fourth, or last; the concept of putting herself and her own wants first, seemed totally alien and self-indulgent.

Chapter 15

Harriet had recovered from her frustration at Jason's ignorance of clear instructions and realised she needed to be the adult and clear up his mess, sweet-talk Lux-Lodge Hotels and Ray. She sat at a table in an exclusive London restaurant to which her father had taken her many times before.

Smartly dressed waiting staff glided across the floor holding plates as if suspended by magic. Columns throughout held the domed ceiling in place. It was painted in homage to the Sistine Chapel, with colourful scenes from the Bible above her head. Golden-winged angels stared down from the columns, pointing their elaborate trumpets at the customers.

She'd thought it terribly *faux rococo* at first, but after eating, had decided it could carry off this slightly fussy décor since the food was simple, comforting and sublime.

Checking her phone, she saw Eric was nearly late. Or was he going to stand her up? It wouldn't be the first time a man had done that to her.

A waitress arrived at her table with one portly grey-suited man and another in skinny jeans, white shirt, leather waistcoat and sunglasses.

'Eric?' Harriet said to the nearest man.

'He's Eric, I'm Ray, the photographer. Owner of Ray Photography. We've emailed.' They shook hands, then sat. 'We're pleased you're meeting us instead of your latest diversity hire, who doesn't know his arse from his elbow.'

She ignored that little dig at Jason. Harriet didn't disagree that Jason had made a pig's ear of it, but she didn't think it was fair to refer to him as they had. She smiled. 'Thank you.'

Eric straightened his cutlery on the table. 'I'm very much a live-and-let-live person, because it definitely does take all sorts, but when *they* start to think they're calling the shots—' He stopped, shook his head, shot a glance at Eric.

Eric winked and nodded.

The mention of a nameless, amorphous mass of *they* alongside professing to being fine with all sorts of people didn't pass Harriet by. 'It's lovely of you to make the time to meet me. Would you like wine? I'm going to have a glass, it is Friday after all.' She laughed.

They did not.

This was going to be harder work than she'd imagined. They ordered wine, sitting in silence as they read the menu.

Ray said, 'Sparkling mineral water for me, please.' After the waiter left, he said, 'I'm teetotal now, since... Well, it's better. I would have thought you'd know that about me.' He sat back in the chair, his long spindly legs spread wide. 'But then again, you don't know much about me, do you?'

Harriet chose to ignore this. It felt like an ambush. Only a very slow and careful one. She was up to this, as long as she remained calm. Though she wished she'd spoken to Jason first; he would have remembered Ray didn't drink. It showed a distinct lack of research and preparation which irritated Harriet.

'What would you recommend?' Eric asked.

At length, Harriet explained how this was one of her favourite restaurants and her father had taken her here many times. She particularly enjoyed their takes on simple British classics, such as spotted dick, jam roly-poly, shepherd's pie, toad-in-the-hole and the like. She was obviously babbling because the men sat in silence, with their menus closed. *This is meant to be easy, what is going wrong?*

The waiter arrived, took their orders, then left.

Turning the wine glass between her fingers, Harriet said, 'I'm so pleased you agreed to meet. I really wanted to put this nonsense behind us. Discuss how to move forward, as we had been working in partnership for so many years.'

Eric looked to Ray. 'And so we're all clear about why we're here, what, as far as you understand it, is this nonsensical issue?'

'You know how long we've been working with your companies. You're of course aware of all the business we've put your way. We've had a long and fruitful partnership. However, the way I see things is we've somewhat gone off course. A little glitch. An unfortunate misunderstanding here and there. Although I wasn't involved before, I do hold myself *wholly and completely* responsible.' Grovel, was what her father had advised. Get in some serious grovelling and lay yourself prostrate in front of them, before moving onto a discussion about the way forward. Her father had taught her well, telling her on numerous occasions how he'd rescued a soured business relationship.

'That's very big of you,' Ray said, sipping his sparkling water. 'Particularly since it wasn't you that did it. Jason, he's called, isn't it?' He raised his eyebrows.

Harriet nodded.

'Didn't have him down as one of them,' Ray made a limp-wristed motion. 'Not after speaking to him on the phone, like.'

Eric's eyes widened, possibly Ray was going further than they'd agreed.

But it was showing Harriet precisely the sort of people these two were, and contrary to how she'd started the meeting, she found herself softening towards Jason's viewpoint.

'Can't tell nowadays can you, which one of 'em are, and which ones… aren't…' Ray drank some water and moved, possibly from Eric kicking him under the table.

Their main courses arrived and everyone ate in silence for a short while.

Harriet had expected them to be chattier, but their silence seemed to imply they'd agreed some kind of game plan. She should have prepared a bit better.

Not to worry, I've still totally got this.

'I understand,' Harriet said, 'your hotel chain has a client with views that make you hosting some of our weddings something of a challenge.'

'We have to balance all our business partners' and clients' needs. If I were to host a conference for the Butchers' Guild, you wouldn't expect them to share space with, for example, a vegetarian charity, would you?'

Harriet shook her head, carefully chewing her food.

'Imagine if, for example, your company were owned by a Jewish family, how would you feel if asked to organise an event for an anti-Semitic organisation?'

'We always reserve the right *not* to work with customers.'

'Precisely,' he said, sipping his wine and narrowing his eyes. 'So you see, how this puts us in a difficult situation.'

'Except, our weddings aren't for any sort of anti-anything organisations or clients.'

Ray poured himself more water. 'Want some? Anyway, it's slightly more complicated than that. I understand your clients' needs, and I, and my company, don't have anything against those people, nor their weddings. We have some very traditional clients, and if they saw our portfolio included, well, those weddings, they'd... Well it wouldn't help us. We have clients who've had three generations of their weddings photographed by a Ray photographer. My grandad did their wedding shots, and now they're asking me, or one of my associates to do it. We have word of mouth, and whole groups of friends come to us. But they're expecting a certain kind of photography, the classic list of shots, like you'd see in a celebrity magazine.'

'Right.' Harriet added pepper to her food, more for something to do other than drinking more wine since this was going so badly.

'And the traditional list of shots doesn't work for your... less traditional clients. We don't have anything against that lifestyle choice, or those people, it's simply a matter of the majority of our clients. No judgement.'

Eric leant his elbows on the table. 'What does it say to children who might be looking at pictures of weddings we've hosted?'

'I don't follow,' Harriet said. She decided to give them enough rope and they may well hang themselves. Although in favour of traditional values, she wasn't against gay people per se, just some of the ways they seemed to be taking over what had been wedding traditions.

'Little James is looking at pictures of weddings we've hosted and he sees two women kissing outside one of our gorgeous lakeside log cabins. Or perhaps there's a picture of two men exchanging rings, one taking the other one's hand. Imagine being James's parent and having to explain that one.' Eric rolled his eyes.

'It was on the telly last time I watched. Parading about, holding hands, kissing each other. Not just TV dramas or films, but reality TV too – real people.' Ray shook his head, miming being sick. 'Like I said, I'm live-and-let-live, do whatever you need to, but not when they're ramming it down our throats on national TV, you know?'

The mention of no judgement, followed by their half-baked ideas about what children should and shouldn't see, told her they were doing precisely the opposite. Perhaps Jason hadn't been so wrong after all. 'Of course.' Turning to Eric, she said, 'This is your final word?'

He shrugged, holding his palms upwards. 'I'm afraid our other client is worth significantly more than you. It's really about the figures.'

It seemed, to Harriet, it was much more complicated than simply the figures. It appeared as if it came down to morals and values. And the ones these two men were showing, as much as Harriet had dismissed Jason's concerns, were stuck in about 1960, as far as she could see.

The waitress arrived. 'Would anyone like to see the dessert menu?'

'I'm all right,' Ray said.

'Watching my waistline,' Eric said, patting his stomach. 'I think I should go.'

Ray stood, winked. 'No hard feelings, all right?'

Eric was standing, buttoned up his suit jacket. 'Thanks for the lunch. You were right, it was delicious.'

They left.

Harriet asked a passing waiter for the bill. How could she have got it so wrong?

After paying, she decided to walk back to the office, giving her precious time to reflect and consider her next steps.

Were they severing all ties with the company, or only refusing certain of their clients? And, when she considered it, did it make any difference? If Lux-Lodge Hotels and Ray Photography were refusing some of their clients, didn't that reflect badly on their other clients, by saying Tailored Weddings were happy to work with suppliers who picked and chose whose weddings they worked on?

Upon arriving at the office, she went straight to see Christopher.

With the door closed, she explained how the lunch meeting had gone. 'I tried everything in the book. Flattery, pleading ignorance, apologising for our misunderstanding, but when pressed, they stuck to their guns.'

Christopher leaned on his desk, shaking his head. 'You've tried your best. I'm disappointed, very.'

'I'm sorry. I thought I'd won them over, that they were going to change their minds.' She shook her head, defeat threatened to engulf her. There was no worse feeling than doing your best and it still not being good enough. 'And...'

'Yes? Is there more?' Christopher asked.

'Some of the things they said, well… I'm a great believer in traditional values, but some of the stuff they said…' She made a *sheesh* gesture with her mouth.

'Like what?' He narrowed his eyes and leaned forwards.

'Limp wrists, confusing children, ramming it down our throats, to name a few.'

'Right. Well, that changes things. Thank you for trying. I wish Jason hadn't taken it online. A private battle maybe we could have weathered, but once it's on social media…' He shook his head.

Harriet did the same. 'What will you do?'

'Find alternative suppliers.'

'Now?'

'Later.'

'He didn't start it.'

'You said. You'll be safe, don't worry. You've been nothing but a model employee. Do go home.'

It was past home time anyway, but the sentiment was something, she supposed.

Chapter 16

'When you said you wanted me to organise our wedding, I didn't realise you were going to be like this,' Jason said to Pete.

'I don't understand the problem.'

'You've asked me to recreate a music concert, but in the form of a wedding.'

Pete shrugged. He'd been to a concert with water fountains, acrobats climbing down ropes, all on a rotating platform, out of which the singer appeared. He said he wanted to appear from the middle, and their guests to be sitting in a circle around the central platform.

Jason knew when he was beaten so decided to return to that later. 'How many people have you got on your guest list?'

'Seventy-eight.'

Jason was starting to get a headache. '*Small and intimate*, you said. I remember you saying the words.'

'How am I meant to choose which of my friends can or can't come?' Pete gave him the look of sadness which Mel had explained he'd used as a boy to get pretty much anything he wanted.

Part of Jason's heart melted, and his brain, the logical part, which had to make this vision into a reality, stopped him. 'That's what an evening do is for.'

'About that. I was thinking we could show a video of the main ceremony to the evening guests. That way they won't have missed it.'

It wasn't a bad idea. 'I like that. But I want you to understand what you've described isn't possible. Not within the bounds of our budget.'

'I've got some drama school friends I could ask.'

'To build a rotating stage, and suspend ropes from the ceiling?'

'Maybe.' Pete grinned. 'The fact that you humour me, even though I know I'm being completely unreasonable is just one of the reasons why I love you so much.'

Jason's heart jumped and they kissed. 'Look, can we at least tick something off the list, make a decision? I've got Adam and Ryan's this afternoon.'

'Can't I come? Please? For inspiration.'

Jason had never let Pete see him while working because he wanted to separate the two different versions of Jason he had. That, and he knew Pete would have a tendency to become over-excited and Jason would already have his hands full looking after the clients, making sure their day went smoothly.

'If it'll help you see what is doable, and what is only within the realms of an international pop princess who's playing the O2, then maybe.'

Pete jumped up and down, clapping, hugged Jason close and kissed his neck. 'Love you.'

'I said maybe. I need to check with the grooms first.' Jason left, and called Adam.

'What's wrong?' Adam asked, with terror in his voice.

'Nothing. I wanted to ask a favour.' A pause, and then: 'I'm going to be there an hour before your ceremony, and then drive on to check the other venue.'

'You don't need to. What can go wrong with a registry office?'

He didn't want to say, if it could go wrong, he'd seen it, so instead said, 'I've got this. So you don't need to.'

'What's this favour?'

'Pete's vision for our wedding is a bit… Anyway, he needs his expectations managing a bit. So I wanted to show him what is possible. In this world.'

'I'd love to meet him. I feel like I know him already.'

'Just to warn you, he's a massive fan of *Simply Dancing*, so he may want to talk to you about that.'

'Fine. But not while we're getting married, all right?'

'I'll bring him after the ceremony.'

'He's very welcome—' Adam said.

'I know, but I think it's for the best. He'll be trying to talk to you as you're exchanging rings.'

'You know best.' Adam ended the call.

On the night they met, Pete had asked for the autographs of the three women from Appledrama, while they were posing for press photos. Jason had needed to forcibly remove him and that was how they'd started talking.

He told Pete what Adam had said, and they agreed to meet at the hotel ballroom Adam and Ryan had hired.

'Is there some big first dance fandango?' Pete asked, his eyes shining.

'You'll have to wait.'

'Can we have a drag queen performing the ceremony for us?'

'Not unless they're legally licenced to perform weddings. Which one?'

'Not sure. Just throwing it out there.' Pete crossed something off his list. 'Can we have a band at the start and then a DJ?'

'Now that, we can do. What sort of music?'

'Classical music during the ceremony and then all the wedding favourites at the party. Do you think I could get one of The Fridays to do an after-dinner speech?'

And they were back in cloud cuckoo land. 'Didn't they split up?'

'Sad times. I wonder if Adam knows them, you know, from his TV show. One of them was a guest judge last season.'

'I'm going.' He kissed Pete goodbye and left.

—

Adam and Ryan's registry office ceremony went smoothly: the guests were directed to one side or the other, depending on which groom they knew best. The grooms walked to the front of the room – there wasn't what you could call an aisle in the council building – one at a time. Adam's mother held the rings. Ryan's father cried. They stood on the steps of the building for photographs as their guests sat next to them, and threw confetti over them.

Now, at the hotel ballroom, Jason adjusted a sapphire blue ribbon tied to the back of a chair. It went well with the white cover and tablecloths.

A banner on the far wall read: 'CONGRATULATIONS RYAN AND ADAM!'

The room was filled with circular tables and chairs. Each table had a centrepiece of a male ballet dancer in a leotard, suspended by a thin piece of wire, giving the illusion he was jumping in the air. Adam had used to dance ballet profession-ally, before moving onto ballroom dancing.

They'd settled on a sit-down meal for one hundred and fifty. Roast chicken dinner and sticky toffee pudding, because 'It's what Mum would have made if she could,' Ryan had said, with a tear in his eye.

Now, the guests were arriving, checking the seating plan at the entrance, taking their seats, shaking hands and opening the table wine.

He was content the ballroom was set up as it should be. Later, half the room would be cleared, revealing a dance floor, where their expertly choreographed first dance would take place. He couldn't wait to see Pete's face at that.

He walked to the entrance to greet the grooms.

Pete arrived first, in a floral white suit, plain blue shirt and smart black shoes. He looked like a walking bunch of flowers and Jason couldn't have felt any prouder.

'Are they here yet?' Pete asked, after they hugged.

'Here they come.'

Four white horses pulled a pumpkin-shaped golden coach into the hotel's entrance. It stopped, and a doorman opened the door.

Adam stepped out first, in a sapphire blue suit, turning to take Ryan's hand as he climbed down from the carriage. Ryan was beaming in his matching suit.

'The ballroom is ready,' Jason said.

'Can I have a photo?' Ryan asked, ''cos I don't think I'm gonna believe this really happened.'

The grooms stood in front of the horses and Jason took photos with Ryan's camera.

'With you,' Ryan said, handing the camera to the doorman.

The three men stood in front of the carriage as their photo was taken.

Ryan cried.

'What's wrong?' Adam asked, pulling him in for a hug.

Ryan took a deep breath. 'I can't… It's here… We did it… Cinderella coach and everything.' He wiped a tear off his cheek. 'It's just so much. I can't…'

Adam hugged him tightly. 'Take a breath, everyone in there's waiting to see us.'

Ryan blew his nose, took a deep breath, glancing at the coach as it was driven away. 'I just didn't think it was possible. I put it on the scrap book, because I've always wanted it. But I didn't think we would.'

'Whatever you want.' Adam pulled him in for a kiss. Then: 'Husband.' His eyes widened.

'Say that again, I like it.'

'Husband.'

'Again.'

'Husband. Husband. Husband.'

Jason gently shepherded them inside. 'You must be hungry.'

'My stomach's like a ball of nerves,' Ryan said.

They were at the door to the ballroom now. Adam held his husband's hand. 'If you don't want to do it, we don't have to. I want you to enjoy today. It's nothing to me, I do it all the time.'

Ryan composed himself. 'I want to do it.'

'Ready?' Jason asked.

They nodded.

Jason opened the door, holding it for them as he said, 'Adam and Ryan are pleased to welcome you to their wedding breakfast.'

–

'Getting any good ideas?' Jason asked, finishing his sticky toffee pudding a while later.

'I like the food. And the blue. And these.' He picked up the centrepiece, twirling it around so the male ballet dancer looked as if he were pirouetting in the air.

After the speeches – both grooms spoke about how they'd met and why they loved one another so much – Ryan's father talked.

A bald middle-aged man stood. He had the edge of a tattoo showing on his neck, and covering his forearms, visible as he'd rolled his shirt sleeves back. 'Didn't think I'd see Ryan happy. Not when he was a little boy, I didn't. He never fitted in. Wasn't like his brothers. Worried what would happen to him. Wasn't sure about him getting into the TV game, why couldn't he just do what his brothers and me did.'

A laugh erupted from the guests. Someone at the back shouted: 'Because he couldn't put a screw in a wall to hang a bleedin' picture!'

Someone further back shouted something slightly rude about screwing.

Both grooms laughed.

Ryan's father went on: 'I've already got four sons, and when we first met Adam, I knew he made sense with my son. I don't understand what they do for a living, no more than I can dance either. But he makes Ryan happy, so he's my son too now.'

The guests stood, gave a toast to the grooms.

Jason looked to his side and Pete was crying.

Tears streaming down his face as he held his hands in front of his mouth.

'What are you like?' Jason kissed the top of his head.

'You know what I'm like.'

He really did. And that was one of the reasons why he was going to marry Pete. As long as they could agree what their wedding would look like.

A while later, during which Jason thought Pete would explode with excitement, they joined the other guests in the ballroom. Half the room had chairs and tables and the other half was the dance floor.

The opening bars of 'Time After Time' began.

Adam stood in the middle of the floor.

Ryan joined him, holding hands, as they danced to a carefully choreographed routine in time with the music. Adam twirled Ryan around, holding one hand. Then Ryan ran to the far corner, waving his arms as if he were flying, he ran towards Adam in the centre and held both hands, as they span around in a circle. It was a mixture of classical ballroom dancing and modern moves that Adam had created himself.

As the final notes of the song filled the room, there was silence. Adam and Ryan stood in the middle of the floor, holding hands, moving closer until they kissed.

The guests clapped and cheered.

'Worth it?' Jason asked.

Pete, once again was crying. More happy tears. He nodded, wiping his cheek with his sleeve. 'Can we do that?'

'You know I can't dance.'

Pete laughed. 'I've seen you throwing shapes in your clubbing days.'

'You've seen pictures of me, in my mid-twenties, gyrating to dance music in a sweaty night club.'

Pete blinked slowly. 'So is that a yes?'

Chapter 17

Mel woke with a coldness on her cheek and a sense of something not being quite right.

She sat up and replayed what had happened. She'd arrived home from a full day of cleaning and poured herself a wine at the island in the middle of the kitchen. After a sip, she'd decided to close her eyes for a moment as sleep seemed more appealing than drink. Resting her head on the granite work surface, she closed her eyes and then she'd gone under. Sleep had grabbed her tightly, taking her away from the busy day, the endless week, the floor scrubbing, the vacuuming, the toilet cleaning, the kitchen cleaning and before she knew it, plunged her deep into unconsciousness.

Her cheek was red from the work surface. Her hair stuck up, the bags under her eyes were large and dark, and seemed to shout: 'Knackered, in all possible ways.'

There's something else I need to do, but I can't remember what it is.

So much for a brave new world of independence and self-bloody-actualisation as a friend from the school had described it. I can't self-actualise my dinner, never mind a new career, whatever that might be.

She'd enjoyed reading Shakespeare and Dickens and the Brontës, all three of them, and what had it done for her?

Sod all, that's what.

Surely being single should be better than this?

The sunlit uplands of being in charge of the house herself didn't seem very attainable, as she struggled to remember her name, never mind what else she should have done tonight.

She collected the unopened bills from the shelf in the hallway. *Why bother opening them when all they'll want is money. Which I can't afford.*

A credit card bill – how can it be that much when all I've done is work and eat?

She checked the app on her phone and, as feared, the bank account was empty, but she'd done nothing that month. How had that happened? A line of deductions filled the screen: mortgage, utilities, and dozens of smaller amounts she didn't recognise.

Only one credit at the top from her wages. Wasn't Steve meant to be paying towards Lily and Thomas? That was definitely what they'd agreed. Or had they? Mel doubted most things at this point. Her memory hadn't been brilliant at the best of times, but now she had so much less time, she felt memories, appointments, dates, reminders slipping away from her with remarkable regularity.

'I've got to dress as a person from history,' Lily had said one morning.

'And you're telling me this now?' Mel had asked.

'There was a letter. Please don't be as crap as Dad!'

She'd seen it, and knew the date was weeks in the future. A far-away concept Mel didn't need to worry about now.

Lily collected it from the cork noticeboard, handing it to Mel. 'You never used to be like this. Dad's not used to doing this stuff, but you, well, it's what you're here for. Normally.' She shook her head.

'That's today?'

Lily nodded. 'I've already said, haven't I?'

How and where on earth the intervening two weeks had gone was anyone's guess. Certainly Mel was completely clueless. She gave Lily a lacey old nighty with a doily over her head and fashioned a sceptre from a broom handle. 'Queen Victoria, in mourning,' she said as they had rushed to the car.

Lily had complained during the car journey, and said, 'Can't you just give up work, and be a good mum again? Surely Dad's not so bad. Why can't you like, let him move back in. Get things back to normal.'

'It's not quite that simple. Besides, your father left me.'

'So, take him back, maybe?' Lily had said, refusing a kiss on the cheek as they'd arrived at school.

Now, the front door opened and Lily and Thomas shouted, 'We're home, Mum!'

Mel met them in the hallway. 'Was I meant to collect you, or take you somewhere?' *Or dress you in any special way?*

They shook their heads and walked to the kitchen to help themselves to food.

Mel followed, watching as they poured bowls of cereal and shovelled fistfuls of crisps into their mouths. There was something she should be doing here, but she couldn't muster the energy to do it.

The cost of the food they were eating flashed across Mel's mind.

'Did you have a play date?' she asked.

Thomas scoffed. 'I'm not five. Dad collected us from school.'

Is it his day? 'Aren't you staying the night?'

'He's having stuff done, so our bedrooms are full,' Lily said, opening a third packet of cheese and onion crisps and shovelling them into her mouth.

Mel carefully removed them. 'Full of what?'

Thomas rolled his eyes. 'Bullshit, that's what. He doesn't want us there. Sally looks at us like we're aliens or something.'

'Language!' Although she didn't disagree with his sentiment. 'Didn't he feed you?'

'Their oven is broken, or something. More bullshit if you ask me.' Thomas slurped the milk from the bowl of cereal. He shrugged. 'Dad bought me a new PlayStation for when I stay there. Can I have a new one?'

'You most certainly cannot. Who needs two?'

'Someone whose parents don't live together.' Thomas shook his head. 'I'll be in my room. Playing on my ancient PlayStation.'

How was she meant to compete with that? 'Why didn't he consult me first?'

'Why are *you* making such a big deal out of it?' He tutted loudly. 'It's bad enough you and Dad splitting up but now I can't have the things I deserve.' He strode upstairs.

This couldn't continue. She was working full time and still they had no money. She couldn't keep this house without Steve contributing more. Especially if she was having the children most of the time. 'I'm going to ring him.' A desire to have a full-on shouting match with Steve overcame her and she picked up her phone from the work surface.

'He's quite tired at the moment,' Lily said. 'He's going to buy me some toys to keep at his place.'

'Is he now?' Mel narrowed her eyes.

'And clothes. We went shopping and he said I could have anything I wanted.'

'Right.' A terrible sinking feeling descended over Mel. This was not what they'd discussed.

'Dad's really tired. He looks kinda messy. Like he could do with a shower.'

'He's tired! I'll show him tired!' Mel rang Steve, and it went straight to voicemail.

Everything felt like such a monumental effort. Why did every step of the way with Steve have to be another battle?

'Any chance of Dad moving back in, Mum?' Lily asked, scrunching up the crisp packets and wiping her hands on her school skirt.

She shook her head. 'None whatsoever.'

'Why not? It's so unfair! Why did everything have to change? It was all good before and then you had to go and ruin it.'

'That's not quite what happened, and you know it.'

'I don't care. You've ruined my life. Dad's buying me clothes and stuff and I don't really want it.'

'Have you told him that?'

'No. They're nice clothes. Besides, he couldn't take them back now that I've worn them. Don't be so stupid, Mum.' She grabbed a large packet of crisps then ran into the living room.

She tried to call Steve again and it rang.

Steve answered. 'I asked them to explain, tonight's not a good time for me, it's—'

'Not a good time? You've only just started having the responsibility of your own children for the last few months, and already you're avoiding it. And you're spoiling them. Absolutely ruining them.'

'They're very unsettled and I wanted to make sure they enjoy their time with me and Sally.'

'By buying their affection. It's so unoriginal. They don't want things, they want you, to spend time together.'

'Buying them things can't harm, surely?'

'You're spoiling them. They've both stormed off in disgust.'

'Aah. I'll speak to them next time they're here.'

'And take back the presents?' Mel asked hopefully.

'I don't think that's possible. Lily has worn the clothes and Thomas's PlayStation is well-used. He spent most of the night on it, I think.'

Mel closed her eyes and shook her head. 'And this is what you believe to be parenting? Christ, give me strength.'

'I'm trying to get them to like me.'

'Most parents do this by spending time with their children, giving them their attention, not buying them off.'

'I don't have time for that. Which is why I wanted to speak to you about—'

'Swapping your days around, yes I know, the kids told me that too.'

'Come on, be reasonable. I'll swap with you later this week. How about Thursday? Oh no, I can't do then. Or Friday?'

'You're meant to have them Friday anyway.' Her tone was becoming more and more terse.

Walking into the living room, she said, 'I'm sinking here.'

'I said you should sell the house and get something more appropriate. Besides, isn't your little job bringing in enough?'

Mustering all the self-control she could manage, Mel replied through gritted teeth, 'That little job is paying for your children to eat, keeping them housed and clothed. I can't go on like this.'

'What do you propose?' he asked.

'You do what we agreed. The mortgage for one.'

'Big, isn't it?'

'Yes. It. Is.'

'I'm already paying rent for this place, so I can't be expected to pay for a place I'm not even living in, can I?'

'Since you walked out, yes, you can be expected to do precisely that.' And in fact she had a solicitor's letter outlining it too.

'Perhaps we should revisit it with the CSA, or via solicitors?'

'I need help now.' The Child Support Agency would take months and by then she'd have lost the house.

'I'll see what I can do.' Steve sounded very laid back.

'You want me to sell this house, don't you?'

A pause, and then, 'It would make things much simpler, don't you think?'

'For who?'

'Us all. Now come on, be reasonable, darling.'

'Don't you *darling* me. If you don't pay what we agreed, I'll be in touch through my solicitor. I don't see why I, and the children, who spend most time here, should uproot ourselves just because of your mistake. This has been their home all their lives. This house is part of me, my history. I have enough upheaval without needing to move as well. Pay the bloody mortgage or I shall engage a shit-hot solicitor who'll tell you to.'

'Is it really that bad?'

'Do you think I'd be having this conversation if it weren't?'

'I'll see what I can do.'

'Sorry, no, that's not good enough. Do as you've agreed. I am remaining in the family home, and you, as the person who's earning ten times more than me, is to pay for a place for your children and almost ex-wife to live. It really is very standard in situations like this.'

'As I say, I'll—'

She ended the call. Unsure how she'd pay for this solicitor's letter, or when she'd have time to ask for it to be produced. But the red-hot fury coursed through her veins. *How could he be so bloody unreasonable?*

Because he wants me to sell the house. The money from the proceeds of selling the house could be divided in two, allowing Mel money to buy her own place, mortgage free, meaning she could support herself and the two youngest on Steve's maintenance payments.

Remaining in the family home, the maintenance he'd agreed to pay would keep her head above water, until she could find something that paid better. And that left her feeling less like a wrung-out dishcloth at the end of each day.

'Did Dad explain?' Lily asked.

She nodded. 'He did. It's all sorted now.' She stroked Lily's hair, kissing her cheek.

'The clothes are nice, but really I just want Dad back here,' Lily said quietly, almost as an afterthought.

'I'm going up for a bath, eat whatever you like.' Striding up the stairs, she then ran a hot bath, closing the door so her quiet sobs weren't audible. Composing herself, she rang the one person she'd hoped to avoid, since she'd already leaned on him too much at the beginning of this mess.

'Pete, I'm not disturbing you, am I?'

'Jason's doing really well, since the launch of Extra Weddings!'

'I'm so pleased.' She didn't want to spoil this wonderful news by forging on with her rather selfish ask.

He told her.

She listened with a lump in her throat at how she should feel happier, but there remained the reason she'd phoned and her deep worries. 'Is he busy?'

'Very. He's very excited to be designing weddings his way, with all sorts of clients.'

'You must be so proud.'

'I am. I love him so much, Mum.'

'I know.'

There was a pleasant silence that Mel knew she had to spoil with her next question. She licked her lips and carefully said, 'I wonder if I can ask a favour.'

'Of course,' Pete said.

She explained, ending with, 'He wants me out of this place, because it's simpler to divide the proceeds. But it's my home. I can't bear the thought of losing it.'

'It is only a house, Mum.'

'I know, but I won't let him win. It's not about the house, it's…'

'The principle?'

'A loan. To tide me over. I'll pay it back as soon as I'm back on my feet.' *If I can find the time to do so.* She closed her eyes and pinched her forehead as a tension headache threatened to arrive.

'How much?' Pete asked.

She'd expected more resistance, given how it had gone when she'd first announced the divorce. Pete and Jason had their own life to pay for, never mind hers as well. 'Are you sure?' Mel asked.

'Our mortgage is very small: big deposit, bought a while ago. Jason is very good at that sort of thing. His company is making oodles of money – must be, he's so busy.'

'Don't you have to check with him first?' Mel asked.

'Of course, but he'll be fine, I know. A loan?'

'Absolutely. Paid back in full once I'm on my feet again. You're sure Jason won't mind?'

'Wouldn't have said it otherwise. Would something every month help? He's always on about having a monthly budget, spreadsheets and everything.'

She could have cried with relief. It wouldn't only help, it would save her. Sanity, life, home, everything. Give her some breathing space to work out what to do next. How to become Mel, rather than mum, wife. 'If you're sure?'

'I'll text you once I've spoken to Jason. If he has any problem I'll pay you out of my wages. He'll be fine, he loves you.'

'Thanks so much.'

Chapter 18

Harriet looked at the empty seat to one side of her desk. She hadn't expected to miss Jason so much. He'd promised to keep in touch and of course work and life had got in the way and a few months had passed and she'd yet to hear from him. But to be fair, she'd not been in touch either.

The amount of work had, thankfully, reduced; she wasn't sure why, but the new clients weren't flooding in like when she'd had Jason charming them.

'I want you to meet Lux-Lodge Hotels,' Christopher had asked her.

'Isn't it better to let sleeping dogs lie?' She'd read the emails and met them to apologise and realised they were obviously homophobic. Even if they used the excuse of a parent company with links to a country where it was illegal to be homosexual, their stance was one of not being seen to endorse that lifestyle.

Harriet was sure it had been blamed on a large client when Jason was here, so this change seemed suspicious. She'd agreed, while crossing her fingers behind her back and had put off contacting the Lux-Lodge Hotels rep for the last week.

Some internet research during a quiet afternoon and Harriet had a handful of hotel chains that seemed to be more inclusive.

She checked their locations, discounting two that only had hotels in London and the Home Counties. They had clients from everywhere in the UK and she'd organised weddings as far as Edinburgh – the castle, pipers, men in kilts and a three-cannon salute – and Penzance, in a stone cottage used as a village hall, overlooking the sea with a reception on a boat. This left her with one chain which was almost as well distributed as Lux-Lodge Hotels.

Knowing she shouldn't, but reckoning she'd be unlikely to get fired for it, she rang the nearest hotel from this chain. 'Can I speak to your events manager please?'

'How can I help?' came a woman's voice shortly afterwards.

'I work for a wedding planning company and we're looking to partner with a hotel chain for many of our venues. I liked the page on your website with events you've hosted.'

'Thanks, it was my idea.'

'It worked. Sorry, I should have introduced myself, I'm Harriet.'

'Elizabeth, but everyone calls me Busy.' A pause, and then, 'So you should totally call me Busy, right?'

Harriet had been holding her breath. 'Right.'

'Why don't you come out of London and meet me? We've got a little forest with log cabins for guests who want to be more self-sufficient, with the reception and restaurant on hand if they need.'

'I'd love to come, but I'm kind of doing this on the secret, because I need all the figures together to show my manager. So I can't hurtle off to…' She peered at the address. '…Hertfordshire, because he'd wonder where I was going. He's a bit…' Harriet thought carefully about how to describe him. She didn't want to air her dirty washing in public, particularly since she'd never met this woman, but she felt they were getting along nicely. 'It's complicated.'

'I understand. The videos are really good at showing what it's like. We do group discounts for a guaranteed number of bookings. If you think you could reach that number.'

'How many?'

'Twelve. During a rolling twelve-month period.'

Harriet had expected them to specify a minimum spend, so this was much better. 'Do you work with other events companies?'

'We do. Is that a problem?'

'Not necessarily. Our clients usually have their dates in mind well in advance. So what sort of discounts are we talking?'

'We start at ten and sometimes go up to thirty per cent. For our favourite clients.' Busy coughed. 'But I'd totally need to send contracts through and everything. But, in principle, those are the figures we work to. Any good?'

'We normally plan thirty to fifty weddings per year, so...' Harriet let that hang there, waiting for Busy to jump in.

'Sounds more like a twenty-five to thirty per cent situation to me. But like I said, I'd have to run it by my manager.'

Harriet smiled, ticking off another question on her checklist. For something she'd been asked not to do, this was definitely going well.

Busy described the last half dozen events they'd hosted, which included two women who'd wanted a pink fairy-tale theme, including decking the ballroom in pink everything, plus an orchestra playing classical music. 'I was totally jell of them.'

Jell? Jealous, obviously. 'Why?' Harriet had been making plenty of notes and had drifted off towards the end. Her head was buzzing with possibilities for working with this chain. It really could be a case of having their cake and eating it.

'It's stupid, ignore me. We've not even met.'

Harriet sat back on her chair, stirring her cold coffee. She'd lost track of time. 'I feel like we've covered a lot rather quickly. Why were you jealous?'

'It's like every time feels like the last, and then I have to do it again.'

What on earth was Busy talking about? 'Don't worry if it's a big thing. Honestly, it's fine not to say.'

'It shouldn't be a big thing, but it is. I'm talking in riddles. Look, whatever, I was texting my...' Her voice went quiet. '...girlfriend with pictures and she said she loved it and... Whatever, doesn't matter.'

This woman is… gay? Lesbian? Which is the right word, Harriet wondered. 'Well, I think that sounds lovely. You're lucky to have someone who wants that with you. I've given up on men.'

'I could make a joke now, but I really don't feel it's appropriate, since we've literally just met.'

Harriet chuckled. 'Will you and your girlfriend marry?'

'Definitely. One hundred per cent.'

A notification for a meeting flashed on Harriet's screen. She'd been on the phone for almost half an hour. 'This has been fun. And useful. Can you send me some details by email, so I can put it together for my boss?'

'Sure. I hope we can work together, Harriet.'

'Same, Busy. Same.' She ended the call with a huge grin, turned the page on her notebook and walked to the meeting room for her next appointment.

See, it really wasn't so complicated, there were other hotel chains they could use without all this baggage. Lux-Lodge Hotels were definitely not being wholly truthful about their reasons. If she'd had the energy she'd have looked into it more deeply, but why waste time on people and organisations like that?

Chapter 19

They were in Jason's study at home and he didn't know what to do. Jason stared at the article and read the first paragraph again.

'Have you read this yet?' Mel asked, pointing to *Weddings* magazine on the table.

'I'm just trying to process this first. How did it happen?'

'You know how.'

Jason had, rather naively, not expected Adam and Ryan's wedding to be of interest to anyone except their friends and family. Adam had promised not to mention it in the press; he was, after all, only the paid dancer, not the actual celebrity who formed the focus of the show.

And yet, all their guests posting pictures on social media and using #adamandryan had created more of a buzz than Jason had expected.

There was an interview with them in *Menz!* a popular gay lifestyle magazine – five pages, pictures of them in their wedding suits, outside their home, in their garden with their dog, answering questions about what they loved most about each other.

Jason's phone hadn't stopped ringing after that, all from Ryan mentioning his name and Extra Weddings. No website or number, but people had obviously googled and found it easily.

Jason had spoken to fifty people the week after that interview, most of them wanting him to plan their wedding.

This had led to a national newspaper writing the article Jason was reading now. It described how they'd met on the TV show and went into some detail about Ryan's family, in obvious contrast to the wealth that Adam came from. The Cinderella coach had sort of sealed the deal.

Simply Dancing Star Weds His Assistant Boyfriend in Cinderella Pumpkin Style Coach

Adam Winchester, a professional dancer on Simply Dancing for the last three years, last month married Ryan Westerman, a production assistant on the show.

The couple met less than twelve months ago, when Ryan brought Adam his rider of cheese and pickle sandwiches. They struck up a conversation about the best fillings. 'It all sort of went from there,' says Ryan, 32, from Basildon.

Adam went to RADA and grew up in a village in Buckinghamshire. His parents, an architect and stay-at-home-mum, were delighted their son found happiness in Ryan.

Ryan's dad said: 'His mum would have been made up to see our son so happy. He's found himself a pukka bloke in Adam.'

Adam, overwhelmed with joy at the wedding ceremony said: 'We got talking about sandwiches and it sort of went from there. He said his favourite fairy tale as a boy was Cinderella, so we knew what sort of wedding car we needed. Jason, from Extra Weddings made our dream into a reality.'

Mel opened *Menz!* at the article. 'What do you want me to do today?'

Jason felt lightheaded. 'You haven't got a paper bag, have you?'

'Why?'

'I think I'm sort of having a panic attack. I feel sick. I need to lie down.' He lay on the floor.

'What's the problem?' Mel perched on the seat.

'Do you know how many enquiries we've had since last week, since that article was published?'

'A dozen.' That was the normal amount, and less than half would become clients.

'Two hundred. Since three days ago. I don't know what to do.' He took a deep breath, closed his eyes again and lay flat.

'Do you really want a paper bag?'

Jason nodded.

Mel ran off and returned with one, handing it to Jason. 'Breath into this slowly.' She rubbed his shoulders. 'Nobody died.'

'Never mind the clients, and it's just me to deal with them.'

'I am here today.'

'But not until next week though.'

'So, what do you want me for today?'

'There were some enquiries about interviews. Journalists I assume. They want the story behind the company. Come and take photos, all sorts. It'll be like a circus. I don't know what to do.'

Mel took his phone from the desk. 'I'll listen to the messages and we can talk about what to do. Journalists, I'm thinking say yes. No such thing as bad publicity. Isn't that what they say?'

It was. Apparently. 'I did a launch party. It was mainly friends and family.' A few local journalists had come because he'd promised free wine. But this was *The Daily Post*, *The Overseer*, *The Visor*, *The Mercury*. Proper newspapers people read all over the country.

'That was before.'

'That was basically my first wedding and now this. This sort of thing doesn't happen. Someone told me most overnight successes take a decade or more. This—'

'How long have you been doing this?'

'You watched me lie down.' Jason sat up, felt better.

'Events, weddings.'

'Twenty years.'

'And now this. Enjoy it. This is your moment in the spotlight. Step into it, make the most of it. Bask in twenty years of working bloody hard leading you to this point.'

Jason shook his head. 'It doesn't feel right. Why me, why now?'

'This is the first year there's two men dancing together on *Simply Dancing*. Last year there was the two women, and two men on the ice-skating programme. They walk amongst us, as Pete once told me.'

Jason grinned, remembering how his colleague had been to buy a wedding card and been struck to find ones for two men and two women. Without pausing, Pete had said, 'They walk amongst us,' and swept majestically out of the office.

They'd laughed very hard that evening, and more when he'd told his mum.

'Since you seem incapable of telling me what you want me to do, I'm going to tell you what you need me to do: I'll check the voicemails, call back all the journalists and schedule in interviews.'

'What shall I do?'

'You deal with the potential clients.'

'Two hundred of them?'

'So, if half say yes, that's one hundred weddings. Two a week for a whole year. Think of the money. No more worrying if you'll make enough each month.'

'I won't be able to do them all myself.'

Mel gestured from her head to toes. 'I'll do a few hours a week for you, if that's any good.'

'It'll have to be.'

'And you'll pay me?'

'Of course,' Jason said.

'You need staff.'

Jason felt a headache brewing at that. He'd probably need an actual office too, if this carried on. Although, they were nice problems to have.

Later, Mel showed him a schedule of interviews with journalists – most of them on the phone, a few wanted to visit him and take photos.

'Don't meet them here,' she said.

'Why not?'

'You don't want everyone knowing where you live.'

'Why not?'

'Oh God, are you really that innocent? After what happened before on social media?'

Jason had assumed that was a one-off and most people would be happy for him.

'I love that you always want to see the good in people. But not everyone is like that. Meet at a café, not here, all right?'

'Right.'

'How are you getting through the clients?'

'I've offered them times to speak to me. It's all I'm going to be doing for the next fortnight.' Never mind he had a wedding to organise, including his own, but that would wait.

That evening, Mel left and Jason thanked her, feeling much more organised than he had that morning with his unmanageable to do list.

–

After one of the interviews, the journalist asked, 'Would you like to do a radio interview?'

'Why?' Jason felt suspicious.

'I think you'd be good on radio.'

'Face for radio, isn't that the joke?' Jason laughed nervously.

'You're very knowledgeable about this and the way you describe meeting clients to work out their perfect wedding is really interesting. If I could, I'd get you on a TV show, talking through one of the scrapbooks you described.'

Jason felt his blood run cold. 'I'm not doing TV.' It already felt big enough, so soon, so he wasn't about to go on national TV. Who did they think he was? He'd enjoyed being the fairy godfather of weddings in the Cotswolds, but to be a what, celebrity – no, not quite – a local face, made him feel embarrassed.

'I'll think about it,' Jason said.

Of course, Pete had other ideas.

That night, when Jason told him about his day, and the offer for a radio interview, Pete said, 'Why didn't you bite his arm off?'

'Because I'm embarrassed. I don't want to make a fuss.'

'You really are dim sometimes. You had a big launch party, a big fuss, and it was great, considering no one had heard of Extra Weddings. And now you're known, thanks to Adam and Ryan, you're not riding this wave of publicity. You need to ring him back now, tell him yes, and do any other publicity you're offered. It won't last forever.'

'Why not?'

'Because it never does. There's always one big thing, for the month, and then everyone moves on. I studied it at uni. There's something about the British psyche.'

'Can you call him?'

'Why don't I suggest we both go on the radio show?'

Because you're not part of Extra Weddings? Although, it would take some of the limelight off Jason, which he liked the sound of. 'Go on then. Tell him I'm planning our wedding too.'

Pete rolled his eyes. 'Obvs.' He held his hand out for Jason's phone.

–

At the radio station, in Oxford, the broadcaster and host, Sean, had chatted to them in the green room, talking about what he was going to ask them. How long they'd have to talk. 'There will be a few breaks when I play music, so you can get your breath back. Just remember to enjoy yourselves and don't say anything you might regret.'

Pete shook his head.

Jason widened his eyes. 'Like what?'

'Don't mention anything about your last job. Why you were fired. It'll just sound like sour grapes. Just say you wanted to create a more modern, inclusive wedding planning company and it was the right time to break out on your own.'

'Can I write that down?' Jason asked, meaning it.

Sean smiled. 'Good one.'

'No, I really mean it.' Pete grabbed his hand across the table, squeezed it.

'You've totally got this,' Pete said, stroking his foot up Jason's leg gently.

Have I? Well, why do I feel terrified?

They put headphones on and moved closer to the microphone as they'd been shown earlier.

The song faded out and Sean said, 'We're lucky enough to have the man who planned that fabulous gay wedding between *Simply Dancing* dancer, Adam Winchester, and Ryan Westerman. If you don't know, just check out hashtag-adam-and-ryan for all the great stuff on the socials.' He nodded, indicating if they were ready.

Sweat ran down Jason's back and his heart was beating loudly in his throat.

Pete nodded.

'So,' Sean began, 'can you tell me how you go about planning a fabulous gay wedding such as Adam and Ryan's?'

Jason bit his bottom lip. 'I think nowadays the gay is silent.' He chuckled.

'Of course. Any wedding. For all your clients. Presumably you take any sort of couple at Extra Weddings?'

'We do...'

The interview passed in a blur and he gained five hundred followers on his social media accounts afterwards.

'Good stuff,' Sean said, as a song started and he removed his headphones. 'You can come again.'

'Was I all right?' Jason genuinely had no idea and couldn't believe it had happened. During the whole interview he'd been running on pure adrenaline and had no recollection of it.

'You have a really personable way about you. Easy, answering questions. Explaining things in a way everyone can understand, and even picking me up for my *faux pas* at the start, in a really clever way.'

'Faux p—'

'Saying it was a gay wedding. When it's really just a wedding,' Pete jumped on.

'Right.'

Afterwards, the media interviews died down, only the occasional request from a local paper, but his client list grew and grew, until he had to partner with another wedding planner to buy in some time from their staff, while he sorted out how to employ his own. Jason retained complete creative control, created the Pinterest boards with them and had oversight of the suppliers, leaving the day-to-day to the staff of the partner company.

He knew it couldn't continue forever, but he didn't have time to process new clients, never mind work out how to make a limited company and start to employ staff. It was a well-known method to have additional capacity during peaks of work in the events business, but Jason knew any mistakes the other staff made would come down to him, and he didn't want to lose the friendly, personal ethos he'd wanted when setting up Extra Weddings.

But that was something he'd worry about another day. Today, he was just managing the mountains of work and longer hours he was working, meaning he saw less and less of Pete.

Chapter 20

That weekend Mel arrived at Jason and Pete's with the two youngest.

Lily was looking forward to having her hair plaited and make-up done by Pete, and Thomas was practically bouncing off the walls at the prospect of playing Jason's latest PlayStation game and comparing notes on weightlifting.

'Why are we waiting, Mummy?' Lily asked.

'Give me a moment, please.' Mel was thinking of the best way to explain to Pete and Jason that despite Steve paying child support, and Pete and Jason lending money each month, she was still only managing money-wise and that wasn't something she could sustain for any length of time.

She sighed. Even staring at herself in the mirror as she put on her war paint hadn't convinced her this would be any easier. She hated asking again, but didn't know what else to do.

'Right, let's do this thing.' Mel left the car, with the children following and after hugs and kisses, they were sitting in the kitchen.

Jason was talking about Extra Weddings and how pleased he was to have made the change.

'Plus, you were fired,' Pete added with a wink.

'That too.' Jason grinned. 'What about you?' he asked Mel. 'Is Steve behaving like an actual adult human being, or still like a petulant child?'

Pete shook his head. 'That's my dad you're insulting.'

'Sorry.' Jason raised his eyebrows.

Mel adjusted her position. 'He's been really good.'

'Really?' Pete asked.

'He's stuck with his times to have the children for the last month. He's paying me more than the CSA advised. I think it's because he's happy. She must be doing something right. Whatever, it's more than I managed.' *God, that hurt. What a waste of those years.* She took a sharp intake of breath.

'You all right, Mum?' Pete stroked her back.

She nodded.

'How's Isaac settling in?'

'Haven't heard from him, so I'm assuming he's fine. I drove him, helped him unload into the halls of accommodation and he couldn't wait to see me off.'

'Bless,' Pete said, dripping in sarcasm. 'Not even a goodbye meal?'

'I offered to make him beans on toast, but he said it was embarrassing, his new friends watching me make him food.'

'What were they like, his friends?'

'A pale boy – man – who looked like he needed a good wash and stank of smoke; two American women were very friendly, asking him about where he lived; and a woman who oversaw her parents unpacking the car and installing her into her room, before being whisked off to eat somewhere.'

'Bet he's dating her by now,' Pete said.

Mel thought for a moment, remembering the looks they'd shared with one another. 'It certainly seemed on the cards.'

'Or they've hooked up and she's realised how much of a tool he is.'

'She was very prepossessing. And Isaac, he's not ugly, is he?'

Pete shrugged. 'He's my brother so it's hard to tell. He's handsome I reckon. Shame he's a—'

'Enough of the brother-bashing. He's finally decided to go to uni after taking two years to work out he didn't want to *not* go. It's a win of sorts, so we should all be happy for him.' She looked about, from Pete to Jason.

They nodded.

'Look, I didn't come here to discuss Isaac's love life.'

'Disappointed. Very,' Pete said.

She took a deep breath, braced herself, she was going to rip off the plaster, get it over and done with. 'I'm gonna say it, okay? Thank you so much for the money. The hours I work for Uncle Jason are helping. And your dad's money is making a difference. But it's not enough. I've done my sums and it doesn't work. Not long term anyway. I'm putting stuff on a credit card every month with no way to pay it off.'

There was silence as Mel held her breath.

'How much?' Jason asked carefully.

She shook her head. 'I'm not gonna lose the house. It's a little bit each week. Food and petrol. But I can't pay it off. It's not like I've gone to a loan shark.'

'We'll pay it off and you can owe us.' Jason nodded and Pete copied.

'I'm not asking for that. I'm not telling you the amount for precisely that reason. It's not going to work long-term. I'm working all week and it just about covers the bills. I'm existing. We're existing.'

'We'll sort it,' Jason said.

'I don't want you to sort it. I want to sort it for myself,' Mel replied tightly.

'How, Mum?' Pete asked.

'There's not any jobs going at your place, is there?' She looked at Pete.

He shook his head. 'They're cutting budgets, recruitment freeze, austerity measures. A trade union's member funded. No cash to splash, I'm afraid.' He shrugged.

'I'm cancelling your standing order.' Mel was horrified.

'It's fine at the moment. Don't panic.' He rested a hand on Mel's as it lay on the work surface.

'Jason?'

He chewed his lip in thought. 'It's still early days. It's going to take a while before I have lots of spare cash.'

'Ignore me, I'll ask the agency for more hours,' Mel said.

'When would you work them? On the eighth day of the week?' Pete asked.

Jason rolled his eyes. 'Or the twenty-fifth and twenty sixth-hour every day.'

'I feel like such a failure,' Mel said.

'You're Superwoman. You're She-Ra, you're the goddess of girl power.'

'I wasn't last Sunday when I slept through my alarm to take Lily to a birthday party and forgot Thomas was at hockey and called Steve, then the police in a panic about where he'd gone. And then he—'

Thomas walked into the kitchen. 'Arrived home wondering why there was a police car in the drive?'

Mel nodded, blushing bright red. 'I'm failing at so many things so often. All the time in fact.' She shook her head. 'I can't juggle it all. I'm bound to drop a ball.'

Thomas hugged her. 'Chill out. No one died.' He kissed her cheek.

She felt overwhelmed by the help and love of her family. Refusing to cry, she sat up straighter, taking a deep breath and looking at the ceiling, blinking furiously.

'Can I see Uncle Jason's new weights?' Thomas asked Mel.

'Ask him.'

Thomas did so.

'Come with me.' Jason led Thomas through the kitchen into the garage where he kept his weights and gym equipment.

Lily had been watching TV in the lounge. She appeared in the kitchen with her pigtails removed. 'I need Pete, Mum.'

'In a minute,' Mel said with more impatience than she'd intended.

Lily's bottom lip stuck out, she looked as if she were about to cry, turning and walked slowly back to the TV.

'I am a terrible mum. If I were me, I'd report me to Child-line.' She sighed. 'I have no patience. I'm always tired. I thought it was better without your dad, but now I'm working, it's as bad. Or worse.' She thought for a moment. 'No, it's a different sort of shit.'

'You're doing fine. Stop being so hard on yourself.'

'I wish I believed that myself.' She sighed, feeling old, irrelevant and outskilled by everyone else in the workplace.

'Believe it. You'll sort it out. You always have in the past.'

Mel looked up. 'Not alone, I didn't.'

Pete raised his eyebrows. 'You've organised four children and a husband, run a house, volunteered on all those PTA meetings, village committees... You're more organised than most chief execs I've worked with.'

She stroked his cheek. It always surprised her that somehow the baby she'd carried and given birth to, was now a hairy-faced man, taller than her. It seemed like a few months ago when she was watching him learn to walk.

'You're very sweet. Whatever, I'll be fine. Something will turn up. It always does.'

'I'm not just saying it, you do yourself down. You're amazing, Mum.' He hugged her tightly.

All these kind words, and Mel felt everything but amazing. An amazing failure maybe.

'Are we eating?' Mel asked. 'I was gonna bake a cake, but...' She raised her eyebrows and tilted her head to one side, hoping it said, '*I'd run out of ingredients, didn't have time to buy them during the week, then ran out of time this morning, so I'm running out of everything that's any use, please forgive me.*'

Pete led her into the living room, switched off the TV and collected Lily's bag, brushing her hair. 'Are you going to do my face, or me do yours?'

Lily thought for a moment. 'I saw something about how they put make-up on over beards.' She looked up at Pete. 'Can we try that?'

'Acne be damned! Of course.' Pete shrugged. 'I thought we'd eat out.'

Mel didn't want the expense but didn't know how to say. She frowned.

'We'll pay.'

'You're already giving me money. I can't—'

Pete put his hand up. 'How much do you think eighteen years of breakfast, lunch and dinner is worth?'

Mel shook her head. 'Don't be silly.'

'You're the one who's being silly. Our treat.'

Lily lined up foundation, lipstick and eye shadow on the table, comparing the colours to Pete's skin tone.

'I could make the cake here, I know where everything's kept.'

Pete put his hand on her lap, gently preventing her from standing. 'There are these places and they sell cakes already baked. It's great.' He looked at the ceiling for a moment. 'What are they called...? Oh yes, shops. Relax, we've got this.'

Mel relaxed her body for the first time since arriving, went limp. She pushed herself back on the sofa, tucking her legs underneath herself. She might not have done much else with her life since giving birth to four humans, but she reckoned she'd done a pretty good job of that, all things considered.

Chapter 21

Harriet arrived at the Kensington restaurant her father had suggested. He never arranged purely social calls, there was always a business reason behind them meeting.

Her father stood, pulled her into an embrace, kissed her cheek. He smelled of woody citrus *Creed Bois de Paris* and hair pomade as usual. He wore a grey suit and white shirt.

She sat, grabbed the menu.

'How are you?' he asked, leaning back in his chair, placing the menu on the table.

'Well,' she replied with tight lips. She knew her father didn't want to know about her love life, or not the way she was going about it anyway. He might pretend to be interested, but as soon as she delved into any sort of details he'd clam up and change the subject.

'Work?'

She shrugged, glancing up from the menu. 'I'm having a starter, are you?'

He waved indicating she should do whatever she pleased. In this particular decision anyway. 'Are you still at the events company – in the East End, wasn't it?'

'Wedding planners. Knightsbridge, but near enough.' She sipped the sparkling water. 'And yes, I am still there.'

'You've more than proved your point with that job. I wasn't sure you'd actually follow through.'

The waiter arrived. 'Are you ready to order?'

'One steak, well done, no French fries and extra greens.' Her father raised his eyebrows at Harriet.

'Foie gras pâté, followed by the fish.'

The waiter left.

Her father rubbed his stomach. 'Aren't you impressed?'

'Still following the doctor's orders, I see?' Her father had suffered a small heart attack and, since it very much reminded him of his mortality, he had been on a much healthier diet.

He nodded and smiled.

'Very good.' A pause, and then, 'What do you mean you didn't believe I'd follow through with the job?'

'I thought you'd get a job, to show me you could, and then... Well, you'd return to how things were before.' He poured them red wine. 'Medicinal, one glass, apparently. Any more than that's not, or so they say.'

She twirled the wine glass between her fingers. The *before* he referred to meant the years post university when she'd tried extremely hard to party all night and sleep all day. In fairness, she'd given it a bloody good try for a few years, and had succeeded until her father had given her an ultimatum.

'I enjoy it,' she said. Not the early mornings, nor the office chitchat – small talk taken to the lowest common denominator so it was almost microscopic talk – but the people and the work, she enjoyed.

'Come off it,' he scoffed.

She sat up. 'I do.'

'Really?'

'*Really*. Being part of a team, pulling together for a shared endeavour.'

'Don't you want to roll over in bed and leave it all?'

She didn't need the money. Her father had bought her the apartment and gave her a generous allowance. She mentioned neither of these things to anyone other than old school and university friends, who'd known her long enough for this not to make a difference.

'Every Monday,' she replied.

'So what gets you up?'

Without a moment's thought, she said, 'The clients. The staff. My reputation.' *Satisfaction in a job well done*, but she kept that to herself since her father would probably scoff at that too, having made his views clear about the wedding industry as a frivolous way to spend money.

'It would almost be a good place to meet a suitable husband, were it not so...' He shrugged.

Her starter arrived and she spread thick wedges of pâté onto thin melba toast. 'Do you want a little?'

'Carbs. Wheat. It's all a no-no since...' He raised an eyebrow and a faraway look flashed across his face.

After swallowing the creamy, buttery mouthful, she said, 'I enjoy creating the perfect day for couples.'

He rolled his eyes. 'Like in those books you used to devour as a child.'

She still read her fair share of romance novels, although kept it to herself. Some days, if it was a choice between a bottle of wine and a book, she'd plump for the latter knowing it far less harmful. Other evenings – more of late – only alcohol would do.

After chewing thoughtfully for a few moments, she said, 'How *is* Aunt Wendy?'

Her father's sister had introduced her to romance novels one summer while staying at her home deep in the Welsh countryside. An entire room with wall-to-wall filled bookcases had always intrigued Harriet until at twelve, away from her parents who had very particular ideas about what girls should and shouldn't read, she'd taken one, settled in the corner, and hadn't moved until she'd greedily gobbled it up, relishing falling in love with the hero and experiencing love and romance alongside the heroine.

'Living in her own little world, as usual, I should imagine,' her father said with a slight sneer.

'Very sensible in my opinion.' She found so much of modern life less than satisfactory, why wouldn't one escape into books every now and then? Harriet made a mental note to arrange a visit.

'Never mind all that, it's no way to move oneself *forward* in life. Pretending one's in a fantasy world of dukes and knights and God alone knows what else.' He looked about impatiently. 'When do you think they'll bring our main course?' He'd gone red in the face, indicating his patience was fraying and he was on the edge of one of his tempers.

'I think my job is like arranging the epilogue of one of those books. But in real life. And I think that's pretty neat, don't you?' The thought had come to her one day after discussing a few clients' requirements and one had mirrored, almost exactly, the ending of a book.

The waiter passed and her father waved his white napkin. He stopped by their table.

'Do you know if there's any danger of me being fed today?'

She caught his eye, glaring at his rudeness.

Reluctantly, he added, 'Please?'

The waiter placed one arm behind his back and held the tray carefully. 'I'll check right away, sir.'

Her father turned to her. 'Any danger of a husband in the wings, or are you still associating with your unsuitable gentleman friend?'

Harriet sighed. 'I'm seeing someone, if you must know.'

'Seeing? What on earth is that supposed to mean? I can see you now. Having eyes means this is a by-product of spending time with someone.' He shook his head.

'It's less serious than dating, more concrete than a fling.' But only just.

'I don't suppose there's any chance of him shifting into the dating arena?'

'Why is that so important to you?'

'You're not getting any younger.'

God, could he be any more from the Dark Ages? Although she loved him, it was sometimes hard to like him. 'Twenty-nine is hardly old. Besides, he'll do for now.'

'Will I perhaps meet him?'

She shook her head.

'Why not?'

Because he's nearly your age. Because he's almost definitely married. Because it's not serious and I don't want to show how precarious it all is. Because telling you I'm really only in it for the sex, and not any chance of the romance, doesn't make sense to me, so there's no chance you'll understand it.

Harriet shook her head. 'No point, I'm about to dump him anyway.'

'Are you?'

Am I? Yes, I am. Once I've found out if he's married, I'm going to summon all my gumption and leave him behind. 'I am. No chance of meeting Mr Right if I'm cluttering up my time with Mr Right Now, is there?'

Her father coughed, obviously relieved they weren't going to discuss any more details of her relationship with this mystery man.

Harriet poured them more wine. 'Why did you want to see me? It's surely not to discuss my job and my love life?'

The waiter arrived with their main courses.

Her father prodded his steak with a fork, once satisfied he began eating. 'It's okay.' He nodded and the waiter left.

Harriet picked up her cutlery.

'You've proved your point with this current venture, I wanted to speak to you about moving onto something more...' He waved his fork about.

Something he could control, something he placed a value on perhaps...

'...fitting,' he said finally.

'Such as?' Although she'd been brought up in the shadow of her father's company, she'd never been too interested since it was something he controlled so strictly, leaving her with little scope to do it her way when the time came.

'What would you feel about being a company secretary?'

'Not much.'

'It's not what you think.'

'Which is?'

'It's not a secretary. It's more involved in governance, issues of transparency, keeping the board running in the proper way.'

'I can't type. I'm not doing shorthand. There are apps for that now.'

He shook his head. 'I've had this prepared, it outlines some of the duties.' He reached into his suitcase, handed her a sheaf of papers.

Glancing at what looked to be a job description, she folded it in her handbag. 'Why now?'

'Aren't you going to look at it?'

'I thought you said I should take over from you when I turned thirty-five.'

'This isn't that. It's dipping your toe in the water. You could do it with your eyes closed. Aren't you going to look at it?'

'Later.' Although she'd expected the lunch to be focused on something business related, she hadn't anticipated this. An actual job offer. Or was it a job order?

'I think you'll find it's a very varied role, plenty of opportunities to influence how the company is run.'

'Why now, why me?' She knew the answer to the latter was because she was his daughter, and more now than in her early twenties, she felt uncomfortable about such nepotism. Having watched others work hard to gain similar roles, she wasn't sure how it would sit with her if she simply slid into a high-powered role on the board of Electrovax.

He outlined the role in some detail, then said, 'The current post holder has retired. I thought we could do with some new blood on the board. Drag us into the twenty-first century.' He chuckled.

'We're quite far into that century, Father.'

'I know. Toe in water job, as I said.'

'I'd like to consider it please.' It wasn't a decision she could take lightly.

'You won't have to apply, the job's yours.'

'If I want it?'

'I thought you'd… I assumed you'd…'

'Are you asking me to do it or telling me?'

'I wanted you to want it. And we have a gap on the board, which I'd rather like you to fill. Does that help?'

She nodded, finishing her food.

They ate in awkward silence for a few moments.

Now she knew it was an offer she couldn't refuse, Harriet almost wanted to turn her father down straight away. But she knew he'd insist she hadn't considered it properly, so she decided to wait to give her decision.

'I'll read this and let you know.'

She wanted to make her own way in life. As much as possible at any rate. Although she knew he wouldn't cut her off, so she'd never *truly* be able to make her own way, she wanted to show her father she had the option to forge her own path, rather than going along with his suggestions like some sort of automaton. And she didn't have the heart to tell him not a single atom of her body was even remotely excited by the prospect of working for a company that manufactured vacuum cleaners. It was, as she knew, his life's work, so she'd always kept that thought to herself too. But it didn't alleviate the expectation that she would take over, in the absence of any siblings.

He clapped her gently on the shoulder. 'It's an amazing offer. Plenty of people's dream job.'

She smiled tightly. *Yes, but it doesn't mean it's my idea of a dream job.* 'If I left, I couldn't leave them in the lurch at Tailored Weddings. They've been very good to me.'

'I'm sure they have.' He blinked slowly.

'I have to line up a few things if I decide to accept. You understand?'

He nodded.

They moved onto other topics as they finished the meal.

Later, after he'd paid, as they waited for their coats by the cloakroom, he said, 'It may not seem this way, but I'm very proud of you. Of how you stand up to me. No one else does, except your mother of course. Doesn't mean I want you to say no though.' He smiled and winked as he slipped on his coat.

Harriet squeezed his arm and smiled. She said nothing, although it was pleasant to be praised for her efforts, even if it was in disagreeing with her father.

Outside the restaurant he looked about for his driver. 'Can I offer you a lift?'

She could have accepted, but she felt the limos and drivers and private jets were a bit passé. Like some kind of hangover from the eighties. Weren't business leaders meant to be men or women of the people nowadays? Travelling with the masses, to understand their needs and wants?

She kissed his cheek, brushing it with her hand. 'I'm going to walk. Love you.'

He climbed into the black limo, ducking his grey-haired head, waving from an opened window, before he was whisked away.

She brushed her hair out of her face, turned away from the restaurant and into Hyde Park, breathing deeply at the scent of flowers and the sight of joggers and walkers and families enjoying the green space.

She knew whatever she chose, eventually her father would support her, and would respect her more for making her own decision.

She hoped.

Perhaps a role as a company secretary on the Electrovax board would satisfy her father's wish for her to be involved, while letting Harriet pursue her own career... Could she really juggle it all?

Her phone rang with Robert's name. Involuntarily she smiled as she answered it. As far as casually seeing someone went, she could do a lot worse.

'I'm lucky enough to have a free afternoon if you wanted to meet,' he said.

She wanted to ask if his wife had let him out to play, but since the last mention of a wife, they'd not spoken. He had then insisted he wasn't married and was free and single and available for her. Taking him at face value would have been much simpler. Except for this niggling doubt deep down in her gut that told her a man of that age, with such limited time to see her, was probably in a relationship.

She bit the inside of her cheek. 'What were you thinking?' She felt sure he'd suggest some afternoon delight at her apartment, to which she'd refuse, obviously. Make him work for it first of course. Except, she knew as soon as they were in her apartment all her clothes would melt away along with her worries, because nothing would matter for the whole glorious time they were together, in her bedroom.

'Late lunch?' he offered.

'Just eaten.'

'Supper? Champagne picnic perhaps?'

'Where?'

'I'm in Hyde Park, where are you?'

'Wimbledon, but I could be with you in two shakes of a lamb's tail.'

He had a habit of using old-fashioned phrases like that. It partly reminded her of her father, which made her feel conflicted about fancying a man her father's age, and also strangely comforted by his experience and knowledge.

'Why are you there?' He seemed to often be in Wimbledon for undisclosed reasons. He also spent time in Surrey, worked in London, although he'd told her he lived in London, but she was still yet to see it for herself.

'Or would you like to come south of the river? Clapham Common?'

'Will I finally have the privilege of seeing your place?'

'Don't see why not.'

Her heart soared. She was going to see his place, and know once and for all if he was married, single, or otherwise. 'Wonderful.'

They agreed a time and place to meet and she ended the call.

Operation Boyfriend is resumed. She couldn't wait to tell friends they'd finally reached this significant relationship marker.

Chapter 22

Jason was prepared for the media circus at this wedding. It made sense because one groom, Zane, was in a boyband from the early noughties, and the other, recently rebranding himself as simply B, had been a children's TV presenter at the same time.

What Jason hadn't prepared himself for was how high-maintenance Zane had been.

'Are you letting in *Hiya* magazine yet?' Callie, Zane's assistant, asked.

'For what?'

'Photos.'

'They spent two hours taking pictures at the town hall.'

'Yeah, they want more.' Callie rolled her eyes. 'Aren't they, like, paying for it?'

There had been talk of a media deal, which Zane had been particularly interested in. Jason thought music would have paid him enough to not sell his wedding like this, but it wasn't for him to criticise – if he and B were happy with it, then who was he to disagree?

They would have been, what Jason described as twinks, back in the day. Only now, at about Jason's age, they were far from twink territory. Greying temples and beards, while trying to hold onto their youth by dressing in designer clothes that were too young for them. Nobody needed to see a forty-year-old man in a low V-neck T-shirt that came down to the middle of his chest.

That, taken in the early noughties, had been one of the inspiration photos they'd provided for their mood board. Jason noticed they'd very much clung onto that look nearly fifteen years after the event.

Zane, the frontman from The Needed, a manufactured boyband, had not heard the word 'no' very often in his life. Jason had worked this out when he'd said that word, after Zane had asked if they could scatter glittery confetti over themselves, with the backdrop of a lake next to a waterfall.

'Why not?' Zane had pouted.

'Because the glitter will ruin the lake and kill the fish.'

'I'll pay for them.'

Jason placed his hands in a praying position, on the table, and closed his eyes as he worked out the best response to this. 'I will lose my licence. I'm signed up to an environmental awareness charter, for sustainable and green weddings. Glitter in a lake isn't either of those things.'

'I'll pay for your licence. I saw it at a baby shower on Instagram. They had balloons that floated off, and they popped them, the glitter went everywhere. It was amazing. I want that.'

That had been the first of dozens of difficult conversations during the planning of this wedding.

They had settled on confetti made from rose petals, scattered over them. It had taken bags of petals, because Zane wanted to pose for photos there, and the confetti throwers – an actual job title Jason had needed to use when requesting them at an events company – had thrown confetti for nearly an hour.

Now, Jason was faced with the dilemma of whether to let *Hiya* magazine in before the grooms, as they'd probably want to photograph the venue without people.

Jason's phone rang.

B said, sounding flustered: 'Have you let them in yet?'

'Who?'

'*Hiya* magazine. It says they're not allowed on site until we're there.'

'They have asked for access to the empty venue. Am I to tell them no?' Jason took a deep breath. It would all be worthwhile.

Additional publicity could do no harm. If he could deal with a precocious narcissist like Zane, he could deal with anyone.

Zane came on the phone. 'Tell them to photograph us as we arrive.'

'They're insisting on seeing the room now.'

'I'm not having them seeing it before I do.' There was chatter down the phone as the two men conferred. Finally, Zane said, 'The contract says they get prior access. Give it to them.' A pause, then: 'Please.'

'Understood. When will you be here?'

'Ten minutes. Tell the photographers to be ready. I'm not doing this bit four times.' A cough. 'Thanks.' Zane ended the call.

Four times referred to the number of takes it had required for the confetti lake waterfall pictures. Jason dreaded to think how long it would take to work their way through the list of photos the journalists had requested of the grooms, their family and friends.

But that wasn't really his problem. He told Callie to let the magazine in.

Jason strode to the front of the yellow brick building. A large country hotel, set in the rolling hills of rural Somerset. It was the only venue with enough capacity for the sit-down meal and rooms for guests to stay, as well as the press.

He leaned against the pillars over the entrance porch and checked his watch. 'About five minutes, everyone,' he said to the photographers standing about.

'Can I take photos?' Pete asked. He'd been quietly standing in the background – much to Jason's relieved surprise.

'Do it subtly. And don't post it. The magazines have an exclusivity clause. If anything gets leaked before they publish, it's all ruined. And Zane will blame me.'

'What about the guests?'

'Handed their phones to one of my staff when they arrived at the wedding.'

'Wow!' Pete's eyes widened.

Jason nodded. 'Right.'

A low-slung hot pink sports car that looked like a thin slice of cake laid on its side, arrived at the hotel gates.

'Is this them?' Pete asked.

Jason nodded.

The photographers ran towards the car, surrounding it, flashes going off all around.

The car slowly drove towards the entrance, stopped. The nearest door opened upwards, like a bird's wing. Out slipped B, in a hot pink glittery suit, feather headdress and red shoes.

The other door opened, giving the impression the car was about to take off by flapping its wings.

Zane exited, legs first, standing to his full height. He stepped around the car in a glittery red suit jacket with long skirt that seemed bigger than the car.

Jason had no idea how it had fitted inside earlier.

Three assistants who seemed to have appeared from nowhere unfurled Zane's skirt, until it was twice as wide as he stood tall, with a long train behind him.

'That's the money shot,' Jason said to Pete, nodding as the two grooms posed in front of the Italian sports car.

Pete joined the photographers and took as many pictures as possible.

B announced, 'We will move inside now.' He took Zane's hand and they walked inside the hotel, followed by photographers.

The speeches came thick and fast, including the publisher of a fashion magazine. She stood, looking diminutive in large black sunglasses and long, black, sleek hair. 'I wanted to say how I know these two men are made for each other. When we featured them in our magazine, I could see they were meant to be together. I'm so privileged to have some small part in documenting their love. Forever.'

Guests clapped, Zane and B blushed slightly, looking about the room as everyone continued clapping.

Next, the manager of Zane's band, a middle-aged man with grey hair and beard, who wore a T-shirt and jeans. He was still very close friends with Zane of course. 'I remember when Zane was an unknown eighteen-year-old. I've never worked with someone who could go from sweetness and light to a volcano in under five seconds.'

Applause and laughter.

Zane didn't look amused.

He continued, 'Of course it's his voice we all know Zane for, and I think it's perfect he's found someone who not only puts up with his capricious nature, but seems to enjoy it.' He paused. 'No, I jest. Zane is one of the most talented artists I've worked with and I knew he'd go far when I first met him in that audition hall in Watford all those years ago. B, I'm sure you'll have your hands full, but it looks like you enjoy it.'

Next came Zane and then B, thanking everyone for coming today, for helping them share in their special day.

No family speeches, which Jason thought interesting. He later read in a magazine interview the men had revealed Zane had been adopted and fallen out with his parents after some negative comments he'd shared about how they'd brought him up. B, it turned out, had lost his mother as a teenager, and had lost touch with his father when he came out.

Jason couldn't believe families still did that: disowned, severed all ties with someone due to their sexuality. His family weren't exactly close, living far away, but he was still on speaking terms with them.

After the speeches, the guests continued eating – smoked salmon and oysters to start, followed by chateaubriand, thickly sliced and served with crushed and roasted potatoes on a bed of green spring vegetables, served with a red wine and beef jus. 'A posh roast,' Jason said, elbowing Pete gently.

By the evening, guests were encouraged to move to the next room, which had a dance floor with tables and chairs. Waiters took orders for evening food from a menu. A hundred new guests arrived, joining the others, making it one of the biggest events Jason had organised.

The press, satisfied they'd captured enough footage, pictures and interviews with the guests and grooms, were sitting on a table together, tucking into their food, pouring each other wine from the table that was constantly replenished by waiting staff.

The music started with a few songs from The Needed playing live, and then The Fridays performed a few of theirs, much to Pete's delight.

'Zane used to date Melly,' Jason said by way of explanation when Pete had asked how exactly he'd managed to get The Fridays too.

Pete frowned.

'Bisexual.'

Pete nodded in understanding.

The two groups were sitting on tables by the stage as other guests queued up to talk to them, and pose for photos together.

The DJ – Princess Louise, very big on the Ibiza club circuit, used to set up club nights in the eighties – was spinning tunes. A mixture of classic wedding fare and upbeat dance tracks.

Pete and Jason danced, relieved it had all gone well and near the end of the night, Jason was basically off duty.

A tap on Jason's shoulder stopped him. He turned.

Zane and B stood, smiling, they were still wearing their wedding outfits.

'I'm impressed you've danced in that,' Pete said.

'Might as well make use of it. Doubt I'll wear it again,' Zane said, then laughed.

Jason introduced the grooms to Pete, they shook hands.

'Have you enjoyed yourselves?' Jason asked.

'Best. Day. Ever,' B said, breathlessly, grinning widely.

'I'm so pleased.'

'Thank you.' B put his hand on Jason's shoulder. 'I know it's not been easy, but you've been awesome.' He turned to Zane.

'Yes,' Zane said. 'What he said. Thank you.'

They kissed each other on the cheek, Jason waved goodbye and they left.

In their car, Jason said, 'Did you get lots of ideas for our wedding?'

'I don't normally say this, and it was very them. Made sense. But it felt a little bit... much. For us, I mean.'

'We couldn't even come close to affording this. It was the most expensive event I've ever organised. Including all the corporate launches I did in London.'

'How much?'

Jason named a figure.

'Shut up!'

Jason put the car into gear and slowly drove out of the hotel's grounds. 'They're getting more than that from the magazine deals.'

'That's an idea...' Pete put his finger on his lips in obvious thought.

Jason said nothing and they drove home in silence as Pete rested his hand on Jason's thigh.

Chapter 23

Steve had asked to meet Mel at a café near the house.

When Mel arrived, Steve was slumped over a table by the window, staring into the distance. *This is not going to be fun.*

Mel greeted him and asked if he wanted another drink.

He shook his head, briefly looked her in the eye then resumed staring into space.

'Okay?' she asked, leaving her jacket over the seat, more as a way to try and work out what was wrong with him than anything else. Depending on his response, that would dictate which drink Mel bought. And the degree to which she'd stick to her no processed sweet comestibles rule she'd introduced since seeing herself from behind in a shift dress.

Steve shrugged, signed, dunked a biscotti into his coffee then lifted it to his mouth. Half dropped into the coffee. It was as if the world had ended. Steve shook his head and tutted loudly.

'I'll get you another biscotti,' Mel offered.

'It's not about the biscotti, it's…'

'I'll be back.' Mel left and decided she'd treat herself to a slice of the black forest gateau, purely medicinal purposes. *Sod the diet and that shift dress.* She reckoned she was going to need it if Steve's mood was anything to go by.

Shortly, she returned to their table, handing Steve three biscotti. 'I explained you'd had a little accident with yours. They were very helpful. They're good here, aren't they?'

Steve shrugged, tearing open a biscotti packet.

This was typical Steve, he wouldn't open up until she prised it out of him. 'What's happened?' He'd not shaved, his hair hadn't been combed and he had a fairly fruity aroma indicating he'd probably not washed for a while.

Mel's coffee and cake arrived. She put the cake in the middle of the table, offering Steve a forkful.

He fiddled with the empty biscotti packet, staring into space over her shoulder.

'Are you okay? You don't seem it. You seem...' She had to be delicate here because if she pointed out he looked a mess, he'd definitely not tell her.

'It must be me.'

Marvellous, we have contact! 'What must be you?'

'Otherwise why would I fuck up two so soon?'

'I'm not following you. Two what?'

'Relationships.'

Right, she thought this would be the problem. 'What's happened?' She forked a mouthful of cake and chewed, reckoning she was going to more than earn the calories this morning.

'Everyone has little fights, you know that. It's part of the ups and downs of a relationship.'

'I don't understand. Why would she leave me?'

'What happened?'

He shrugged. 'I don't know. She walked out.'

At least he hadn't cheated on her with someone else. She always suspected Steve wasn't a serial cheater. If so, he'd have surely done so earlier in their twenty-five-year marriage. 'What did she say?'

Steve pulled his phone from his pocket and read out from a note. 'I don't want another piece of jewellery, I want you.' He placed the phone on the table.

Mel pulled it closer so she could read the note. Nothing more. Although this sounded familiar.

'She had new clothes, jewellery, shoes, a car, I'd paid for her place to be decorated how she wanted it. New kitchen, boiler, double glazing, her place is... was a bit of a state, you see. Holidays, we'd gone on at least three, Maldives, Florida, and Australia was booked and then this happened.'

'How were the holidays?' Mel could guess what he'd done wrong, but wanted to ease into it gently. Didn't want to scare the horses, or the ex-husband.

'Expensive.' He shook his head tutting loudly, opened a biscotti and carefully dunked it into his coffee, chewing thoughtfully in silence.

Let's try another tack. 'When you were on holiday, what did you do?'

'Ate out, sat by the pool, swam, she read a lot of books. Seemed not to enjoy it as much as I thought. Always ringing friends back home.'

'What about you?' she asked carefully.

'I was there, I'd paid for it, what more did she want?'

'Were you working while on holiday?'

'I had a deadline. The project would have failed if I hadn't. It was last minute. She really wanted to go, so I said I'd bring my laptop with me. It was a compromise.'

'Did you tell Sally you'd need to work while on holiday?'

'Might have done. Probably. Look, I don't remember, all right? I reckoned I'd fit a few hours in before she got up to sit by the pool.'

• Mel had heard that one before, dozens of times. Every family holiday Steve had remained in the villa working for almost the whole day, only emerging for evening meals and some breakfasts. She'd given up complaining since he always insisted if he didn't do it he'd probably lose his job. Mel believed he preferred working to spending time with his family, but she hadn't thought about that too deeply since it filled her with sadness. For both Steve and their family.

'So you got a few hours' work in and joined her by the pool?' Mel knew the answer to this.

'Some days, yeah.' He shook his head.

Mel smiled. 'But you've been having the kids at weekends, what's she like with them?'

'I take them out to eat, while she stays at home. Didn't take much interest in them to be honest.'

'Right,' Mel replied evenly.

'She wanted for nothing. Just like you. I worked so hard so she had it all.'

'You ate out together, and had date nights, of course.'

He nodded. 'Of course.' He coughed. 'When I moved in, not so often. Okay, so lately, not at all.'

This sounded familiar too. 'Why did you stop?'

'Because I'd got her, I didn't need to carry on the pursuit.' He looked up with bloodshot eyes. 'I suppose you're going to tell me I got that wrong too?'

'Our house is beautiful. It sounds like you did the same for Sally's home too.'

'Correct. So why am I living in a hotel? I did what my dad taught me. I got it all right. Except the cheating on you. Sorry.'

Mel remained silent. Christ, if Steve couldn't learn from his mistake then she wasn't about to help him. How could a man, whose job was almost too complex to describe, be so bloody thick?

'She chose the new kitchen and the Mercedes and the new three-piece suite for her lounge.'

'Does Sally have children?'

He shook his head. 'She wants to wait until she's thirty. Work out who she is beforehand. What's with all this working out who we are? I'm me, I go to work, I pay for everything. That's it. You raised our children. That's how it's always been. Mum and Dad made it work okay for fifty years.'

'They did. I suspect Sally wanted to spend time with you. Just like I used to.'

'How am I meant to do that when I'm working to pay for all the things?' Exasperation crossed his face.

'I always said I'd live in a small house; the cars were nice but didn't mean as much to me as seeing you.'

'That's what people say. They don't really mean it. Everyone likes nice things. Everyone.'

'Not at the expense of someone they love.' Because she had loved him. Very much indeed. Otherwise she wouldn't have had four children with him.

'So what should I have done?'

Mel fiddled with her cake, forking in a mouthful to stop herself providing an answer. She still felt something for Steve, but she was fucked if he thought she should help him learn from the same mistakes he'd made with her, only this time with his new girlfriend. *Spend time with her, with us, but that ship had most definitely sailed.*

'What should I do?'

'I'm thinking.' The financial security, the five holidays a year, new cars every three years, five-bedroom house, were all wonderful. But not at the expense of having a husband to spend time with. Of having a man who not only fathered, but parented their children with her. She allowed herself quiet admiration for Sally having reached this conclusion much sooner than Mel herself.

'Do you think she'd have me back?'

'I've never met her, so it's hard for me to say.' She bit her tongue from pointing out what was blindingly obvious to her, but Steve was totally unable to see for himself.

'Right.' Steve fiddled with the napkin on the table, tearing it into strips. 'I'm stuck, I thought you'd know what to do.'

This was definitely getting into weird territory. 'I don't know how you and her are together. Don't want to really. This is for you to sort with her. I can't be this person for you any more. It's not fair.'

Steve put his head in his hands, closed his eyes and muttered something. After a short while, he asked, 'Were you happy?'

For a long time, Mel hadn't been happy. But she'd sort of become used to it, a bit like back pain or similar. She'd learned to live with the unhappiness, keeping busy, and accepted it was her lot. But Sally had obviously had a much lower tolerance for unhappiness.

'We had some great years together,' Mel said finally, not wanting to hammer any more nails into Steve's coffin of his own making.

'Politician's answer. That's very kind of you.' He sat upright, rubbing his red eyes and stroking his stubbly chin. 'Let's try it again, this time honestly please.'

'If you're asking me if you could have been a better husband and father, yes, you could. If you're asking me if you gave me and the children everything we ever wanted, yes you did.' She stopped herself. *If you're asking me if we'd have liked you to be more present, then yes, I can't deny it would have been lovely, but I'm not telling you now, so you can take that to improve your current relationship.* She hadn't been happy for years, she realised. But telling Steve this now was pointless.

Steve picked up his fork. 'Can I have some?'

'Of course.' Mel sat back in her chair and watched him eat half her black forest gateau, chewing thoughtfully they sat in silence.

He stood, left money on the table.

'I've paid for mine,' Mel said.

'It's for you.'

'No need.' She pushed it away.

'Sorry.'

'What for?'

He smiled weakly and put the money in his wallet. 'I'm an idiot.'

'You are. You're also a man trying to do his best for his family. I wish I'd been more forceful.'

'I wouldn't have listened.' He coughed. 'Because I'm an idiot.'

'Maybe try *not* to be the same idiot this time around.'

'I'll try, but I'm still me.' He left.

Steve may be still him, but Sally was definitely not Mel. Although she refused to give him the answer on a plate, she didn't wish them harm. Steve being happy would be a better father to their children.

Mel ate the remains of the cake alone with her thoughts. Steve had never stood a chance, basing his husband and father model on his own father's. But he was right, he wouldn't have listened, even if Mel had complained about him being a workaholic. He'd have insisted he was doing it all for them. Plus, he loved his job, and convincing someone to leave that for the messiness of a family was always difficult. At work people listened to him, did as he asked. At home, Steve wasn't the family's chief executive, he was the second in command, next to Mel. So was it any wonder he'd avoided it?

Chapter 24

Harriet pulled the duvet up to cover her breasts. There were no books, ornaments, pictures, anything personal within this one-bedroom flat in Wimbledon to indicate it belonged to Robert.

Robert was making clattering noises in the tiny kitchen, having volunteered to make something to eat.

Last night they'd eaten a very substantial dinner at an exclusive restaurant on the King's Road, followed by too-substantial amounts of wine at a small bar nearby. By the time the bar had closed they were irretrievably pissed, giggling at something Robert had said as they hailed a taxi for his apartment.

She blushed and grinned as a memory from last night flashed across her mind. That was something about the older gentleman, she appreciated, much more likely to know his way around a woman's body than some inexperienced clumsy twenty-something.

She shuddered at a particularly dissatisfactory night with a man her own age where she'd ended up in her place ('I'm afraid I live with my parents!' he'd said), which should have set alarm bells ringing. After a few unsuccessful attempts at foreplay she'd proclaimed he didn't need to bother, she'd simply manage on her own. And he'd scuttled off to the bathroom – a pale white bottom the last she saw of him – before her front door clicked shut.

At least Robert knew what he was doing bed-wise.

He arrived in the bedroom carrying a tray, a single red rose in a mug and mint chocolates spread like a fan across a white plate.

It wasn't quite cordon bleu, but at least he'd tried.

He placed the tray on the bed. He wore baggy blue-and-white-striped boxer shorts and grey socks. His chest was broad with dark grey and black hairs forming a pattern over his pectoral muscles. *At least he has them.* No six pack, but instead a rounded stomach. Not that she could talk, she'd never had anything approaching abs and had a decided she disliked them on men, making her feel far too inferior if she slept with a man who was slimmer than herself.

Hadn't he removed his socks last night? When we were... Oh dear God, what am I doing?

'You look pensive,' he said, sitting on the bed as it creaked slightly.

'Nothing. Splendid. A rose. Wonderful. And chocolate. I feel like I'm in one of those adverts where the woman says she likes a certain kind of chocolate and the man scales a wall to deliver them to her.' He had definitely tried. It's just there was something else niggling her about this whole situation and she couldn't bite her tongue any longer.

He helped himself to a chocolate mint, offering them to her.

She took two. The alcohol high had long since worn off, replaced by a dull hangover, and somehow it all felt much less like one of her favourite books and more like... Well, a bad Mike Leigh film. She needed something to ease her passage back to reality.

He knelt forwards and kissed her. A chocolatey tongue and lips weren't quite what she'd wanted now reality was encroaching into what had seemed like a good idea at the time.

She pulled back. 'Sorry, I'm not a *massive* fan of mint choc actually.'

He looked so crestfallen. 'You should have said.' He stood. 'I'll fetch us some different chocs. Name your favourite. I shall procure the best money can buy.' He pulled on his shirt and trousers. 'Whatever the Waitrose local has, but anyway!'

She slipped on her clothes, covered by the duvet, retrieving them from the floor. It wasn't the socks he'd left on last night. It wasn't the dad bod – she quite enjoyed that actually. It wasn't his grey hair – it made him look rather distinguished. It wasn't even the fact he was not far off the same age as her father. He had money, he knew a good wine from a crap bottle of plonk. He'd promised her a weekend in the Cotswolds on numerous occasions but had yet to follow through – busy weekends of overtime apparently. It wasn't his odd sense of humour, which could be endearing in the right time and place.

Confident she was suitably dressed to have this conversation, she climbed out of bed.

She couldn't shake off the niggling feeling he was lying to her. And yet, up until now, she'd wanted to believe he was telling the truth.

He stood by the door, dressed. 'I shall return forthwith.' He raised his eyebrows. 'Would you like to come with?'

'No. What I'd really like is for you to tell me the truth.'

'About?'

'This place. Your life. Why there's no personal belongings here. Why you're unable to see me at the weekend. Take your pick on which to begin.' She folded her arms across her chest.

He went red-faced, shifted uncomfortably from one foot to the other. 'This is my *pied-à-terre* for when I work late. I stay here in the week. I have a country pad in Surrey.'

'Good, we're making progress. Presumably you have children?' *And a wife*, but she decided to hold that back for a little more. He'd already flatly denied it, which if it turned out to be a lie, was a deal-breaker. Being able to lie, while looking someone in the eyes was a line Harriet wouldn't cross again. Not since the man she'd been seeing in the first year at university who'd also been dating at least three other women, and had denied it, vehemently, on a number of occasions until she caught him red-handed, with another girlfriend at the student union bar.

Ugh.

He nodded slowly. 'Two children. Boys. They're at boarding school in Sussex. It's not cheap. One of the reasons why I'm always working so hard.'

She didn't dislike him for that. It was, after all, an admirable quality to give one's children a good education. 'And who else lives with you in this Surrey home?' She stared him directly in the eyes.

He looked at the floor. 'Shall we get some more wine?'

At seven o'clock in the morning? 'I don't want more wine. I want answers. I know you've denied you're married once, but I'm asking you again: are you married?'

'Separated. Practically like siblings. Different bedrooms. Have done for years.'

Harriet felt the hot rage building up as her face heated and the blood rushed in her ears. The hurt, betrayal, her wasted time at investing herself, her affection, her hope that this would become something more, something that may, one day, lead to a family, all combined in her stomach.

She rushed to the bathroom, clutching her stomach and was almost sick in the sink. Her stomach tensed with anguish, pain at Robert's lies and at her own naivety for not following her gut instinct much sooner.

Relieved she wasn't still naked and in bed, she collected her handbag from the floor. At least she'd used protection, becoming pregnant among this great galloping mess was the last thing she needed. She walked to the door.

He ran ahead, blocking her exit. 'Please, hear me out. We are separated. She doesn't—'

'If you're about to say she doesn't understand you, save your breath. Do you think I arrived with the morning's sunrise?' The betrayal still stung but her rage was overtaking it.

'It's true. She doesn't understand me.'

She tried to push him aside, but he remained resolutely solid. 'Are you going to keep me here against my will, or are you going to let me leave? Or would you prefer I tell your wife about our assignation?'

The colour drained his face and he stood open-mouthed.

'As I thought.' She nodded. 'Siblings my elbow.' So predictable. Why, after how he'd behaved maturely, treating her like a princess in so many ways, would he now turn out to be a total toad. *Men, they're so predictably disappointing.* Couldn't he have at least been original with his bloody deception? She pushed him aside, opened the door and ran out to the street. Worried for a moment he'd follow, she ran a few hundred yards away, jumped into a taxi, giving her address.

And it wasn't until her breathing returned to normal that she realised how wretchedly stupid and gullible she felt. Disgusted with herself at being so easily taken in, for not seeing what was in front of her eyes all the time, she arrived home, poured herself a large glass of wine, even though it was eight a.m., drank it, repeated this a few times, while taking deep breaths and feeling absolutely wretched, stupid and idiotic, and then called Sophie. 'You were right,' she began.

'Was I? About what? I usually am.' Sophie laughed.

'Robert *was* bloody well married. As you warned me.' Harriet shook her head. 'How could I be so bloody stupid?'

'Do you want me to come round?'

'I'll be fine. I am fine. Bit shocked.' The betrayal hurt most.

'Sure? I can be in a cab and there within the hour. I'll tell work it's a family emergency.'

Harriet looked at herself in the mirror, her make-up was streaked, her face blotchy and red from crying in the taxi. She felt somewhat like a family emergency, but she didn't want anyone to see this mess, her shame for being so swept along by Robert's surface charms. 'Can we talk on the phone instead?'

'That, I can definitely do.' Sophie waited for Harriet to set the conversational topic. This was an all too well rehearsed routine when one of them had been let down by a man and the other would be there to catch the other, in whatever way they needed most.

'At least I can move on now,' Harriet began. 'No more hanging around.'

'Dive straight back in, is what I say. Fishing in the dating pond.'

'Maybe I'll give Dad's suggestion a go?' She shrugged. 'I'm shrugging BTW.'

Sophie laughed. 'Sure you don't want me to come round?'

Harriet shook her head. 'No one deserves to see me looking like this. Besides, I must go to work.' Shower to wash off the sadness and guilt, cleaned teeth to get rid of the red stains from all the wine. *I'll be fine.*

'Ring in sick.'

Harriet shook her head. 'I need to keep busy. This is helping.' She wiped a tear from her cheek.

A pause, and then, 'Didn't your dad have some eligible bachelors he wanted to push your way?'

Harriet rolled her eyes. '*Dozens* by all accounts.' Saying it filled her with dread.

'So maybe give them a try?'

'Perhaps.' She bit the inside of her cheek, not wanting to say what she was thinking: getting to know a man, putting herself out there, laying herself bare to a man, sleeping with him for the first time, all of which she found terrifying. The thought of doing it again and again, running along beside them, thinking he was on the same track, and then being told out of the blue, sorry it wasn't working, or that he was married. Harriet felt completely unequal to it.

'Chin up,' Sophie said.

'I'm staring at the ceiling.' Harriet looked down and poured more wine down her throat, the taste combined with the thrill of doing so at this early hour and no one being able to castigate her was quite addictive.

Chapter 25

'I don't know what to do.' Jason arrived home.

'What?' Pete asked. 'Not another one?'

Jason, feeling dejected, nodded. Another fake client meeting. They'd email him, even speak on the phone and arrange to meet, and wouldn't turn up. He'd wasted days on these over the last few weeks.

Ever since the publicity from the two celebrity weddings, there had been such a thing as bad publicity.

His social media followers had increased by tens of thousands each week. At first he knew everyone who followed him, but now that was impossible.

'Can't you take payment from them?' Pete asked.

'Before they ask me to arrange their wedding?' Jason shook his head. 'No. It's not how you do things.'

'So, what are you going to do?'

'Block up the letter box for a start.'

'How would that help? The deliveries will still come here.'

Jason pinched the bridge of his nose, closing his eyes. 'At least the packages wouldn't get inside the house.'

Over the last few weeks he'd been delighted to open packages including a dead rat, a dead bird and what he hoped was a dog or cat poo.

'When did the last one arrive?' Pete asked.

It had arrived that morning, two male dolls holding hands with a note that read: 'Adam and Eve not Adam and Steve'.

Jason felt his fists clenching involuntarily. 'Today.'

Pete stood behind him, leaning his head on Jason's back.

Jason involuntarily relaxed.

'What was it?' Pete asked quietly.

Jason shook his head. 'Doesn't matter. Shall I tell the police again?'

'Why?'

'So they can do something this time.' He'd reported it to the police who'd said that as the packages didn't pose an immediate threat to life, they couldn't prioritise it. Yet. Jason hadn't told Pete all the details because he knew how upset Pete would become, having been mercilessly bullied at school.

'Can't do any harm,' Pete said.

'They basically told me I had to wait until it was a firebomb or anthrax until they'd do something.' Jason felt himself tensing up again.

'Did you tell them it was a hate crime?'

'I explained about Extra Weddings and the publicity we'd got.'

'And?'

Jason turned.

Worry clouded Pete's face, as he'd expected. 'Shall we move to Mum's?'

'I'm not letting these people chase me out of my home. I understand if you want to move out.'

Pete shook his head. 'I'm staying with you. But let's sort out the letter box asap.'

'I'm doing it now.' Jason had put it off because it had been a while since the last-but-one package, but after this morning's delivery he knew he needed to do something.

'Now-now?'

Jason left the room. 'Now-now.'

He blocked up the letter box in the door, and installed one on a pole, at the far end of the drive, with their house number clearly visible.

Jason continued with his work, keeping an ear open for the door or letter box, but nothing came all day. Perhaps he'd moved past the worst of it.

That evening over dinner, Pete said, 'Why aren't you eating?'

Jason had moved his food around his plate but hadn't eaten much. His stomach was tight with worry as he thought about tomorrow's deliveries. He had parcels regularly arriving with samples for clients: wedding favours, flowers, chocolates, samples of fabrics used to decorate... They arrived most days. Perhaps he should have set up a PO box address, but he'd not had the time nor expected to face this.

'Some days I wish I was back at the old place.' Jason pushed the plate away.

'Come on, you don't really mean that.'

'At least their homophobia was against some clients, whereas this is about me. My business. Feels more personal.'

Pete stood, cleared up the plates and offered Jason more wine.

Maybe it would help him sleep. He'd struggled for the last few weeks. Busyness and the constant worry about what he'd find on the doormat, meant he was struggling to get three or four hours decent sleep a night. He felt as if he'd aged a decade in the last month.

'Small one for me,' Jason said with resignation.

'Isn't trolling illegal now too?' Pete poured the wine, led the way into the living room.

'Depends.' Jason sat on the sofa, with Pete leaning against him.

'On what?'

'What is it, and besides, half the accounts you can't track back to a person. They have no email address linked, and if they do, it's a fake one. No profile pictures, always with a long string of numbers in the profile name. It's like Whack-a-Mole.'

'Has the trolling stopped?' Pete asked.

'No. But I'm better at dealing with it.' At first he'd found it so unbelievable that actual human beings, hiding behind their computer screens, could think and say those terrible things. So he'd bitten back. Replied to them, trying to argue, to reason, to explain why they were wrong.

213

'I can't believe some people can be so wrong, so full of hate,' he said now.

'The internet.' Pete shrugged.

'I know, but it's so stupid. Why would someone think that two men or women getting married in the UK affects their marriage to someone who lives in...' He checked his phone. '...Arkansas.' Jason wasn't completely sure where that was, except in the US.

'How are you dealing with them now?' Pete asked.

He'd hoped he would have learned from his social media pickle with Lux-Lodge Hotels, but Jason couldn't become a different person. His natural tendency when faced with wrong was to try and fix it, correct the person, reason with them.

'Do not engage,' Jason said.

'That's it?'

'Block, ignore, block again.'

'So that sounds like an improvement.'

Jason smiled, determined not to let this take over their evening. 'It is. I'm fine. They can't hurt me. Sticks and stones and all that.' Jason pulled Pete closer, hugging him tightly, kissed his cheek. How and why would anyone think what they had was anything other than love? 'See what's on?'

There was a silence. Jason knew that names couldn't hurt him in the same ways as physical violence, but being on the receiving end of such hatred, against him and him alone, was starting to take its toll. He was questioning whether he should carry on with Extra Weddings or just walk away, move into events that weren't so controversial as same-sex marriage ceremonies. A book launch, or a new car maybe. Nice, unemotional corporate events.

'Right.' Pete switched the TV on.

Jason stared at the moving images, not really paying attention as he tried to push to the back of his mind the messages he'd received today on social media. He could screenshot them, post them publicly, but then he'd be banned for sharing hate speech –

even though it wasn't his messages he'd be sharing. Even trying to have a reasoned debate had got him suspended a few times. He needed the socials to publicise his work. Without them, he'd struggle to reach new customers.

He switched his phone off and put it face down on the sofa's arm. Wasn't it much simpler as a teenager in the nineties – no internet, no mobile phones, and when they had arrived, they did nothing but text and call. And now, everyone has a pocket computer, with access to everything and everyone in the world. Which had been wonderful, but it also meant the madness, hatred, abuse, could come from everywhere and anywhere.

Pete had fallen asleep, leaning on Jason's chest. He stroked his hair, kissing it gently.

The only way to beat these trolls is not to feed them. Do. Not. Engage. Block and move on. Jason resolved to try this, but it didn't make receiving the abusive messages any easier.

Chapter 26

That evening, Steve video-called Mel. She'd made dinner, Lily was in her room reading and Thomas using his PlayStation in his room. It was almost as if all they wanted her for was food and shelter.

No, it had been a long day, she was tired and overwrought.

So seeing Steve's face and name on her phone wasn't met with much enthusiasm. 'I've had a long, shitty day, is this urgent?'

'Nice to hear from you too,' he replied, standing in front of a mirror and wardrobe she'd not seen before.

Mel poured wine, having resisted so far, but this, she felt, would warrant some. 'Sorry. Are you calling to ask about changing days for the kids? 'Cos if you are can you please just not? I don't have the head space to deal with that right now. They're your kids as much as mine, and you should stick to the pre-arranged times for you to have them. It's only fair—'

'Sorry to interrupt, but if you'll let me get a word in, I'm not calling about the kids. Well, not directly anyway. I've been thinking about stuff.'

This ought to be interesting.

'If I could do it again differently, I would. Except I can't.' He stared unblinkingly at her.

'Do what differently?'

'Husband, father, everything.' He coughed, looked away for a moment then continued: 'So what I'm saying is, will you take me back?'

'To live here? I thought you were at Sally's place.'

'She threw me out. I'm in a hotel.'

Aha, so I'm the final choice available, in extremis, so to speak. 'Are you asking to move in, or to get back together?'

'I've always loved you.'

What? 'Say that again, will you?' It was at least something that he admitted to always loving her. But it definitely felt a touch too late to be having this particular conversation.

'I have always loved you,' Steve said slowly. 'And I know I took you for granted. Stupid of me.'

'Right...' She sounded unsure, but wasn't hating him admitting he'd been wrong and that he had always loved her. She wished he'd shown her in other ways, better ways than just buying everything. Spending time with her and helping with the kids would have been a start.

'You were there in the background making sure everything ran smoothly while I went out and earned the money. I didn't know you were so unhappy for so long.'

To be fair, neither did Mel. She'd got used to feeling nothing much. Which, once she had put it behind her, she saw had been dissatisfaction, unhappiness, restrictions of a life half lived. 'It wasn't *all* your fault,' she said.

'It was.'

There was a silence and Mel wished she'd been recording the call so she could listen again. It didn't feel real, Steve coming to her and practically laying himself prostrate in front of her, admitting his failings and telling her he'd always loved her.

Steve bit his bottom lip, took a deep breath, staring into her eyes. 'Please will you take me back?'

Take him back. Take? Him? Back? Is this a dream? Am I imagining this? He puts me through all this heartache to leave me and now this? She controlled her breathing as she considered this for a moment. She'd been with him most of her adult life and, from observation, didn't think people, especially Steve, could or would ever really change. A small admission of guilt here, or a proclamation of love there. But deep down, Steve would still be the same workaholic Steve, and she would quickly revert back to doing everything else. And resenting him for it.

'Well,' he said, 'what do you say?' He stared at her with large brown eyes, filled with contrition.

Oh God, he's not going to cry is he? She swallowed, chose her words carefully. 'I will *always* be here for you. You can *always* call, I'll see you. But as a friend. Only. We will *always* have the kids in common.'

'I love you. Always have. Losing you has made me realise what I took for granted from you. I'm an idiot.'

Mel bit her bottom lip. This was a lot to take on for a Wednesday night. 'An idiot is a bit much. Be fair on yourself. There were two of us in the marriage. I could have spoken to you.'

Steve shook his head. 'Wouldn't have listened, would I? 'Cos I'm an—'

She put her hand up to stop him, she couldn't bear him repeating that he was an idiot. Again. 'If you were still with Sally, would we be having this conversation?' She suspected what it all boiled down to was that he couldn't bear the thought of being single, without a woman by his side.

'She was a mistake.'

'You wanted to leave me, for her. What happened? Had you temporarily lost control of your senses? Did your brain put itself onto low power mode and your dick took charge?'

'Course not.' He sounded contrite, and his face looked it too. Steve's face always told the truth, even if his mouth was lying. 'I fucked up. Massively.'

She thought for a moment. Steve was obviously hurting, flailing probably, thrashing about for something to blame, for some way he could fix his mistakes. But sadly, she didn't think this was the way to do it. Besides, she knew she no longer loved him.

'What do you think?' he asked.

'I'm thinking.' *How to let you down gently.* 'You're sure Sally doesn't want you back?'

'She won't return my calls. She put all my stuff in black bin bags and left them on the lawn.'

'How hard have you tried to speak to her? If you want to fix the past, maybe you need a different future to the past you messed up with me.'

'That's a no, isn't it?' Desperation tinged his voice.

'You loved this woman. You left me for her. You left your children for her. And now, suddenly you want me back. You must understand why I'm being a bit cautious.'

Steve cried, tears flowed down his cheeks and he wiped them with his sleeve.

'The definition of insanity is repeating the same thing and expecting a different outcome.' She kept her tone as bright as possible, given the circumstances.

Steve was not a crier. In their whole marriage, she'd seen him cry twice: once at his mum's funeral and once was something to do with football which Mel didn't even pretend to understand.

Steve's quiet sobs grew louder. 'I'm so sorry,' he said between deep breaths.

'Are you thinking of taking your own life?' she asked calmly. She'd done an online course about this, and apparently mentioning suicide did not make people more likely to do it. It meant she could really understand where Steve's head was.

A loud sniff, and then, 'No. Don't be daft.'

Sweet relief washed through her. Steve's crying had really knocked her off-kilter and the last thing she wanted was for him to do anything stupid on the basis of her rejection. 'I'm not going to say yes or no to you now. But I think you should reflect on how someone can go from being the person who makes you leave your children and wife, to someone you can happily walk away from, within the space of a few months.'

'You think I should give it another go with Sally?'

She nodded slowly. 'If you tried as hard with her as you are with me now, I don't think we'd be having this conversation. Much as I'm touched you'd like to try again.' But her feelings for

Steve were only that of a close friend, someone she'd brought up a family with.

Steve sniffed, blew his nose loudly on a tissue. 'You're probably right.' Another sniff, a cough and then, 'You don't mind if I give Sally a ring?'

'I'm telling you to do that. Although I'm flattered you want to try again, I think we both deserve better than being each other's second choice, don't you?' Mel felt that summed it up pretty well.

Steve chuckled quietly and nodded. 'I'll collect the kids on Friday night, if that's still okay?'

'Of course it's okay. You're their dad. Always will be.' *And my ex-husband. Always will be.*

'Sorry, got a bit emotional back there.' He laughed nervously.

'You know everyone still wants you in their lives, except differently from before.'

'Doesn't feel like it sometimes.' He looked glum, stuck his bottom lip out and shrugged.

'Well, they do. Me included. So you're stuck with me, all right?'

'Yep, look, gotta go.' A pause, and then, 'Thanks. Appreciate it.' He waved in the awkward way, with a smile that he'd used to give her when leaving for work every morning.

'See you Friday.' She ended the call feeling exhausted, as if she'd been fighting in a boxing ring for the last fifteen minutes.

She'd been fighting to maintain her independence, to not just fall back on what she and Steve knew, even if it wasn't the right decision.

She tidied the kitchen, turned off the TV as her eyes drooped closed.

Checking first on Lily, tucking her into bed, asking how her story was, she said, 'Dad will see you on Friday.'

'I like seeing him.'

'That's good.'

'I wish we did stuff like we do here.' She snuggled under the duvet.

'Like what?'

'Normal stuff, eating in his house. Watching TV.'

'What does he do with you and Thomas?'

'Pizza Hut, McDonald's, KFC.'

Mel kissed her good night, switched off the light. She'd talk to Steve about keeping their children amused with more than junk food. But it would wait for now.

Thomas's bedroom was lit with the TV screen as he'd disappeared into the world of the PlayStation.

Mel sat on his bed. 'Off.'

He pressed a button and the room fell into darkness, he turned on the bedside lamp.

'Do you enjoy seeing Dad?'

Thomas shrugged, sitting up in bed.

'What's that supposed to mean? He's your dad, isn't he?'

Thomas nodded. 'Doesn't feel like it.'

Mel frowned. 'Like what?'

'He takes us out to eat, bowling, ice skating, roller-skating, activities. But he, I dunno… We don't hang out together. Like this.'

'Sleep.' Mel kissed his cheek, he pulled away.

'Really?'

'Really.' She could almost feel him as he moved away from being the little boy to a young man, feeling embarrassed by her and not wanting mummy kisses. It broke her heart a little, but that's what happens with kids.

Undressing in her bedroom, it occurred to her, she understood how much Steve must be struggling to suddenly have to begin parenting, rather than providing. This was probably linked to their earlier conversation and Mel felt sure he wasn't asking to get back together for the right reasons. He was, she admitted, very sad and confused, which she wanted to support him with.

Brushing her teeth, she stared at her reflection. Tired, old, clueless.

Shaking her head, she said, 'No way.' No way did Steve really want her back. And her heart had moved on too. Being single wasn't so bad really. Although having someone to cuddle up to at night wouldn't be bad either…

The brief thought had morphed into a vague dream of going back to university and finishing her English degree. Even as a dream it felt impossibly unreachable. As she climbed into bed, reaching over for her book on the bedside cabinet, she considered how on earth was she supposed to fit reading proper books, studying and writing essays in between work, the children, Steve and God only knows what else life would throw at her?

Mel managed to read three pages before she fell asleep, the book folded face down on the duvet.

Chapter 27

Harriet stood outside South Kensington Tube station.

Her father had shown her pictures of Sebastian, which was why she'd agreed to the date in the first place. But she wanted to be sure he lived up to his photo in real life, so if she saw someone holding the required red rose, and he had a face like a bag of spanners, she'd quietly slip back into the Tube station.

A grey-coated man appeared on the other side of the busy road, carrying a red rose. He ran across, darting between the slowing traffic as the lights changed. He was tall, with thin willowy limbs and light blond hair styled into a floppy centre parting.

His face lit up as he saw her carrying a yellow rose.

Too late to leave now.

As he strode closer, she decided there was no need to slip away.

His jaw was pleasingly square, covered in the requisite beard of every man that age, blue-green eyes and a friendly smile completed her assessment: he did not, in any way, resemble a bag of spanners.

'Harriet!' He held out a large hand.

She shook it and thought perhaps her father's suggestion of dating some eligible bachelor sons of his friends was maybe not the worst idea she'd ever heard. 'Sebastian!'

'You can call me Seb. Better for when you're shouting it in the throes of passion!' He grinned and winked.

God, did he just say that? As a joke? Harriet chuckled nervously.

'Is it Harriet, or Haz, or Harry maybe? I was bonking a nurse called Harry in my first year, such great fun. Sorry, shouldn't have mentioned my ex. Well, she wasn't really an ex, we only saw each other without clothes. Wanted to keep it all on the down low, you know?'

And he's a talker too. At least I won't have to make all the conversation. That's something anyway. 'Shall we?' She nodded towards the Victoria and Albert Museum where they'd agreed to see an art exhibition. Her father had said Sebastian was something of an art buff and hence suggested they meet there for the date, before eating in a Polish restaurant next to South Kensington station.

Seb reached out, grabbed her hand, strode across the road, holding up his hand to stop traffic as it screeched to a standstill while they threaded their way between cars to the entrance of the V&A.

Harriet reclaimed her hand. 'Thanks.' She bit her bottom lip.

'Gets the blood pumping, don't you think?' He nodded back towards the road.

'I prefer a strong coffee.' Harriet strode up the steps into the building. This was going to be a long evening.

For someone who apparently enjoyed art, Seb chose a display of pre-historic artefacts and spent the whole time commenting on the drawings of cave people in scanty loincloths. He wasn't so much offensive, as very puerile. He darted from one display case to the next not reading anything, simply laughing and beckoning Harriet over to share his next hilarious joke.

'Where now?' he asked.

'Do you have to be somewhere?' *Perhaps it would offer an escape route from this date.*

'I'm on a late shift.'

'At the hospital?' Harriet asked, wondering why he'd not mentioned this before. Her father had certainly said Sebastian was a doctor a few times.

'UCLH. Second year doctor in training. I'm specialising in cardiothoracic, I'm practically a surgeon.'

Harriet knew if he was in his first or second year's training he'd be as specialised as a French hypermarket selling everything from brie to bicycles. He'd also be as near to being a surgeon as she was. She raised her eyebrows. 'When do you start your shift?'

'I'll check my watch.' He angled it towards Harriet.

Of course it's a Rolex. Mentally she rolled her eyes, wishing she could beam herself up and reappear at home. This was how she'd chosen to spend her precious Saturday. All for her father.

'Two,' he said finally. 'It's very accurate, this watch.'

She smiled tightly, determined not to rise to his Rolex bait. That gave them over an hour.

'Do you mind if we eat first, and then see your paintings?' He grinned.

Harriet felt sure that face had got away with, not quite murder, but very near, on numerous occasions. His grin was one of confidence become arrogance, cosseted by the sure knowledge his family could buy him out of any problems he ever encountered.

'Of course,' Harriet replied tightly.

He grabbed her hand and led her away.

'I've a table booked at Pierogi's,' she said to the back of his head.

He shook his head. 'Dumplings and lots of pork. I don't think so.'

Harriet would later castigate herself for not objecting sooner, but at the time she didn't have the energy, and her reasoning went that if she played along with Seb, the sooner they'd eat, the sooner he'd go and the sooner she'd return alone to her 'odd looking paintings' as Seb had described them, also known as Expressionism.

They ended up at a tiny restaurant accessed via some elaborate secret door knock, where the waiting staff behaved as if they were doing you a favour simply by being there.

Seb ordered a foamed something followed by a black ink something else. Harriet listened as he explained how his dad had helped set this place up.

Harriet chose the simplest and largest thing on the menu, having seen waiters carrying enormous white oval plates containing tiny portions and reckoning they couldn't bugger about too much with spag bol.

'Do you enjoy food?' Seb asked after a particularly rambling account of how he'd got into medical school, involving his parents, a laboratory named after his grandfather and an incident with a Bunsen burner during the sixties.

Harriet had, during the whole interminable interlude, drifted off and been imagining what Sophie would say about this date. Sophie had been on her fair share of terrible dates, having been Tinder-ing furiously for the last few years. She had, at one point, told Harriet she'd reached the end of Tinder.

'I'm really looking for someone who enjoys it,' Seb said now.

Harriet had drifted off, smiled, asked, 'What?'

'Food.' He cut enthusiastically into whatever sat in the middle of his bath-sized plate.

'Yes, I enjoy it. Clearly you do too.'

'Do you cook? Me, I could burn a hard-boiled egg if I tried. Not that I do. Try, that is.' He guffawed at his joke.

For the first time in a long while, Harriet found herself interested in the conversation. She leaned forwards, twirling great swirls of pasta and tomatoey meat sauce on her fork. 'Surely it comes in handy since you're away from home studying to be a doctor?'

'Surgeon. The doctor's block is catered. I'm staying there for next year. Special dispensation.' He tapped his nose knowingly.

Special dispensation for being a useless article. 'What made you agree to meet me?' She was curious, more to see if it amounted to anything more than being instructed to do so by his father. It seemed his parents oversaw pretty much everything Seb did. She wondered if he had to report back to them weekly.

'Mother said I ought to start searching. I am twenty-seven, so...' He shrugged.

He looked much younger than his years and Harriet wondered why it had taken him so long to reach his second year of medical school. She feared asking this would result in another convoluted story, which she neither had the time nor the patience to endure. 'What would you say is your perfect date?' She felt it less on the nose than asking what he wanted in a girlfriend.

He thought for a moment, snapped his fingers to summon a waiter. 'This is soft. Is it meant to be soft?'

'It's *purée de pomme*. It's intended to be soft.'

'I'd like a new one.'

The waiter took a deep breath. 'It will be the same, sir. I—'

'Look, I don't need a lecture, I want some more of the purée stuff. All right?'

The waiter smiled tightly, bowed and left.

Seb shook his head. 'They need to be told who's in charge. I don't think he knows Dad's the reason why this place exists. Why he's got a bloody job.'

Harriet had used to behave like this with waiting staff, until her father had admonished her *very* severely, suggesting she needed something to do with her time other than partying and living off his allowance. 'You need to understand what hard work is,' he'd said, although he was still given to rudeness at restaurants.

'This is a pretty perfect date,' Seb said. 'Bit of culture, bit of nosh, and then perhaps a bit of how's your father.' He winked.

Harriet closed her eyes. *Oh God. I can't bear this. I should walk out and tell him he's an unspeakably unbearable human being.* But she couldn't bear to be as rude as him. Glancing at her watch she reckoned she'd have another ten minutes before he left.

'Not that I'm expecting that this afternoon,' Seb said winking again and grinning like an idiot. 'I shall be nose to the grindstone, knee deep in patients.'

Is he going to ask me what my perfect date would be, she wondered.

'Silence.

'I went to Windsor Boy's of course. Otherwise our fathers shouldn't know one another.'

'Did you enjoy it? Dad hated boarding, but said overall it was—'

'Character building.'

'Yes.' Her father said public school had given him a confidence he'd never had elsewhere. Plus a determination to succeed.

'They almost flung me into the local comp. Could you imagine?' He shivered. 'Mixing with the hoi polloi. I'd have been the only one to do so at medical school. Well, unless you include old Dustbin Kev, and he doesn't count. He's rather the exception not the rule.'

Dustbin Kev, dare I ask why?

'His father works for the refuse collection service at the city council. Couldn't believe how much those men earn, it's far above market rate as far as I can see. Literally throwing money into the dustbin.' He finished his food, letting the cutlery clatter onto the plate. Summoning a waiter, he said, 'Could you get a shift on with the dessert please, only I've got a busy afternoon saving lives.' He winked to Harriet once the waiter left.

At the time Harriet hadn't accepted her father's assessment of why she needed to get herself a job. But Seb was clear evidence of what could have happened otherwise. He'd clearly never done anything for himself in his whole life.

She didn't pay attention to what he said during dessert, simply smiling and nodding while his mouth indicated he was still talking. About himself, of course.

Finally he paid, making a big show of his platinum credit card, hugged her as they stood. 'It's been lovely. I knew it wouldn't be as bad as I'd thought.' He chuckled. 'I've really enjoyed talking to you.'

Harriet nodded. During the whole interminable two and a half hours, he'd seldom asked questions of her. It had been like being on a chat show hosted by and about Seb.

He left after promising he'd be in touch, having begged her to exchange numbers. Having ploughed through the whole terrible date, she felt it foolish to withhold her number and cause a scene. She planned to simply ignore his calls, sending a message to him via their fathers that she'd gone off the idea of dating.

She almost gave him the wrong number, but, showing the first bit of intelligence since they'd met, he rang her to check, and they smiled as she ignored her ringing phone in her handbag.

How they'd laughed. Her cheeks had been stiff with a fixed grin all morning.

The waiter asked if she needed anything, collecting the receipt and bill.

Harriet held his shirt sleeve. 'Can I say, I'm sorry about how he spoke to you? I would say he's my friend, but really, he's not.'

The waiter shrugged. 'We're used to it, serving food like this.'

Harriet left, checking Seb wasn't about. As she sat on the Tube back to her apartment, she saved his number in her phone, naming it 'Unbearable Seb' and blocked it.

Her father asked how the date had gone and Harriet said, 'He doesn't want a girlfriend, he wants someone to look after him while giving him sex on tap.'

Her father began to say something and Harriet said, 'Think very carefully about what you say next, please.'

'Will you see William? I've promised his mother. She's so excited to put to one side the question of him being... a poof who's rather too preoccupied with his appearance. Somewhat... like a peacock.'

Harriet sighed. *Poof.* 'We don't say that word now. Besides, would it be so bad if Wills were?' She'd had many gay friends at university and enjoyed their company. It was the taking over of marriage and what it meant to be a man and a woman that she couldn't agree with.

'Not as such, no. But his mother has rather got her heart set on a traditional setup for him.'

'I shall meet him.' It couldn't be any worse than her date with Seb.

–

Harriet and Wills had been corresponding by text in the fortnight leading up to their meeting. Harriet had insisted, since she felt sure if she'd done so with Seb she'd have cancelled the date.

Satisfied Wills was neither a snob nor in search of a cook, cleaner and sex doll in human form, by dint of his polite texts, constant stream of questions about how she was and what she'd been doing, Harriet agreed to meeting.

They met outside the cinema, and Harriet was impressed at Will's muscular physique. Dark brown hair, a neatly trimmed beard on a Disney hero-esque square jaw plus brown eyes with the longest lashes she'd ever seen, had her sure the date would go well.

They chatted about the weather, their journeys, the film, while queuing.

He declined popcorn, soft drink or sweets, offering to buy Harriet some, which she thought generous.

They sat in near silence throughout the film, which Harriet took as a good sign since watching while someone talked over the film was one of her pet hates.

As they left she found herself wanting to spend more time with him, in complete contrast to her date with Seb, which she took as a good sign.

'Do you want to grab something to eat?' she asked.

'Yes.' A brief check of his watch.

'Do you need to be somewhere?'

'I'm teaching later, but it's… later, so…' He shrugged and smiled.

Perfectly straight white teeth. His eyes looked kind too. Harriet felt sure he'd make a good father, especially if his pert behind was anything to go by. She'd allowed herself a little peek at the cinema when he'd walked to the gents' loos.

And he's a teacher. She didn't remember her father telling her. 'What do you teach? Primary, secondary?'

'Body shaping.'

She frowned. Didn't sound like a teacher she'd heard of.

'In a gym. I'm a PT too.'

'PT?'

'Personal trainer.'

'Dad said you're a model.' He looked like a model. She was sure she'd seen his face before, which was why he felt so familiar. Definitely the face of some designer sunglasses. Or jeans maybe. Both perhaps…

'I am.' He gestured for her to lead. 'Where are we eating?'

We, she liked that. Giving her the choice and him going along with it. This was looking up, as every minute passed.

She chose a pizza chain and he agreed, without blinking. She could get used to this.

Having ordered, she looked up. 'What about you?'

The waitress stood eagerly by the table.

'Can I have a large bottle of still mineral water? Please?'

Manners, nice.

'Anything else?' the waitress asked.

Will handed her the menu, shaking his head.

The waitress left.

'Aren't you eating?'

'I am. Not this stuff.' He removed a silver sachet from his backpack. 'With water, it's a complete meal.'

Harriet inspected it with scepticism. It promised to be a complete meal nutrient- and vitamin-wise. It came in three delicious flavours, could be made by adding water, or if one felt particularly adventurous, milk.

She handed it back. 'Why?'

'It's easier. When I'm between jobs, I can eat it and then I don't have to worry.'

'Tell me about this class you teach at the gym.' *God, this is starting to feel like hard work.*

He explained how long it lasted, how many people usually joined, how long he'd been teaching it, why it was useful for removing fat and building muscle. After what felt like an hour, but was in fact long enough for her pizza to arrive, he said, 'What do you like doing?'

Saying shopping, make-up and partying felt a little shallow, having listened to his impressive dedication to all things health orientated. 'Not much really.'

'You look very pretty.'

She smiled. *He really is very handsome.*

'Do you go to the gym?'

She shook her head. 'I used to do this gymnastics thing...'

'Right. I like the ropes. And jumping.' His eyes lit up.

His face was definitely one a luxury brand would pay handsomely to advertise its goods.

'When did you last do it?' he asked, adding his white powder to the water and stirring it.

'Five.'

'Years ago? Equipment has moved on so much since then. It's all linked to your personal stats.'

'Five, I was five. It was something I did as a child.'

'Right.' He sipped the milkshake concoction.

She cut her pizza, offered him a slice. 'Sure?'

He shook his head. 'Can't.' A large hand rubbed his flat and no doubt hard stomach.

Abs to die for. She reckoned he'd look splendid naked. Like those Greek statues she'd seen at the British Museum, all sharp lines and bulges in all the right places.

'What do you like to watch on TV?' she asked, desperate for something to talk about.

'Whatever's on at the gym. Usually music videos.'

They did which gyms he preferred and why, the various food supplements he could have used and why he'd settled on this one. Then, in a last-gasp attempt to rescue the evening because he was so damned pretty Harriet couldn't believe he could be so dull, she asked, 'What did you think of the film?'

'Nice. I liked it.' He checked his watch. 'Look, do you mind if I leave money because I've gotta go?' He mimed being on an exercise bike, put money on the table, kissed her cheek and left.

She was about to say he didn't need to pay since he'd not eaten anything, but he'd gone. She allowed herself one last look at his pert behind in tight jeans and muscular back in a T-shirt as he walked outside. He waved and appeared as if he'd stepped out of a Hollywood film. Impeccably dressed, groomed, in such good shape. But sadly, that was all he had to him.

Harriet hadn't been convinced of the received wisdom that people were either clever or attractive. Although, now she thought of it, her school friends did confirm it. However, at Cambridge she'd been surrounded by people who disproved the theory. Perhaps, she reflected as she left, it was because she'd simply never met anyone as strikingly handsome as Will.

She didn't mind being left to talk, but she needed something to work with. Will seemed to drift through life thinking everything was *nice* and *okay*, and never seeking to get underneath the surface of anything.

She rang Sophie as she walked to the nearest Tube station. Harriet had, she now realised, somewhat marched herself and Sophie up the hill of hope having seen Will's picture and conducted a thoroughly pleasant text conversation beforehand. This made it much harder, when confronted with him in the flesh, to accept he wasn't as he seemed.

'And?' Sophie asked, excitement in her voice.

'I may sleep with him.'

'What was he like?'

'Movie star, CGI good-looking.'

'Definitely bed him I'd say.'

'If only to confirm what I believe.'

'Which is?' Sophie asked.

'That the best thing about him is his body.'

'It's a good start, surely?'

'Not if he has all the personality of an Electrovax 330.'

Silence, as her friend obviously considered this.

'Are you still there?' Harriet asked.

'Definitely bed him. When a man is so buff yet thin personality-wise, it's the only answer.'

Harriet sighed. 'I don't think I'm really sure of the question to which he's the answer.' She'd had enough of dating. Of following her father's suggestion.

'Is it possible to date a man your father suggests for you?'

Harriet laughed. 'I shall dip my toe back into Tinder. Are you going to join me?'

'If I must, I must.'

'That's settled, I shall tell Dad I've had enough of his match-making.'

'Fancy going to Belle's on the King's Road?'

'Now?'

Before, Harriet would have said yes, but that was when she had nowhere to be and nothing to do all day every day. Since being something of a woman with responsibilities, she'd left behind her days of practically living at the club with a group of other privileged twenty-somethings unimpeded by the usual constraints of work and responsibilities.

'Saturday?' Harriet asked.

'If you want. Although we may have a date.'

'We'll bring them.' Harriet smiled at the image of her and Sophie bringing their Tinder dates to Belle's, the members-only club where one could dance until daylight with the mid and low list celebrities of the moment.

'I've got to go,' Sophie said. 'I'm expecting a call.'

'Who from?'

'From whom…' Sophie laughed. 'That would be telling.'

'Love you.' Harriet ended the call. If Sophie thought she'd duck out of their Tinder pact, she was going to be very much mistaken. Although based on her friend's secrecy and tone, she reckoned Sophie would soon be whisked off to Planet Boyfriend, which would hopefully be orbited by the Moon of Fiancé and soon end up within the Galaxy of Husband.

God, why is it so hard to find a decent eligible man?

She threw change into the guitar case of the busker outside the Tube station, ducked inside into the warmth and on her way home, sat on the train contemplating her evening.

Chapter 28

Jason looked at the time, he was due to meet Pete for dinner in ten minutes. And it took twenty to get there, making him… ten minutes late already.

He had a pile of invoices to send for work he'd done weeks ago, needed to place orders for flowers, wedding cars, photographers and menu options for at least six weddings.

I'll do the invoices, that way I'll have money to order the other parts.

He sent a message to Pete: *run l8, can u order 4 me pls x*

> **Pete**
> I'm here

> **Jason**
> c u soon x

No reply. No kiss either. Jason didn't have time to think about that. He started on the first invoice, checking the amounts once, twice, three times, making sure he'd used the right template and none of the words were underlined with squiggly red lines.

When he arrived at the restaurant, Pete was standing by the till and paying. 'You came, then?'

'I said I'd be late,' Jason said, taking Pete by the shoulders and pulling him in for a kiss.

Pete squirmed out and shook himself away. 'No you don't.'

'What's wrong?'

'Thanks,' Pete said to the cashier, then walked outside.

Jason followed. 'I was just coming. I wanted to have dinner with you.'

Pete pursed his lips, checking the time on his phone. 'You messaged me nearly an hour ago. It's fine. We just won't bother next time.'

'Don't be like that. Talk to me.'

'That's what we were meant to do earlier. Instead I ordered two pizzas, ate one, alone.'

'What happened to the other one? I'm starving.' Jason's stomach rumbled at the mention of food. He'd lived on black coffee all day, too busy to take a lunch break – he'd been running on caffeine and adrenaline for twelve hours.

Pete sighed, shook his head. 'They offered to put it in a box.'

'And?'

'I said they could keep it.'

'Why?'

'Because I wanted to. Because you weren't here to have a say. Because I wanted to deliberately do something that would piss you off.' Pete stared at him.

'Very adult.' Jason ran into the restaurant, asked if the spare pizza was still available.

'We threw it away,' the cashier said after checking in the kitchen.

It wasn't a big thing, but it was a thing, and as Jason felt hangry, it was not improving the situation.

Pete stood with his arms folded. 'And?'

'It's gone.'

'I'm going home.' Pete turned and walked away.

'Where are you going?'

'Home, I said. Or are you ignoring that too?'

'What's that meant to mean?' Jason asked, feeling both starving and frustrated at Pete's behaviour.

'We said we'd have dinner. A date night and you ignored it. You said you'd be here shortly, and turn up an hour later.' Pete shrugged.

'I'm working really hard to make Extra Weddings work.'

'Maybe you need to work a bit harder to make us work. You have time to organise everyone else's weddings, but not ours. When's the last time we talked about our big day?'

Jason couldn't remember. It had been before the trolling had started. Before Zane and B's wedding probably, when the workload had him up to his eyes every day. '*We* can do that tonight,' Jason offered.

'Too little, too late. I don't want to talk about getting married. You hardly see me, why would I want to marry someone who's never there?'

Wow. That hurt. Jason felt winded. 'I'm setting up a new business. It's basically me with some help here and there. It all rests on my shoulders. It needs to be right.' Surely Pete would understand that.

'I miss you. I miss the old Jason.'

'He's gone. I can't go back there. The nine to five Jason doesn't exist any more. I thought you wanted this for me.'

'I prefer that Jason. To this one. Sorry. There, I said it.' Pete leaned against the wall, looked to one side.

'I don't know what to say. I'm busting a gut here and you're saying, what, you want me to chuck it all in and get a normal job?'

Pete sighed, worried his bottom lip. 'What I also don't understand is why we've never got any money.'

All the more reason not to waste the pizza, but Jason didn't say it.

'How are you planning all these high-profile weddings and we have no money? Aren't they paying you?' Pete narrowed his eyes. 'It's a good job we've got my salary, is all I'm saying.'

It really wasn't all he was saying. Jason felt like crying with frustration. 'I have to pay the suppliers, the venue, the flowers, the car, so the clients don't need to worry. And then I add my mark-up on top.'

'Right. So where's this mark-up?'

'I haven't had time to invoice yet.' So basically they'd been paying out deposits for hotels, flowers, cars, catering for the clients, and hadn't yet received any money from the clients.

'Have any of them paid you?' Pete stared, open mouthed.

'A few sent me money before I invoiced. Look, when you have the choice of paying a deposit for your client's dream venue, or sending an invoice for a wedding you did eight weeks ago, it's always gonna be the first that wins.'

'Why?'

'Or the client loses out on their dream venue.'

'We're a gnat's chuff away from losing our house.'

'What?' Jason spluttered. 'How?'

'Money coming out of the account to pay for this hotel, that hotel, these flowers and sometimes there's not enough to cover the mortgage.'

'You should have told me.'

'I tried,' Pete said carefully.

'When?'

'A few weeks ago. You said it would be fine, money would come in soon.'

'You should have nagged me.' Jason couldn't believe this – his house, their house, they'd nearly lost it. This wasn't happening.

'I messaged you. Multiple times. Me nagging, and you'd have responded so well to that.' Pete gestured from Jason's head to feet twice. He shook his head and laughed.

'Am I that scary?'

'Sometimes,' Pete said in a small voice.

Jason felt even smaller. His heart was crushed, his blood ran cold. Obviously he was older and larger than Pete, but he never felt he wore the trousers in the relationship, it felt very much a relationship of equals. Or it had, up until now.

Jason looked at the ground, kicked the pavement. 'I'm sorry.'

Pete shrugged.

'Do you want me to walk away and get a normal job?' He would, if Pete wanted, if it meant they didn't argue like this again. If it meant he wouldn't make Pete feel too scared to speak to him.

'No.'

'So what do you want?'

'It's complicated.' Pete said, making eye contact for the first time since Jason had arrived.

'Tell me. Talk to me.' They had always discussed everything, no secrets, an open conversation about all their decisions, so why was this so different?

Pete swallowed. 'I wanted this for you. I really did. But if it means I never see you, and we have no money, then…' He blinked away a tear. It fell down his cheek. 'Selfish, right?'

'Not necessarily.' He held his hands out, gesturing for Pete to stand close, so they could hug, so he could press Pete's head onto his chest and he could kiss the top of it.

Pete stood still. 'I miss you.'

Jason worried they'd gone too far, that Pete had fallen out of love with him, that they were so far apart there was no way of finding their way back together again. 'Same here.' But it was only when he allowed himself time to stop that he realised how much.

'The old you. The you that used to tell me about your day every evening. The you who didn't spend most evenings in the study, working. The you who had enough money for us to not worry about it.'

'I miss him too. But I can't do this any other way.'

'Let's go home. There's a pizza in the freezer.' He looked up at Jason and smiled.

There was a glimmer of the old Pete, the grin, the joy, the love. 'I'll make it.'

'You've had a long day. I'll make it.' Pete scoffed. 'Make it — put it in the oven for twenty minutes.'

'Right.'

They drove home separately and Pete sorted out the pizza for Jason. He knew he had a dozen things to do, waiting for him upstairs in the study, but instead, he sat at the dining room table, eating his pizza, while Pete nibbled at a slice Jason had given him.

Instead of skulking off to finish some work once they went up to bed, Jason closed the study door, took Pete by the hand into their bedroom and said, 'Shall we talk about the wedding? *Our* wedding,' he said with feeling as he looked into Pete's eyes.

'We could. It's late though.' Pete narrowed his eyes, gesturing for Steve to come closer. He switched the light off and they kissed.

And then thoughts of weddings and debts and clients and overdrafts were gone. It was just Jason and Pete in their bedroom...

Afterwards, they slept like spoons, Jason the big spoon to Pete's small one.

Pete kissed Jason's hand, said, 'I love you. If I didn't, I'd just leave.'

The next morning, Jason emerged from the shower, Pete was still sleeping soundly. He placed a kiss on Pete's forehead. Something had to change, and it wasn't going to be his fiancé.

Chapter 29

Mel was at the employment agency, not quite with her tail between her legs, but definitely in need of gainful employment.

'You've got a face like a smacked arse. Nobody died, did they?' Dawn frowned.

'Not yet,' Mel said with a glum tone.

'I've plenty of cleaning work. Shall I book you in for this afternoon?' Dawn drummed her long red nails on the desk. Her hair was golden blonde with dark roots, her lipstick matched her nails.

'I've got three children, do you have any care work going?'

'Do I have any care work going?' She lifted a large box file from the floor, followed by three others.

'What are they?'

'I was gonna say they're all the requests for care work, but they're on my computer. They're three folders I've been meaning to sort through but haven't had the time.' She smirked. 'Do I have care work? Take your pick. Nursing home, rest home, domiciliary care, hospitals.'

'Don't I need qualifications?'

Dawn shook her head and put the folders to one side. 'I reckon you could do with something much better than that.'

'What?'

'A bloody good night out.'

'You remember I told you I'd just lost my job, well,' Mel raised her eyebrows, 'that.'

'Don't worry. Let's get this sorted, and then we'll go out.'

'Tonight?'

'Good a time as any.' Dawn shrugged, adjusting her gold necklace on top of a red and black leopard print blouse.

Mel didn't think she'd be able to say no, so said: 'Can I phone my son to let him know I won't be home to do the dinner?'

"Course. How old's he?'

'Fifteen.'

'He'll be chuffed he's got the night to himself. Teenaged lads in their bedrooms, best left alone, or so I've heard.' Dawn winked.

'What?' There was something about Dawn's over-familiarity that endeared her to Mel, meant she wanted to go along with whatever Dawn had suggested.

'Ring him then.'

She rang Thomas, explained she wouldn't be home, asked him to tell Lily to text when she was home, and said he could heat up something from the fridge.

'There's a pizza in the freezer. I'mma have that.' He said it as a statement more than a question.

'Have some salad with it.'

'Tomato and peppers are on it.'

'Tell Lily to let me know she's got home okay, will you?'

'*Or* you could text her,' Thomas didn't even try to keep the irritation out of his voice. 'Shall I tell Dad you're leaving us home alone?'

'Do you want him and Sally to babysit?'

A pause, and then: 'Nice one, Mum. Bye.' He ended the call.

'Sorted?' Dawn asked.

Mel nodded. 'Do I need any qualifications?'

'Your four kids,' Dawn said, 'are qualification enough. As long as you don't mind getting your hands dirty.'

'No fear,' Mel said and they completed the necessary paperwork.

That night Dawn took her to a wine bar — glass tables, chrome pillars, leather sofas — and said, 'What are you drinking?'

'White wine. Chardonnay, small glass,' Mel said, looking around and thinking she was very underdressed.

'Piss off.'

'Sorry, what?'

'When's the last time you went out?' Dawn perched on the arm of the sofa, swinging her legs.

Mel thought for a moment, narrowed her eyes in concentration, trying to remember when Steve had last taken her out. Or when she'd met some of the school mums for drinks. Or perhaps the village mums she'd gone out with. She swallowed. 'Does a barbecue count?'

'Does it bollocks! Out-out. Wine bar, pub, nightclub out. Sparkly top, full make-up, skinny jeans, heels, jewellery, getting home in a taxi and falling over in the hallway as you take off your shoes.'

Lily was ten, so she reckoned it had probably been sometime before she was born. Although Thomas would have been a little boy then, maybe she'd asked someone to babysit. 'Over ten—'

'Ten months ago?'

'Years,' Mel said quietly with shame she'd not considered before. 'Before Lily was born. I think I asked Steve to babysit and I went out with the girls from uni.'

'What did you study at uni?'

'I didn't finish. I dropped out. Pregnant with Pete. English lit. Kept in touch with the old gang though. This was a big do, someone had gone back to school, MA in something. Anyway, then.'

'What year?'

'I had an old phone, only it wasn't old then. Not a smart phone. What do you call them?'

'A dumb phone?'

'2011.'

'Fuck off, 2011!' Dawn stood. 'Fizz, okay?'

Mel nodded.

'Steve looking after his own kids isn't babysitting, that's called being a parent.' She shook her head. 'Nibbles? Something to line the stomach?'

'If you want. I won't stay long. Just a drink and then I'd better get home.'

'Girl, you've spent your whole friggin' life at home. They'll be okay without you. Breadsticks are good, absorb the alcohol. Bottle of fizz it is then.' She left for the bar, laughing to herself and shaking her head.

Mel texted Lily telling her she was out tonight.

Lily
Out? U never go out

Mel
In a bar with Dawn

Lily
Whos she?

Mel
Employment agency – new job

Lily
Right

Mel
Are you home yet?

Dawn returned with a silver tray upon which was a metal ice bucket with a bottle of fizz. 'No go with the breadsticks. So I thought we'd have this, then go for some grub somewhere else.'

'It's okay, we can just have this.'

'You've not had a night out since smartphones were invented and you're skipping the food. No. You really need to treat yourself a bit more. A lot more.'

'I'm fine. My life is okay.'

'Not judging by your face when you arrived.' Dawn filled the tall glasses with fizz, toasted: 'Here's to going out-out!'

Mel wasn't completely sure what that meant, but she toasted and drank and drank some more, and soon found herself telling Dawn about her marriage, why Steve had left, and how she'd just got used to doing things for others and never thinking about herself.

Dawn was talking, waving her hands animatedly, something about the masks you wear on a plane and how you should always put yours on first, before anyone else's.

Mel wasn't quite sure what Dawn meant, but she nodded and listened.

Dawn stopped speaking, swaying from side to side. 'What happened to the breadsticks?'

246

'They didn't have any.'

'Thassit.' Dawn clapped. 'We were gonna do something else. What was it?'

'What?' Mel asked, feeling very light-headed and strangely ravenously hungry. 'Are you hungry?'

'That's what I was saying. Let's get some of that stuff, what you have when you're hungry.' Dawn narrowed her eyes, leaning her head on the table.

'Food?'

'Thassit!'

As they left the bar, waving at the staff, pouring themselves into a taxi that had appeared from nowhere, Mel felt joyfully, irretrievably pissed, as if she were careering through life at a hundred miles an hour, without a plan, without any responsibilities, without an endpoint to the evening. And for the first time in over a decade, she remembered feeling like this as a teenager, before kids, responsibilities and timetables, schedules, mortgage payments, packed lunches, school runs. Just when Mel had been Mel and not all the other things she'd collected in the intervening twenty-five years.

Somehow they got to an Indian restaurant. There was an incident involving a pile of poppadoms, naan bread and a lot of laughing, and the mild-mannered and very understanding waiter bringing a jug of water.

Mel drank it as if she'd never had water before. Her throat was dry; it was probably the bread and poppadoms. Definitely that.

Dawn persuaded her to try a different curry from her usual. 'Live a little!'

There was a moment when they'd finished their food, drank enough water to sink a battleship, where Mel felt not completely pissed as she had before leaving the bar but nicely merry and tipsy and she leaned across the table, a comforting warmth filling her body, as she grabbed Dawn's arm. 'Thanks.'

'Tha's all right. My pleasure.'

–

Mel woke the next morning, with a hangover that could have felled an elephant. She was dressed but in her bedroom. So she'd somehow managed to get home last night. At what time, she was yet to find out.

She moved slowly, removed her clothes, stood under the shower until her limbs felt able to move properly. Slipping on a dressing gown, she then walked downstairs.

She sat in silence in the kitchen, first with a fizzy paracetamol and then with an orange-flavoured drink that promised to revive and refresh and replenish her. Mel reckoned she could do with all of those things, and some.

Lily, in pink pyjamas, walked into the kitchen, shaking her head. 'What happened?'

Mel wasn't one hundred per cent sure, so she said, 'I went out with a friend.'

'Out? But you never go out, Mum.'

'Is Thomas up yet? You've both got school.' *Am I over the limit for driving, still?*

Lily shrugged, helped herself to cereal and sat in front of the TV.

Thomas, wearing a T-shirt and boxer shorts, walked in, grabbed the cereal and helped himself. 'You look rough, Mum.'

'Morning to you too.' She eyed up the food suspiciously, knowing she ought to eat something but not sure if her stomach would manage it just yet.

'You must be knackered,' he said casually.

'Going out is more tiring than I remember.' She sipped some water.

'Especially if you get in at three a.m.' Thomas laughed.

'Three o'clock in the morning! Isn't that night-time still?' Lily asked.

Mel's eyes widened. Surely not? That wasn't possible, was it? 'Get dressed will you, we need to leave in fifteen minutes.'

She turned away from the children, made herself a strong black coffee and returned to her room.

After the school run, she returned to bed, with more painkillers and some fizzy water, emerging at lunchtime when she felt more human.

Dawn rang: 'How are you feeling?'

'Okay, considering.'

'What?'

'Three a.m. apparently I got in.'

'First time you've gone out in a decade and you're complaining?' Dawn scoffed.

'I'm very grateful. Thanks. Next time it's my treat.' Mel smiled at the sure knowledge that she and Dawn would be very good friends.

'I'll hold you to that. Once you're earning again. Which is why I rang.'

'Right.'

'Still interested in care work?'

'Definitely.'

'I've arranged for a placement for you at a local nursing home. Two days to be shown what it involves. A morning shift and an afternoon/evening, that way you'll experience the full range of activities you're doing for the residents. If you don't like it, no harm done, but otherwise, you'll be ready.' A pause, and then: 'Game?'

'Yep.' Mel nodded confidently. She could do anything and she knew it.

—

She decided on domiciliary care, which meant visiting people in their homes, helping them get up, washed, dressed, preparing their meals and then putting them to bed again. The hours were more flexible than shifts at nursing homes and hospitals, and Mel liked the idea of working in people's homes, same as when she'd been cleaning.

It was hard work, not brilliantly paid, but with mileage and flexible hours, plus plenty of job satisfaction, Mel enjoyed it. And after a week of working next to Lorraine, an experienced carer, Mel was assigned her own 'ones' which were clients she could look after alone. She'd been caring for 'twos' which were people requiring two carers at the same time.

One evening, after she'd finished her fourth client's bedtime routine, seeing he was safely clean and dry and tucked up in bed, Mel arrived home. She quite enjoyed the uniform of blue tunic and black trousers or blue dress. She'd been asked by the neighbours, walking to her car one morning, if she was a nurse. Mel had proudly explained, 'I'm a care assistant, in people's homes,' and driven off.

Chapter 30

Harriet finished her white wine and watched the queue outside Belle's, at the hoi polloi waiting to be let in. Sophie and whatever his name was, would soon be here, and they'd stride past the queue and into Belle's.

Magic.

Harriet shivered with anticipation and excitement. Or was it cold, since she'd poured herself into a very short dress, after having a long bath and a sloe gin cocktail?

Harriet checked her hair in the window. A newly high-lighted French bob, revealing her slender neck, all the better for the men to kiss, so she hoped.

No sign of Sophie. Harriet checked her phone as it lay on the table. She'd swiped right so many times her thumb ached from RSI. She'd dated a few men from there, and they were either too young and immature, wanting more of a mother figure, or only interested in sex. Not that Harriet wasn't a fan of sex. In her early twenties, she'd used to gulp great gallons of it, feeling invincible, from party to party, bed to bed. Sophie had become quite worried at one point, coming over all school marm-ish and telling Harriet she'd never find a husband that way, to which Harriet had said she wasn't looking for one.

Only now, on the precipice of thirty, her thoughts had turned to something more stable than only fun. A man she could take home to meet her parents without worrying he'd embarrass her at breakfast by scratching himself, or breaking wind loudly as they poured the tea. Both these had happened to

Harriet, which her parents seemed to bring up with remarkable regularity as a reminder of her unsuitable taste in men.

Dating, Harriet felt, had become like a second job. So assiduous had she been with her hunt for the perfect man. And yet none ever measured up to her thirty-seven-point checklist.

Harriet checked it on her phone. She needed it to hand for every date she went on. Sophie had said, 'You're setting yourself up for failure.'

'It's how I found my apartment.' Her father had thought her mad, presenting him with a list of two dozen must-haves. But, biding her time and increasing her father's budget, lo and behold, she'd found the perfect apartment. She'd reminded Sophie of this.

Sophie had smiled, shrugged and mentioned her current beau whom she'd stumbled into, quite by chance, at work.

Harriet remained to be convinced. Especially since there were no eligible men at work. They fell into one of two camps: married or gay. She wondered how Jason was getting on.

A taxi stopped outside Belle's and a man who she recognised from Sophie's pictures as Tom, in shirt and trousers, exited, followed by Sophie in a very small, very expensive red cocktail dress. He held her hand and the door, making sure she was safely on the pavement before paying the driver.

Sophie waved, tilting her head towards Tom.

Harriet paid the bill, thanked the waiter and went out to meet her friend.

She hugged Sophie then shook Tom's hand. He placed a hand in the small of Sophie's back as she led them past the queue waiting outside Belle's.

Sophie flashed her membership card and the bouncer let them in.

Harriet walked down the steps, handing her fake fur jacket in to the cloakroom. She literally couldn't wait for another drink and to dance away her worries.

She found a booth opposite the bar, Sophie sat opposite, placing her handbag where Tom would sit when he returned with drinks.

Harriet watched him talking at the bar and couldn't help herself wishing it was the two of them, Harriet and Sophie, as it had been since university.

'You look amazing,' Sophie said.

'Same.'

Sophie nodded towards the bar. 'I hope you don't mind me bringing Tom.'

''Course not.' He was nice to look at from a distance, and clearly Sophie adored him.

'We only see each other at weekends because he's so busy with work during the week. And I like my own time, of course.' Sophie grinned. She was positively beaming and Harriet felt churlish at resenting Tom's presence.

She decided to get to know him better. Not that she hadn't tried. Only it had taken Sophie this long to emerge from her Tom–Sophie bubble to see Harriet. She thought wistfully about her terrible dates and nights she'd spent alone, when Sophie was doubtless enjoying herself with Tom. A shard of envy struck through her.

Jealousy and coveting what someone else has are such unattractive emotions, darling, her mother had told her. *I love Sophie, Tom is making her happy, therefore, I shall learn to love Tom.*

On cue, Tom arrived with a silver tray containing a bottle of champagne, three glasses and a red rose, held between his teeth. He pretended to be a waiter, placing it carefully on the table, opening the fizz very gently, pouring it expertly, then presenting Sophie with the rose as he knelt.

Harriet admitted he was pretty bloody perfect.

Sophie accepted the rose, kissing him. Turning to Harriet, she said, 'Sorry I said we wouldn't be too mushy tonight.'

Tom sat next to Sophie.

'Good choice, Tom,' Harriet said, making eye contact with him. 'Nicely done.' She winked at him and smiled.

He nodded, pulling Sophie closer, as they toasted to the night, to old friends, new ones and having lots of fun.

'So where did you meet?' Harriet asked Tom.

He frowned. 'Hasn't she told you?'

Sophie blushed. 'I've not seen my dear Harriet in too long. What with work and...' She snuggled closer to Tom.

He coughed, then told their meet-cute story. It involved an investigative journalism assignment Sophie had been working on, a police station and a misplaced cat stuck up a tree.

Harriet found herself smiling as Tom held her attention, pausing every now and then to check inconsequential details with Sophie, before continuing.

'Which is how we met,' he said finally, kissing her lips.

She'd never seen Sophie this happy. Harriet could only be happy. Although she wished she had the same, she knew Sophie's happiness wasn't somehow taking away her own chances of finding romance.

The champagne gone, Harriet slid to the edge of the banquette. 'I'm going to powder my nose. Drinks?'

With their order, she left them staring into each other's eyes as she toured the club. It was smaller than she remembered. Perhaps because now she was less drunk than her typically inebriated state when she used to come here in her twenties, before her father had thrust responsibilities into her lap.

She was grateful. She waited for the barman to make their drinks. Quietly, she left theirs on the table, tapped Sophie's shoulder, then left them alone, taking her drink and resuming her tour.

Standing by the side of the small, raised dance floor, she saw a well-built man, her type. He wore a fitted blue shirt, well-tailored trousers, short hair and a bushy beard. He danced very well, moving unselfconsciously; closing his eyes, his limbs gyrated in time with the music impressively well.

A woman, obviously his girlfriend, touched his forearm, whispered in his ear, then left.

Maybe not his girlfriend.

Another man who'd been leaning against the wall opposite Harriet, walked towards the well-built one. He was casually dressed in green T-shirt and jeans – Belle's didn't allow those before, standards were slipping. His slender arms waved in the air as he danced through the crowd, closer to the built man. Slender man had the grace and movement of a dancer perhaps. His jeans were tight, muscular limbs, and his bare arms slender and graceful. He was less Harriet's type, but she couldn't take her eyes off them.

Friends.

The slim man grabbed Built man's hand, twirled around, and pressed himself against his friend's chest.

Very close friends…

Harriet sipped her drink, not taking her eyes off them.

Built man wrapped his arms around slender man's waist, pulling him backwards, then he placed a kiss on slender man's neck.

Gay friends…

Harriet looked around the room, expecting everyone else to be looking on in horror. No one was looking, except herself.

The way they unselfconsciously danced together had something bubbling up in Harriet's stomach. The same feeling as when she reached the happy-ever-after of her romance books. Similar to how she'd felt watching Sophie and Tom in their love bubble.

Harriet finished her drink, strode onto the dance floor. She closed her eyes to the music, to the moment, occasionally catching the two men out of the corners of her eyes, but mostly dancing in her own world, as the world of Tinder, bad dates, and her increasingly unenjoyable job, all fell away.

A hand grabbed her arm, bringing her back to the moment, away from why her job wasn't as enjoyable any longer…

'Sophie,' Harriet said, hugging her.

They danced together, Tom twirled Harriet around, much to Sophie's delighted cheers. He quickly returned to Sophie, holding her hands, as if to make it absolutely clear he was hers.

After a while they sat in the quieter room and Sophie went to the bar.

Sitting opposite Tom, Harriet knew she had to make an effort. If she soured this relationship, it could ruin her friendship with Sophie.

'Nice moves back there,' Harriet said.

Tom shrugged. 'Thanks. I'm having a great time.'

'Didn't you expect to?'

'Of course, yes. I just… Nothing. Doesn't matter.' He blushed, suddenly becoming interested in the drinks menu on the table.

This was as difficult for him as Harriet. Their friendship dwarfed Tom and Sophie's relationship. 'I'm going home in a bit.'

'Stay. She wants you to enjoy yourself.'

'I am. I'm not going yet. Look, if you want to be alone, kick me under the table, all right?'

He shook his head. 'It's not like that. Stay, will you?'

She nodded, wanted to touch his forearm to reassure him, but decided it wasn't appropriate. Instead, she said, 'I will. But one gentle kick and I'll leave. Not leave in a huff, slip off home. Give you some space.'

'Thanks. Appreciated.'

'I assume you know I'm a wedding planner.'

'More interesting than what I do.'

'It's okay.' Less than before, but she wasn't going into that now. 'What do you do?'

'At the moment, anything that makes Sophie happy.'

Harriet smiled. He really was perfect. 'Good answer.'

Sophie arrived with drinks. 'What's a good answer?' She looked from Harriet to Tom and back.

'Nothing. I'm going to leave you two love birds alone.'

'You don't have to, does she, Tom?'

'Stay,' he said.

'Don't feel like a gooseberry. You're not a gooseberry. I came out to see you. You sounded so...'

Disappointed was the best word Harriet had for her state of mind when she'd explained to Sophie she was tired of dating, hadn't seen her in weeks, and could they go out to dance away their worries.

'I'm fine.' Harriet meant it.

'Her last proper boyfriend was married,' Sophie said to Tom. 'Two children, house in Surrey, living a double life.'

'True story.' Harriet shrugged and laughed briefly. She had now very much put that incident behind her.

They finished their drinks, danced together, then Harriet left them alone, dancing to a slow tune, kissing Sophie and Tom's cheeks, saying, 'Love you both. I'm going home.'

They hugged her goodbye, waved her off.

As Harriet collected her jacket she saw one of the men from earlier. The slender one stood in the queue in front of her.

Feeling slightly emboldened by the alcohol, elated at Sophie's happiness, she tapped his shoulder.

He turned. 'Excuse me?'

'This is a bit random, but it's late, and I'm a bit drunk so I hope you'll forgive me.'

He stared at her, raised an eyebrow.

'I saw you earlier, with your... friend. I wanted to say you looked very happy. It's nice. To see you together.'

The queue shuffled forwards one place.

'I mean,' Harriet went on, knowing she was making a pig's ear of this. 'My friend, Sophie, she's here with her boyfriend. And I'm happy for her. I'm happy for you and your... boyfriend. Love, well it's all around apparently. According to the song.'

'He's not my boyfriend.'

Harriet's face fell. *Oh shit, I've committed a massive faux pas.*

'He's my husband.'

'Amazing.'

'I'm his husband.'

'Sorry, I don't normally do this sort of thing. But I saw you dancing and, well, I wanted to say how well you fitted together.' *Is that a tad over the top?*

'Thanks.'

'I'm a wedding planner.' She explained, in an awkward and garbled way, the problems they'd had with the hotel chain and photographer, without naming names.

'Same with our wedding.' A sadness crossed his face.

Without thinking whether it was appropriate or not, she pulled him into a hug, and they stood for a short while. Separating, she said, 'Sorry. I didn't mean to upset you. I want to apologise.'

'It wasn't your fault.' He laughed briefly.

Harriet knew this, but she felt complicit, and saw her views had been very old fashioned. *Of course gay people and lesbians – and bisexual people – all wanted to marry. Why wouldn't they?*

He was at the front of the queue, handed two tickets and took two jackets, and was met by his husband at the bottom of the stairs. He smiled at her, said something to the larger man, then they climbed the stairs holding hands.

Harriet nodded goodbye as he walked off. She shrugged on her faux fur jacket and carefully walked up the steps, through the narrow doorway and onto the pavement.

It was neither dark nor light. The time before the next day really began when and while most of the nocturnal fun was still going on. She hailed a cab, climbed in, gave her address and snuggled up in her jacket, leaning her head against the window as the lights of London whizzed past.

She let her eyes droop as the cars passed outside the window. She had really got it wrong at work, hadn't she? Standing up against Jason, when she should have sided with him.

I must text him, see how he's getting on, in the big world after Tailored Weddings. A world that seemed more interesting than the world in which she'd stayed.

She paid the taxi driver, tipping him generously, thanking him as he waited for her key to unlock the door, seeing her safely inside as she wobbled on high heels.

I can't catch love by running after it. The perfect man doesn't exist. It's not like finding the perfect home, holiday. I'm getting it all wrong.

Sipping a pint of water by her bed as she snuggled under the duvet, on her phone she opened her thirty-seven-point check list for men.

No more romance, no more running after the perfect man.

Her thumb hovered over the delete button. She smiled, thinking about Sophie and Tom, probably arriving home together now. Then the two men, who'd looked so well suited.

Delete.

With a sense of relief at finally letting go of finding the perfect man, accepting it wasn't meant to happen for her, she replaced her phone on the bedside cabinet, switched off the light and fell asleep.

Chapter 31

The ceremony was completely non-religious, a humanist service held in the university hall where the women had met thirty years ago.

The bride wore a white fairy-tale dress – well, one of them did. The other bride wore a grey morning suit and cap, with a cane and monocle – she was a massive *Jeeves and Wooster* fan.

'We met at uni,' Beatrice had said when Jason had spoken on the phone.

'What do you want your wedding to feel like?'

'Half like a library at uni and half like a pair of floral wellington boots that people wear to music festivals.'

Jason had smiled, he reckoned he could work with that. 'Can you bring me your scrapbook ideas when we meet and we'll take it from there?'

The ceremony was taking place surrounded by wood-panelled walls filled with books. Neither bride had living parents – that, Jason found out, had been one of the reasons they hadn't married before – their parents wouldn't have been supportive.

'We've been living in sin for thirty years,' Caroline had said when they arrived with the scrapbook.

'Didn't your parents suspect anything?'

They both shook their heads.

Caroline said, 'They didn't suspect anything because they were so sheltered. Couldn't imagine us being anything but two friends who'd just not quite managed to find the right man yet.' They laughed.

'Took me twenty years, so I suppose that's believable,' Jason grinned.

They'd had a registry office wedding a few weeks ago, to get the legal part completed, and Jason hadn't been involved.

Now, the ceremony had ended, it was short and humanist, conducted by a celebrant the couple knew. Each woman had described why they loved the other, the life they'd shared together and why it had been important to wait until now to marry. They explained now their parents were gone – definitely *gone* and not in Heaven, Jason noticed – they were free to publicly show their love for one another in front of those who were special to them.

Jason followed the brides outside the building. There was a park nearby, where they were having photos taken.

The photographer was a uni friend, who'd studied photography and now took natural, unposed photographs. No list of groupings or poses as with so many wedding photographers, just documenting the day as it happened.

Jason stood in the background watching the women as they sat on a bench, Beatrice held the long dress out of the way as Caroline sat. They kissed on the bench. The guests took photos and Vee, the photographer moved to the front to capture the best image.

Satisfied all was going smoothly, Jason left, nodding almost imperceptibly as Beatrice acknowledged his departure. He checked his social accounts – a few more trolling posts from different accounts. He blocked them and they came back, just as vile and just as many.

Do. Not. Engage. He put his phone away, determined not to let them spoil his day. He had a job to do and he was bloody well going to do it.

He arrived at the house the brides were using for the reception. Their budget was small, but Jason believed everyone could have their dream day on whatever budget and it was his job as fairy godfather to make it happen.

The front door was opened by a friend of Beatrice's, Mary. She wore an apron, her hands were covered in flour.

'I thought you'd have finished by now,' Jason said, staring at the kitchen in disbelief.

The wooden table had multiple mixing bowls, bags of flour, sugar, cartons of eggs and every surface was covered with what he presumed to be cake batter.

'Tea?' Mary asked nonchalantly.

'Don't you need to…?' He gestured at the kitchen.

'I buggered up the sausage rolls. And the fairy cakes. Burned to a crisp.' She held a tray of coal-like items he presumed were at one point cakes. 'So I'm making more.'

'They'll be here within the hour.'

'Milk, one?'

Jason surveyed the scene before him, looking out of the window at the marquee they were using for the reception.

'Milk, none, thanks.' At least the venue itself was ready. 'Do you want me to ask them to delay? The photographer could make them take longer. They look amazing in their outfits.'

Mary handed him a tea. 'I saw.' She showed him a picture posted on socials as they'd left the registry office. A bride in a white dress, with the other bride in top hat and tails, holding her train. They were smiling and staring into one another's eyes.

'First week at uni, they met. Never spent more than a couple of nights apart since.' Mary sat, crossing her ankles and sitting back.

'Honestly, I'll ask them to delay. Do you want me to help?' He wasn't a great baker, but whatever needed doing for a wedding, on the day he'd roll his sleeves up and do it. First rule of wedding planning.

Mary stood and showed Jason the pastry and sausage meat, setting him off alone after showing him how to make a sausage roll.

She returned to a large mixing bowl and electric whisk where she mixed sugar and butter, then added flour and eggs gradually.

Mary told him, in snippets, over the course of the next half an hour while they worked together: 'Beatrice is a year older than Caroline, and they met at the student union bar. They weren't dancing because all the men were annoying, and well, men. Beatrice had told all of them to piss off. Caroline was looking for the exit because she'd lost her friends from their halls of accommodation and wanted to go home. Beatrice persuaded her to say for just one drink. And thirty years later...'

They had the sausage rolls in the oven when the doorbell rang.

Jason had sweat pouring down his face. *Skin of the teeth job, this one.*

Vee, the photographer, burst in first, turning around to capture Beatrice and Caroline as they walked inside.

Beatrice grabbed Jason's arm. 'Why's there bits of coal on the table?'

'Everything all right?'

'We've waited thirty years for this, I'm not having slack Mary buggering it up for us. I love her to bits, but she's so laid back she's horizontal most of the time. What's she done?'

'Minor event with an oven. Sorted now.' Jason's phone dinged indicating another message. Probably another troll. *I'll leave it until later.*

Caroline arrived, laughing and burst between the two of them. 'What's up?'

'Talking about the food.' Beatrice glanced out of the window. 'Festival's all ready. Do you have your boots?'

'I'm going to change. If I keep this on once I start drinking I'll fall arse over tit.' She laughed, pausing to catch her breath. She held onto Jason's sleeve. 'In case I don't say later, when I'm... pissed. Thanks. This is awesome. Everything we'd wanted. Can't believe we met thirty years ago this week.'

The date had been one of the other very specific requests Beatrice and Caroline had for their day. Tailored Weddings wouldn't have bothered with a client with such a low budget

– it was peanuts in comparison to the big celeb ceremonies he'd organised – but to see their faces, it was worth it. Even if, sometimes Pete didn't think so.

A woman excitedly pulled at Caroline's wrist. 'Come on, let's go outside.'

'I was going to change first.'

'Make the most of it, wear the dress all day. When else are you gonna wear it?'

Caroline shrugged. 'She's not wrong.' She left for the garden.

'Cheers,' Beatrice said, shaking Jason's hand firmly. 'If I don't see you dancing in the dance tent later, I'll hunt you down, find you, and drag you in for a boogie. Understood?' She winked at him, grinned, then left.

He knew she meant it. Jason circled the house, checking everyone knew the wedding festival was outside in the garden. He moved outside, ensuring the tents each had their required equipment and were set up correctly.

The buffet was soon demolished, with guests sitting on picnic blankets in the 'eating' tent, as music played quietly from the 'dancing' tent. There was a queue for the 'weeing' tents, as with any good festival.

Mary found him, pressing a warm sausage roll into his hands. 'Try that. Your taste buds will love you forever. You've not eaten yet, have you?'

He had not. Usual nerves, wanting to make sure everyone else was happy before himself. He took a bite and the flaky pastry melted in his mouth, the succulent pork meat was flavoured with pepper and mace that emphasised the taste, with just enough of a kick.

'Am I right? Or am I right?' Mary asked.

'You're right.' He handed back the rest of the sausage roll. 'I've just got to check on something.' He left the house, sat in his car and checked the stream of social media trolling he'd received. People had tagged his accounts in the brides' pictures, so he was still getting abuse, even though he'd not posted anythingtoday.

Ugh, he really couldn't win. What was he going to do? He shook his head, closed his eyes and lay back in the seat for a moment, considering what to do next.

A bang on the car window startled him.

Mary said, 'What you doing, skulking off here? Music's on. Beatrice says if she doesn't see you dancing soon, she's going to hunt you down.'

Right. Jason opened the door and stepped out. 'One dance.'

He left at one a.m. after dancing for two hours, periodically pausing for water and squash, despite all the guests pressing wine on him for putting on such a perfect day.

The highlight was Beatrice's speech: 'I was a fresher and I'd heard about "fuck a fresher" week.'

The guests laughed.

'Little did I know I'd be her fresher to fuck. And still here, thirty years later.'

Caroline kissed her. 'I know how to pick 'em.' She punched the air, holding her cane aloft and swinging her monocle on its chain.

Now, Jason sat in his car, composing himself for the drive home. He sent Pete a text to say he was just leaving, and no he'd only been drinking water and lemonade all night. Although he didn't feel it, there was a light joyfulness floating about his head from all the dancing.

A notification flashed on his phone.

It was Harriet, messaging him: *Hi Jason, do you want to grab a coffee sometime? H x*

Precisely the sort of vague, shall we go on, we must do lunch, type of message he had fuck all time for now. What did Harriet want?

Chapter 32

Mel held the letter. It was from the University of London, confirming her place to start in September on their BA English literature and language course.

She'd applied, just to see if she could, encouraged by Dawn one night when they were having a quiet night out in a wine bar, and not going out-out.

'I'm over forty, what's the point in going to uni?' Mel had said.

'So what? I was over forty when I started this business. And look at me now. Best decision I ever made.'

'It'll take three years. I'll be nearly fifty when I finish.'

Dawn chewed on a breadstick. 'You're gonna be nearly fifty anyway. Time ticks on, right. Just look at my face.' She briefly pulled the skin tighter around her eyes. 'If you want to do it, do it. It's your life.'

'Seems a bit...'

'If you're about to say self-indulgent, I'll slap you. Or at least gently poke you with these.' She held up her long red nails. 'You've spent over twenty years putting others first, and being an afterthought in your own life. God love 'em, you have beautiful kids, but what's *your* plan? Wait until the littlest is at uni and then what? There'll be grandkids coming soon after, you wait.'

'Maybe,' Mel said.

'And, three Bs is three bloody Bs. More than I managed,' Dawn had said.

So Mel had promised she would apply and Dawn had nagged her every time they spoke, asking if Mel was still a secondary character in her own life, or whether she was finally letting herself have a main character moment.

Mel hadn't expected to hear back from any universities. Her two years of English degree had impressed some and disappointed others. A phone interview with a few heads of faculty had given her the opportunity to explain her love of reading, writing and language, plus talk about what she'd studied decades ago. Unsurprisingly, the texts hadn't changed much, and a lot of what she remembered was useful in these discussions.

Which had led her to now, one evening alone, at home, clutching the letter from her favourite university, the one with a college exclusively for night classes, meant for people who worked while studying.

Her job as a carer had confirmed how much she *needed* human contact, hearing people's stories, meeting them face to face, talking about nothing and everything. Her friendship with Dawn too, had shown her if she didn't make time for fun in what she wanted to do, nobody else would. All the things she'd missed when dropping out of university to have Pete, she knew she needed now.

She'd worked through the application process, surprised as she moved through each stage, not expecting to make the next step, except now, here she sat, with an unconditional offer in her hand. Unlike other students, who had to wait for their A level results, Mel had hers, from a quarter of a century ago, but three Bs were still three Bs.

And the only thing she needed to work out now was how she'd fit studying in among working and Mum-ing, plus how she'd afford it. Tuition fees now were no joke.

It still felt a bit self-indulgent, why did she need an English degree, at forty-six, nearly forty-seven? She was perfectly okay as she was: a job she enjoyed, parenting Lily and Thomas and sharing that with Steve, plus looking after the house. Her house.

Steve had signed it over to her with some financial jiggery-pokery which, even now, Mel didn't quite understand, but she'd accepted it, calling Steve and thanking him. He'd seemed happier, was back with Sally now.

Thomas arrived in the kitchen. 'What are you doing? Come watch TV with us.'

She folded the letter away. 'Coming.' She swallowed. She was being stupid, even thinking she could do all this. It was a silly fantasy.

Thomas stood by the table. 'What are you doing? It can't be work.'

She shook her head. 'Nothing.'

'Is Isaac defo coming tomorrow?'

Mel nodded. She'd told him it was important he come home, even if it was only for a few days of his week off. 'And Pete and Uncle Jason.' Her whole family was going to be there for a meal she'd arranged to coincide with Isaac's reading week – while she longed to experience her own glorious week in which to read and study – so he could come home.

'Sweet.' Thomas stood next to her, putting his arms around her for a hug. 'Thanks.'

She blinked, feeling a little overwhelmed with emotion. 'What for?'

'Tomorrow, everything you do.' He shrugged.

Wiping a tear from her cheek, she said, 'It's okay. It's what I'm here for.'

'I know.' He pulled back from the hug, stuck his hands in his pockets, staring at the floor and toeing it. 'Thanks though.' He left, taking big, nearly adult strides into the living room.

She packed away the papers, tucking the letter between two cookery books.

'One of your programmes is on. Shall I record it?' Thomas shouted.

'Be there in a minute.' She blinked away more tears. They seemed to be coming from nowhere.

'It's starting!' Thomas shouted.

Mel drank water, wiped her cheeks, then joined them in the living room.

Lily snuggled close to her on the sofa. 'Have you been crying?'

Mel shook her head. 'Hay fever.' She sniffed, looking up at the TV as her programme started. Normally she watched it alone, but today the kids wanted to watch it with her.

She really was lucky, so why would she do anything to unbalance things?

—

The next day, Jason and Pete were helping in the kitchen.

'You seem quiet, Mum,' Pete said, putting his arm around her shoulder.

'Everyone together, it's been a long time.' Except Steve, although she had invited him and he'd said he was taking Sally away for the weekend.

The front door opened, and then a deep voice she knew to be Isaac's, shouted: 'Give me a beer.'

She ran to the entrance hall where he'd dumped his bag on the floor.

He looked taller and broader and definitely had more beard than when she'd driven him to uni for the last term.

He hugged her and kissed her cheek. She held on tightly, his back hadn't been this broad before, had it? And he didn't smell the same, something else, not like when he'd been a teenager. She inhaled deeply over his shoulder.

'Mum, are you sniffing me?' he asked.

She shook her head. 'Pleased to see you.' Still holding tightly, they stood in the hallway for what may have seemed too long. But for Mel it was right, she needed to remind herself what she'd achieved in her life, *without* going to university.

Isaac released from the hug and stepped backwards. 'You totally sniffed me.' He shook his head.

Mel blinked away tears of joy. 'Beer's in the fridge. Your room's ready.' She'd smiled at the memory of his childhood football club bedspread and single bed, wondering if he'd enjoy coming home to sleep. She picked up Isaac's bag.

He appeared next to her, clutching a bottle of lager. 'I'll take that.' He strode upstairs, three steps at a time.

Mel returned to the kitchen where she helped Pete with the last few dishes.

Shortly, they were all sitting around the dining room table, eating, passing food from one end to the other. Mel looked around at her four children and Jason talking and eating happily. She'd done this. She'd done something worthwhile with her life and didn't need to worry about university.

Isaac helped himself to seven roasted potatoes. 'Has anyone else found out why we're all here from Mum?'

Pete shook his head. 'Three-line whip, apparently.'

'What does that mean? Is it naughty?' Lily asked.

Thomas whispered something into her ear, laughing.

Lily's eyes widened. 'Is that true, Mummy?'

Mel said, 'It's not. Whatever he told you it's a lie. Aren't I allowed to have all my family together, once in a while?'

'So this is because you fancied it?' Isaac shovelled great heaps of food into his mouth.

They were going to eat her out of house and home, and she couldn't have been happier. 'Just because,' Mel said with a smile, sure she'd made the right decision to ignore the university offer.

Jason handed a folded piece of paper to Pete, whispering into his ear.

Pete read it. 'Jason wants to ask a question, Mum.'

Mel waved for him to do so.

'Pete has a question,' Jason said, squeezing Pete's hand.

Pete sighed, unfolded the paper. 'Is today anything to do with this?' He waved it about.

'What is it?'

'From the University of London.' His eyes widened.

Mel stood, ran around the table and tried to snatch it from him. Her cheeks heated. Why didn't she file it away, why hadn't she destroyed it? Perhaps there was a part of her wanting the children to know. 'It's private, can you hand it to me, please?'

Pete did so. 'It's great news. I'm very proud of you. We all are.'

Isaac shouted, 'I would be if I knew what it was.' Another three potatoes onto his plate as he continued eating as if it were his last meal.

Mel felt stupid for even applying when there was no hope of her making it work. She shook her head, folding the paper and placing it in her pocket. 'It's nothing,' she said, and left the room so they didn't see how emotional she was.

Standing in the kitchen, she shook her head.

Pete joined her. 'Come on, it's great news, Mum. You're always telling us to blow our own trumpets. Well, this is a massive great trombone, or one of those big ones. Whatever, it's good news.'

'Is it?' she asked, bordering on angry, upset and over-whelmed.

'Isn't it?'

'I can't. I shouldn't have applied in the first place. Never expected to get anywhere.'

Isaac joined them. 'What's wrong?'

'It's not good news apparently?' Pete said.

'What isn't?'

Mel handed him the letter.

He read it, hugged her. 'This is amazing news. What's the problem?'

Mel waved in the air. 'This. Lily and Thomas. My job. How am I meant to do it all? I can't. It's impossible. People like me don't drop everything and go to uni. I'd be twice the age of everyone else. Never expected I'd get this far. Knowing I could, that's enough for me. It's nice. I'll keep it in my folder.'

'What folder?' Pete asked.

'I keep cuttings of stuff you've all done that I'm proud of. Pictures I print out. Newspaper clippings, pictures of your reports from school.' Sometimes she'd leaf through it, reliving the small victories each of her children had gone through.

'Getting a place at uni isn't worth shit if you don't actually go,' Isaac said.

'Well, I disagree.' Mel folded her arms, feeling very stupid all of a sudden.

Pete put his arm around Mel's shoulder. 'Mum, sorry to say this, but you're talking bollocks. You've got to go.'

Jason joined them. 'What's going on?'

Pete explained. 'And we're telling her she's wrong. She has to go.'

Mel threw her hands in the air. 'I've ruined the meal. It wasn't meant to be about me. It was to be about all of you.'

Pete said, 'It's okay to have things be about yourself. In fact, you deserve it. You've done so much, still do, for us, and now this is for you. You've got to do it. It's time for something, this thing, to be about you.'

'Nice try.' Mel turned to walk back to the dining room. 'I live in the real world, not a fairy tale.'

'What's stopping you?' Jason asked, blocking her way.

'You too?' She looked him up and down. Why was she surrounded by giant men?

Jason smiled, folding his arms across his chest. 'Let's sit down and work out how to make this work.'

'Everyone?' She looked from man to man, from son to son and to de facto son-in-law.

'Everyone.' Pete led her back to the dining room where he explained the news Mel was trying not to share. 'Mum really wants to go, but doesn't think it'll work.'

'It won't. I wouldn't mind going. If it could work. Which it definitely won't.'

Ten minutes later, Mel sat in amazement as her children organised her life.

Jason and Pete agreed to help with school pick-ups for Lily and Thomas, when Mel would be in London at the lectures. Isaac said he'd help out during his reading week and university holidays if Mel needed to study, while he was home. Thomas offered to take Lily to school on his own, which Mel wasn't convinced about, but said she'd think on for a while.

Pete said, 'Dad's going to up his thingummy payments so you can cut back on your hours.'

'Why did you ask him?' Mel was angry at this being taken out of her hands.

'Because I knew Dad would help. If you asked. And I knew you wouldn't ask, so I asked for you. Texted him earlier.' Pete smiled.

She couldn't remain angry any longer.

'How long is the course?' Isaac asked.

'Two years. They said I could start the second year because my two years counted towards their first year. Points transferred or something. I have to send them my essays from my old uni. They're handwritten. God, how embarrassing.'

'Nobody cares, Mum,' Isaac said. 'Everyone's getting on with their own lives, no one's gonna give a shit if your old essays are handwritten or not. I mean it was like the seventies, so nobody had laptops, right?'

Mel laughed. 'I'm not that old. Nineties, but you're right, there were no two-hundred-pound laptops then.'

It had taken a while, but one by one they'd made her believe, with everyone's help, she could make this work. 'What about my home care clients?'

'Dawn will totally understand you cutting your hours.'

'Maybe I'll stay as they are and see how it goes.' She couldn't bear the thought of handing over some of her clients to someone else. She reckoned she could juggle it all.

'Happy?' Pete asked her.

She nodded vigorously. 'So apparently I'm going back to uni.'

'Even if we have to put you in a cab ourselves. We'll manage without you. You need to do you, right?'

Excitement at this new venture she felt she maybe deserved bubbled in her chest. Anticipation, anxiety and enthusiasm to get back to what she'd always loved so much mixed together and she began to say thanks to everyone.

But as they were talking, some had started carrying plates to the kitchen, others were wiping the table, a shout from the kitchen came – something about the dishwasher – and Mel sat quietly in the middle of the buzzing activity, almost convinced life would go on without her doing it all.

Chapter 33

Sophie had suggested they have cocktails, after last time when they'd gone to Belle's and had such a great time.

'I'd prefer if we didn't,' Harriet had said uneasily.

'I shan't bring Tom, if that's what you're worried about. Playing gooseberry again.'

'It's not that. He's splendid. Very handsome. Much more. It's just…' Harriet couldn't say it, because then it would be a thing and it was most definitely not a thing. It was, at this point, simply a feeling, a slight worry, something she'd noticed but hadn't yet been able to describe to herself, never mind anyone else.

'Tell me. Do,' Sophie said. 'No secrets, remember.'

A swear they'd made to one another at university and that had, up until now, been kept, as far as Harriet knew anyway. 'Afternoon tea, is what I thought,' Harriet said brightly.

'And you'll tell me everything when we meet?'

'Of course.'

Now, Harriet sat in the ornate tea room at Claridge's waiting for Sophie.

Sophie arrived, greeting the waiter in his black suit and white shirt, nodded towards Harriet, and then she sat at the table. 'Free top-ups of tea, sandwiches and cakes.'

Harriet raised her eyebrows. 'Indeed.'

'Assuming that doesn't apply for shampoo.' Sophie placed her expensive blue handbag on the floor next to her feet.

Harriet had tried to fall out of the habit of using their old boarding school slang, since it marked her out so obviously as being frightfully posh.

Sophie stood, reaching her arms out. 'How the devil are you?'

Harriet copied, and they embraced, kissing on both cheeks, as was their usual greeting.

They sat.

Sophie picked up the menu. 'Is something wrong? You're not ill are you?'

Harriet shook her head.

'Preggers?'

Another shake of the head.

'Why all the mystery? No secrets, remember.' Sophie raised an eyebrow.

The waiter arrived in his butler's uniform. 'Are you ready to order?'

'I am.' Sophie stared at Harriet. 'You?'

Harriet turned to the waiter. 'Would you mind if you gave us a moment, please?'

He left.

'I deleted my checklist,' Harriet began quietly, staring at her menu.

'About time too, I reckon.'

Harriet wasn't sure what she had been thinking, believing she could find a husband in the same way as she'd identified her apartment. 'How many of my thirty-seven points do you think I'd tick?'

'For me, all of them.' Sophie grinned.

'I worked through it for me and even I only scored twenty. On my own list.' She shook her head. 'I am such an idiot.'

'You're not. Continuing to use the list to no avail would have maybe made you one. But not now.'

Harriet felt the crushing weight of realising you were incorrect about something you'd held as an inarguable truth for so

276

long. 'I realise I've been terribly wrong about a great deal of things lately. Well, not lately, generally.'

'Growth. It's good to learn from one's mistakes. Look at me with the banker who I fell off.'

'And the rest.' They shared a look.

Sophie had fallen off the man while in the bedroom and had broken her hip. But what had been a great deal more painful was the fact that he'd broken her heart. Very badly indeed. He'd completely and utterly failed to commit to her and, after dating for three years, had, quite out of the blue, announced he didn't want to be with her any longer. Sophie had been in hospital, recovering from the broken hip and Harriet had never seen her at a lower ebb.

'You seem very quiet. Shall we order and then we can get stuck in?'

'I'm not having champagne,' Harriet said simply.

'Fine, but I am.' Sophie was glancing at the menu, occasionally looking over the top at Harriet.

'I'm not having it ever again.'

'Bit drastic, don't you think? One killer hangover isn't enough to put you off for good, surely. It's the best cure for one, apparently. Mother and Father swear by it — small glass of the stuff the morning after and they're prancing about as if they were teenagers once again. It's miraculous.' Sophie put her menu down.

'I'm not having it ever again, because I can't. I mustn't.'

'Ah. Understood. I did wonder if you might be... a little... But if you think you are, then that's preferable to an...' Sophie waved about for a moment.

'Intervention?' Harriet said glumly.

'That's the one.'

'I can't be this sad all the time any longer. It doesn't help.'

'Being sad, well of course it doesn't.'

'Drinking.'

'Depressant, apparently. Terrible stuff. I shouldn't touch it again. In fact, I'll have what you're having. Tea, I'm assuming.' Sophie studied the menu with a great deal of fake interest.

'Have what you want. Don't mind me. You drinking isn't going to change anything for me. I'm just letting you know that as of now, I'm not.'

The waiter arrived, took their orders – champagne afternoon tea with cakes and scones for Sophie, and Darjeeling tea with the same for Harriet – and left.

Sophie shifted in her chair. 'Not very comfortable are they?'

'I thought the same.'

'What else have you been wrong about?'

'Sorry?' Harriet asked, relieved the conversation seemed to have moved onto more familiar territory.

'You said you were wrong about a great deal of things lately. One being…' A pause, as she swallowed. 'That.'

'Yes, and well, there were three.' Counting on her fingers, Harriet went on: 'That. My thirty-seven-point list for men. And Jason's concerns.'

'Jason at work?'

'He's left now.'

Their drinks arrived. Harriet waited for her tea to brew, while Sophie eyed up the champagne. Finally, they toasted – the champagne flute against the china cup – as Harriet went on. 'He had this sort of campaign against two of our biggest suppliers. I thought he was being over-sensitive. You know, campaigning and making everything about his being gay.' She rolled her eyes.

'Yawnarama.'

'Indeed.' Harriet sat up in her chair, making herself more comfortable. 'Except not. Except he wasn't. And in fact that's another thing I'd got pretty wrong too.'

'How so?'

Their food arrived. They set about cutting the scones in half and slathering them generously with Cornish clotted cream and strawberry jam after debating which should go on first.

Harriet, after taking a mouthful, said, 'I don't care which goes first, as long as there's jam and cream and a scone, I'm very much here for it.'

'Right.' Sophie took a bite.

Harriet swallowed her mouthful, had some tea. 'He has never made everything about his being gay. He was just, being himself. No one would accuse us of making everything about us being heterosexual women, would they?'

'A man might.'

Harriet shrugged. 'Except, it's not as conspicuous as when people come out. We've never come out, have we?'

'Not even in the debs' ball sense, no.'

'But Jason had. Anyway, I met the suppliers, and they, well, some of the stuff they said, I couldn't believe. I'm all in favour of a joke, but not when it's at someone else's expense. I've never minded gay people, it was always about eroding traditions, traditional institutions. The proper way of doing things. But...' Harriet felt deflated all of a sudden.

'What?'

'Look how far that's got me. Doing things the *proper* way.'

'Sorry.'

'Not your fault at all. Anyway, so I need to apologise to Jason.'

'For that? I'm sure he'll live without the apology.'

'For that. I'd never believed people would discriminate against people just for who they loved. It happens all the time. I spoke to a man in Belle's. Same thing. It's unbelievable.'

'You were wrong, people make mistakes. What else?'

Harriet felt guilt and shame wash through her. She stared at the carpet then collected one of the mini strawberry tarts from the top of her multi-tiered cake stand. 'There's more. I'm so ashamed.'

Sophie grabbed her hand across the table, holding tightly. 'It can't be that bad.'

The shame and regret made Harriet almost feel sick. She shook her head, as the icy feeling of what she'd been doing, for so long, dawned on her. 'It can.' She cried. Huge tears rolled down her cheeks, collecting under her chin then landing on her blouse.

Sophie handed her a napkin. 'Oh dear, you have got yourself in a real pickle, haven't you?'

Harriet nodded, blinking away more tears. She shook her head. 'I didn't mean to. It sort of grew and grew. With the other thing, I used to do it after I'd...' She waved about.

'Got drunk?'

Harriet bit her bottom lip. 'I don't deserve his forgiveness. I'm not sure I'd forgive me.'

'You must. Now you've admitted you have a problem, you're on the road to returning back to the Harriet I've known for most of our lives, and loved very deeply.'

Harriet blushed. She didn't deserve Sophie's love, support, nor Jason's forgiveness. So, as they asked for top-ups of sandwiches, cakes and tea, Harriet told her about her rage about Jason leaving her to fix the mess he'd created, at how jealous she'd been at him setting up his own business, and how, all around her were happy couples and yet she seemed singularly incapable of maintaining anything approximating a healthy adult relationship, despite searching very hard and for a great deal of time.

'Father wants me to take on a position on the board.'

'Ah.'

'Quite. And I haven't the heart to tell him I not only don't want it, but I don't want what he has planned for me in five years' time.'

'Don't you think he's picked that up, since you're making your own career plans?'

'Refuses to see it. Completely blind. I can't let him down. And yet continuing, knowing I won't do it, I'm letting him down.'

'What if you told them?'

'I wish I had a brother. I can imagine Father enthusiastically teaching him everything he knows about running Electrovax and letting me get on with my own life, undisturbed.' She imagined how that would feel, just for a moment, and felt lighter.

'You've told me. Just do that with them. What's the worst that could happen?'

'I'll probably grow into it, in five years.' She had a great deal of growing up to do and no clear way in which to do it. She supposed admitting she'd been wrong about all these things was a first step.

'Why didn't you tell me how unhappy, how overwhelmed you were?'

'Because I didn't need to. Because I had... that.' Harriet winced, looked at the champagne flute.

'Oh my darling, you didn't need to face this all alone.'

'I know that now. But for so long I'd become used to feeling so wretched about everything and that took it away and then I'd wake and it would all be there still.'

'How do you feel now?'

'Better. For telling you. For not passing out and waking up in my hallway.'

Sophie sat back, covered her mouth with her hands. 'Seriously?'

With such shame, Harriet nodded.

Sophie walked around the table, kneeling next to Harriet and gave her a hug for a very long and tender moment.

Chapter 34

Jason checked the show guide. He'd done two halls and still had three left to visit.

He was at the biggest wedding fair in the UK, held at an events venue in the East End of London.

He'd found sustainable and environmentally friendly food suppliers who worked with local farmers to tailor the menu to what was available near the venue. He'd met a wedding dress designer who exclusively used vintage clothing to upcycle into modern, unique designs. Her online shop included a video consultation for bespoke commissions if the brides so wanted.

A UK-only florist had caught his eye – cutting down on air-miles and using polytunnel technology to produce a broader range of blooms than normal in the UK. Flower designs could be specified by type, or as was more often required, colour palette. They would do their best to match clothing colours, or suggest an alternative.

Jason's head was buzzing with ideas.

Men's wedding outfits were so often an afterthought, which, when there were two men getting married, felt like such a shame. Jason headed towards the third hall and a stand that promised men's outfits for all sizes and types.

Jason described the outfits his grooms had worn during the last few months.

The owner – a St Martin's College student who'd set up the business during his final year – showed pictures of men on the red carpet at recent film premieres and award ceremonies. 'I did those.'

'All of them?' Jason asked.

'All of them.'

'Why is this the first I'm hearing about you?'

'My marketing manager isn't very good.'

'Ah,' Jason said.

'We split up.'

'Professionally or personally?'

'He was my boyfriend. I caught him in bed with my friend.'

Jason hadn't expected this, but knew this man was sharing because he obviously felt he could with Jason. 'Ex-friend, I'm assuming?'

'Correct. Anyway, so this is me trying to get my name out there, until I can find someone else to do my publicity. You don't know anyone, do you?'

'I have a few clients who'd love your clothes. If they buy them off you, we can make sure it's everywhere on our website and social media.'

'That would be amazing.' He held his hand out. 'Lawrence.' He shook his head, flicking his fringe out of his eyes. 'I feel like I've over-shared. Sorry.' He laughed nervously.

'Jason.' He shook Lawrence's hand.

They exchanged business cards and Jason promised to point his next few clients his way.

Jason made his way through the remaining halls, picking up ideas and business cards like a child in a sweetshop. With a bag of freebies and his brain buzzing with ideas, he left the exhibition hall, towards the taxi rank.

There were half a dozen black cabs waiting. He strode towards them, holding out his hand and bumped into someone.

'Sorry, I'm trying to—' It was Harriet. *What's she doing here? Why has she bumped into me?*

'I've been trying to contact you.'

The messages, asking to meet. Yeah. 'Sorry, I've been up to my eyes. Are you okay?'

'You know.'

He didn't actually, but wasn't too inclined to ask further. 'How did you know I was here?'

'Twitter and Instagram.'

'So you, what, waited by the exit all day, until I came out?'

'Pretty much.'

'I'm sure there are laws against that sort of thing.'

Harriet looked away. 'I needed to tell you something.'

'Isn't that what direct messages are for?'

'I needed to tell you this to your face.'

A sense of dread filled Jason's stomach with butterflies. 'What have you done?'

'You've been getting quite a few trolls, lately, haven't you?'

Jason narrowed his eyes. 'How do you know that?'

'It's on your accounts. When you share them, screen grab.'

Of course. 'So why did you have to come here to tell me that?'

'Because it's me.'

'The trolling?'

'Yes.'

'All of them? You can't be all of these accounts. There's hundreds.'

'Not all of them, but I started it. Made a new account, did it again once you'd blocked me. Once you start trolling, the other trolls join in. It's like a competitive sport, to see who can make the person react in the worst way, so they get cancelled.'

Jason felt sick. 'Is this a joke?'

'I wish it were.'

'So why are you telling me?'

'Can we go somewhere to talk?' She sounded sorry.

Jason was trying to process this. 'There's a pub next to the station.'

'I wondered about the library.'

'The library. Why?'

'It's better if I'm not in pubs. Takes away the temptation. Restaurants are okay, because there's food. But pubs, well they're only really there to sell alcohol and I'm better if I'm not drinking it.'

'There's a café over there, and you're buying.' Jason shook his head, leading the way.

Once seated with their drinks, Harriet said, 'I am so, so sorry. There's no excuse for it. I am a terrible person.'

'Those things you wrote in my private messages. The way you antagonised me. Did you get some sort of sick pleasure out of it?'

'At first. But then it just became something I did. A habit. And a lot of the time it wasn't me, it was other trolls.'

'Well, that's all right then.'

'It's not. I brought them out from under their bridges.'

'I was being sarcastic.' Jason stared at her.

Harriet was hunched over, looking older than before, it was almost as if being this angry about such ridiculous stuff had aged her.

'You were right about Lux-Lodge Hotels and Ray the photographer. I should have taken your word for it.'

'I did tell you.' Jason stared at her, narrowing his eyes for a moment. How much of this was performative, and how much was really Harriet wanting to right the wrongs she'd done?

'I should have listened. Like I said, I've been getting a lot wrong lately.'

'What else?'

'Doesn't matter.' She looked away, shook her head. Tears filled her eyes and she blinked them away. 'Can you forgive me?'

Jason thought for a moment. He believed if someone apologised you should accept it. Afterwards their changed behaviour showed if they really meant it. 'I didn't think you'd be capable of some of that anger and poisonous words.'

'I am so sorry. What do you want me to do? I beg you, whatever it is, I'll do it.'

'I'd like you to do something to help a charity for LGBT people.'

'Whatever it is, I'll do it.' She sat up.

'I'm assuming you're not short of money, so I won't ask you to donate that.'

'I can. As well. How much.'

Jason named a figure he thought reasonable to make up for all the time he'd spent fighting Harriet and her followers' poison. 'I want you to volunteer for a youth group, get to see the problems young people face about this stuff. I'm pretty sure it won't have changed much since I was a teenager.'

'I'm not... Won't it seem a bit odd, me volunteering for them?'

'If it's too hard, then don't worry.'

'No. I mean it. I'll do it.'

Jason gave her the names of a few LGBT youth groups who had followed him on social media.

They had finished their coffees and Jason really wanted to get home to see Pete. But he sensed Harriet didn't want to be alone. There was a sadness about her, a sense of being lost and not able to find her way, that he'd not noticed before.

'Was the show good?' Harriet asked.

He showed her his bag of goodies and business cards. 'Lots of great ideas. You should take photos, use them at your place.'

Harriet bobbed her head from one side to the other.

'Why not?'

'They have a way of doing things and I'm not sure they're open to changing that.' She shrugged. 'How's Pete? I'll leave you. Get back to your evening with him.' She gathered her bag and coat.

Jason put his hand on her arm. 'No great rush. I can stay for a bit. Was gonna suggest the pub but...'

Harriet tipped her head to one side. 'Sorry. I was just going to go home.' There was a sadness in her eyes at that.

Jason imagined her large apartment in the portered block she so often talked of. Returning to an empty home, where she'd sit with her own thoughts.

'There's another café down the road, towards the tube station,' Jason said.

She nodded vigorously. 'Thanks.'

Jason gathered his belongings together.

As they walked, Harriet said, 'This is very kind of you. I'm not sure I'd have forgiven me. Still haven't in some ways.'

'You should always forgive yourself, if you genuinely are sorry.'

'I am. Very much. Mortified.'

They arrived at the café.

'I'll get them again. I'm so grateful for this. Really am. It's the evenings that are the hardest, I've found.' She walked towards the counter.

Jason sat. He was really doing nothing, just having another coffee with an ex-colleague. But the thought of her alone in her place, fighting the urge to drink had his heart squeezing with sympathy. He texted Pete: *gonna be late, having a coffee with Harriet x*

> **Pete**
> Harriet from work Harriet?

> **Jason**
> yes

> **Pete**
> y?

Harriet returned with their drinks. 'I'm so grateful for this. I hope I'm not spoiling your evening plans.' She sat. 'How did you know about these youth groups?'

'They follow me on the socials, and I used to go to one. It's how I came out.'

'I never really understood that, not fully. I know what it is, but I've never had to do something like that. When did you do it?' She leaned her elbows on the table and sipped her drink.

'Last time was yesterday.'

She frowned. 'I thought you came out years ago. You're not much older than me, are you?'

'Forty.'

'Twenty-nine. Right. So yesterday, was it a big thing?'

Jason had been waiting home for someone to fix the dishwasher. The engineer arrived and asked Jason if he was staying in cos the missus had asked him to.

'Right,' Harriet seemed fascinated. 'What did you say?'

'I showed him a photo of me and Pete. Said he's my missus. Or we're both it. Or neither of us.'

'And then what?'

'He fixed the dishwasher.' Jason chuckled.

'Of course.' A pause, and then Harriet said: 'I thought you did it once, and that was it. I'd never really appreciated it's continuous.'

'It is.'

'I think I'm going to enjoy working with the youth groups. I've already sent them a DM on Twitter.'

Jason smiled.

Chapter 35

In a greasy spoon café near her university library, they sat at a Formica table, the smell of bacon, sausages and toast wafting through the air. This had become one of Mel's favourite places to hang out during the late afternoon, before her evening lectures started.

'Are you really sure?' Mel asked.

Jason had offered her a permanent job at Extra Weddings. A wedding planner, similar to Jason's role, but without all the legal responsibility shenanigans that terrified her.

'I wouldn't have asked otherwise,' Jason said.

'I don't think I can.' Mel stared at the table.

'I'm paying myself minimum wage, because it's my company. Pete hooked me up with an accountant, apparently, that and dividends is the way to go.' He shrugged. 'I'm leaving it to them.'

'I like my job at the moment. It's flexible. What would my clients do if I left?' And it was regular money, every month, the same amount, give or take. As much as she loved Jason, Extra Weddings was a bit of an unknown quantity. Whereas Cotswolds Care had guaranteed her work as long as she wanted it. Dawn said the clients had nothing but good things to say about her, and she was a senior carer, shadowing new staff for their first week as part of their training.

Jason pushed a letter across the table. 'Have a read, see what you think.'

It outlined the job, hours and rate of pay, which was about double what she earned at the moment. The prospect of being paid so much strangely terrified her. *I'm not worth that. No way.* 'You really think I can do all that?'

'I know you can. Whatever hours you want. We can work it around studying and the kids. As long as I know when you are and aren't working, it'll work. Project management. You're brilliant at it.'

She knew her way around Word and Excel, but project management, not so much. Mel blushed. She shook her head. 'You're giving me all this flannel because you need someone.'

'You've spent most of your adult life organising four kids and a husband, and yourself. Is it any surprise you're good at it? The launch party, I gave you a list of what needed doing and you got stuck in.'

Once he'd given her the contacts, Mel had loved it, felt like organising her own wedding. 'Can I think about it?'

'Of course. In your own time. I'm getting more clients every week, I'm managing okay at the moment, but soon there's going to be too much work for me to handle. Which is a great problem to have, obviously.'

She folded the letter into her handbag. They talked about he and Pete's wedding plans, which Mel was helping with of course. 'I can't wait.' She was so pleased to have Jason as a proper son-in-law, to see Pete settled, so happy and secure.

Jason checked the time on the wall clock. 'I've got a meeting.'

'And I've got a lecture.' Mel smiled. 'Who would have thought I'd ever say those words?'

'Me. I always thought you could do whatever you put your mind to. Which is why—'

Mel nodded. 'I get it. No more pushy salesman, okay?'

Jason held his hands up in a sign of surrender. He hugged her goodbye. 'I'll get this. Business expense. So my accountant tells me.' He grinned and winked.

Chapter 36

'I feel like I'm working in a sausage factory,' Harriet said in their café on Saturday morning.

Sophie raised her eyebrows. 'Is that rude or something?'

'I'm doing the same wedding again and again.' She shook her head. 'Boring. Like a production line.'

'What does your boss say?'

'Not interested.' Since being told she couldn't pursue the business relationship with Busy's hotel chain, Harriet didn't have the energy to fight it again. She'd been told there were reasons why they had to continue working with Lux-Lodge Hotels. Quite what they were, Harriet hadn't got to the bottom of.

'Do you have to stay? Hasn't your dad got something else you could do?'

'I politely told him to stuff it. I'd rather not have to go back, on bended knee.'

A look of mischief crossed Sophie's face. Of course.

'Talking of bended knee – I still can't believe you didn't ask me to organise your wedding,' Harriet said.

'I am sorry. I am contrition personified. Please do forgive me. But when Tom suggested having it on the beach in California, I could hardly say I'd rather it be in a hotel in Oxford.'

'You could have.' Harriet smirked.

'And I would. If I'd wanted it.'

Harriet was to be the maid of honour, and one of only a dozen guests Sophie and Tom were inviting. They both wanted to hear the ocean and feel the sun's warmth on their skin while promising to love each other forever.

Harriet thought it a touch dramatic, but knowing Sophie, who would live on a sun-drenched beach if she could, it made sense. Plus Tom, apparently, unbeknownst to Sophie initially, was something of a surfing professional, so almost had webbed feet and hands.

'What else is going on with you?' Sophie asked, and her tone implied she meant 'in the love department'.

'I'm having my apartment completely redecorated.'

'You've not long had it done, surely?'

Harriet didn't want to go into the reasons, those being her complete about face from the pastels, pinks, blues, and fairy-tale ethos of her naive early twenties, and instead facing her thirtieth birthday with a modern woman's apartment in cool whites, chrome and a bathroom reminiscent of a spaceship. She knew Sophie would persuade her otherwise, but Harriet's mind was made up. It seemed foolish to have a bedroom with floral wallpaper, silvered antique-style wood furniture that could have come from the Palace of Versailles and a four-poster bed inspired by Cinderella, especially when she was alone in the bed.

'Five years ago,' Harriet said.

'Good to have a project to focus your mind.' God, Sophie's tone was so pitying. Harriet knew it was well-meaning, but the last thing she needed was her engaged friend's pity.

'I think I shall tell them to stuff it.'

'The decorators? I thought you'd had terrible trouble landing one.'

'Work.' If Jason could fling himself out of work for his well-held principles, she, with her father's allowance, sure as hell could too. Guilt at letting it rumble on for so long, before taking a stand, stabbed through her.

'I should. Sounds like you've outgrown it.'

'I have, rather.' Harriet nodded, thinking she really should resume the hunt for a reputable decorator who could meet her stringent specifications.

Chapter 37

'Are you sure you've made your final decision on these?' Jason asked, pointing to the checklist Mel had designed for them.

Pete ran his finger down the paper. 'Flowers, car, venue, catering, music, decorations, dancers, wedding favours, seating plan.' He nodded. 'I think that's it.' He bit his bottom lip. 'What about a stag do?'

Mel walked into the room, carrying a tray of hot drinks. 'You haven't asked me to organise that. And in all fairness, it's not quite within the remits of a wedding planning company.' She glanced at Jason.

Jason nodded. 'She's right, you know.'

Mel handed out the drinks, then sat at her desk. 'Would you like me to handle this?'

Pete looked from one to the other. 'What did we decide about the unicorns? And rainbow table decs? Did my friends from college say they can do the dancing?'

'It's all here.' Mel pointed to a spreadsheet on her screen.

Pete pouted briefly. 'I preferred the scrapbook stage to this.' He motioned at Mel's computer.

Pete had embraced the scrapbook stage completely. He'd created a whole book, filled with clippings, snippets of lyrics, pictures of celebrities, pieces of wallpaper and fabrics, filling more than two dozen pages, whereas the original brief had been one piece of A2 paper.

Jason stood. 'I've got to check out a car supplier who promises to have everything we'd ever want. I'm asking them if they have a pumpkin-style coach.'

Pete put his hand in the air. 'Can we have one of those?'

Mel checked her computer screen. 'I thought you'd settled on... a classic Citroën from the seventies.'

Jason raised his hand. 'I chose that.'

'I know, but I'm just not sure if it says Pete and Jason, quite enough.' Pete looked at his mother.

'Can I leave this with you, Mel?' Jason kissed Pete on the lips, then Mel on the cheek. 'This is me, leaving, and removing myself from this discussion. Okay?'

They both nodded.

Pete had been talked down from basically staging a pop concert in front of which he and Jason would be married. Mel had done a great job of managing his expectations, although they still had plenty of touches that were purely he and Pete. He was enjoying it, now he wasn't the one who was doing the organising. Having Mel working for him part-time was a literal life-saver. She seemed to do much more than he managed, despite working fewer hours. Perhaps it was because she was an organisational ninja and could type faster than Jason could speak.

Jason stood by the door, listening to Pete and his future mother-in-law and employee talking about their wedding. He caught the odd word like 'colour-coordinated' and 'unacceptably drab', and Pete saying, 'But if I can imagine it, Jason said you can create it. It's there, on your website.'

Mel raised her voice slightly: 'I'm just not quite sure we're going to persuade Appledrama to perform, just for your wedding...'

Jason left with a smile, wondering what delights the wedding transport company would hold. He really did have the best job in the world.

Chapter 38

'Can I borrow your notes for the last lecture?' Gareth asked.

Mel was in the university library late one evening, after her lecture had ended. She found staying there meant she was more likely to complete the work, before the pull of the house and its endless chores took hold. Plus, it meant more time hanging out with fellow students and discussing all the things she loved about the course. She'd forgotten how much she loved learning, acquiring knowledge, new ideas, different ways of seeing things. Debating how you could interpret a text.

Gareth and her were on the same course, and about the same age; she'd not asked Gareth his date of birth quite yet, but she'd sat next to him in a lecture six weeks ago and they'd shared a joke when the lecturer's profile picture had been a pink aardvark from a children's TV show they both knew.

At the same time they'd said, 'Cyril Sneer.'

'I wondered what he was up to,' Gareth said.

'A reformed character.'

'Who doesn't love a happy ending?'

The lecturer said, 'Is there something you'd like to share with us all?'

Mel felt the heat rising on her cheeks as she blushed, shaking her head.

'We like your profile picture.'

'Thank you for that incisive comment. I hope next time you'll keep discussions limited to the subject in hand.' She turned towards the screen and moved to the next slide.

Gareth winked at her and smiled.

Mel had felt a light sort of flutter in her stomach. His blue-green eyes had wrinkles around the edge, and his silvery grey short hair and a neatly trimmed grey beard meant he had the look of a middle-aged Sean Connery. He suggested a coffee after the lecture and Mel, so grateful to meet a student her own age, had agreed. They fell into an informal arrangement of sitting next to one another in lectures, putting the world to rights in the university café, where they agreed to meet most mornings, and as now, studying together in the library.

However, on this night, despite all her best efforts at better planning, she had an impending deadline for the most critical essay of this term, and she was being asked by Gareth if he could borrow her last set of notes.

Mel nodded, removing them from her folder, shuffling them opposite her, where Gareth sat.

'Thanks,' he replied.

'If I can read this book, and the next one, take notes, I'll be halfway to getting this done, leaving me...' She checked the date. 'Shit, leaving me two days until it's due in.'

Gareth seemed remarkably relaxed, considering he'd missed the last lecture. He seemed to find nothing, at all, in any way stressful. Greying beard, hair and muscular forearms that even now distracted Mel when she was trying to concentrate on, what was it again? Milton, imagery about something or the other...

Mel looked up, allowing her gaze to linger on Gareth's well built forearms. *How does he make a polo shirt look so bloody good? If I wore something like that, I'd look like a sack of potatoes with arms.*

Most of her adult life spent with one man, only looking at others, knowing she wouldn't touch, meant she was rusty at this. Whatever this was.

He's not flirting. He's being a man. Her jaw tightened.

Gareth raked his hand through his neat hair, smiling, the polo shirt tightening on his chest in a way Mel found pleasingly sexy.

God no. Not in the library!

'What are you smiling about? Aren't you panicking too?' His effortlessness was really irritating today, for some reason.

'Nothing.'

Mel sat up, she needed a break from the books and the writing.

God, his eyes are smiling too. Actually smiling. Who has eyes that do that? Christ on a bike, I think I fancy him.

Mel looked away. *No I don't.* 'Come on, laughing boy, what's so funny?'

'Boy, I've not been called that since...' He blushed. 'I'm thinking someone who had already done two thirds of this degree ought to be panicking less. And maybe know she's really good.'

'How do you know?'

'I've seen all your grades this term.'

This sounded a little creepy. Mel narrowed her eyes. 'Noted.'

'I've sat close, so I can see your grades when they hand out the marked papers. I wait until you've sat and then decide where to sit.' He looked away, smiling a little.

'Is that supposed to make me like you?'

'It's supposed to make you understand why I'm about to ask you for your number.' Gareth smiled.

Mel didn't believe him. Even though he'd said it, this wasn't what happened to women her age, particularly her. Being propositioned in the university library late on a Thursday evening. *What does he think this is, some bloody rom com?*

He was still staring at her, smiling his big wide grin and twinkling his huge blue sparkly eyes.

'Go on then.'

'Will you give it to me?'

'I beg your pardon!' She tried to keep a straight face and failed. What would the children say if she told them she'd been propositioned in the library, on a Thursday night?

'Your phone number.'

'Possibly.' *Definitely. If he actually asks. Which he won't.*

'Can I have your number, please?'

'Why?'

'Because I'd like to have a drink with you. And then maybe eat a meal together.'

'Why?' This wasn't happening. Couldn't be. She refused to believe it, despite evidence in front of her eyes, very much to the contrary.

'Because you're amazing and you're attractive and I want to get to know you.'

'Go away!' She waved him off, shaking her head. 'I'm forty-six, divorced, four kids, about two foot too short for my weight, and having a midlife crisis by coming to uni when I'm old enough to know better.'

He smiled, staring straight into her eyes. 'So can I have your number please?'

Mel scribbled it on a piece of paper, handed it to him. 'Do what you want.' She looked to the ceiling. 'Is this being filmed? Are you doing it for a bet? That's it, isn't it, you've been asked to pretend to ask out the oldest, most dowdy-looking woman on our course, and if I agree, you win a yard of ale, or something.'

'On my mother's life, I'm telling the truth.'

A tiny prickle of intrigue coursed through her body. *Perhaps he's not lying.* 'Okay, supposing that's true, what's a man like you doing being interested in a woman like me?'

'I could ask you the same thing.'

'Piss off! Look at you, you're nice…' She bit her bottom lip as she thought about much better adjectives to describe Gareth the silver fox who sat next to her in every lecture, and who, up until now, she'd thought only wanted to be friendly for her superior notetaking skills.

'Widower, two grown-up kids, boring job, developed a fascination with sport as part of a full-on midlife crisis.' He raised his eyebrows.

Mel reckoned she had very little to lose by giving him her number. It would make arranging to meet around the university campus much easier. The thought of sleeping with someone other than Steve terrified her, but she tried not to think about that as she watched Steve writing his number on a Post-it and handing it to her.

'Have you finished with my notes?' she asked.

He handed them back in silence.

They worked diligently until the library closed. Jason and Pete were looking after the children tonight, so Mel didn't need to rush home.

They packed away their papers, books and folders and walked towards the exit. Mel didn't know whether to do a big formal goodbye or a little wave and turn and then leave.

God, why is this so complicated? It's been so long since I... did this.

'Do you have to be anywhere now?' Gareth asked.

Mel turned. 'My son and his partner, Jason.' She watched to see if he reacted.

Nothing.

Good. 'His partner, Jason, and my son, are looking after my two youngest. I've got work tomorrow, early. Seven. But now, I don't have to be anywhere. What were you thinking? I'm not hungry, are you hungry? Or maybe we could have a drink.' She stopped herself from babbling. *This is what happens when I'm nervous.* And now Gareth had mentioned phone numbers and all the other stupid stuff, Mel didn't know how to behave. Before, when they'd been friends on the same lectures, Mel knew where she stood. Hadn't made a fool of herself as she was now.

Gareth stood closer, held her arms. 'I'm going to hold your hand. Is that okay?'

Mel blushed, nodded, smiled, closed her eyes. Because, even if she'd told herself she wasn't interested in doing all this again, now she was standing inches away from Gareth, she admitted he was handsome, and the thought of him holding her hand wasn't the worst thing she'd ever heard.

He took hold of her hand. 'There's a pub.' He nodded. 'If you feel like it? One drink.'

Mel smiled, almost giggled, grinned inanely. Nodding.

'Is that a yes?' He squeezed her hand.

She nodded. *I definitely feel like it.*

They walked a short distance to a Victorian pub on the corner, with smokers outside, a busy bar and mostly full tables. The smell that hit her sent memories crashing through her mind. That beer, warmth, people scent. She'd used to do this sort of thing after lectures, the first time. That was where she'd met Steve. He'd bought her a drink and then—

'There's a table,' Gareth nodded into the corner. 'I'll get the drinks.'

The joyful memory mixed with sadness of where she and Steve found themselves now, combined with the reality of Gareth being gentlemanly made Mel's stomach bubble with excitement and anticipation. 'Okay.' She smiled weakly.

'You all right?'

Mel swallowed. 'I've not… in a long time.'

'We can go somewhere quieter.'

That felt worse, somehow. Mel shook her head, looking at the swirly patterned carpet and blushing. 'It's fine.' She walked to the table and sat, watching Gareth leaning against the bar.

If I'm already doing the unbelievable thing of going back to uni, what difference is another ridiculously unreal thing like having a drink with a man?

She checked her phone for messages about the children. Nothing. A nod in recognition at a woman she knew from her course, a smile at a young man she'd spoken to about Shakespeare, and if she closed her eyes, ignored the mobile phone, and the fact she'd gone up three, maybe four dress sizes, she could almost imagine she was back at uni in 1995. The excitement and anticipation of anything being possible had been addictive back then. And somehow in the intervening decades of becoming Mum and Wife, she'd lost that.

Chapter 39

On Sunday evening Harriet visited her parents' London apartment. Father was in town for a board meeting and Mother was eyeing up Knightsbridge for a spot of shopping.

The doorman nodded in recognition as she unlocked the front door, leading to the grand, airy entrance hall.

The key turned easily and she slipped inside, shouting her arrival. She slid across the parquet floor into the oak-panelled library, filled with green leather high-backed chairs and book-lined walls punctured by large, airy sash windows.

'What's happened?' her mother asked, looking up from a game of cards on a green velvet table, kissing her cheek. 'Are you pregnant?'

'Who is it?' Her father arrived to join them. 'Are you?' He stared at her.

She'd hoped for a warmer welcome, but it wasn't entirely their fault since she so seldom visited. Partly because they were often not in London and partly because she hadn't the stomach for another lecture on why she ought to have accepted the job her father had pushed under her nose and why her mother couldn't understand why she seemed unable to find herself a husband as she was now thirty.

Harriet sat in a chair, preparing herself for a twin-track lecture.

Her father leaned against one, looking stern.

'I know I said I didn't want to be told what to do with my life. And I was perfectly capable of making my own decisions.' *In love and her career* were unsaid, but implied.

'Darling, are you pregnant?' her mother put her arm around Harriet's shoulders.

'I am not. Chance'd be a fine thing.' She chuckled to herself.

'Not for lack of trying on my part,' her father said, huffing.

'I think I've made a terrible mess of things.' She'd kept her sadness to herself for so long, and now, these two people who'd known her for the whole thirty years Harriet had lived, deserved to be told.

'You are pregnant!'

Unable to marshal her anger any longer, Harriet snapped, 'I am *not* pregnant. Unless you're hoping for an immaculate conception, that will not be happening any time soon.'

'What is it, Harriet?' her mother asked.

'I feel rather at sea.' She knew having her apartment redecorated and getting a new job was her regular remodelling of herself, which she tended to do every five years or so. Except the last time she'd done it, she'd rather hoped it would be the last incarnation, expecting to be moving into the countryside manor of the beau she was marrying. She kept reinventing herself, trying to work out who she was – without Electrovax, without her parents' mores and values weighing her down, trying to be her own woman. But it was so bloody difficult. Adulting – her parents would hate that word – was so much harder than they implied at school, and university even.

'Tell us,' her mother asked carefully. 'One thing at a time.'

And so, she did. She told them about falling out with Jason, over something she now knew she'd been on the wrong side of. She told them how her job bored her and she'd finally realised they weren't the sort of company she wanted to work at and how she'd started sabotaging her role there. And then finally, having managed to keep her emotions in check, she let them all come spilling out, tears, gasped breaths, blinking away the sobs, she admitted she was so terribly, awfully painfully lonely and feared she would never find someone who'd love her as much as her parents loved one another, as much as Sophie and Tom for instance.

She took a deep breath, feeling relieved and slightly embarrassed at her histrionics.

Her father said, 'I shall call that so-called boss of yours, instruct him that due to irreconcilable differences, you will part ways and will not be working your notice. And then you can walk into my board secretary role at Electrovax. I've still not filled it.'

Her mother looked at him, then at Harriet. 'I rather think you're somewhat missing the point.'

Harriet sniffed. 'I don't want you to sort out my problems for me. I wanted to tell you, so you can offer suggestions. I don't want to be saved, Dad, okay?'

He smiled tightly, nodded.

'I expected by now, with all the fortune I have from being part of this family, I'd... Well, I'd have things much more sorted than they seem to be at the moment.'

Her mother patted the sofa and Harriet joined her. 'I'm over twice your age and I often feel at sea. Most days in fact.'

Harriet nodded, feeling slightly better.

'I didn't meet your father until I was your age. Many frogs were kissed before. Many.' She rolled her eyes.

'I worry I shan't be enough. I'm so picky about boyfriends – why, I'm hardly perfect.' She told them about the thirty-seven-point list she'd discarded.

Her mother pulled Harriet to her bosom for a hug, rocking from side to side and stroking her hair.

Harriet felt strangely serene and it reminded her of being a small child. She closed her eyes and imagined she were ten, about to disappear to her bedroom and play with her dolls.

'Has it occurred to you that you could simply *stop*?' her mother asked.

'What?' Harriet asked.

'Searching, trying, wanting, hunting for a man.'

It had, which is what she'd told herself, and Sophie. But when she was alone again, she knew that was ridiculous – at her age she only had so many more viable eggs if she wanted to start a family. She thought she did want one. Had looked on as friends had produced offspring, wondering what sort of mother she'd make. But she didn't want to do it alone, go to some sperm bank and pick a father as if she were buying a new laptop. And she wasn't getting any younger, her grey hairs would start coming through soon enough. Wrinkles around her eyes, saggy bits and expanded others.

Harriet explained this.

Her mother said, 'Stop. Just stop.'

Her father nodded. 'Stop.'

Stop.

Harriet felt herself go limp as she let go of all the plans she'd made, all the expectations others had of her, and allowed herself to return to thirteen-year-old Harriet.

They ate her favourite supper from when she was a child – fish-finger sandwiches, jelly and ice cream – and she slept in her old bedroom, with its candyfloss pink walls, My Little Pony wallpaper and duvet set and summer-sky-blue carpet.

The next day, she went to work, armed with her father's advice and emailed Christopher outlining her case:

> Dear Christopher,
>
> This decision hasn't been taken lightly, but I'm afraid I do not feel able to work in line with Tailored Weddings' values. I have been put in a compromising position with some of our clients, and I find myself having to lie to them. For this reason I would like to tender my resignation.
>
> I have evidence about Lux-Lodge Hotels' and Ray Photography's views about their outdated attitude to some of our clients. If taken further, these could be very damaging to this company.
>
> Yours sincerely,
> Harriet

She'd made sure to print out the evidence in the previous few weeks, in both disbelief that she was forced to accommodate their views and as a potential parachute out of the company.

Her desk phone rang. It was Christopher asking her to meet him in his office shortly.

Harriet sat in Christopher's office, clutching her email giving her notice and a few copies of the incriminating evidence. She was going to walk out, but it felt a little childish and unnecessary. They'd given her a job, so she at least owed them time to find her replacement.

'You don't need to hand deliver it,' he said. 'Your email will suffice.'

Nice that he cares so much. Harriet sighed slightly, handing him the letter.

He scanned it. 'Noted.'

'Don't you want to know why?'

'I presume you've got another job.'

'I have not.' *Why isn't he discussing the content of her email? The accusations, mentions of evidence.*

'Ah. Well, now you've given this to me, I'm afraid wheels will be put in motion. Once they've started it's rather difficult to stop them.'

So he didn't even want to persuade her to stay. Why had she wasted so long with these people? 'I feel like all the weddings are... the same.'

Since Jason had left, most of the rainbow clients had moved too. Subsequently they'd changed their website pictures to give a very traditional view of the weddings they preferred to organise. Of course they couldn't say outright they didn't cater for those clients, but Harriet had been told to point them in the direction of other, more avant-garde wedding planners.

Christopher said, 'I sense this is important to you. I thought you were better than to be swept up with others' hobby-horse pet crusades.'

'I think Jason was right.'

'It's for the best you're leaving us.' He shook his head, shuffling her letter uncomfortably.

'Hindsight is a wonderful thing, but they had principles, which is more than I can say for myself at the time. You think these weddings are cutting edge, modern, progressive. They're really not. They're weddings. And whatever's keeping this place clinging to the hotel chain and photographer and their backwards views, it's preventing this place becoming a modern events company and wedding planning department. Which is why it's time for me to move on.'

'Wonderful. If you'd please close the door on your way out.' He was clearly keen to end this.

She left the room, returning to her desk fizzing with rage. She'd wanted him to disagree, argue, explain why they'd chosen this way forward, picking and choosing their clients. It was exactly the opposite of how a modern company should work.

She walked to a meeting room where someone from HR handed her a piece of paper. It confirmed she would not release anything in relation to the internal memos about what she'd referred to in her email, or anything else to bring the company into disrepute. It listed a figure, plus her notice period payment and owed annual leave.

It wasn't much, given her father's position, but it was, to most people, a significant chunk of money.

'If you sign this, you can leave today, with this money. I'll give you a cheque today. But you can't tell anyone anything about this company. Or you will be in breach of this agreement.'

'I'd like to think about it. And take advice, please.' She stood. 'Okay.'

Harriet collected her personal items from her desk, flung them into her handbag and walked out.

She would have made great use of the money, everyone could, regardless of their position. But it would have been tainted. She'd been on the wrong side of the moral argument once before; she wasn't going to make the same mistake again.

She left the building, head held high. 'I've walked out,' she said triumphantly to Sophie on the phone.

'I hope you got a good pay-off.'

'Nope.'

'Wish I could afford to refuse money.' Sophie laughed nervously.

'I couldn't afford not to refuse it.' After a pause, Harriet said, 'Morally, I mean.'

'I got that. Well done. Didn't mean to snipe. I could do with a bit more cash. Who knew weddings were so expensive?'

'I feel like you've sort of set me up for this… but I did. How's it going?'

'You sure you want to hear? It sounds like you've had quite a day of it.'

'It's done now. I wanted to tell you.' *I've missed you. Didn't want to see you with Tom, but now I realise that's foolish, because you're my best friend and I love you.* 'Missed you.'

There was a silence, and then Sophie said, 'Let's go to Belle's, us two. Stay up until the sunrise, drink champagne in Hyde Park, walk back to your apartment and fall asleep on the sofa with lashings of buttered toast.'

It had been years since they'd done that, and although Harriet knew it was unlikely they'd repeat those nights, having the shared memories comforted her. Sophie's happiness was Harriet's happiness.

Finally, Harriet said, 'Yes. Definitely. And definitely want to hear how the wedding's coming on, even if you declined my professional services. I need to know since I am, after all, maid of honour.'

'And master of ceremonies.'

'Quite.' Harriet nodded, smiled as she walked away from the office for the last time. Unsure what she was going to do next, but certain it would be better than what lay behind her.

Chapter 40

Jason looked out of the window onto the street. He was on the phone with Mel, discussing a client's requirements.

Mel finished her long description of potential ideas for the clients' dream vision. 'I'll pop it in a handover email unless anything comes up between now and next week.'

'They won't want me, they'll want you. You're their wedding planner, not me.'

'Say that again.'

Jason grinned and did so. 'I wish I'd known what Pete was going to be like with ours.' He rolled his eyes.

'How long have you been together? Why is this a surprise?'

Jason had lived with Pete for three years, but he'd not witnessed Wedding Planning Pete in action before. 'If I could hand it over to someone else, I would.' Except Pete would never forgive him. Jason was balancing the requirements Pete kept making against the moments of joy where they'd sample a menu together, or try on outfits and Pete's face would light up causing Jason's stomach to fill with butterflies and reminding him, all over again, why he loved Pete so much.

'I'm going now, boss,' Mel said with a smile to her voice. She ended the call.

Jason's charms had tempted her to work with him. Plus the hours were more flexible than the care work. He'd offered her more hours, but she'd remained firm, wanting to give herself time to study and enjoy her final year at uni.

Jason saw Mel's handover email pinging into his inbox, as promised. She was so organised it put him to shame. Jason preferred to wing things much more than he ought, but it had got him this far, so why change the habit of a lifetime?

He replied to Mel: *log off, enjoy your days off! The Boss xx*

Her out of office said she'd be back on Monday and for any urgent queries to speak to Jason, chief executive of Extra Weddings.

Chief executive, even reading it now, made him pinch himself. He'd done this. They were small, but growing and he was taking on more clients every week.

If he left now, he'd reach the gym before it was too busy with the after-work crowd. A clear calendar, and the rest could wait until he returned, later. Smiling at literally being his own boss, Jason made for the gym.

An hour of running, weights, rowing and then a quick swim and Jason left, red-faced, feel-good hormones buzzing through his veins.

If I get home now, I can clear the decks before Pete arrives home…

Staring at his phone, checking emails, he bumped into somebody. 'Sorry.' Jason looked up.

Harriet.

He checked, since she was out of context. He'd only seen her at a desk at work, or in London and here she was, standing outside of his gym, in the Cotswolds, far from her usual stomping ground of West London.

Why?

'Fancy seeing you here! How are you?' He put his phone in his pocket.

'Stalking you actually,' she said looking at the ground.

'What? Again?'

'I've been stalking you on the socials. I know you tend to come to this gym at this time.'

Jason frowned. He didn't know how to respond.

'Sorry.' She shook his hand firmly.

He pulled her into a hug. No hard feelings and all that. 'How are you?'

'I'm well. I really wanted to talk to you.'

'Now?' he asked.

'If it's all right.'

He put his bag on the floor.

'I'm sort of adrift still. In many ways.' She hung her head.

He squeezed her shoulder. He really hadn't expected to see her again, never mind this. He wasn't sure what to do. 'Do you want to grab a wine or a coffee?'

Harriet bit her bottom lip. 'Wine sounds lovely, but I'd best stick to coffee.' A pained expression crossed her face.

'Coffee it is.' Jason smiled, led them to a bar.

Perched on a copper-covered shelf by the window, Jason told her about Extra Weddings and planning his marriage to Pete.

'I'm so pleased for you. It's wonderful news. Really wonderful.' She looked away for a moment, took a deep breath. 'Are you still seeing the older man?'

She shook her head, looking at the floor. 'I'm taking a sabbatical, a leave of absence from all matters of the heart. From everything actually, work too. I've decided to cover all those whimsical, silly, romantic parts with matt and gloss white paint. No more pink or floral, I shall be grey shift dresses and power suits.'

'What now?'

She explained about having her apartment redecorated in a more mature colour scheme, befitting someone of her age. Jason nodded and thought it spoke volumes of her real feelings, but didn't think it polite to say so.

'Aren't you still at our old place?' Jason asked.

She shook her head, lifting her empty cup. 'Another? Or a wine maybe?'

'I shouldn't.' He checked the time, Pete would be home now, wondering where he was. 'Let me text him so he doesn't worry. Small wine for me.'

'Of course.' She left for the bar.

Jason texted home, explaining he'd bumped into Harriet, wouldn't be long. Pete replied: *ok x*

She'd definitely said something about taking a sabbatical from work too, as well as romance. He believed the former was much more possible than the latter. And her face at refusing wine spoke volumes too, but he didn't want to intrude.

When Harriet returned with a glass of white wine and something sparkling in a tall glass, she said, 'I got you a large one, only buttons more than small. I've got to think of these things now.'

'Now you're... unemployed?'

'Yes, I walked out.' She raised her glass.

'No wine for you?' Jason raised his too.

She shook her head. 'Best not.'

'Are you okay?'

'I am now I'm not drinking.' She smiled brightly.

He left it at that, knowing if Harriet wanted to talk about it, she definitely would. She'd always struck him as such a bubbly person, but perhaps that had been more alcohol than personality.

Harriet explained why she'd left, how much she regretted not doing so when he had. 'It wasn't the same when you left. Sausage factory weddings.' She sipped the sparkling cordial.

He drank more. If he had any more he'd have to leave his car here and ask Pete to collect him. 'All the same?'

'Yes,' Harriet said, banging a hand on the table. 'You under-stand. I knew you would.' She shook her head. 'So boring. All the same. White Rolls Royce, sit-down fish/meat/veggie options, disco. First dance one of the same bloody half dozen songs. I couldn't do it any more.'

'What will you do now?' He finished his large glass of wine, his head felt light. Definitely not driving home. 'Fancy some crisps?'

'Definitely. Or we could grab dinner?' She shook her head. 'You've got plans. With Pete. Ignore me. Go now, I'll finish this and go home. I wanted to tell you in person that I'd left. I've done that. No more need for you to put up with me.'

'Let me call Pete; we could eat at mine.'

'You don't want me cluttering up your evening.' She dismissed it by waving her hands.

'Stay.' He walked away, explained to Pete what had happened. 'We're having a great time. I didn't know whether we should eat out, or bring her back home.' In a whisper he said, 'She's quite broken. Underneath. And I'm a bit pissed...'

'Bring her back. Plenty to go round. Do you want me to collect you?'

'I'll get a cab. Pick up my car tomorrow.' And with a wide grin at the sure knowledge he had the best fiancé in the world, Jason returned to their table, explained the plan.

Harriet blushed, shook her head. 'I don't want to impose. I shouldn't.'

'I insist.' He banged her glass with a fork. 'Finish up.'

They arrived at Jason and Pete's house. Harriet looked through the window as Jason paid the driver.

'Are you sure?'

'He wants to meet you.' Jason stood on the pavement, holding his hand for Harriet.

'If you're sure.' She stood, straightened out the wrinkles in her dress. A deep breath, head high, shoulders back, she followed Jason inside.

Jason and Pete kissed in the entrance hall. Pete shook Harriet's hand.

'Can I have some lime cordial and soda, please?' Carefully, after removing her heels, wobbling on one foot then the other, she walked to the kitchen where she leaned against the work surface.

'I could do with some more wine,' Jason asked loudly.

Pete presented Jason with a pint glass of water, and Harriet with her drink. 'You've been having a great time by the looks of it.' He turned and checked inside the oven. 'Beef casserole with dumplings, lots of green veg. Okay, or are you veggie?'

Harriet shook her head.

'So what have you been talking about? Having a good catch-up about old times?'

Jason explained as they moved to the dining room table.

Harriet sat, holding onto her glass as if her life depended on it.

Jason helped Pete with the food, doing a sort of kitchen dance as they so often called it, twirling and moving around one another without bumping together; Jason knew which parts Pete would want help with and vice versa. Jason felt Harriet watching them. He turned and glimpsed, out of the corner of his eye, her sitting, staring at them, smiling. He wondered if she'd ever been in a gay couple's house before.

They sat at the table, Pete waved for Harriet to help herself.

Jason stood, resting his hands on Pete's shoulders, kissed his cheek as he sat.

'Thanks so much for this,' Harriet said, blushing, staring at them. 'I'd have been happy getting cheesy chips at the bar. I was so pleased to see you.'

'She stalked me on social media.' Jason paused.

'I'm always telling him not to post his location,' Pete said. 'Especially if he's there at the same times.'

Harriet nodded. 'This is basically how I did it.' She smiled.

As Harriet spoke about what had happened at the wedding company, why she'd left, Jason noticed how her gaze followed them every time he touched Pete. He wasn't going to change his behaviour in his own home. If it made her feel uncomfortable, that was her problem.

'So what's your plan now?' Pete asked.

Harriet sat back, looking from Jason to Pete twice. She shrugged, leaning forwards, nodding at the bowl in the centre of the table. 'Can I?'

Jason nodded. 'Of course.'

As she helped herself to seconds, she said, 'I could see what my dad has for me at Electrovax. He wants me on the board. But it always feels like cheating, you know?'

Harriet had briefly mentioned her family were something big in white goods, but Jason had assumed it wasn't much.

'Asking for help isn't a bad thing,' Pete said.

'I was so bored at Tailored Weddings, same old same old, every bloody wedding like one of those things you make cookies out of. You cut them out. What's it called.' She sighed. 'I'm not much of a cook.'

'Cookie cutter?' Jason asked with a smirk, putting his hand on top of Pete's on the table and squeezing.

'That's it!' Harriet looked at their hands for a long moment.

'Do we make you feel uncomfortable?' Jason blurted, without thinking.

Pete pulled his hand away. 'Rude!'

'Not in our house it isn't.'

Harriet took a deep breath. 'I was going to say, but didn't know how to. But I'll say it now. I think you two are adorable. A-dor-able. There, I said it. I can't stop looking at how you two are with each other. All I can say is I wish I could find someone who loves me as much as you two love each other.'

Jason hadn't expected that. Not at all. He didn't think there was much more to say, making a point she'd changed her views felt like putting her on the spot for justifying why she'd done so. People learn, grow, change, which should be applauded. 'What's for pudding?' Jason asked.

'Bread and butter pudding.' Pete stood, stacked plates and carried them to the kitchen.

Checking Pete was out of earshot, Harriet said, 'I'm sorry if I made you feel like that. I couldn't stop looking because you're so sweet together. I've never seen you in that way. At work.'

Harriet stood, carried crockery to the kitchen.

Over dessert, served with custard, Harriet said, 'Reminds me of school dinners. And the cafeteria when I was at Cambridge.

I was in catered halls. It was always food like this.' She gobbled a large mouthful. 'Never have it at home.'

She reminded Jason of a much younger girl. Beneath the strong exterior, Harriet was as clueless as everyone else. 'Work for me.'

'I'm between jobs, but I'll be okay.' She blushed, chewing her next mouthful. 'I get an allowance. It's embarrassing really. I work for the people, the endeavour, the purpose it gives me. Which was why I left Tailored Weddings.'

'That works out well. I'm a start-up business, the money's not great, but there's plenty of variety, opportunity to use your creativity at this endeavour.'

'All different types of wedding?'

'All different types of people too.' He explained the ethos of Extra Weddings. 'And the people there are good too.'

'Right.'

'Come and work with us, will you?'

'Go on then.'

They shook hands.

'It's less money, more hours, but you'll be working with me again.'

'Sounds perfect.' She beamed across the table.

Later, after she'd left, Pete said, 'I wasn't expecting that night to happen.'

'Same.' Jason shrugged.

'You reckon she'll fit in?'

'I do. She's what we need. Who'd have thought it, eh, Horrible Harriet working for me.'

'I'd forgotten your nickname.'

Jason bit his bottom lip with guilt. 'Not to her face.'

'Obvs.'

Chapter 41

Gareth was sitting in their corner, at a desk for two. He'd reserved a seat with his jacket.

Mel sat, reaching out to squeeze his hand. She didn't like making a big show of them being together, not in the library anyway. Felt a bit... ostentatious. Except she really wanted to kiss him, feel his arms around her, inhale his soapy, woody scent she enjoyed so much. *God, I'm like a bloody teenager, it's a good job I'm not telling anyone this.*

She told him about working for Jason.

'You're enjoying it?'

'I didn't think I was good enough. I felt comfortable doing the care work. Why change things?'

'Because you are good enough. Better than.' He smiled.

Her stomach filled with butterflies. All this change in her life was amazing, but after decades of stasis, she wondered if she were somehow losing part of who she was. She needed regular reminders that she was good enough and she could continue trying new things.

'How was Dawn about you leaving?' he asked.

'Pleased for me. Said she knew I would move on to bigger and better things.'

'As you deserve.'

He'd admitted he could never do her job – too squeamish – which had surprised her since he had two daughters. It turned out his ex-wife had done all the day-to-day raising of them and he'd, like Steve, done light duties and handled the money.

Am I dating a man who's too similar to Steve? Is this setting myself up for heartache so soon? 'I'm gonna think on it. Shall we go?'

They walked to their lecture where they received their grades for the first essay that went towards their final degree grade.

The lecturer put them face down in front of each student.

Gareth got a sixty-three per cent with some really encouraging comments. He was beaming.

Mel knew she'd messed it up. She'd got herself in something of a tizz about the sources she'd used online. Last time, there wasn't anything online; in 1995 the internet didn't exist. She'd assumed all references needed to be from books. And then after handing it in, she was sure she'd tackled the question entirely wrongly, focusing on aspects they hadn't covered in the lectures and using a completely inappropriate theory to deconstruct it.

'Aren't you going to turn it over?' Gareth pointed to her essay.

Mel shook her head. 'I can't.' If she failed, it would be clear, once and for all, she didn't deserve her place here. In some ways it would come as a blessed relief and she could return to her old life.

'Do you want me to check for you?'

She slid it across to him, nodding.

He checked, smiled, then grinned broadly. 'Ready?'

Mel took a deep breath.

'Seventy-five per cent.'

She snatched it from him. 'Bollocks.' There, in black biro, a large '75/100' at the top of her essay. She scanned the comments as her vision blurred. Blinking furiously, she stared at the ceiling air ducts, concentrating on not crying.

'You're amazing. When are you going to start believing it?' Gareth kissed her cheek.

The lecturer was at the front of the theatre, his first slide on the screen signalling he was starting.

Mel pushed the essay to one side, and turned to her whizzy new Netbook Isaac and Pete had bought her to begin the next challenge.

Later that evening, after attending two lectures and returning to the library to collect books, they were eating at a Mexican restaurant near the university.

Gareth had insisted on taking her out to celebrate the essay grade. Mel had thought it a bit showy and unnecessary, but acknowledged she'd spent her life without pause for celebration of her achievements, so this was her time.

They were halfway through their second bottle of wine. It went well with the tortilla wraps they filled with steak and pepper slices, guacamole, sour cream, cheese and refried black beans.

'Are you coming back tomorrow?' Gareth asked nonchalantly as he assembled his third tortilla wrap.

'What for?'

'The talk on women in fiction. The panel looks brilliant.'

It wasn't part of their course, but it sounded really interesting. 'I'm working.'

'It's at three. I've booked the day off. Weren't you going to as well?'

The memory of that conversation scuttled across her mind. She'd written it down and then left and it had slipped away. Mel checked her work rota for tomorrow. 'I didn't book it off.'

'Not to worry.' Gareth looked disappointed. More than seemed appropriate. He looked away, stroking his beard in thought.

'There will be others.'

He nodded and they continued the meal in easy conversation. Except Mel couldn't help noticing Gareth seemed different.

He paid and they were saying goodbye outside the restaurant when she sensed something was on his mind.

'What?'

'Nothing,' he said.

'I'll ask again and that's it. I was married to someone who used to play this game. I'm not playing it any more.' She stroked his cheek, gently pulling his face up so they made eye contact.

'I've booked tomorrow off. We talked about how you'd do the same. I thought you could stay, and we'd go to the talk together.'

Stay. At his place in London. 'Right,' she said carefully and swallowed.

'I'm not rushing you. It's fine. I didn't tell you I was hoping you'd stay over. This is me asking you now. You've got a job, a life. I'm an idiot.'

'You're not.' She bit her bottom lip. The thought of doing anything more than kissing with Gareth both excited and terrified her. She'd spent twenty-five years with Steve and had no idea what to do.

'I *really* like you. I—' He seemed to have a frog in his throat 'And I'd like to...' He looked away. 'Carry on liking you and seeing you and dating you.'

Excitement and nerves bubbled up in her stomach. They'd been dating – saying the word felt stupid at her age – for three months. Since the start of this term. It wasn't as if going to bed with Gareth hadn't occurred to her in her alone time, when she remembered his kisses, the way he placed a hand in the small of her back, how he held doors open for her and dozens of other small gestures.

'If you can't come back to my place tonight, I understand. I should have... I am an idiot.' He turned to her, staring into her eyes. His were blue-green and shining. 'I want to know you'd like to... When the time is right.'

Mel nodded. She held his face close, pulling him in for a kiss. His beard rubbed against her face, he opened his mouth and she inhaled deeply the scent she knew to be Gareth as her mouth opened, tasting him, hinting at so much more they could do together. Heat uncoiled from her stomach to her core. 'Yes.'

Gareth nodded, smiling, his eyes twinkling so much. 'Can we walk to the Tube station together?' He took her hand.

As they walked, Mel's nerves seemed to subside as the immediacy had passed while the promise remained. The anticipation of what they'd do together hovered excitedly over the horizon. The anticipation and excitement of sex, and how joyfully fun it could be – if she could remember – made her smirk. Except not her, not at her age, their age.

At the station, she turned towards him. 'I don't want you to build this up into something big.'

He frowned.

'I'm not... It's been a while. I don't do it too well.' Steve hadn't said this, but she'd sort of got out of practice between the kids and his work and being tired, leaving them with occasional, perfunctory lovemaking, which always had her worrying she wasn't doing it quite right. 'I don't know how to do this. At our age...'

'I'm sure that's not true. I hear it's like riding a bike, once you get going.' He grinned at that, staring deep into her eyes. 'I'm clueless. We can be clueless together. Bumped heads, falling on the floor. It's fine. As long as it's with you, it'll be great.' He nodded. 'Okay?'

She felt a quiet degree of confidence she'd not expected. A sense of being safe in Gareth's strong and gentle hands, in them rediscovering this side of their lives together, in all its glorious, awkward, middle-aged splendour. 'Yes.' And then she kissed him, fully open mouthed, eyes closed, leaning into the moment and in anticipation of so much more they'd discover together when it was right for them. She turned, with butterflies in her stomach and desire uncoiling from her centre at the kiss, and she walked through the ticket barriers, down the escalator and onto the Tube train.

–

It was a bright Tuesday night at Gareth's place when Mel finally stayed over. She'd arranged childcare for her almost-adult children. Gareth sorted out a taxi back to his apartment, a converted hospital in Greenwich. There he lit candles, poured wine and they talked, ate and Mel had never felt so loved and cherished.

In a sudden moment of boldness, she sat on his lap, unbuttoning his shirt, running her hands through his dark grey chest hair, on the contours of his body. He gazed up at her with a look of love and caring. She took his hand and led him into the bedroom, where she allowed him to undress her, garment by garment, alternating with her removing his clothes one item at a time as she appreciated his body. His skin was warm, his stomach blessedly free of abs and six pack, slightly squashy around the edges like hers, and covered in grey and dark hair over his chestthat had her unconsciously licking her lips and stroking it.

They stood naked in the gentle candlelight she'd insisted upon, feeling sure it would better cover a multitude of her body's sins than the harsh overhead lights.

They kissed, and then she followed his gently tugging hand as he led her to the bed, bathed in gentle candlelight...

Afterwards, Mel wanted to tell everyone how wonderful she felt, how much she was enjoying being with Gareth, how she hadn't realised that was how it could be. But she didn't, she held the memory quietly to herself and told Gareth instead. 'Well, I enjoyed that very much.'

'Like riding a bike.' He winked and stroked her hair and she rested her head on his chest.

'I wondered, if you'd like to carry on doing this.'

'What now? You'll need to give me a while, but as soon as I can, I'm up for another bike ride.'

She shook her head. 'Not that. I mean us. Together.'

'As boyfriend and girlfriend?' he asked.

'Do people say that at our age?'

'People can do anything at any age.'

She nodded. 'Yeah. As boyfriend and girlfriend.'

'I reckon that sounds wonderful.' He kissed her and to her surprise, he was ready for another bike ride much sooner than she'd anticipated.

Chapter 42

A week spent with Aunt Wendy, in her pastel pink thatched cottage in a remote part of Wales, as Harriet had hoped, did her the world of good. She joined Wendy twice a day for long, galloping dog walks as the three gun dogs ran around them. Harriet helped make a cake and then decorated Wendy's conservatory as they listened to the radio and chatted about Harriet's father, Wendy always bemused by how they could be related.

It took her until the second day to tell Wendy what was wrong. She'd been up since the sun rose, curled up reading in the corner of Wendy's third bedroom given over to her book collection. All walls had floor-to-ceiling bookshelves, with four others in the room, forming a zig-zagged barrier between the window and the sofa.

'I shan't ask you again, your father refused to tell me what had happened. Said you'd tell me in your own good time.' Wendy stood by the door, holding a tray of tea in the early morning light.

Harriet looked up from her book, carefully inserting a bookmark and laying it on the soft sofa next to her. 'Where is he?'

Wendy sat at the far end of the sofa, offering to pour the tea from the pot. Carefully checking it was strong enough, she then added a splash of milk into the bone china cup. 'Who?'

'I'm at sea. I rather believed I'd have life much better arranged by this age.'

'Who are you searching for?' Wendy replaced the cup and saucer onto a small table.

'I thought I knew who I'd marry. I could imagine what he looked like. Since I was a teenager, sneaking in here to read your books.' She shrugged, sighed, shook her head.

'You're not going to blame me, are you?' Wendy smiled. 'When my parents died, they got me through. Saved me, I've no doubt.'

'What about Uncle Howard?'

She interlaced her fingers, placed them on her lap. 'He was...' A long pause, a sigh, a shake of her head, and then: 'Absolutely useless.'

Harriet didn't know if she could laugh or not.

Wendy nodded, smiled. 'Honestly. Chocolate teapot territory. Carpet fitter's ladder environs.'

Harriet giggled slightly.

'He was the love of my life, I shall never find a man like him. But with grief, he wasn't much help.' She placed her hand on Harriet's thigh. 'I was nearly forty when I met him. He'd been married before, if you can call it that – they never saw one another between his work and her falling in love with the town's headmistress. And then one day, he moved into the village and I met him at the post office in the town. Posting a pile of Valentine's cards for my nieces and nephews. He was in for his car tax disc.' She rolled her eyes. 'Decades ago.'

Harriet hadn't heard any of this before 'Headmistress? They were...'

'Moved to a small village in Yorkshire and opened up a B&B. Apparently it's very popular with women who like women.' Wendy shrugged. 'Live and let live, I say. Howard certainly agreed love is love, whatever flavour of it tickles your fancy.'

Well I never! Lesbian affairs in the seventies! Harriet nodded.

'I told Howard I wasn't interested, I'd got used to my own ways and wasn't keen on him getting under my feet.' She stirred her tea. 'He wouldn't take no for an answer. Persistence paid off for both of us. Thirty-two years he was under my feet.' She blinked away a tear. 'Don't give up on love.'

'Too late.' Harriet untucked her legs from beneath her. She'd explained her plan to de-sentimentalise her apartment, in recognition of leaving behind her sickly-sweet obsession with romance and all that entailed. 'He, whoever he is, is obviously not coming. Or I'm simply far too exacting. You've seen how particular I am about my toiletries and clothes, is it any wonder I want perfect when it comes to a husband? So I shall keep my chin up and march on, as you did after you lost Uncle Howard. I always held you in such admiration, forging your way in the world alone like that. I thought you far more impressive than Mother, seeming to live in Father's shadow.'

'You don't know what goes on in anyone else's relationship. You can only see what's visible. Being independent was wonderful, but I was lonely. I had dozens of friends with which to amuse myself – groups, holidays, nights in the village pub. But I'd always return to the dogs. Uncle Howard used to drive me potty, but I'd give everything to have him getting under my feet again.' She stood. 'Coming into town with me? Market day.'

The last time she'd visited, Harriet had been desperately trying to get a good enough phone signal to call her boyfriend. She'd driven herself spare with wondering if he'd been in touch, climbing up the nearest hill and holding her phone above her head. Refusing to admit to anyone at the time nor asking to borrow the landline for it seemed terribly not feminist of her to await a man like that. And yet she'd not been able to help herself.

Harriet shrugged.

'I'll see if the butcher's has any lamb mince and we can make your favourite, shep pie. The butcher's lad is running it better than his father ever managed. Big strapping man, plays rugby for the club in town. Looks splendid in a pair of shorts. They did a charity calendar, posing with only a rugby ball to cover their modesty.' Aunt Wendy blushed.

Harriet admitted that had piqued her interest. Even if it would obviously never lead anywhere. Except in one of the books she'd been devouring, it would have been the hero and heroine's meet–cute. She nodded. 'If I must.' *When am I going to get my meet-cute?*

Wendy stood. 'There are some things in life at which you can try too hard. You're better off playing them by ear. It's not like a job interview, you know. Love doesn't work like that.'

Chapter 43

Jason knew this wedding was going to be a challenge when one of the brides, Bridget, a TV presenter who'd worked her way up from being a production assistant, handed over a checklist at their first meeting with a shortlist of suppliers for each of the main elements, including websites and phone numbers.

'It's all in there,' she'd said.

Jason had said, 'If we could start with the scrapbook, mood board, I usually find that helps. We have a set process here, which we've found works best, to really get to know our clients' needs and dreams. If you can imagine it, dream it, we can make it happen.'

Bridget rolled her eyes, crossed her legs and faced away from Jason. 'I said this wasn't right. *If you can dream it, we can make it happen*. Next thing you'll be saying you run on fairy dust.'

Oli said, 'Give them a chance.'

'If I see anything mentioning live, love, laugh, I'm leaving, laughing at you and not loving it.'

'Bridge, will you please behave?' Oli said firmly.

Harriet had obviously sensed Jason was slightly feeling adrift, so leaned forwards. 'I think what Jason's trying to say, is we like to start big picture and then narrow it down as you've so ably done here.' Harriet put aside Bridget's list.

Oli, the other bride, another TV presenter, held Bridget's arm and exchanged a stern stare. 'I said they'd know what to do.'

Bridget folded her arms.

'She won't have a male voice on her satnav, it's all very sensitive.'

Bridget went bright red. 'Why did you have to tell him that?'

'It's useful context in terms of your behaviour. They don't mind, do you?' Oli looked from Jason to Harriet, seeking reassurance.

Harriet reached into a nearby filing cabinet and retrieved two scrapbook mood boards. 'Some clients prefer to do these online, others, well, they like it old school.' She laid them out on the table.

They were in the one meeting room of the tiny office Jason had moved Extra Weddings into. Now he had himself and four other employees, including Harriet and Mel, he'd found trying to do it all remotely hadn't really worked.

'I like this,' Oli said, examining the handmade scrapbook. 'So it's anything?'

'Anything that has the right… vibe. Sorry, I always giggle at that. It feels a bit… naff. You understand what I mean, though?'

Bridget took a photo of the two mood boards. 'Where do you start with it?'

'Anything that means something to you both. Where you met, a song, an album, a film. We can build the whole concept around that if you want.'

Jason wasn't really needed but Harriet hadn't wanted to take the meeting on her own. She seemed to have lost some of her confidence since returning from the visit to her auntie's place in Wales. She hadn't said much about it, but Jason imagined not having alcohol as a crutch may have affected her.

'Where did you meet?' Harriet asked the brides-to-be.

Bridget rolled her eyes. 'Haven't you seen, it's in all the papers, if you can call them that.'

'I don't…' Harriet smoothed her dress on her lap.

Jason sensed she felt nervous, as if she'd said something tactless and wrong. 'I met my boyfriend—'

'Fiancé,' Harriet said.

'Fiancé, at a book-signing for his favourite pop group from the eighties – even though he wasn't born then.'

Oli looked up briefly. 'For those who haven't read the version the papers have printed, which isn't completely true and misses out some key details: I was opening a village fete... Why anyone would come to watch me cut a ribbon and tell some questionable jokes using lots of innuendo is anyone's guess. But they did. I was filming a show about driving around the British Isles in an old British car, stopping at places to sample the things they were renowned for. Cheddar cheese, Red Leicester, Melton Mowbray pork pies. The village fete was near where they make the jam.'

'Tiptree?' Harriet offered.

'And,' Bridget went on, 'I was filming a gardening series nearby. Had to stay over and my crew said Olivia was at a thing nearby, did we want to check it out.'

'Same production company,' Oli offered by way of explanation.

'What was she like?' Jason asked.

'Don't know,' Bridget said. 'Didn't go.'

'We were staying in the same hotel – the cheapest one for miles around, so of course that's where we were booked in. Public broadcaster, so we must always be seen to be spending the licence payers' fees well.'

'We all ate together, and we ended up in the bar until closing.'

'Then what?' Jason asked.

Bridget blushed.

'Right.' Jason raised an eyebrow, catching the look of mischief between the two brides-to-be.

There was a silence into which Bridget and Oli chuckled.

'That sounds wonderful,' Harriet said. 'Is there anything you'd like to incorporate from that into your big day?'

They talked at length, and Jason watched Harriet do what she did best, and do it very well. She had developed a rapport with the two women and they were soon shaking hands, kissing cheeks, swapping socials details and promising to follow each other.

Harriet showed them out of the office.

Mel had done the research for their premises, Harriet had visited the shortlist and Jason left them to decide on the best option. Up to him, he'd have continued working from his study forever, but Harriet and Mel had become sick and tired of meeting in cafés and having to arrange similar to meet clients.

Six months of planning, three attempts at their mood board, once electronically on Pinterest, twice using pens and paper and Bridge and Oli's wedding day had arrived.

Jason had told Harriet he didn't need to be there, it was her wedding, her day, he trusted her completely.

'I think you should,' she'd insisted.

'You're much better at this than you think.'

Harriet, never one to accept praise, shrugged and said, 'Whatever, please come.'

Jason and Harriet arrived at the church grounds. They were set up like a church fete – stalls, tents, chairs and tables in the middle. A dance floor tent.

They hadn't been able to have the marriage ceremony in the church, it wasn't yet allowed, but the vicar had agreed to a blessing in the grounds, after the legal and very brief ceremony in the registry office.

The brides stood in the church doorway, a flower wreath covering it around the edge. The vicar asked them to repeat their commitment to one another and she blessed them, in the name of the father, the son and the holy ghost.

Both women had been brought up in a religious household and had struggled with that since coming out later in life, so Jason had been really impressed how Harriet had managed to work with the vicar to do what was allowed and provide an important spiritual element to the wedding.

There wasn't one wedding cake, but instead a table of wedding cakes made by their guests, each with cocktail sticks and labels describing them.

A bowling alley was keeping the children and plenty of adults occupied in one corner.

The main stage, a raised platform with lights and speakers, sat in the centre of the grounds.

The church provided parking and toilet facilities, as well as bell ringing as the guests arrived.

A table had photos mounted on three panels of the brides throughout their lives, with descriptions, dates, one bride on each side, with their lives together on a third panel in the middle.

The closest friends of the women wore superhero outfits, all with capes.

Oli was dressed as Wonder Woman and Bridget as Xena, Warrior Princess. They shared a love of illustrated comics and one of Bridget's most frequent phrases, particularly at work, was: not all heroes wear capes.

Jason worried the other guests may have found the superheroes disconcerting, but since each table was named after a different comic character, it made sense.

The green four-by-four arrived and first Xena stepped out, then Wonder Woman.

There was no press permitted and they had barricaded the roads towards the church and kept everything top secret, including no socials on the day itself.

It felt a bit of a shame because Jason knew it would be great publicity, but he respected the brides' wishes.

Bridget and Oli walked through the churchyard to applause from their guests, the superheroes standing closest and posing for photos.

There were four speeches: Bridget first. 'I wasn't going to come to the meal at the hotel that night. I'd had enough of people. I was just divorced. Done with men and relationships. But Oli showed me a different way to do things.'

A double entendre-appreciating cheer went up from the crowd.

Oli's dad spoke next – a slim white-haired man in his seventies in a grey morning suit. He spoke about how love was love. 'Oli was always a bit different. She was never going to have an ordinary life. So when she started being paid for being opinionated and rude, I wasn't surprised. She'd been doing that since she could speak. I'm so happy she's found someone who can argue back. Because I lost the ability to do so, years ago. She's as fast as a whip and as sharp as a knife and I'm so happy that Bridge can keep up with her.'

Oli stood, thanked her father. 'There isn't a wedding cake, as there is also no groom or groomsmen, but instead we have six bridesmaids. I wanted to thank them all. Can they please come up to the front?'

Six girls, aged from three to eleven-ish, walked to the front. They wore princess, prince, superhero outfits, whatever they wanted. The unifying theme had been 'Whatever makes the girls feel powerful'.

The guests clapped as they were named one by one, curtseying before returning to their seats.

Bridget stood. 'The cake stall is now open for everyone to help themselves!'

The music started to play in the far corner of the grounds, filling the dance-floor tent.

'I hope you're taking lots of pictures,' Jason said to Harriet.

She nodded. 'When do you usually slip off at these things?'

'Depends.'

'On what?'

'If I need to fix stuff, if I'm having a good time or what else I need to do. You've totally seen it through, you don't need to stay now. Just check with Bridget and Oli that everything's okay, and then we can leave. Unless you want to stay?'

'I love a wedding. But sometimes they make me sad, you know? Actually, you probably don't, because you have Pete.' She waved it away. 'Ignore me. It's hard, you know.' She indicated the table covered with bottles of wine.

Jason hugged her. 'You're doing great. You've totally got this.'

'I have. But it doesn't go away, you know? The wanting.'

Jason couldn't imagine wanting a drink and not being able to have one, so he smiled weakly and nodded. 'Shall we have a massive slice of cake?'

'Splendid idea.' Harriet led the way towards the cake tent. She cut herself a slice of chocolate sponge and Jason some carrot cake with cream-cheese frosting.

They took them back to the main tent where people were eating and dancing.

Bridget and Oli didn't want the whole first-dance fuss, so the music had started halfway through the sit-down wedding breakfast — toad-in-the-hole with creamy mashed potato and onion gravy or nut roast with vegetables — and by now there were children dancing in small groups, with parents swaying from side to side.

They walked up to Jason and Harriet's table. It was one of the most bizarre experiences in Jason's life, catching Wonder Woman and Xena, Warrior Princess approaching from the corner of his eye, with a small village church in the background, as children ran around the maypole and morris dancers performed outside the tent.

'We thought you'd have left,' Bridget said.

'We can totally go if you want us to,' Harriet said with a smile.

'No, I mean, you must go to these all the time, doesn't it get a bit... boring?'

Harriet shook her head. 'Not at all. Tiring, complicated, messy, absolutely. But boring, never.'

Jason nodded. 'Same.' He bit into the carrot cake. Something didn't taste right. There was a spicy edge to it. Not the cinnamon in the cake, but something else.

'Is that nice?' Oli asked him.

'It should be.' He didn't want to make a fuss, perhaps it was the coffee he'd had earlier… He took another bite. Yep, odd. Not nice. 'I think I've had too much cake.'

'Mine's delicious,' Harriet said.

'Can I?' Bridget pointed at the carrot cake. She took a bite, screwed her face up, then spat it out.

'Is it off?' Harriet asked.

'Cream cheese.'

'Off?' Jason asked.

Bridge shook her head. 'It's not off, but it does have garlic and herbs in it.'

Jason's mouth fell open in horror. 'I'm so sorry.'

'This is my fault,' Harriet added.

Bridge laughed. 'It really isn't.'

She had taken charge of cakes, contacting their baking friends and asking them to make their favourite cake for the cake tent, in place of one wedding cake. Bridget had explained she hated wedding cake: 'Who actually enjoys fruit cake? Not me. Never. Let's have cakes people actually like. And some choice. Otherwise it's wedding cake or nothing. No.' And she'd promised that she totally had this.

Oli said, 'Who made it? Is it who I think it is?'

Bridget nodded.

'What are we going to do?'

Jason stood. 'Nothing, we'll sort it.'

'Honestly, it's fine. Doesn't matter. It's hilarious. My mum refuses to wear glasses. She'll have grabbed the cream cheese and not read the label.' She clapped, laughing and held her stomach as the chuckles continued coming in waves.

'I'm so sorry. Is everything else okay?' Harriet asked after Bridget and Oli had stopped laughing.

'It's wonderful. It's perfectly us. It's messy, it's British, it's quaint, it's totally not celebrity.'

It was the least celebrity wedding he'd ever seen for two celebrities. He told them. 'What will you do about the papers?'

'I'll post some pictures this evening and they can use that as the story. Thanks for keeping it all quiet. I know it must have been hard.'

Jason smiled. Pete had been pestering him constantly as soon as he'd mentioned they were planning a celebrity wedding for two women. Pete had taken to guessing their names until Jason could bear no more. But he'd kept it confidential since the two women's privacy had been so important and he'd have been mortified to have spoiled that.

'If you ever want any endorsements, celebrity anything, hit us up.' Oli looked at Bridget. 'I'm totally speaking on your behalf and we've been married, what, less than two hours.' She shook her head.

Bridget kissed her. 'It's fine with me.' She smiled at her. ''Cos it's you.'

Oli laughed nervously. 'Sorry. We seem to have stepped into a Richard Curtis rom com.'

'Nothing wrong with that,' Harriet said, raising a fist, which she bumped with Oli, then Bridget.

Jason felt so happy that he'd helped make this happen, that he did this for a living, that he felt a tiny tear appearing at the corner of his eye.

'Very kind of you,' Jason said. 'Thanks.' He stood, they said goodbyes, hugging and kissing cheeks.

They walked away from the church fete as lights strobed, showing a rainbow on the spire and 'Come On Eileen' played.

'It's not a wedding until that comes on,' Jason said as they reached their cars.

'Second rule of Wedding Club,' Harriet said.

'What's the first one?'

'If you can dream it, we can make it happen.'

'Of course.'

Harriet looked back at the party in progress as a melancholy look clouded her face. She took a deep breath. 'It's fine. I'm fine. I'm taking Mother's advice. Weirdly, for the first time.'

'Which is?'

'To stop.' Her shoulders relaxed as she leaned against her car.

'Stop what?'

'Doesn't matter. It's silly. Go home. Say hi to Pete from me, will you?'

He didn't want to ask her back to theirs for the evening because she'd know it was a pity invite. She'd caught him out like that a few times. 'Stop what?'

'Wanting, all of this.' She nodded back at the party.

Jason held her tightly in a hug. 'See you Monday.'

'Aren't we interviewing for an office manager?'

Jason climbed into his car. 'I think you're interviewing for an office manager.'

Harriet slid into her car, waved goodbye and beeped her horn loudly as she left.

And Jason hoped with all his heart, that Harriet, once she stopped wanting and searching, would find love, just as he had in exactly the same way.

Chapter 44

Mel was deeply submerged in an essay, books splayed out, laptop whirring away, on a blissfully quiet Saturday in an empty house. She'd warned the eldest two that alternate Saturdays were her time, unless by pre-arrangement, on pain of death. This was her quiet Mel time, to study, be, reflect.

She used to think that being a mum would be her life's work, that it would be enough for her. The four children were her proudest achievement. But since returning to study, finding her own career, she knew although raising a family had been joyful, messy, worthwhile, they hadn't been enough. Not through any fault of the children, not even Steve, but her own. She'd allowed herself to believe she had no time for anything else, was too scared to try and fail, was too old to bother, so hadn't pursued it.

But now she had what she'd heard others refer to as a balanced life: family, friends, love, career, learning, all bringing her joy in different ways.

Love.

Steve had Lily and Thomas, Gareth had left earlier that morning, having stayed the night.

The memory made Mel blush and smile.

He'd kissed her at the door, said he'd see her at uni on Monday evening.

She glanced at her handwritten notes, checked the thick textbook's index and flicked to another page, ready to make more notes. She had developed a process for essays, starting with writing notes on all the sources, then sketching out a skeleton of an essay structure, linking which references she'd use. Then she'd dive into the laptop and write.

It was much more long-winded than most of her fellow students, but then again, she was much longer-in-the-tooth than them. It worked for her, giving her As and Bs throughout.

Her coffee cup was empty. *Later, I'll finish this book's quotes first.*

The doorbell rang.

She ran to answer it.

Steve stood with Lily and Thomas either side.

'But it's… isn't it?' She checked the time.

'Lunchtime Saturday we said.' Steve showed her on a spreadsheet on his phone.

'Right.' She stepped aside, gesturing them inside.

Steve stood in the hallway. 'Everything okay?'

'I thought you had them until tonight. Doesn't matter.' She stepped backwards. 'Coffee?' Her concentration had been broken now, so may as well be civil.

Over coffees, Steve asked how her studies were going.

'Good. It's hard, but good.'

'Do you want me to take them? If you're up to your eyes, I can take them now and bring them back, when shall we say? Tonight? Tomorrow night?'

It had taken him a while, but Steve was both enjoying and becoming better at looking after his children. It made Mel happy to see how he'd changed. 'It would be amazing. It's got to be in on Wednesday and I'm working and then I've got them until your Wednesday night.'

'No worries.' Steve smiled, looked about the kitchen. 'It feels nice in here. You've got it nice.'

She'd redecorated. When Harriet had been struggling to find someone to do her place, she'd passed on the man's details. Harriet had nothing but positive things to say about him.

They sat in silence as the children watched TV in the next room.

'I'm really pleased for you. What you're doing. Uni, it definitely suits you. I should've told you to carry on when I got you pregnant.' He looked down.

That was a different time, their priority had been the new baby and there didn't seem any way she could carry on studying while Steve supported them. 'Hindsight.' She shrugged.

'I never saw how much you did, do, used to. For the kids, the house.' He shook his head. 'Sorry.'

'What for? It's all water under the bridge now.' Mel felt embarrassed at this sudden outpouring of emotion from Steve, it was so unlike him.

'If I could do it again I'd do it differently. Be a better husband, dad.'

Mel wasn't convinced. She nodded at their mugs. 'More?'

'Better not. Trying to cut back. Sally says it makes me hyper.' He stood. 'Tomorrow night then?'

'If that's okay.'

'I think I owe you quite a bit of childcare, don't you?' He picked up the mugs, rinsed them and placed them in the dishwasher.

Mel held onto the table in shock. Who had killed her ex-husband and replaced him with this man? 'How's Sally?' It had taken Mel a long while to be able to ask without gritting her teeth. But seeing how she'd somehow created Steve 2.0, Mel couldn't help but have a little admiration for her.

'She took me back, so I can't be getting it totally wrong.'

'Absolutely.' Mel felt sure if she hadn't forced him to try harder with Sally, he'd have begged her to take him back, and she'd have probably agreed, for an easier, if unhappier, life. But some relationships weren't meant to last until death us do part. She and Steve had worked well to create a family, but it was both their faults she'd somehow disappeared, lost Mel.

Steve called the children's names, they soon arrived. 'Change of plan, Mum's studying, so you're stuck with me until tomorrow night.'

There was a bit of complaining about Thomas having started a game on the PlayStation, and could Lily bring her dolls this time, but soon they were picking up their bags, saying goodbye to Mel and walking to his car.

'Thanks,' Mel said to Steve in the hallway. 'How's work?' She didn't want to ask any more personal questions, she felt they'd inadvertently covered a lot over coffees.

'They assumed I loved working all hours.' He chuckled. 'Thought I enjoyed working on holiday.' He shook his head. 'Hindsight, eh?' He looked at the floor.

She knew there was no likelihood he'd ask to get back together, but she couldn't help feeling sorry for him now. 'Better you find it out now than when you're sixty.'

'Take care, eh? Tell Gareth to look after you.'

She nodded. 'Say hi to Sally from me.' They'd not met, but maybe, sometime in the future, Mel could imagine all four of them together. She allowed herself a tiny curl of her mouth at the edges.

'Will do. She says hi back, asked me to tell you.' He waved, turned and walked to his car.

Harriet closed the door and wished she and Steve had talked like that when they were married. Maybe they wouldn't be divorced now, she thought wistfully. But then again she wouldn't have met Gareth. Probably wouldn't have had the drive to go back to school.

Maybe they needed to separate so they could both become the people they were now, the couple who'd had the discussion as improved individuals.

That had to be the case because Mel reckoned anything else too sad to think about. Too painful to imagine an alternative life where Steve was the new Steve and she was the new Mel and where they were still together. Where Steve wouldn't have looked elsewhere and had an affair.

Best not go down that road, she stopped herself, and returned to the essay.

Chapter 45

Harriet walked from room to room in her apartment. The walls were blue-white, orange-white and green-white. In truth, only she could tell the difference since she'd chosen them. Sophie had said she liked how it was all white, white, white and Harriet had explained their slightly different hues.

She stood in front of the drawers in her kitchen. *Am I really going to do this?* She held a hammer in both slightly shaking hands.

It didn't make sense. Not her destroying a perfectly good set of drawers, but the reason why.

Paul.

She entirely blamed Mel for Paul. No one had given Harriet a firm quote for the decorating work; she wasn't sure why, she simply had very exacting standards and an inflexible time frame in mind.

Mel had recently redecorated her home and after a work video call, where Mel had given Harriet a tour of the house, Harriet had explained her trouble securing someone.

So Mel shared Paul's number and duly, on the time and date arranged, Paul had arrived at Harriet's apartment to provide a quote. None of the others had done anything of the sort, simply ignoring her emails.

Paul had strutted about her apartment, having only reluctantly removed his dirty work boots after Harriet had exclaimed he couldn't possibly enter wearing those. So about her rooms he'd strutted, bending and reaching in his large pocketed tight work trousers showing off, very well, Harriet noticed, his muscular behind and thighs.

Paul was measuring her rooms with a red laser contraption, writing things on a scrap of paper, pursing his lips, chewing his cheek and stroking his roughly unshaven face – *unkempt facial hair is so unflattering* – in what Harriet assumed was thought.

Having inspected the final room and placed his laser contraption into his tool belt, he said, 'Any chance of a cuppa? Only I'm parched.'

Reluctantly, Harriet obliged. A short while later, producing a tea pot, she handed him one of her workmen mugs she kept beneath the sink, giving herself a china mug covered in pink flowers.

'Do you think you'll be able to do it?' Harriet asked, pouring herself tea – milk second of course.

She watched in horror as Paul half-filled the mug with milk, added the tea,, then removed one of the bags from the teapot, swirling it about in his mug.

Savage.

She'd decided she didn't want this man in her apartment any longer, never mind paying him to redecorate it. Even if he made her think ridiculously impure thoughts involving his tool belt falling off, his trousers sliding down to reveal slim hips and a touch more of his bright underpants that occasionally flashed above the trousers.

It's been far too long since I've even been kissed by a man. Perhaps time to return to Tinder.

She could find no earthly reasons why Mel would have recommended him. She must ask Mel, precisely where she'd dug up this man.

Paul sipped his tea. 'Aren't I good enough for a nice mug?' He inspected his, then glanced at hers.

No one had ever said that before. She blushed. 'I think it's better you leave, please.'

343

'Fair enough, but I saw your email and, I don't mean to be rude, but you're never gonna find someone to do the work for you like that.'

Averting her gaze from his muscular arms, Harriet resigned herself to a cold shower that night. 'Why not?'

'There's no way one man can redecorate a place like this within three days, all because you don't want to be inconvenienced.'

'You're wrong.' She took his mug from him, brushing his rough fingers, causing a shot of electricity to course through her arm.

'Only way you can do it so quick is getting a team of six men to do it.'

'So why don't you do that?' Harriet found herself softening, not wanting him to leave, but also not quite wishing he remain.

'Can I show you?'

He's here now, might as well. She nodded tightly, putting his mug on the work surface.

'I'll have that.' He picked it up, led her room by room, explaining about wallpaper removal, issues with her coving, the light fittings, skirting-board problems, sipping the tea all the while, talking with enthusiasm and a grin she didn't dislike, until finally they returned to the kitchen.

Harriet felt rather small. No one had bothered to explain precisely *why* her ask was unrealistic, they'd just ignored her. But Paul, for all his faults – and they were many and various as far as Harriet could see – had taken the time to explain what *really* needed doing in her apartment, and was now, on a piece of paper she'd fetched him, leaning against the breakfast bar as he wrote her a quote for the work.

'Why don't you sit?' She pulled a stool out from beneath the bar. Although she'd been rather enjoying the view, it didn't feel very dignified simply ogling him as he stood there oozing masculinity from every pore of his body.

He hopped onto it, returning to the quote, deep in concentration as his tongue stuck out and didn't seem to notice what Harriet was doing.

Harriet wanted to leave him alone to his work, but she didn't want to stop watching him. He had a kind of urbane rough-around-the-edges quality that fascinated her. Totally unselfconscious with himself, his confidence oozed in his movements, the way he stood, but he somehow managed not to be arrogant or patronising.

He had – Harriet saw as she read his quote, written in capitals with interesting spelling, some letters back to front – gently led her by the hand through the issues and explained them, so when she'd finished reading, she had no option but to say, 'When can you start?'

'Have a think about it. No rush.' He slurped the last of his tea, put the mug next to the kettle. 'Sorry about the spelling, I hope you get the gist.' He looked away.

'Made perfect sense.' Harriet held the quote and nodded. 'Monday?'

It had started a fortnight later, seven a.m., Monday morning, with her supplying him with endless pots and mugs of tea while he decorated. Then at the end of one particularly long day, he was covered in tiny white freckles of paint and said, 'Mind if I wash these before I go?' His hands were speckled white. As was his neck, from where he'd removed his T-shirt earlier with the windows open during one of the hottest days they'd had that year.

Harriet wasn't sure where to look when she'd returned with tea to find him standing bare chested, paint roller in one hand and tray of paint in the other. 'It's looking good, don't you think?' he asked with a grin.

On the tip of her tongue, as she'd taken in his tanned chest with dark hair, was *not too bad*. Which was far too coarse to verbalise, so she'd looked about the room at the walls, window sill and proclaimed quietly, 'Very nice,' before shuffling away from this distracting sight and retreating to the safety of her bedroom, thence for a brisk walk in the park.

As the day ended, she showed him to the kitchen sink and returned to inspect his work in the spare bedroom. Despite wanting to, she could find no fault with his flawless 'cutting in', as it was called apparently, where he used a small paintbrush for the edges, having covered the ground with a roller.

Content she was happy for him to continue, she returned to the kitchen.

He was scrubbing himself rather enthusiastically.

'Are you finished?'

He held up red hands, still spattered with paint flecks.

He was clearly educationally backward or something, otherwise he'd have known to use something in addition to scrubbing. Tutting loudly, she offered the use of her tea tree shower gel, returning from the bathroom and handing it to him.

An embarrassing squirting noise later, he rubbed it on his hands and forearms, then totally unselfconsciously, slid off his T-shirt and began soaping up his chest, which was speckled with the same white marks.

Harriet looked away, feeling bad for intruding on what should be a private experience for him. She blushed and faced the window, wondering if this was some elaborate plot to get her into bed, in the style of those dreadful seventies soft porn films called *Confessions of a Window Cleaner* and the like.

He was splashing water all over her tiled floor, suds and mess were spreading out in a semi-circle from the sink.

'For goodness' sake.' She tutted loudly. 'Why don't you have a shower?'

'Wouldn't want to inconvenience you.' He turned to face her looking quite clueless. And adorably handsome, with his soap-covered torso and arms, still visibly muscular and causing Harriet's eyes to dart over them at quite a pace.

'Towels in the cupboard next to the bathroom. You know where it is.' She pointed and stared at the ground.

He walked past, apologising profusely for his mess.

Finally, he emerged from her shower, redder skin from his frantic scrubbing she presumed, but without any white specks. It occurred to her after he'd left, having apologised profusely, surely he knew paint sticks to skin, so why would he have removed his clothes?

The weather, probably.

The next day when he'd asked to put his packed lunch in Harriet's fridge, she took one look at his sad-looking plastic container of something or other and said, 'If you don't cover yourself in paint today, how would it be if I made lunch?'

He was doing something with his painting paraphernalia, his broad back facing her, and he leant forwards, showing the two globe shapes of his buttocks in the white dungarees he seemed to have chosen for an odd reason on that day.

In response to his silence, Harriet said, 'Not to worry if not. Otherwise I shall eat out. Get out of your way.' *I wonder if Sophie's free for lunch…*

'Lunch, if you're happy to, would be great. If it's okay with you. Don't have to make a habit of it. 'Course not. It's your home and I'm working in it.'

Oddly rambling response for such a simple question, Harriet thought, but replied, 'Fine,' and took herself away to her bedroom where she took three video calls with clients about their dream images of their weddings, made copious notes and soon it was lunchtime.

Their first lunch was so surprisingly pleasant that it became a regular occurrence. Every day in fact when Paul was there.

To her surprise, he was fascinated by her job, why she'd moved to this apartment, her family business and, even when Harriet felt sure he was going to pull out the classic, 'What's a girl like you doing without a boyfriend,' he didn't. Instead, he asked: 'My sister reads those books you like.'

Her eyes narrowed as she leant forwards for another spoonful of soup.

'On the shelves, I saw them when I first came round.'

She waited for some snippy comment about either him not reading, or why didn't she read proper books. Thickly buttering a piece of bread, she said, 'Right.'

'I don't read much. Sports biography for Christmas, couple of books for my summer holiday by the pool.' He shrugged.

She waited for the next part, carefully cutting her bread in half.

'She used to nick Mum's off her when we were kids. My sister. Loves 'em still. When I was having a difficult time.' He stopped, swallowed carefully, mopped up the soup with the bread, chewed it for a moment, swallowed.

His lips appear so plump, sitting in contrast to the dark blond beard. Stop it!

'She suggested I read, take my mind off stuff.' He tapped his head.

Harriet's eyebrows rose in surprise. 'Really. And?'

'They weren't for me, but I did read. Helped me focus on one thing, instead of trying to do seven at the same time.' He shrugged. 'Anyway, I think it's cool you've got shelves of 'em.'

'I used to steal them from my Aunt Wendy.'

As the weeks passed, Harriet became used to subtly gazing at his mouth, wondering what his lips would feel like. They talked favourite films, TV shows, music, and sometimes Harriet found they'd extended their lunch until well into the afternoon. She'd jump up, dash back to her laptop when her mobile phone rang.

One morning, once Paul was starting on the bathroom, removing the ill-advised floral and pink tiles and replacing them with plain white ones, Harriet said, 'I'm going out to visit some clients, probably have lunch out. But help yourself from the fridge.'

The look of disappointment on his face was obvious. 'I'll get something from a cafe.' He said it to rhyme with 'naff'. It used to make Harriet wince slightly, but now it made her smile.

'Honestly, the fridge is groaning with food. Please eat it.' After a pause, when she admired him kneeling, reaching upwards to do something with her old tiles, revealing a rectangle of tanned stomach – with dark hairs, Harriet added, feeling the heat rise in her cheeks, 'Not everything though.'

'Gotcha.' He turned and resumed his work.

'Spare key by the door, if you do need to leave,' she shouted, then closed the door, with an odd contented feeling. This man, who, up until a fortnight ago, had been a perfect stranger, whom she'd been put in touch with through Mel, she was now offering him the food in her fridge, the spare key for her flat and goodness knew what else. She didn't go any further with such a ridiculous thought because as she arrived at her car, she noticed one of the tyres was flat.

Inspecting it more closely, she kicked it. Definitely flat.

There was a spare wheel somewhere. Determined not to be the stereotypical clueless woman, she opened the bonnet: no sign of a wheel there. It must be in the boot. She opened the rear of the car, lifted the carpet to find a small green canister resting in a circular shape that looked as if it should contain a spare tyre.

Harriet reluctantly admitted defeat. She checked in the glovebox for the breakdown card she'd been given when buying the car. A short phone call revealed her cover had lapsed two years ago, and did she want to renew it. The person added, 'But we can't assist until two days after the cover starts.'

Harriet shook her head, feeling a tension headache beginning to spread. 'Thanks.' She ended the call.

She called Mel to explain she was going to miss her client meeting. 'Can you meet them please? Explain I'm having car trouble.'

'Is Paul with you?' Mel asked.

'He's doing my bathroom. When I say those tiles were ill-advised, I am not joking. Honestly, what was I thinking—'

'Paul will know what to do.'

'I know, which is why I'm paying him to decorate the bathroom.'

'The tyre.'

'I don't like to ask. It's hardly within the bounds of reasonable for someone who's plastering your walls, is it?'

'If you don't ask him, I will.' After a pause, Mel said, 'He won't mind. His dad runs a garage.'

Paul hadn't told her this, but then again, why would he? He'd been too busy asking about her, making her laugh. Making her smile.

'Are you still there?' Mel asked.

Harriet swallowed as what had been staring her in the face, yet she'd managed to not notice, came bounding over the horizon in white dungarees, a tool belt, cheeky grin and the kindest eyes she'd ever seen. 'I'll see if he can help.' She ended the call, then walked back to her apartment, pausing on the doorstep as she tried to make sense of why she both really wanted Paul to help her and why equally she wished she didn't want his help so much.

'I'm back,' she shouted in the hallway.

Paul stuck his head out of the bathroom doorway. He had white dust in his hair, on his nose and yet he still looked good enough to play a lead in a Hollywood film.

God, where did that come from?

Right.

Harriet explained what had happened.

Paul stood, leaning against the door frame confidently in such a way that Harriet both felt reassured with his presence and irritated she couldn't deny how attractive he looked.

'Of course,' he said, following her out.

He opened the boot, removed the canister, connected it to the flat tyre, pressed it and somehow it inflated. 'You'll need to get a new tyre.' He replaced the canister and closed the car's boot.

'Thanks.'

'Don't mention it.' He strode back to her apartment with maybe a little spring in his step.

Harriet drove to do as he'd suggested, and learned not an inconsiderable amount about flat tyres, run flats, inflation apparatus, and left having bought breakdown cover.

Not for any reason other than needing to make sense of her feelings – away from Paul – Harriet went for a drive, parking outside Mel's house.

She hadn't thought it all through enough, so Harriet drove off, hoping Mel hadn't seen her parked outside. She'd think Harriet was weird. Which, given she was debating asking Paul out when she arrived home, wouldn't be too far from the truth.

Harriet remained away from home most of the day, going shopping, sitting in a café alone, remembering and writing down her long since deleted list of requirements for a man, and confirming, without any doubt, Paul didn't tick any more than five of her boxes. And yet…

She arrived home and he'd finished removing all of her ill-advised tiles, had smoothed the wall and lifted half the floor tiles. He'd stacked them neatly in the corner.

There she found a note, written in his large blocky letters using pencil: *I got urjent job tomorrow. B back Mond – P :-)*

Harriet had sat on the loo, with the seat down, staring at the note with a deep disappointment lodged in her guts at not seeing him tomorrow, and had known, beyond any doubt, she was developing feelings for a man entirely unsuitable, with nothing in common and who'd substantially disappoint both parents were they ever to meet him.

The final week of his working at her apartment, she'd practically embraced him on the Monday morning, such was her pining for him that Friday, having become very much accustomed to him being around for the previous three weeks.

She dared not discuss this with anyone, for it made no sense. Although she did, on his final Friday night, open a bottle of sparkling grape juice, which he'd agreed to as a celebration of his finishing the work. She had toasted with her juice and he'd done so with a can of lager she'd bought, when he'd mentioned it to be his favourite tipple.

They had walked from room to room, admiring his handiwork, her entirely calmer, more adult apartment. She'd complimented him without reservation and had longed to be able to say, 'Can I kiss you?'

But she found, since she hadn't drunk any alcohol, she could not.

He crushed the cans and neatly put them in her recycling crate and then leaned against the wall by her front door. 'See you then.' And he had left, wearing his white dungarees and tool belt, carrying his bags and boxes of tools, walked to his small white van and drove away.

For some reason, Harriet had shouted to herself at her stupidity. At her inability to voice what she'd wanted. At the injustice of the universe throwing Paul her way while also ensuring he was entirely unsuitable, yet making sure she wanted him very much indeed. A lone tear rolled down her cheek and Harriet picked up one of his crushed cans and knew she was entirely lost to this ridiculous matter of her heart winning over her head.

Which was why, now, determined to return Paul to her apartment at any cost, she found herself gleefully smashing up three drawers on the pretext of him refurbishing her otherwise entirely satisfactory kitchen.

With a crash, the drawers splintered and cracked, dropping in pieces to the floor. *I am insane*, she told herself.

Later, surveying the mess she'd made in the kitchen, on the phone she told Sophie, 'I'm insane.'

'Wind back a moment, please. Why do you want him to return when he's finished? Three weeks, wasn't he there?'

Nearly five weeks. He'd been called off twice for urgent plumbing jobs, returning a few days later. 'Twenty days.' Not that she'd been counting. She totally had.

'Oh-My-God.' Sophie laughed. 'Have you accidentally walked into one of your aunt's novels?'

Harriet shook her head. 'I know, right. It makes no sense. We make no sense. He probably doesn't even like me. But, you should have seen him topless.'

'Here's an idea, why don't you call him, and ask if he'd like to have dinner.'

'To discuss my new kitchen?'

'I know you're quite invested in the kitchen story, since you've wrecked yours. But at this stage, I feel like being honest with him is probably gonna be better.'

'What if he's not interested?'

'You find someone else to fix up your kitchen.' Sophie paused. 'Look, he's probably terrified of making a move since, you know, he's in your home, wouldn't want you to feel uncomfortable. Doesn't want to be accused of hashtag metooing you. There's all that to consider.'

Literally none of that had even crossed Harriet's mind. She was so used to meeting men in situations where dating *was* the activity, she'd become so out of practice with serendipitous situations such as this. She told Sophie. 'I shall call him.'

'Best to, I think. Oh and can you send me a pic of him? Preferably shirtless.'

'What do you think I am? Do you imagine me secretly snapping pictures of him while he worked?'

'Did you?'

'Considered it. He's H-O-T. But wimped out. Felt a bit...' *Icky, dishonest, wrong.*

'Right. Go, do, you find man.' There was a banging noise.

'What's that?'

'I'm banging my chest. Caveman. Isn't that what he's like?'

Harriet rolled her eyes. 'Going now.'

She decided calling him, right now, felt too fast. So she busied herself all weekend thinking of reasons why she shouldn't, why he wasn't suitable, why she didn't want to see him again. And then on Monday lunchtime, when she held his business card, with her fingers poised over her mobile phone, there was a knock on the door.

You have got to be joking. This is going to be him. I am actually living in my own romance novel. She glanced out of the window and his van wasn't there.

Relief and disappointment washed through her, at not inadvertently disappearing into the ending of one of her aunt's novels. *Must call Aunt Wendy and see how she is.*

Before she could reach the door, it opened.

Paul.

Harriet's heart beat faster, she felt like Christmas and her birthday had arrived at once. Taking a breath to calm herself, she said, 'I was… My kitchen… It's…'

He handed over her keys. 'I left these in my van. Wanted to return them.'

'That's very kind of you. It's good you're here, I was—' She stopped herself. Walked forwards, pulled him closer, and kissed him.

His hard body pressed against hers, she inhaled the tea tree scent she'd become used to now, perhaps he used her shower gel.

'I wanted to do that. Sorry if I was a bit forward. Should have asked first. But, you know, girl power.' She punched the air, still reeling from the perfect taste and feel of their kiss.

Paul grinned, looked down. 'Can I?'

She nodded.

This time, he kissed her and dipped her backwards like they were ballroom dancing. She closed her eyes, allowing herself to become completely lost in this moment. His strong arms held her, suspended her as she was almost horizontal, his lips and tongue made her melt to her core.

Ending the kiss, he stared into her eyes. 'I have a confession.'

'Right.' *So do I*, she thought.

'I kept your keys so I'd need to come back.'

Harriet stepped aside, gesturing to the smashed kitchen drawers. 'Yours is less insane than mine.'

He laughed, pulled her close for a hug, another kiss that took her breath away, and she reckoned maybe if she were living in one of her books, she could deal with that. If Paul were the hero to her heroine.

'Do you want to grab some lunch?' He nodded outside. 'I've only got the van. But I've got a sheet on the passenger seat.'

'Where is it parked?'

'Round the corner, why?'

Harriet grabbed her keys as she left. 'I… Nothing. Let's eat.'

He took her hand as they walked to the lift, held on tightly as they descended. And by the time they'd eaten lunch, Harriet had long since forgotten her thirty-seven-point check list, and added one thing to her list: *take Paul to meet Mum and Dad.*

For she knew if they met him, they too, would fall completely for his charm, looks and good nature. Because when you boiled it all down, it was impossible to categorise, whether someone worked with you, based on where they'd gone to university, their job, if they could name all the English prime ministers or kings and queens… Because when you knew, you knew.

And finally, Harriet admitted to herself, as he squeezed her hand and her stomach flipped as he stared at her with a look she knew to be love, she knew.

Chapter 46

It felt like a lifetime ago when Pete had proposed, but equally the time to plan had flown by. Between their busy jobs, looking after Pete's younger brother and sister while Mel studied, their very own Extra wedding day had arrived.

Jason, in a white suit, stood at the front of the registry office room. Pete had been very disappointed they weren't allowed to decorate it so he'd really gone to town with the hotel's ballroom. Jason grinned at the memory of Pete's design, which Harriet had made into reality.

The celebrant adjusted his glasses, nodded and the music began. ABBA's 'I Do, I Do, I Do'.

Pete, also wearing a white suit, appeared at the door, his arm looped with Mel's. Mel wore a bubblegum pink skirt suit that accentuated her curvy shape. She beamed with such pride as they took their first step towards the front.

Pete had wanted the sides to be mixed up since he didn't agree with whose friends were whose; his view was any friend of Jason's was a friend of his. So their friends were jumbled sitting on the wooden benches either side of the central carpet leading to Jason.

He swallowed, glad he'd opted not to walk to the music since he had two left feet. He didn't have anyone who could have accompanied him, so had decided to remain still.

'Steadfast, like a rock,' Pete had said when he'd suggested it.

Pete and Mel were standing next to Jason.

The celebrant nodded and Mel curtsied, removing a pink silk cushion from her bag and placing two platinum rings on top. She quietly sat on the nearest bench, turning to wink at her son.

Pete looked at him, grinning so widely he could almost not contain his excitement.

Jason held his hand, squeezed it. Mouthed, 'Love you.'

Pete made a heart shape with his hands, nodding at Jason.

Jason almost, but not quite, cried. He didn't cry. But all the build-up, the planning, the decisions about everything to make it a perfect day, had led up to this moment.

A breath caught in his throat. He swallowed, composed himself.

The celebrant looked from Jason to Pete, checking they were okay to begin.

Almost imperceptibly, they nodded.

The service began, the description about how important marriage was, as a solemn vow to one another, for the rest of their lives. 'Does anyone know of any lawful impediment why this marriage should not take place?' He'd explained to them this was part of the service and had to be said, although in his nearly twenty years of doing it, not once had he heard any objection. 'It's not like in the films,' he'd said.

Now there was silence.

'Phew!' Pete said, smiling broadly.

Jason raised his eyebrows.

'Who has the rings?' he asked.

'That's me,' Mel said, standing from the front bench, carrying the silk cushion with its two rings.

The celebrant took them.

'With this ring, I wed you, promise to love, honour and protect you, forsaking all others, for as long as I shall live.' Jason felt a lump in his throat. He caught Mel's eyes and she winked, putting her hand on her heart and pointing to him.

'Do we have the other ring?'

'Me again!' Mel stepped forward, handing the second ring to him.

Pete repeated the words and Jason slipped the ring on his finger. Pete had at first wanted matching wedding rings, but when Jason had pointed out he didn't wear any jewellery, whereas Pete was dripping in it, he'd changed his mind. They held hands. Jason's plain platinum band shone in the lights. Pete's row of diamonds set in platinum sparkled.

As did he. Both in Jason's eyes and everyone who knew and loved him.

'You are now husbands.'

The crowd cheered and clapped.

Jason leant down and kissed Pete. A light kiss on the lips, as the applause continued. Pete pulled him closer, whispering in his ear, 'I love you so much.'

Jason nodded. 'Same,' he said as the word caught in his throat.

They posed for photos taken by the best photographer on the Extra Weddings roster. The guests took pictures with their phones.

Jason couldn't stop smiling. He'd done it, he had the best husband in the world.

The opening bar of 'All The Lovers' by Kylie began and Pete almost combusted with joy. Jason's heart leapt at the way Pete's joy was infectious, how his never-ending appetite for everything sparkly and rainbow coloured had been embarrassing as a child, but as an adult he really embraced it, accepting without reservation, who he was.

Mel had confided in Jason the signs were always there even when Pete was a little boy. 'What other four-year-old asks for a My Little Pony for his birthday every year until we give him one?'

They walked along the red carpet, smiling and waving as more photographs were taken.

Outside the plain registry office building in the centre of Oxford, they posed on the steps as pink confetti was thrown on them for more photos.

'Everyone knows where we're going now?' Pete shouted.

Harriet's voice, amplified by a public address system said: 'The directions and postcode of the hotel are on your invitations. Otherwise follow that car.' She pointed to a curvy car sitting low on its wheels.

Pete wasn't fussed about the wedding car, but Jason wanted to make the most of his options, so his brief had been the most Extra, zany, quirky car possible.

When Harriet had shown him pictures of the large Citroën from the seventies with its swivelling headlights, suspension that sank when the car rested (and apparently President Mitterrand had owned one), Jason knew this was the car for them.

The driver held the door open. Pete climbed in, Jason followed onto the squashy leather seats.

'All right, husband?' Pete asked, looking about the car.

'Very all right, husband. You?'

'I thought you'd got a classic car.' He stroked the leather seat. 'This feels... modern.'

'It's older than me, and much older than you.'

Pete shrugged, looked out of the window and waved at Mel. 'What do I know? Ignore me.'

They arrived at the country hotel a short drive from the city centre.

Busy, the events manager, greeted them. 'Hello.' She held the door as they slipped out of the car. 'Modern car, nice.'

Pete said, 'See, it's not just me.'

'Did I say something wrong?' Busy asked.

'No. Let's get this party started!'

Busy led them through the lobby into the ballroom. It had pink fabrics hung from the ceiling, rainbows projected on the walls. Giant inflatable unicorns were tied to the pillars and each table had a pink unicorn stuffed toy, glittery pink tablecloth and seat covers. Rainbow bunting hung from each corner across the room, crossing in the middle. It was quite a lot to take in. Jason was used to it now, having seen the designs Pete had come up with. 'When Harriet asked which colours you wanted, you weren't supposed to say all of them,' he'd joked.

'And why not?' had been Pete's reply.

So here they were, standing in a living incarnation of Pete's dream wedding. It was a little much for Jason, but he loved it because he loved Pete, and besides, Extra Weddings.

Jason and Pete sat at the top table, flanked by Mel and Gareth, who wore a kilt, waistcoat and white shirt with a jacket. Jason noticed his very impressive thighs and Pete asked, 'What does a true Scottish man wear under his kilt?'

'You'll have to ask your mum.'

Harriet, as matron of honour, chief organiser and all round go-to for when Jason was finding Pete a little too much, sat on the other side of Pete and Jason. She'd brought Paul, who had more than a touch of the Bradley Cooper about him and was holding Harriet's hand on the table.

On another table, Steve was grinning widely, taking it all in. Lily and Thomas, behaving very well, dressed in a fairy tale princess dress and waistcoat and trousers, sat next to Sally who held Steve's hand. Isaac wore shirt, tie and trousers, sitting next to a girl he'd met at uni.

After the food – fish, meat and vegetarian options, all sourced from within twenty-five miles of the hotel – the speeches began.

They wanted it to be less like a traditional wedding, and more like how American weddings allow anyone to speak if they want.

Harriet went first. She stood in her elegant cerise shoulder-less dress. Since it was Pete's favourite, she'd accepted wearing the same colour as Mel but she'd refused to call it bubblegum pink. 'I am the last person who expected to be doing this. For many reasons. But when Jason asked me to organise, be matron of honour, I couldn't refuse. I've never met two people more suited. I used to be a bit cynical about love.' She shook her head, gazing at Paul.

Paul winked and smiled at her.

Harriet blushed. 'Not any more. I'm all about love. How it comes in many different shapes and sizes, and how no matter who you are, you can't deny these two men are in love.' Harriet handed the microphone to Mel.

Mel stood, removed a piece of paper from her jacket. 'Jason has been part of my family, and in Pete's life, for more than three years. Now I'm so thrilled to be able to call him my son-in-law. He's a wonderful boss, a great boyfriend and I know how happy he makes Pete. These two are more generous and kinder than anyone would believe. I owe them so much and I hope I can be the kind of mother-in-law Jason doesn't make jokes about.' Everyone laughed, and Jason squeezed Mel's shoulder.

After the speeches, the chairs and tables were cleared away to make room for the dance floor.

There was dancing, small children wearing smart clothes skidding across the dance floor and being told off by their parents. There were aunties and uncles boogieing with people half their age. There was an elderly relative on Pete's side who stood open mouthed as Pete and Jason did their first dance.

Jason watched over Pete's shoulder as Mel nudged the man and he looked on at the others.

Their first dance was to 'Only You' by Yazoo because Pete had loved it ever since the Christmas episode of *The Office*.

They held each other, slowly shuffling in a circle as the music played. When it ended, everyone clapped, the tempo sped up with 'Summer of '69' and the dance floor filled with guests.

Later, when they'd drunk and eaten their fill and danced until their feet hurt, Pete took Jason to meet Mel and her man.

Mel wiped her eyes. 'I can't stop crying. Sorry. It's all so lovely. I can't believe it. It's… magic.'

'That it is,' Gareth said, pulling her close into a hug.

Pete hugged her, shook Gareth's hand. 'I'm not calling you Dad, okay?' He winked, kissed Gareth's cheek.

Gareth stood with wide eyes, unsure what to say. 'Fine with me. Your ma here is a very clever woman.'

'They don't want to hear about uni stuff, not tonight.' Mel shook her head.

'You.' He nodded at Pete. 'Thomas, Lily and Isaac, they are why she's clever.'

Mel blushed. 'Go away.'

They stood in awkward silence for a few moments.

'Talking of which,' Pete said, heading off to give Isaac a high five. He picked Lily up and danced with her to 'Roar' by Katy Perry, which Pete had taught her the dance moves to.

Jason felt such pride and love for his extended family, he swallowed the lump in his throat. 'Where's Thomas?' Jason asked.

Mel nodded to a table where he sat with a girl on his lap, his arm around her, their mouths locked together.

'Aren't you gonna stop him?' Jason asked.

'Why? He's sixteen. He doesn't want his old mum embarrassing him.' She chuckled.

Jason left them and joined Pete and Lily on the dance floor. They danced until the music stopped, taking breaks to talk to all their guests. Jason later said it felt like being a celebrity because everyone there knew him. He'd never had an experience like it. Smiling with satisfaction, he realised he really did have the best job in the world, spreading happiness like this to others. As long as they could dream it, he and his Extra Weddings colleagues could make it happen.

After slipping away, avoiding prolonged goodbyes, Pete had taken Jason's hand and said, 'I need you for something,' and led him away.

They presented themselves at the reception desk and Busy led them to their room.

It was a log cabin, secluded in a small wooded area, the other side of a man-made lake with a fountain in the middle.

'Enjoy,' she said, handing them the key.

'We will,' Pete said, opening the door, taking Jason's hand.

The door clicked closed. 'What did you need me for?' Jason asked.

'Forever.' Pete kissed him.

And Jason kissed him right back.

Acknowledgments

There's a few people who deserve a damned good thanking for helping make this book happen.

To Tim, for supporting my writing, for celebrating the successes, for always being there when I needed support, for making dinner, feeding the cats, all while I'm writing. For spending time amusing yourself when we're together, at home and away, and I'm *still* writing. Thank you. Love you.

To the Romantic Novelists' Association (RNA) as an organisation it's been wonderful to introduce me to other authors and publishers. Without the invite from Kiley Dunbar to speak at the Love Writing Manchester event in February 2020 (in Before Times) I wouldn't have met Keshini Naidoo and Lyndsey Mooney and this book almost definitely would not exist.

Members of the RNA's Rainbow Chapter in particular who've helped with so much about my writing and this book in particular. Mary Jane Baker and Rhoda Baxter deserve large glasses of whatever they fancy, on me, next time we meet.

To the Essex Writers Group, Lucy, Zeba, Karen, Alison, Kelly, Andrew, Sophie, Sarah who've been with me through ups and downs of my writing journey, read my pages and cheered me when I've had cause for celebration and bolstered me even more when I've felt at sea. In particular to Virginia Heath who, when I had a minor meltdown as I thought the edit for this story was impossible, quietly reassured me it was indeed not impossible, it would not be as bad as I'd imagined, and that I needed to take a deep breath, brace myself and face it head on. Which was precisely what I did. The book is so much better thanks to the edit, thanks to Keshini and Danielle for this too.

To my author, editor, reader friends within the male male romance genre who have supported me on this new venture writing as Charlie Lyndhurst. A special shout out to a few people who've been at the end of the phone, shared a bottle of wine or a cup of tea at key moments: Ali Ryecart, Sue Brown, Clare London, Derek Farrell and George Loveland.

Aimee who designed this wonderful cover – it's so perfect for The Grooms Wore White. Thanks to everyone in the Hera Books team including Danielle, Gareth and Vicki for editing and proofing so carefully. And finally, and most importantly, thanks to Keshini Naidoo and Lyndsey Mooney for giving me the opportunity to work with Hera and bring this book to the world.

Love and light,
Charlie Lyndhurst xx